OF WEIGHT LOSS & WITCHES

BY MARJORIE JOSEPH

Scripture taken from the HOLY BIBLE, NEW INTERNATIONAL VERSION®.
NIV®. Copyright © 1973, 1978, 1984 by International Bible Society. Used by
permission of Zondervan. All rights reserved worldwide.

Higher Ground Books & Media
P.O. Box 2914
Springfield, OH 45501-2914
www.highergroundbooksandmedia.com

Because of the dynamic nature of the Internet, any web addresses or links
contained in this book may have changed since publication and may no longer be
valid. The views expressed in the work are solely those of the author and do not
necessarily reflect the views of the publisher, and the publisher hereby disclaims
any responsibility for them.

Any people depicted in stock imagery are being used for illustrative purposes only.

ISBN (Paperback): 978-1-955368-60-5

Printed in the United States of America 2024

OF WEIGHT LOSS & WITCHES

BY MARJORIE JOSEPH

Chapter One

"So, how did you hear about Brookline Bariatrics, Evaniese?" Doctor Edward Bergstrom asked Evaniese Spencer, while she sat in his office in the late morning in January of 2016.

Evaniese had no idea what Dr. Bergstrom was thinking. But, it didn't matter in one way or another. *She* felt mortified just being there. Evaniese was tired of being overweight. All her life she'd done everything in her power to manage her weight.

However, at that point, even her best efforts seemed to be working against her. The number on the scale was moving in a direction counterproductive to her goal. For a while, she had done pretty well, and had managed to lose a significant amount of weight. However, for the past three years, Evaniese's weight loss endeavors had fallen by wayside.

It was a new year, and Evaniese was resolved do bring about some changes. Being fat had been the bane of her existence for as long as she could remember. In 2003, she found a very doable low-carb diet. The regimen seemed to work for a while. Following that plan, she took off one hundred and thirty pounds. However, the routine was no longer effective. Admitting to defeat was indeed a shame.

Evaniese was now in her mid-forties. Undoubtedly, her age and hormonal imbalances were huge factors as to why the diet plan had lost its effectiveness. Having stalls on her weight loss journey wasn't anything new. However, at that point, Evaniese had to contend with *continuous* weight gain. It didn't seem to matter what she ate, or how much she exercised.

After a moment of pause, Evaniese told Dr. Bergstrom, "I work through the hospital, and I heard about the Bariatric Group here." Her caramel skin flushed in mortification, as she nervously stared about the room.

"Well, allow me to be the first to tell you just what a wonderful decision you've made by coming to us! Our Bariatric group is one of the very best in the country!" Pushing back into the leather armchair, Dr. Bergstrom smiled with a sense of dignity.

"Okay…," Evaniese said uneasily. "That's good to know. Congratulations!"

"Thank you. I'm proud to be affiliated with Brookline Hospital!" Dr. Bergstrom gave an affirming nod. "So, you're interested in submitting to one of our procedures?" his eyes fastened to Evaniese's.

"Yes." Evaniese nodded. "I think I *might* need to." She frowned.

"I'm sure the nurse has filled you in on some of the procedures we provide here. So, you probably know about the Lap-Band, the Gastric Bypass, the Duodenal Switch, and the Vertical Sleeve Gastrectomy. We also offer the Balloon. Have you decided which one might be right for you?" Dr. Bergstrom grimaced in urgency.

"Given all the information, I've decided to go with the Vertical Sleeve Gastrectomy," Evaniese asserted. This time around, her eyes didn't waver from Dr. Bergstrom's intent stare.

"Very good." Dr. Bergstrom smiled. "With the sleeve, the patient is expected to lose 3 to 5 pounds a week. There's no sporadic maintenance, as you would see with the Lap-Band. The procedure is also minimally invasive, and considerably less intrusive than the Gastric Bypass, or the Duodenal Switch. The nurse *did* explain…?"

"Yes, she did," Evaniese said. "The nurse also mentioned the number of medical *clearances* required to have the surgery." Evaniese folded her hands in her lap.

"Yes, there *are* quite a few steps. However, we can schedule your appointments together," Dr. Bergstrom reassured.

Evaniese nodded in agreement. "The nurse wants to schedule an Endoscopy first. She wants that done in a couple of weeks?" Evaniese questioned, staring warily at Doctor Bergstrom.

"Yes… The Endoscopy will be performed right here through Brookline's surgical team."

"I understand." Evaniese nodded.

Inwardly, she was apprehensive. She'd never had a surgery, let alone an *elective* procedure. The entire concept was foreign to her. However, she was convinced that having the procedure was in the will of God for her life.

Still, a part of her doubted she could actually go through with it. Evaniese vowed to continue praying for courage and strength. Yet, in spite of the uncertainties, she felt excited over the prospect of having a brand-new body, even if she wasn't thrilled about the idea of going under the knife.

"Well, tell me a little bit about your history, Evaniese…," Dr. Bergstrom asked with a pleasant expression on his face.

Roused from reflection, Evaniese snapped to attention, and gave the doctor an inquisitive look.

"Tell me a little bit about yourself," Dr. Bergstrom reiterated.

"Honestly, ever since I can remember, I've always struggled with my weight. Thirteen years ago, at the urging of a friend, I started a *special diet*. Being a person of faith, I feel as if God guided me through the process. At the time, I had ballooned up to 330 pounds. Through this special diet, I was able to take off in excess of a hundred and thirty pounds."

"That's amazing! How did you manage that?" Dr. Bergstrom's face sparked in intrigue.

Evaniese smiled thoughtfully. "Well, first and foremost, my faith has a lot to do with it. My relationship with Jesus Christ means *everything* to me. So, when I found myself at that weight, I was honestly terrified. So, I prayed diligently on the matter. Over time, God showed me the steps I needed to take in order to see a turnaround."

"And, what was it that you thought God showed you, dear?"

"Well, at the time, I had a very interesting conversation with a friend. I don't remember now how we got on the subject, but we were discussing different diets. One of the things we covered in that conversation was reducing carb intake." Evaniese felt a lot less self-conscious at that point, as she steadied her gaze into Dr. Bergstrom's.

"Okay. Sounds sensible enough. And, that worked for you?" Dr. Bergstrom's brows knitted broodingly.

"Yes, it did…for a long time. I incorporated a low-carb diet with exercise. I started using my treadmill at first. However, when my treadmill stopped working, I started jogging on the street. I ran four to five times a week." A reminiscent smile stretched across Evaniese's face.

"That sounds amazing, and *inspirational*. You said this plan worked for a long time. Do you have any idea what changed?"

Sadness puckered Evaniese's face. "That plan worked for years. That is until recently. I'm not sure why that is."

Evaniese remembered running up and down *Vail Avenue,* near her home with ten-pound weights strapped to both ankles. She even took a nasty fall the first time she wore them.

"What's been happening recently, Evaniese?" Dr. Bergstrom gave her a sympathetic look.

"It's difficult to know. I've been keeping up with the diet. However, instead of *losing*, I've been steadily *gaining* weight." Tears gleamed in Evaniese's eyes. Inwardly, she prayed for God's strength. She didn't want to fall apart, but the circumstances were indeed heartbreaking.

Have there been drastic changes to your routine?" Dr. Bergstrom began taking notes in a chart.

"Not really. I can only conclude that my body's no longer responding to the diet, and the exercise routine," Evaniese groused, disheartened.

Dr. Bergstrom sighed. "Unfortunately, there are a few things to take into consideration. For starters, there's your age. Another might be how much sleep you're getting nightly. You said you work through the ER here. Do you work the late-night shift?"

Evaniese nodded. "I work from 3-11 p.m. So, I get home pretty late. I'm usually famished by then."

"Do you snack a lot once you're home?"

"I do snack, but they're usually healthy snacks, like almonds and rice cakes. I do stay up pretty late, and snack until I'm able to fall asleep," she admitted.

"So, the late-night snacking *could* play a significant role in the weight gain. Through one of the medical clearances outlined, we'll check out your Thyroid levels. Evaniese, let me ask you this?" His face creased in solemnness. "Have you also been under a lot of stress?"

Evaniese took stock of her circumstances. The past few years had been extremely stressful. Working through the hospital had brought about a number of personal setbacks. Then, there was her *current* situation. Initially, Dr. Nathan Andrews seemed *romantically* interested in her. From the outset, God revealed that the young doctor was tied into her destiny. However, since Evaniese had received that revelation, Dr. Andrews had pulled away, rather than drawing closer.

Evaniese had worked through Brookline Hospital's ER for the past seven years. The hospital was located in the town of Amber Hills, Indiana. Evaniese worked through the Registration Office. Seven years earlier, she put her work as a teacher on hold, and decided to try something new. As an added incentive, Evaniese had better medical insurance working as a PAR (Patient Access Representative) at the hospital than when she worked through the school. The job was stressful, and the pay left a lot to be desired. But, for the time being, Evaniese knew God wanted her there.

For that very reason, in spite of how difficult the job itself was, Evaniese resolved to use the medical insurance provided to have the surgery. The way she saw it, the surgery would be the culmination of her struggle. Then shortly after, she'd resign. Evaniese had grown tired of being abused, and taken for granted by Paula Rivers and Ann Ridges.

Paula was the Director of the Admissions Department, and Ann was her assistant. To put it bluntly, both were *horrible* bosses. From the outset, the pair had mistreated her. Yet, in spite of the challenges, Evaniese knew it was where God wanted her. Even so, from the very beginning, working there could only be described as a trial by fire.

Two years prior to Nathan Andrews stepping on the scene, Evaniese had met another doctor by the name of Jeremy Carter. As a woman of faith, Evaniese had waited a very long time for God to bless her with a Godly spouse. Hence, the reason why she was in her mid-forties and *still* waiting. Love had evaded her so many times. Adding insult to injury, she often found herself victimized in romantic relationships with the wrong men.

When Evaniese first moved out to Amber Hills, she found a good church-or so she thought. To this day, she continued to attend *Fresh Anointing Church*. It was at the church she met Brent Peterson. Brent was a very wealthy, and incredibly handsome bachelor. It took a while for Evaniese to understand why God had led her to that particular church. However, the more she prayed on the matter, the stronger the impression she received that Brent was her God-ordained spouse. So, for a very long time, Evaniese believed Brent was the *one*.

However, after holding out hope for close to five years for Brent to make a move, Evaniese took matters into her own hands. After service one late morning, she approached Brent, and asked if he felt a connection between them. Much to her surprise and *chagrin*, Brent put her on blasts. The man vehemently rejected her, and spelled out in no uncertain terms he felt no such connection. He also emphasized how she wasn't his *type*.

Worse yet, Brent embarrassed Evaniese by announcing to everyone at the church how uncomfortable she often made him feel. Brent said she was much too *affectionate* during the meet and greet segments of the service. He threw her under the bus, and told their Pastor, Richard Carvers, *she* was the reason for his sporadic lateness, and tenuous church attendance.

Evaniese was devastated! Prior to that infraction, she and Brent were cordial. In the past, they'd had chummy talks and friendly exchanges. However, about a year after Brent ostracized and alienated Evaniese, he stopped attending church, and disappeared from Evaniese's life altogether. Falling out with Brent in such a shameful and public manner, had impacted Evaniese in a negative way. It was like pouring acid into her wound, because she'd sincerely fallen for him.

And so, as a result of the whole church debacle, Brent was no longer in the picture. However, about a year later, while working through Brookline Hospital's ER, Evaniese remarked a shift in her relationship with a certain Dr. Jeremy Carter. Long before Evaniese was hired to work through Brookline's ER, Jeremy Carter had been there for a number of years. However, in 2011, something undeniable sparked between them. Unexpected, it was a total game-changer for Evaniese.

With a new romantic prospect on the horizon, Evaniese felt hopeful again. She was more than ready to put the painful experience with Brent behind her. For a while, it seemed, Dr. Carter was *into* Evaniese as well. For starters, he frequented her office, and flirted incessantly with her.

Jeremy also followed Evaniese around the hospital. It didn't seem to matter where she wandered on hospital grounds, Dr. Carter would always *mysteriously* pop up, even in the most unexpected places. His behavior confused Evaniese. Yet and still, she couldn't say she hated having the good-looking *younger* man show interest in her.

Sadly, Evaniese would realize soon enough that Dr. Carter wasn't the person she thought. The first red flag was when Evaniese overheard Jeremy and one of his work colleagues talking inside the ER. When the PA asked Jeremy if he was interested in Evaniese, like a school boy, Jeremy had vehemently denied having any interest in Evaniese. Furthermore, he affirmed Evaniese wasn't his *type*, and he boasted of *other* romantic prospects outside of the hospital.

That scenario taught Evaniese a great deal. One of the things Evaniese walked away with from that experience was, even if she had a beautiful face, her body-type and monetary status, were unsuited for Dr. Carter. The most humiliating aspect of that circumstance was that Evaniese felt led by God to tell Jeremy how much she liked him. Tragically, the night Evaniese told Jeremy *I love you*, he viciously censured her. Notwithstanding, he told her he was already in a *committed* relationship. Evaniese was even more confused. And yet, in spite of what he'd said, he couldn't stay away from her.

As if the matter wasn't agonizing enough, just when Evaniese thought things were about to change, Jeremy resigned from his position in the ER. Evaniese was shattered when Jeremy left the hospital. Jeremy left, ignorant of the fact that Evaniese loved him more than she'd ever loved anyone else before. Evaniese was convinced he loved her too, even if he kept denying it. Shortly after Jeremy's departure, Evaniese was the victim of two separate automobile accidents-one of which was a near-fatal four-car crash, which she herself had caused.

So, Evaniese *had* known stress, suffering and heartache. Her relationships prior to meeting Brent and Jeremy had also resulted in heartbreak. In her early twenties, she was engaged to her very first boyfriend. However, her then fiancé had cheated on her, and had left her for a mutual friend. An even bigger slap to the face was that the two were married.

Then, there was her *abusive* relationship with Alistair Connors. Evaniese had suffered at Alistair's hands for four long years. For all intents and purposes, she was his ragdoll. Alistair would throw her into the closet, then pull her out again whenever he felt like playing. Evaniese couldn't even count the number of times he stood her up for dates.

Once, Alistair even stood her up on her birthday. He had no problem spending weeks-and even months at a time without calling her. Then, he'd mysteriously resurface again. Evaniese lived out that nightmare, honestly believing that Alistair was tied into her destiny. So, she was well-versed in sorrow and disappointment. In her early twenties, she succumbed to her first bout of MDD (Major Depressive Disorder).

It was now 2016, and Evaniese still couldn't get a handle on how *sad* she truly was. Even if she wasn't having a recurrence of MDD, she had been sad for quite a while. Evaniese had turned a corner from dealing with such gripping depression and anxiety. However, she was ready to admit that she in all likeliness suffered from Dysthymia, a less debilitating, yet persistent underlying depression. She was essentially living and functioning in a depressed state.

However, things changed up again. About two years after Jeremy left the hospital, Nathan Andrews happened on the scene. Evaniese was stunned when Nathan waltzed into her office, and openly asked her out. After praying on the matter, Evaniese realized that it wasn't a random act. God had brought Nathan into her life.

Evaniese couldn't have been more confused. Nathan was the *third* man God had revealed to be tied into her destiny. Evaniese was also skeptical of what she felt God telling her. After all, nothing had panned out with Brent or Jeremy. To the contrary, her connection to both men, had left her with a shattered heart. And, for all of the suffering and frustration, Evaniese didn't have so much as a kiss to show for it.

Dr. Nathan Andrews waltzed into Evaniese's life after her disappointment with Jeremy Carter. Nathan breezed into Evaniese's office one afternoon in September of 2014. Evaniese was absolutely breathless when she saw him for the first time. Moments before Nathan stepped into the registration office, Evaniese saw him. He was standing across from the ER's nurse's station. Her initial reaction to seeing him was that he looked a lot like, and reminded her of Jeremy. Both were extremely good-looking. On that fateful afternoon, the last thing Evaniese expected was for Nathan to step into *her* office. She was sitting at her desk when he came in to use the copier.

"Good afternoon, I'm Dr. Andrews!" he announced, with a captivating smile. Nathan was about 5'11, with a muscular upper build. Being Indian, his complexion was café au lait, and his eyes were maple. The combination made for one of the most handsome men Evaniese had ever laid eyes on!

While Nathan stood there, Evaniese found herself entranced. However, she tried to play it cool, and forced herself to speak. "I'm Evaniese," her voice wavered.

"It's nice to meet you, Evaniese! What a pretty name!" Nathan complimented. "Well, I'm new to Brookline Hospital. So, I came in here to properly introduce myself." He smiled openly.

"Welcome to Brookline! It's nice to meet you as well!" Evaniese tried to sound confident, even if she was totally bedazzled.

It was then she realized Dr. Andrews had also seen her from across the nurse's station. All the same, she was perplexed, because she'd spent less than a minute inside the ER. "I hope you like it here!" Evaniese smiled, with reddened cheeks.

"I have a feeling I'm going to like it here...a *lot*." Dr. Andrew's eyes fastened flirtatiously to Evaniese's.

"Oh, is that right?" Evaniese looked away timidly. "I have a feeling *we're* going to like having *you* around here as well." Her eyes had relinked to his.

"Thank you! I'm happy I got to meet *you* this afternoon, beautiful Evaniese!" Nathan uplifted. "Maybe, we can grab a coffee sometime…?" His eyes delved furtively into hers.

"That would be nice," Evaniese said, pleasantly surprised.

"Bye, now." Nathan turned away hesitantly, and ambled over to the office door.

"Bye," Evaniese said quietly. Her heart raced, as she watched Nathan step back into the ER.

Evaniese was amazed, and surprised that such an incredibly good-looking and *significantly* younger man, had flirted with. Not only had he flirted with her, but he'd asked her out. It felt nice to have the attention of a younger man, especially since she was forty-six years old at the time. Of course, Evaniese had never looked her age. She was frequently told she looked like she was in her late twenties. Hence, that afternoon in September of 2014, marked the beginning of her relationship with Dr. Nathan Andrews. However, it didn't take very long for things to go south.

About a week later, Evaniese bumped into Nathan for the second time. He came down to the Emergency Room in order to admit a patient. Evaniese was responsible for the patient's admission paperwork. So, she found Nathan right outside the patient's room. He was just as flirtatious as he was that first time. In a gentle way, he took Evaniese by the arm. Pulling her aside, he told her how she'd made his day by looking so lovely and smelling wonderful.

Yet, as much as Evaniese enjoyed Nathan's attention, in her heart and mind, it felt as if she was being unfaithful to Jeremy. At the time, she honestly believed she had to remain true to him, even if he was no longer a part of her life. After all, *both* Brent and Jeremy were tied into her destiny. So, by some misguided sense of loyalty, she felt constrained to honor both past relationships.

It took a while, but the more she prayed on the matter, the more confident Evaniese felt to move forward with Nathan. According to what God had shown her, *he* was also tied into her destiny. At that point, Evaniese felt like a contestant on a dating show. And, Nathan was *bachelor number three* so to speak.

From the outset, Nathan made it a habit to come and sit with Evaniese in the registration office. The second desk to Evaniese's right hand side, was free when Nathan stepped into the picture. In fact, that desk had been vacant for close to two years. So, Nathan *always* had a viable desk and desktop computer to use to complete his hospital admissions.

Doing the job of two people, and leaving her to fend for herself in a ridiculously busy ER, were ways in which Evaniese's bosses took advantage of her. There were days she found herself unable to go to the restroom, even if she needed to. However, when Nathan started hanging around the office with Evaniese, he temporarily stifled the craziness and the disparities of her job. From the start, he kept hinting at how much he wanted to take Evaniese out. He would say things like, "What are you doing this weekend, Evaniese?"

Evaniese would wait for the open-ended question to be filled in with something like, "Would you like to…?"

Nathan always seemed to be on the *cusp* of asking. However, he never quite sealed the deal. All the same, Evaniese remained faithful in prayer and fasting, knowing Nathan Andrews had an important role to play in her life. He was the *third* man tied into her destiny. Of course, Evaniese was still trying to process how she was linked to the three good-looking and successful men.

All her life, she'd prayed for one love and *one* spouse. So, the scenario was completely bizarre, but nonetheless true. Even more puzzling was that Nathan started wearing a *wedding ring* on his finger shortly after God confirmed he was *her* guy. When they first met, he wasn't wearing a wedding band. Yet, about a month or so after the encounter, things changed. The guy who'd flirted with-and had asked her out, had a new narrative. The storyline was that of a wife whom he talked about all the time.

By then, Evaniese's heart was already vested in him. After the pain and disappointment she'd known in the past, Nathan represented a beacon of hope. Sadly, all her hopes and dreams were dashed. To her chagrin, the more she prayed on the matter, the greater clarity she received that Nathan was her guy, irrespective to the wedding band, and the wife he spoke so often of. Evaniese found it odd that Nathan never called his wife by her first name, and she dared not ask him what it was.

By Nathan's account, he was a married man. That was his story, and he was sticking to it. Evaniese was crushed when things changed with Nathan. It hurt all the more, because at the time, she'd already developed feelings for him. Wanting the relationship with Nathan to get off the ground, she kept waiting for God to iron out the wrinkles.

Incidentally, Nathan actually gave Evaniese his phone *numbers*, and even his email address. It was a courtesy she wasn't extended from Brent or Jeremy. On the one occasion she had to call Jeremy, Evaniese had asked one of the nurses for his number. And, Brent never allowed her to get close enough to ask.

Evaniese and Nathan texted from time to time. However, unlike the way things were at the beginning, he started keeping their talks strictly platonic. At that point, Nathan only seemed interested in talking about their respective faiths. Nathan, being from India, believed in the practices of the Buddhist religion, while Evaniese always emphasized faith in Jesus Christ is the *only* way to salvation (John14:6). Sometimes, Nathan answered her text messages right away, but there were times it took days for him to respond. Then, there were the times he didn't respond at all.

So, as she sat in Dr. Bergstrom's office that late morning, Evaniese assessed her relationship with Nathan. She'd dealt with his erratic behavior for the past two years.

In that span of time, there had been moments where she was hopeful of a connection. However, two years had elapsed, and she was *still* waiting for him to make a move. Evaniese kept hoping he would stop talking about his *elusive* wife, and ask her out, but he never did. So, in that moment, Evaniese ascertained the correlation to her ballooning weight, and the heartache she'd endured in her past and current relationship.

So, while sitting in Dr. Bergstrom's office, Evaniese finally answered his loaded question, "Yes, absolutely. I *have* been under a *lot* of stress."

How on earth could she itemize the ways in which her heart had taken hits? It was far too difficult to interpret. Evaniese just offered Dr. Bergstrom a neutral smile. "How much time do you have?" she asked humorously.

"Wow! I'm sure there's a lot to unpack there." Dr. Bergstrom frowned in commiseration. "So, in addition to one's age, hormonal changes and sleep deprivation, trauma and emotional distress, are triggers for *emotional* eating. One of the most important clearances required for the surgery is submitting to a few counseling sessions with a psychologist. Having those sessions will help you to unpack those issues, and to identify the underlying causes for this extreme shift in weight in the past few years."

"That sounds promising." Evaniese smiled. "I'm so sorry, Dr. Bergstrom. I realize you don't have that kind of time. Believe me, it would certainly take a moment to unpack all of my issues." She shook her head in negation. "*So* much has happened." Evaniese pushed back into the armchair.

"I understand. There are a lot of factors to consider with any Bariatric procedure. Part of the process is a monthly weigh-in. We will no doubt submit the claim to your insurance company, but they need to see that *you're* doing your part in taking the weight off on your own." Dr. Bergstrom's expression was solemn, as he began to go over some of the foods she would need to avoid on her weight loss journey.

"I understand," Evaniese acquiesced. "Do you foresee any problems with my insurance?" She frowned in jeopardy. She had to ask. Quite honestly, she didn't think she'd be able to lose any weight on her own. After all, failure to manage her weight, was exactly what had brought her there. Hence, the reason why she wanted to submit to weight loss surgery.

"Don't worry. We'll handle the technicalities with your medical insurance company. Your part is to focus on not gaining any *more* weight in the interim, while you muddle through the clearances required." He smiled hopefully over at the beautiful, but sad young woman.

Evaniese sighed, relieved. "Okay… I will do my very best. Is there anything else that needs to happen today?" she quizzed.

"The nurse will come out in a little while for your first weigh-in."

An internal alarm immediately went off for Evaniese. She and the scale had had a sketchy relationship in the past. For all intents and purposes, the scale was an enemy. Evaniese wasn't psychologically prepared to see the number. She knew she'd gained a significant amount of weight in the past few years. *Was she prepared to face the truth about just how much?* Evaniese avoided getting on a scale at all costs. However, with this new undertaking, she was going to have to become reacquainted with the enemy. "Oh, okay," she acceded.

"You already have all the paperwork. If you have any questions or concerns, please don't hesitate to call or email this office."

"Thank you, Dr. Bergstrom, I will." Evaniese stood to her feet.

"It was nice meeting you today, Evaniese! Good luck with everything! I think you're making a very good decision."

Evaniese issued a timid smile. "That remains to be seen."

"Trust me when I say you definitely are." Dr. Bergstrom gave her an encouraging wink.

Moments later, Evaniese stood on the digital scale waiting for her weight to come into focus. She cringed in shock, and embarrassment when the numbers calibrated 244 pounds. From the time she'd gotten down to a size ten back in 2009, she was up by 64 pounds.

"You can step off now," the nurse told her, and noted the number in Evaniese's chart.

"Thank you," Evaniese said thickly, fighting back tears.

She couldn't help thinking that the beautiful, thin, twenty-something, Caucasian nurse, was judging her. Evaniese was mortified. Although she wanted to ask if the number on the scale was correct, she was too embarrassed to open up her mouth. She'd wanted to remain in denial, but the truth was staring her in the face. More than ever, she had to follow through with her plan to undergo the procedure, before she found herself back up to 330 pounds.

***

"I think Dr. Andrews might actually like her," Nia Brighton said. She was one of the physician's assistants who worked through Brookline Hospital's Emergency Room. She and her work colleague engaged in conversation, while on break in the ER breakroom.

Janice Hubert, another nurse, shook her head contrarily with a dubious expression on her face. "You *really* think he likes her? Evaniese is so fat," she berated.

"Well, some men like bigger women," Nia argued.

Janice shook her head in negation again. "Nah! There's no way. I *can't* see him being interested in her. Something tells me Dr. Andrews threw that wedding ring on fast, because he probably thought Evaniese was mistaking his kindness for interest." Janice issued a cunning smile. "He *also* put it on, because every woman working through the hospital are throwing themselves at him."

"Yeah, I agree with Janice, Nia. Dr. Andrews put on that wedding ring to keep the women at bay…especially Evaniese. *Maybe*, he was being nice to her in the beginning, but he killed that noise fast," Nurse Kyla Dwyer assessed.

"Whatever the case, I'm so relieved he's keeping that overweight witch at arm's length (I'm also glad that medium I connected with help me put a spell on her so that she can stay fat). "I can't stand her. She's a big girl, but she's so pretty. She's also smart, well-spoken, prim and proper. '*I love Jesus!*'" Kyla parodied.

Evaniese had shared her faith openly with everyone in the ER. So, they all knew she was a Christian, but Kyla just thought of Evaniese as a *Jesus freak*. *What woman would still be waiting for God to bless her with a good husband at the* **tender** *age of 46? What woman would remain celibate for that length of time? What on earth was wrong with Evaniese?* Kyla judged that Evaniese didn't drink, smoke, party, curse or even date for that matter.

"I can't even lie. Evaniese *is* gorgeous! What gets on my nerves is that everyone who comes across her desk is *always* telling her how pretty she is. I'm also sure she's a little stuck up, because she's a former teacher. Even so, right now, she's just a glorified ER Receptionist," Nia vilified.

"Evaniese *does* has a beautiful face! She's shapely, but that shape is way too full (And I will see to it that it stays that way). She dresses well, smells nice, and does a good job around here. Still, that doesn't mean she *deserves* someone like Nathan Andrews (She will only get close to him over my dead body)," Janice susurrated, backhandedly.

"You got that right. If none of *us* got a guy like Nathan Andrews, that woman isn't going to either," Kyla delineated. (I saw a medium, and she helped me put a hex on Evaniese, so that she will never lose weight. I also saw to it that things fell apart with Jeremy Carter)

"If Ms. Evaniese Spencer didn't get anywhere with Dr. Carter, she's certainly not going to get anywhere with Dr. Andrews. That heifer doesn't get to do better than any of us," Kyla established. A ripple of laughter echoed from the hollow of her throat. "Have you noticed how much weight she's gained lately? She wasn't *that* big when she first started working here."

"I *know*. It's like watching someone pump helium into her body," Nia added, and shook her head nonsensically. (The spell is working. It's obvious she *can't* lose any weight).

"I tell you… Some people have absolutely no self-control. Then, again, I think Evaniese might be *depressed*. I would be sad too if I was a forty something, Christian, waiting on the Lord to bring the right man into my life. Looks like God forgot all about her."

"Poor Evaniese. She couldn't get anywhere near Jeremy, and she's certainly not getting her hooks into Nathan. I don't care how smart or pretty she is. I don't even care how good she is at her job. My husband's a regular guy. And, if *I* didn't get a prince charming, she's certainly not getting one," Janice concluded.

"Well, I doubt we have to worry about her getting close to Dr. Andrews. He's been working here for two years. Not only has he failed to take her out, but purporting to be a married man, he keeps that wedding band on his finger. So, that ship has sailed," Kyla scorned. "Poor, beautiful, but fat Christian Evaniese," she said sardonically. "No matter how beautiful a face she has, she will always be fat-shamed for obesity."

***

"Who is your insurance carrier, sir?" Evaniese went over routine registration questions with a new patient. It was almost 6 p.m., and she'd just registered a woman brought over to the ER for severe abdominal pain. Evaniese was only three hours into her shift, but if felt like a lot longer. In the interim, she'd accomplished a great deal.

The ER was congested and busy. It had been that way from the outset of her shift, and didn't show any signs of slowing down. As it stood, she had admissions paperwork completed for six patients. Evaniese wanted to rush over to the ER breakroom to use the ladies room. But, she couldn't. There was no one else to keep up with the steady influx of work. If she stopped, she'd fall terribly behind.

"You can have a seat out in the waiting room, sir. They'll call you in shortly," Evaniese told the middle-aged gentleman, after updating his information in the computer. Clearly in pan, his face warped in discomfort. So, Evaniese gave him a sympathetic look, as she set the hospital information band on his wrist. "Feel better."

"Thank you," the gentleman muttered, and walked deliberately back out to the ER waiting area.

A few more admissions were called. So, Evaniese had more paperwork to handle. Opening up her desk drawer, she pulled out the forms in order to get started.

As she prepped paperwork for the patients and their families, the office phone rang once again. "Brookline ER, Evaniese speaking...," she answered.

"Hello, Evaniese," Paula River's voice was subtle. She was the Director of the Admissions Department, and fundamentally Evaniese's boss.

Upon hearing Paula's voice over the line, Evaniese's heartstrings immediately tightened. Whenever Paula called during her shifts, it never meant anything good for Evaniese. Evaniese automatically started praying in her heart. Paula wasn't a very nice person, and undoubtedly an unfair boss. Nevertheless, Evaniese prayed for wisdom to handle whatever Paula threw her way.

"Good evening, Paula!" Evaniese said temperately.

"How are things looking down in the ER?" Paula asked glibly.

Overwhelmed and stressed, Evaniese suppressed feelings of frustration. "It's extremely busy, but I'm holding my own," she tried to sound upbeat.

"Well, I'm calling to tell you about a few problems noted in a number of your registrations."

"Problems?" Evaniese questioned, perturbed.

"Yes, you've made several errors processing the correct insurance information. You've also neglected to fill out the box indicating the patients' primary care physicians. That information has been left out without any notes on a number of your registrations. I have printouts of at least twenty-five of those errors. I am currently holding them in my hand," Paula deprecated.

Evaniese blinked back tears. She always worked so conscientiously to ensure she wouldn't make egregious errors. Evaniese tried not to be so hard on herself. After all, she had to work the busy ER registration office all alone.

Rather than becoming exasperated, she took a few deep breaths to maintain aplomb. "I'm sorry. I will try to be more careful in the future, but it gets extremely bus-"

"It doesn't matter how busy it gets, Evaniese. It is your *responsibility* to fill out those registration forms correctly in the system. There are no excuses. That's what you're *paid* to do," Paula censured. "Now, if you can't handle the work...?"

"I will be more cautious about filling in all the gaps," Evaniese reassured, with tears stinging in her eyes.

"Ann and I will still need to set up a meeting with you. There are a number of other discrepancies we've stumbled upon in as far as your work."

"Oh, okay...," Evaniese acceded.

Inwardly, she was falling apart. *How on earth did my life become this? God, I know you have something better out there for me. You said you wanted me to work here, but I don't know how much longer I can stand this,"* she reflected.

"I can come in a few minutes earlier during the week- that is if you need for me to come up to the office," she told Paula.

"Ann and I will let you know when we decide," Paula said curtly.

"That's fine," Evaniese said. "By the way, is Gail coming down for my fifteen minute break?" Evaniese brought up.

"No. I've decided that Gail is to stay up here in the admissions office. So, as of today, she will no longer be coming down to offer you a break. You're only entitled to you dinner break, and that's that," Paula settled.

Evaniese's heart dipped down to the floor. "I understand," she conceded.

"Desiree has pointed out that you come in exactly at three to relieve her. You should come in a little earlier," Paula added.

Desiree was Evaniese's coworker who worked from 7 a.m. to three p.m. Evaniese was responsible for relieving her every day.

"I understand," Evaniese granted, wiping tears away from her eyes.

"So, it's *really* busy down there?" Paula asked rhetorically.

At that point, Evaniese was irritated. She had a ton of work to do, and her dim-witted boss refused to get off the phone.

"Evaniese," Dr. Morris popped his head through the open registration office door, "do you have admissions paperwork for Jonathan Masters?" he asked impatiently, with flustered cheeks.

Startled, Evaniese addressed him, while Paula was still on the phone, "I should have it for you in just a minute," she said softly, trying to keep aplomb.

"Jonathan Masters is going up to the fourth floor. So, we need that paperwork right away," Dr. Morris said urgently, and gestured for Evaniese to get a move on it.

"Paula, if you'll excuse me, Dr. Morris is asking for paperwork..."

"All right, Evaniese. Like I said, you've got to do better. I will be emailing you the details of this meeting Ann and I want to have with you."

"Okay," Evaniese said passively.

"All right then," Paula said deliberately.

Evaniese stared heavenward, and rolled her eyes in frustration. She couldn't believe how clueless her boss was. The ER was bustling, and she had no time to dally over the phone. Evaniese grasped that Paula Rivers had absolutely no idea what she went through regularly down in the ER. No doubt, the woman probably wouldn't have lasted five minutes in her shoes. Evaniese had to tinkle, but couldn't leave her desk, because all kinds of demands were made of her.

Moments later, Evaniese rushed into the ER, and handed the complete registration packet over to Dr. Morris. As she strolled back over to her office, she saw Nathan sitting at the second registration desk. Even if she had mixed feelings about seeing him, Evaniese's heart lashed.

From what she understood, God had revealed Nathan Andrews as *her* guy. However, the circumstances-and even Nathan himself, seemed to be speaking a totally different story. Even from a good distance away, Evaniese could see the stupid wedding ring on his finger. So, the internal conflict resonated. *Why had God placed her in such a cruel situation?*

Evaniese was very attracted to Nathan. So, *friendship* was the very last thing on *her* mind. For a while, it seemed Nathan had wanted more than friendship too. However, he'd since recanted, and was singing a different tune. He continued to maintain that he was a happily married man. And yet, as it would seem, he also wanted to keep his connection to Evaniese intact. Evaniese was 46 years-old, and had waited all her life for the right person to come along. That said, she really didn't need any more *friends*, especially ones who looked like Doctor Nathan Andrews.

All of her past relationships had failed. She'd opened up her heart to Brent and Jeremy, but both men had vehemently rejected her. Even so, Evaniese wanted to remain obedient. She wanted to trust God through this seemingly impossible and excruciating process with Nathan. In spite of the consternations, she walked back into the registration office.

"Evaniese!" Nathan announced, beaming. He veered towards the open doorway to look at her. "I knew you were around here somewhere. The air smelled of your sweet perfume!" Nathan stood to his feet.

"I didn't know you were working through the hospital today," Evaniese said nervously.

Her heart strummed all the more, as she took a moment to size up how incredible Nathan looked in his navy-blue designer dress suit. He looked as serene and enigmatic as a cool overcast day. His dramatic dark hair and bronze eyes, made her heart somersault, and the butterflies danced a new jig in the pit of stomach.

"Yes, I'm here today. In fact, I came in earlier than usual. There are a lot of patients to admit to the hospital. And, the bulk of them are down here in the ER," Nathan's voice resonated. Slipping his arms cautiously about Evaniese's waist, he crushed her to himself. "It's so nice to see you!"

Evaniese awkwardly wrapped her arms around Nathan, and squeezed him in return. It felt nice to touch him, and to be touched. Yet and still, she knew the hug probably meant something totally different for him than it did to her.

"It's nice to see you as well! I've missed seeing you these past few days." Evaniese automatically released her hold from about his waist.

Nathan pulled back, but still stood in close proximity to Evaniese. "Yeah, same here. It's strange whenever I work through the hospital, and I don't get to see your beautiful face!" Nathan gave her an impish wink.

Evaniese smiled. "Thank you. I actually look for you too whenever I don't see *you* around," she admitted.

She longed for the fulfillment of God's promise, and for Nathan to make a definitive move. Changing the status of their relationship was what she wanted more than anything else. However, two years had passed, and she was quickly losing heart.

"Well, that's good to know, because it's really nice having a *friend* like you around here. Thank you for always being so nice," Nathan said with an open smile.

Evaniese offered him a cordial smile as well. She then walked past him, and sauntered over to her work desk. Slipping into the armchair, she turned towards Nathan. "I'm glad we're *friends* too." Evaniese's heart crashed in disappointment.

Again, *friendship* wasn't what she was after. She couldn't help noticing how Nathan's muscles rippled with every move he made through his attractive attire. A lot of the hospitalist didn't wear hospital robes or gowns on their shifts. Nathan was one of those who enjoyed dressing to the nines. In fact, whenever he worked through the hospital, he always dressed as if he was conducting a photoshoot for some trendy men's magazine.

"How have you been?" Evaniese asked Nathan, while simultaneously trying to focus on her work. It was always that way. They usually chatted, while working at their respective desks.

"I've been good! My wife and I were in Hawaii last week," Nathan gladly announced.

Evaniese offered a halfhearted smile. Inwardly, she was crushed. "Oh, is that so? That sounds amazing!" she tried to sound upbeat, as she blinked back tears. Just then, all of the disappointments of her day seem to overwhelm.

During her consult for Bariatric surgery, the first weigh-in revealed she was close to 250 pounds. As much as she'd tried to manage her weight over the years, she'd failed miserably. Hence, the reason why she felt compelled to submit to weight loss surgery.

Then, there was her current job. She often felt beleaguered by Paula Rivers and Ann Ridges. They took advantage of her, abused her, and yet expected her performance to be flawless. And now, she found herself sitting next to incredibly handsome and young Dr. Nathan Andrews. Nathan was about sixteen years her junior. Upon meeting him, he'd hinted at *liking* her. However, in a relatively short time, he'd taken it all back. At that juncture, he kept referring to her as his *friend*, and talked about a *wife* all the time.

"Oh, my *wife* and I had an amazing time in Maui. We've always wanted to go. Have you ever been?" Nathan veered from the computer monitor at the desk to look at Evaniese.

"No, I haven't been. Sounds nice. Maybe, I will get to go one of these days." The rubber smile stretched across Evaniese's face.

"You've definitely got to get out there, Evaniese. Life's too short not to do the things you enjoy," Nathan said with an irrepressible smile.

Inwardly, *he* felt conflicted. He had to keep up the pretense of wanting to be friends with Evaniese. It was the *only* way he could stay connected to her.

He'd asked Evaniese out when he first started working through the hospital. Meeting her for the first time felt like a dream come true. She was beautiful, smart, kind and everything amazing! She was a full-figured, but extremely beautiful woman! To Nathan, it made no difference that Evaniese was considerably older. In his opinion, they looked to be about the same age.

Though, it didn't take too long for some guy by the name of Brent Peterson to start stressing him out about Evaniese. Brent had warned Nathan to stay away from her. The man said Evaniese *belonged* to him. So, Nathan had to find a way to redirect. He'd started the rhetoric of being a married man. Things being what they were, any *romantic* inclination he might have had towards Evaniese, was an impossibility.

Truth be told, Nathan was head-over-heels in love with her! Against all he believed, he acceded to the fact that he couldn't have her. So, the only way he could continue to spend time around her, was to discourage anything other than the platonic. For that reason, Nathan maintained he was married. Upholding such a claim, delineated that he and Evaniese had to respect the boundaries.

Evaniese met Nathan's eyes expectantly and forced a smile. "Yes, I agree. I certainly do need to get out there more. I honestly don't want to miss out on anything in life." Evaniese continued multitasking at her desk.

"And you *shouldn't* miss out. You're too smart, too beautiful, and much too kind not to get all the things you want in life." Nathan gave her a playful wink.

Evaniese smiled faintly over Nathan's compliment. His words offered hope. That was, until he opened up his mouth to speak again.

"I want you to be just as happy as my wife and I are. I would want that kind of happiness for you."

"Thanks, Nathan." Evaniese nodded compliantly.

That conversation with Nathan only added insult to injury. Evaniese wasn't having the best day, and couldn't wait for her shift to end. As soon as it did, she'd be able to go home. Once there, she'd get down on her knees, and cry out to her Heavenly Father for strength and deliverance. Evaniese couldn't fathom this sad chapter of her life being the end of the story. She prayed that God would lighten her load, meet her needs, and give her the victory in all the areas of her life.

***

"I've noticed Dr. Nathan Andrews has been spending a lot of time with Evaniese down in the ER," Paula Rivers spoke to Ann Ridges. Paula had called an impromptu meeting in her office.

"Oh right... He's the new hospitalist," Ann affirmed. "I've seen him around. He's extremely handsome!" she added.

"Yes, quite young and extremely good-looking! He's also been spending utterly too much time down in the registration office with Evaniese." Paula's face rumpled in annoyance. "I wonder what's going on there. Are they friends? *From what I've heard*, he's married."

"That's what I've heard too. Still, from what I understand, he and Evaniese have been *close* since he started working here," Ann explained. "He sits with her at the second desk down in the ED every chance he gets. That desk has remained unoccupied for the past two years," Ann pointed out.

"Well, it might be the right time to hire someone to help *poor* Evaniese out after all. I don't want her getting any closer to this doctor," Paula said grudgingly. "I wouldn't want Evaniese getting any ideas-if you know what I mean." She scowled in displeasure.

"Of course... I know *exactly* what you mean. You want to hire someone new for the second registration desk?" Ann's expression was solemn.

"Yes, it might be time to give Evaniese *exactly* the help she's been asking for. I don't like that Dr. Nathan Andrews is frequenting the registration office. Hiring someone else to work the shift will discourage that."

"I totally agree. So, I'll start interviewing potential employees as early as the end of the week," Ann established.

"The sooner the better. This *friendship* Evaniese has with Dr. Andrews has to be nipped in the bud at all costs," Paula contrived, with a calculating expression on her face.

"I'm already on it," Ann encouraged.

***

"I had a nice time with you tonight, Brent," Celia Douglas told Brent.

Brent had just walked her to her front door after their date. Now, he was saying goodnight. It was the third time he and Celia had gone out.

The beautiful blonde-haired and blue-eyed beauty was confused. Since meeting Brent a couple of weeks ago, he hadn't even made an attempt to kiss her.

"I had a nice time too, Celia," Brent said pleasantly. Hunching down, he pressed a generic kiss to her cheek.

Celia draped her arms about his neck, inched up, and pressed her lips to his. However, the moment her lips bridged to Brent's, he tensed up.

Brent found himself halfheartedly responding to Celia's kiss. In a corner of his mind, all he could think about was Evaniese. Society dictated how wrong she was for him, but Brent couldn't stop thinking about, or wanting the beautiful, full-figured African American woman.

Brent gently pulled out of Celia's loving grasp. "I'll call you later," he said croakily, inching away.

"Okay. That sounds nice," Celia's voice wavered. She was totally disheartened. "Thank you for dinner."

No matter how hard she tried, she couldn't seem to capture the attention of the handsome and affluent man. Brent Peterson was one of the most eligible bachelors in Amber Hills, and Celia was chomping at the bit to snag him.

"You're welcome!" Brent said deliberately, as he continued to pull away. "It was my pleasure!" Brent distanced himself even more decidedly at that point. "Goodnight," he said, before turning and walking over to his limo.

"Goodnight." Celia's face wrinkled in disappointment and uncertainty.

The fact that Brent had rushed away was a slap to the face. Before long, she saw him get into the automobile. Opening up her front door, she slipped inside the house. With her back pressed up to the door, she surrendered to tears.

***

Later back at his mansion, Brent staggered into his bedroom. Having had one too many drinks after his date with Celia, he was *three-sheets to the wind*. Drinking himself into a stupor was uncharacteristic. However, it mollified the sting of despair he grappled with since losing Evaniese. In so many ways he'd lied to her. He told Evaniese she wasn't his type, and that he couldn't have been any less interested in her. Those lies had destroyed his life, and had left him with a bleeding heart.

Brent couldn't fathom Evaniese forgiving him after such a blatant rejection. Aside from repudiating her, he'd made racially charged comments, and compared her to hamburgers and Filet Mignon. Consequently, she was the former of the two food choices. Making matters worse, he'd gone on a rant on how some people liked *hamburgers*, while others preferred *Filet Mignon*. Now, while sitting on his bed, wasted, tears were in Brent's eyes.

"I was scared. I lost Evaniese, because I was too scared to stand up to my family and friends," Brent groused and bawled. "I was terrified to take a stand, and tell her the truth. The truth is that I love her more than anything in the world. I lost her, and it's all because I wasn't strong enough to tell *everyone* else to take a hike. Now, those darned doctors at Brookline have their eyes on *my* girl.

"God, Evaniese is still *my* girl, even if we haven't spoken for the past six years. She's still mine, and belongs to me. God, help me. I don't know how to fix what's broken between us. I love her, Lord! Please, help me find a way to fix it." Brent set the glass on his nightstand, fell down to his knees, buried his face in his hands and wailed. "Please, show me how to fix it, Lord. I messed up, and I lost the most precious thing in the world to me.

"I've made up my mind. If *I* can't have her, no one else will. I had to deal with that Doctor Jeremy Carter. He had a *thing* for Evaniese, so paying him off to leave the hospital was the right move. Now, I've had to drill it into that Doctor Nathan Andrews that Evaniese belongs to *me*.

"No one's taking her away from me. I ran those other men away. Honestly, I'm *not* sorry I did," Brent admitted to God. He realized only God could help him out of the mess he'd created. Six years ago, on an afternoon at the church, he'd told Evaniese she meant absolutely nothing to him. Sometime later, he proved it by leaving *God is for us Church*. Regardless, Brent remained hopeful. Perhaps, God would help him find his way back to the right path.

Chapter Two

"We *definitely* need two containers of heavy whipping cream," Ginger Regel told Evaniese on a Saturday afternoon. They were picking up a few things at the *Health Fair Supermarket*.

Evaniese found herself both preoccupied, and a little distracted in the produce aisle. Her thoughts were a million miles away. There was so much happening in her life at that juncture. Even if she'd asked her friends to come along on her shopping excursion, Evaniese could hardly remain engaged in the task at hand. She had a lifestyle vlog on her YouTube channel. And later, she would upload a video sharing her special recipe for homemade cream of spinach soup.

"Evaniese, does the recipe call for parsley?" Deanna Corley asked.

Ginger and Deanna were Evaniese's best friends.

"Don't even bother asking her, Deedee." Ginger rolled her eyes in annoyance. "Evaniese is in a totally different zone right now. I don't know why she asked us to tag along, when she's completely MIA."

"Huh…?" Evaniese said, hearing only the last few words Ginger had said.

Both Ginger and Deanna stared curiously over at Evaniese.

"I'm so sorry, guys. Did you say something?" Evaniese was roused from reflection.

Since her consult with Dr. Bergstrom about the weight loss surgery, she'd been unable to think of much else. Evaniese was eager to get the medical clearances out of the way as soon as humanly possible. In her heart and mind, the surgery represented her saving grace.

However, she had yet to tell her closest friends about her life-altering resolve.

"Evaniese, Dee and I asked about the ingredients for the soup. Are we getting parsley? I thought I heard you mention parsley, but it isn't on the list," Ginger clarified. "Then, again, you would have heard what we said, if you weren't in a totally different headspace. What's going on, honey?" Ginger's face wrinkled, pertained.

"Yeah, you've been distant all morning." Deanna ambled over, and stood right in front of the shopping cart. "I mean, if you don't feel like company, I totally understand."

Evaniese shook her head contrarily. "No, it's nothing like that." She offered a temperate smile, as she took a moment to size up her besties. Ginger and Deanna were gorgeous! Both were thin, and had amazing bodies. Neither was plagued by obesity and weight issues.

Evaniese could honestly admit she envied *anyone* who didn't have to struggle with their weight. Ginger was about 5'7", Caucasian, strawberry-blonde hair and pretty green eyes. Deanna stood at about 5'4, and had a coffee complexion. She was curvy in all the right places, and had amber eyes. In Evaniese's opinion, her best friends were perfect. For that reason, she felt conflicted about telling them about her decision to have weight loss surgery.

"Then, what's going on, Niecy? Is there something wrong?" Ginger prodded.

Evaniese stalled for a moment, and anxiously fiddled with the cart handle. "Nothing's wrong, actually. In fact, things are right for the first time in a while. I've made a life-altering decision this year! It's something I haven't even told my family about." Evaniese looked over at her friends at intervals.

"Niecy, are you okay?" Deanna set her hand on Evaniese's arm in concern.

"I'm fine." Evaniese nodded and smiled. "So, this past Thursday, I took a trip over to the hospital's Bariatric Center."

"What?" Ginger's eyes widened in shock. "You talked about it in the past, but are you actually thinking about having surgery?" Bewilderment veiled her face.

"I've decided to go through with it." Evaniese nodded confidently. "I've been on the diet roller coaster for a while now, and nothing's worked. And, you both *know* how hard I've worked to take off the weight."

"Hold on a minute here. Are you serious? You want to have surgery?" Deanna kept shaking her head, incredulous and nonplused.

Evaniese's smile was taut, as she stared between her friends for positive affirmation. However, it seemed, Ginger and Deanna were on the fence.

"Niece, whatever happened to the Atkins Diet?" Ginger asked, clearly rattled by Evaniese's announcement.

"I've been on *some form* of the Atkins for years, Ginger. None of that's working for me," Evaniese argued.

"But, have you tried other diets out there? You could try Weight Watchers. Weight loss surgery is such a drastic measure," she disputed.

Evaniese suddenly felt defeated. She'd just shared how excited she was over her decision with her besties, and their response seemed lackluster. Evaniese had hoped for their total support and understanding. However, their reaction was anything but.

"I've already filled out the forms. I'll have to get a ton of medical clearances out of the way, before I'm approved," Evaniese explained. At best, she anticipated a delayed spark of joy from her buddies.

"Oh, okay, Niecy…," Deanna halfheartedly acceded. "If that's what you want… Honestly, I really don't think you're that *big*. Diet and exercise are key to getting healthy. Weight loss surgery is something you can't take back. It's either they reroute your intestines, cut your stomach, or stretch it out in some way…" Deanna had an awkward smile on her face, as she tried to deliver her words with finesse. Somehow, she was failing miserably at the task.

"Yeah, Niecy, Dee's right. I've heard horror stories of people who've had WLS. Some of them wind up regaining all their weight back, and with interest. I could refer you to my personal trainer," Ginger added, rubbing caringly on Evaniese's arm.

Evaniese's heart plunged to the floor. Yet and still, after praying on the matter, she refused to allow her friends to discourage her. God had shown her that submitting to the Vertical Sleeve Gastrectomy procedure was the *right* thing to do. All the same, she couldn't say she wasn't hurt over Ginger and Deanna's discouraging words.

In spite of their contrary stance, Evaniese smiled all the more. "I honestly believe submitting to the procedure is in the will of God," she settled.

"Okay, honey." Ginger's smile was strained. "If that's what you want to do, we're behind you all the way."

"Of course, you've got our support, Niecy," Deanna stated diffidently.

"It's important for me to know the two of you have my back. As it is, the process is long and drawn out." Evaniese stared pleadingly into the eyes of her friends.

"Yes, of course you do," Ginger affirmed, and wrapped her arms about Evaniese.

"Group hug…?" Deanna's face puckered emotionally, as she looked from Evaniese to Ginger. "Bring it in," she encouraged them, and crushed them both in her arms. "I've got your back, girlfriend," she told Evaniese, as they pulled away.

Evaniese smiled, and caught the tears brimming over her eyelids with her fingertips. Guffawing, she tried to rule away the sappiness. "I'm so glad you guys have got my back. That means everything to me!" She stared lovingly, and sympathetically at her closest friends.

"Now, are we shopping for your soup recipe on the vlog or not?" Ginger perked up.

"I'd love help in putting the recipe together. So, let's get everything on the list. And yes, totally grab a bunch of parsley. I can't let my subscribers down." Evaniese smiled hearteningly.

"How many subscribers are you up to now, Niece?" Deanna searched the list, as they promenaded the store, quickly grabbling the items needed from the produce aisle.

"Almost 122K," Evaniese expressed with a sense of dignity.

"That's awesome! Girl, I'm so proud of you! Your YouTube channel *blew up*," Deanna uplifted.

"Well, I had to do *something* for a little extra money. The hospital pays almost nothing," Evaniese admitted.

"Well, keep up the good work! I'm *sure* those YouTube royalties help a lot," Ginger added.

"No doubt. I thank God for blessing me with *other* hobbies." Evaniese smiled, feeling fortunate. It meant the world to have the support of her friends.

And yet, there was *one* prayer God had yet to answer. Evaniese longed to share a life with someone special. She'd chronicled her relationship with Nathan. He'd changed drastically from the time they'd met. It honestly broke her heart. She had no idea what transpired between them to make him withdraw. Nathan had done a complete one-eighty. How much he'd changed still confused Evaniese. It was cruel that he seemed to want to stay connected, while simultaneously keeping her at bay. Adding insult to injury, Evaniese didn't have the option of walking away.

If God hadn't shown her Nathan was tied into her destiny, Evaniese could have dealt with his illusiveness. Furthermore, she could have even tolerated his blatant disregard for her feelings by bringing up a wife all the time. Nathan undoubtedly knew Evaniese liked him. All the same, moving on from Nathan wouldn't have been so difficult, if God hadn't mandated that she not give up.

Therefore, not having the option of walking away, left Evaniese in a furnace of affliction. She was in love with a man who maintained he was married. He'd told her he was only interested in being friends, while her faith dictated something else. The struggle was tearing Evaniese apart. And yet, even if she wasn't in a loving and committed relationship, she had hope. By submitting to the weight loss surgery, at least *one* of her fondest dreams would be fulfilled. She would finally be thin.

***

"Hey, sweetheart! How are you?" Aaron Sellers, Ginger's boyfriend was at her front door later that Saturday in the evening to pick her up for their date. "You look beautiful!" he praised, and slipped his arms about her waist.

Ginger forced a smile, and pressed a kiss to Aaron's cheek perfunctorily. She instinctively draped her arms about his neck, and relished the feel of his arms around her.

Aaron was her boyfriend of a year, and Ginger cared a great deal about him. He was a handsome and successful banker. Besides, he was kindhearted and thoughtful. So, he should have been the perfect distraction. Nevertheless, Ginger only had *one* thing on her mind that night.

Earlier on over at the supermarket, Evaniese had announced her plan to have weight loss surgery. The concept still gnawed away at Ginger. Evaniese was extremely beautiful! Being overweight, however, was the bane of her existence. Evaniese's weight problem was the one thing Ginger felt she and Deanna had over Evaniese.

"*Deanna and I could always say Evaniese was on the chunky side. Aside from that, Evaniese has everything going for her. Evaniese was totally perfect! What if she becomes as thin as Deedee and me? What if she becomes even thinner? Wow! I really don't know if I'm ready to deal with a new version of Evaniese.*

"*Evaniese can't become competition for me and for Deedee. As it is, I have to worry about* **Dee** *whenever we go out. If Evaniese loses the weight, she'll have it all. If she overcomes her weight issue, she'll be on equal footing with me and Dee. I really don't know if I'm prepared to handle that...*" Ginger's thoughts raced.

Confused by Ginger's lack of animation, Aaron pulled away and asked, "Are you okay, baby?"

Ginger gave him an exaggerated smile. "I'm fine, honey. Are we all set to go?" she evaded, avoiding eye contact with her boyfriend.

Inwardly, there was a storm brewing. Ginger assented to the fact that Evaniese *was* a great friend. However, the one thing she couldn't accept was Evaniese Spencer-*the fat girl* in their circle, becoming competition. Ginger didn't have it all figured out. One thing she knew for sure was that she didn't want to deal with the *thin version of Evaniese.* If that happened, Ginger knew for sure Evaniese would be the most *beautiful* one in their circle as well.

"I'm all set to go, sweetheart," Aaron reminded, nudging Ginger away from the front door. He slipped his arms around her waist again, as she shut the door closed. "I missed you so much today!" he said, beaming.

"I missed you too, baby," Ginger said, and planted a quick kiss to Aaron's cheek.

As Aaron helped Ginger into the car, there was only one thing on her mind. Evaniese could *never* be skinny. She was the *fat one*, and Ginger wanted it to stay that way. Evaniese was probably one of the most beautiful women in the world! Her only flaw was that she wasn't a size two or four.

Ginger felt conflicted. Although she recognized her feelings were wrong, she couldn't stop obsessing about Evaniese's resolve. Ginger worried it would change the dynamic of their friendship, and *not* in a good way. In her assessment, the friendship with Evaniese and Deanna *only* worked if Evaniese stayed the fat girl. Deanna was the shapely voluptuous vixen, while she was the beautiful blonde.

If Evaniese had the surgery, Ginger worried she'd surpass them both in status. So, on the way over to the restaurant with her boyfriend, Ginger couldn't stop obsessing about what Evaniese's resolve would do to their friendship. Evaniese would undoubtedly lose a ton weight after the procedure. So, Ginger found it difficult to be happy for, or to support her.

***

"Ellis, Ellis, over here. Can you give us a shot from the left?" the press and media demanded, doing all they could to get Ellis Roman's attention.

Ellis had just stepped outside of the theater from the premiere of his movie *Deadly Roulette*. It was the latest and greatest project he'd work on with Director, William Fold. Ellis was proud of the movie, but it always felt strange watching himself on the big screen. In spite of that fact, he was slowly but surely getting used to it.

It had been a long but remarkable night! Stepping out on the red carpet with Kierra Spalding earlier on, the press had taken hundreds of photos. Kierra was already headed over to the premiere after party. Even so, Ellis was grateful he and Kierra had agreed to attend the party separately.

Spending the entire night of the premiere with Kierra, was a bit too close for comfort in Ellis's opinion. So, he definitely needed a little breathing room. The thirty-five-year-old actor, activist, philanthropist and producer, often grew weary of the spotlight. There were times he just wanted to disappear. However, being a Hollywood A-lister hardly fostered privacy. Also, as a bachelor, he was *expected* to switch up the women in his life as frequently as his designer wear.

"Ellis, Ellis, look this way…," the entertainment reporters, and the media continued to shout his name. "You're really *owning* that suit, Ellis! Great look!"

"Are you and Kierra an item? She's been on your arm for a number of recent events," a reporter from *Entertainment Buzz Magazine* noted.

It was the second time that reporter had made that inquiry. Ellis had ignored him the first time. However, this time around, Ellis decided to rejoinder. Smiling diffidently, he shook his head comically over the young journalist's inquest. "Kierra and I are great friends."

"Still, we're clambering to know. Are you dating your *friend*?" Another entertainment representative probed.

"Since your breakup with Mia Sobel, Ms. Spalding's the only other woman we've seen on your arm," yet another tabloid reporter commented. The woman seemed eager for Ellis to reply.

"Thank you for coming out tonight, and for covering the premiere of the movie," Ellis said graciously. "Your support is greatly appreciated." That said, he took quick strides over to the waiting limo. His driver, Dylan, automatically opened up the car door.

"Ellis, Ellis, how does it feel to have the number one movie in America? And, will you collaborate with William Fold again…?"

"Ellis, Ellis…," the press kept calling out.

Before Ellis slipped into the limo, he waved, and offered friendly smiles to the mob of correspondents scrambling to pounce on him.

Ellis settled into the back seat of the automobile. He sighed, as his back pressed into the plush leather material.

"Where to, Ellis?" Dylan asked from the driver's seat. "Are we going to the after party?"

Ellis's face strained in frustration. However, he softened, and offered Dylan an amiable smile.
"Unfortunately, I have to put in appearance. Apparently, I'm not allowed to skip out on my own after party," he said farcically.

"You don't sound very excited about attending." Dylan turned, and gave Ellis a curious smile. He then veered back towards the open street, and cautiously began rolling away from the area.

Ellis chuckled. "Can you tell I just want to go home at this point?"

Dylan laughed. "Yeah, it's pretty obvious."

"I'm going to have you to standby after you drop me off at the club. I'll go in for a few minutes, then pull a quick disappearing act," Ellis contrived.

"What about Kierra? Isn't she meeting you there?" Dylan inquired, perplexed.

"Yes. The plan is to spend a few minutes with her, then pull out just as soon as I can. You *know* how much I hate that entire scene. So, I'm not staying one minute longer than I have to."

"I got you, Ellis," Dylan reassured.

"Thanks, man. I really appreciate it."

***

"You totally killed it in that movie, Ellis!" Vanessa Noble walked over to Ellis's table inside the Nosey Neighbor Club at the after party. She was a very prolific actress in the industry, and quite beautiful! Many A-list actors were either trying to work with, or date the blonde-haired, blue-eyed beauty. Ellis himself was a great fan of her work. She had won an *Oscar* and a *Golden Globe* for her outstanding performance in the movie, *Ghost Leaks*.

Ellis set his drink down for a moment, and offered Vanessa a warm smile. He was there with Kierra, but she'd stepped away for a moment. "Thank you so much for liking the movie, and for coming out to support me tonight. That's such a compliment coming from you!" Ellis stood to his feet in acknowledgement of the young lady.

Vanessa walked around the table, and eliminated the space between Ellis and herself. "It's nice to finally meet you!"

Ellis took Vanessa's hand in his, and pressed a kiss to it. "The pleasure's all mine! I'm a huge fan of your work! In fact, I *have* been for a while. Your performance in *Ghost Leaks* blew me away!" Ellis admitted.

"Why thank you!" Vanessa chimed, as she sized up the gorgeous actor standing in front of her.

Ellis Roman was every woman's dream. Describing him as handsome was a total understatement. *Beautiful* was closer to the truth when one spoke of him. Ellis was tall, muscular, and had the sharpest features she'd ever seen on any man. With skin the color of butterscotch, copper-colored eyes, and dark, thick wavy hair, he was the dream! He also had the perfect body. Ellis naturally had the six-pack most men killed themselves to acquire at the gym.

Vanessa was a staunch fan, and had been for quite a while. Eager to attend the premier of *Deadly Roulette*, she'd pulled out all the stops to get her name onto the guest list. Vanessa had seen Kierra Spalding walk away from Ellis' table. So, she was using this little chunk of time to connect to Ellis. She was crazy about Ellis. So, she didn't care in the least whose toes she had to step on to get closer to him.

"*I* should be praising *you*, Ellis, for your work in the movie. Very impressive!" Vanessa winked and smiled at him.

"I appreciate that! Still, having such outstanding colleagues in the industry, inspires me to step up my game," Ellis said, grinning. "Would you like to have a seat?" he asked cordially.

Vanessa looked warily about for an indication of Kierra on the prowl. With no sign of the beautiful brunette, Vanessa tuned back into Ellis with a flirtatious smile. "I would love to!" she dallied.

"Can I get you a drink?" Ellis asked courteously.

Ellis undoubtedly admired Vanessa's work. Nevertheless, he was ready to cut out, and leave the after party. Yet, he couldn't be rude, neither could he blow off one of the biggest names in the industry. There was no telling if he and Vanessa would collaborate on a future project.

"Sure," Vanessa agreed, setting down at a chair across from Ellis.

Ellis was suddenly aware of the blare of music, the laughter, and the bustle all about the extensive club. The upheaval made him want to run away, and find solitude someplace else.

Ellis called one of the waiters over, and requested a drink for Vanessa. "What will you have?" he asked politely.

"Gin and tonic with lemon," she said, not once taking her eyes off of Ellis.

"Very well, Ma'am. I have one right here," the waiter announced, and handed her a drink from off his tray.

"So, how long did it take to wrap up work on the film?" Vanessa propped her right hand under her chin, and stared dreamily at Ellis Roman. The man was unquestionably causing quite a stir in Hollywood.

"We worked for about six months on different locations. We were in British Columbia for the first three, then we traveled to Greece and Australia for the remainder of the movie," Ellis explained.

"I knew I recognized the landscape for all of those pretty winter scenes. I knew those shots were from BC. Brilliant!" Vanessa praised.

"*I* also happen to think the scenery was breathtaking! Then again, it's *William Fold*, so you can only expect the best from him," Ellis raved.

"I agree," Vanessa said, mesmerized.

She couldn't help admiring how perfect Ellis looked in his black designer *Armani*. It was also difficult to stop staring at his perfect mouth. It didn't really matter what he said, just watching his lips move, and listening to his rich voice, was bedazzling. Ellis was a walking dream.

"*I* have to agree with you there. William Fold *is* one of the best in the trade," Kierra's voice infused the air, as she breezed back over to the table.

"Kierra," Ellis acknowledged, and immediately stood to his feet.

"Hello, Vanessa," Kierra said curtly, with daggers issuing from her eyes. She was no fool. The blonde vixen had designs on her date.

"Hello, Kierra," Vanessa feigned cordialness with a pretentious smile. "You look lovely tonight! *Who* are you wearing?"

"Thank you! My dress is a *Vanderhuff original!*" Kierra informed matter-of-factly, slipping her arms through Ellis's, and propping closer to his side.

"Well, it's lovely!" Vanessa painted another smile on her face. "I was just telling Ellis how much I loved the movie," Vanessa said uneasily.

Kierra set her arms around Ellis's waist, and posted herself to his left flank. She then began to stroke graspingly on his arm. "I respect William Fold as a director, but a director's only as good as his actors. After all, he *was* working with *Ellis Roman*." She stared proudly and territorially up at Ellis. "Ellis is a total natural! I doubt, he's capable of choosing a bad project," she praised, clinging all the more to him.

Ellis smiled awkwardly, unsettled that Kierra was handling him like property.

"Yes, Ellis definitely has a gift," Vanessa granted. She then pushed back in the chair, and stood to her feet. Displeasure and exasperation veiled her pretty face. "It was nice meeting you tonight, Ellis," her voice wavered

"Yes… Likewise, Vanessa." Ellis gave Vanessa a sympathetic look.

Vanessa reached down, and got her drink from off of the table. "Thanks for the drink." She gave him an alluring wink.

"You're welcome!" Ellis said

"Bye, Vanessa," Kierra said icily, as she watched Vanessa saunter away.

"I wasn't even gone five minutes…," Kierra muttered, and pressed a kiss to Ellis cheek.

"*Just* making conversation," Ellis refuted. He and Kierra weren't an item. They were casual friends. So, her possessive behavior puzzled him. "I admire her work, and I've always wanted to meet her," he admitted.

"I'm sure she's *always* wanted to meet *you*." Kierra remained glued to Ellis's side.

Just then, Ellis's phone went off. He knew it was Dylan. He'd asked Dylan to call him, so that he'd have an excuse to leave the party. Ellis had met his party quota for the night. He'd put in the time, and had hob-knobbed with his peers. Now, it was time to call it a night.

"If you'll excuse me, Kierra," he said politely. "I have to take this."

Ellis pulled his cell out from the inner pocket of his suit. "Roman here," he announced. "Yes, uh-huh. I understand... Tonight...," Ellis improvised, because Dylan wasn't saying a word. "Right now?" He glowered in urgency. "Sure."

"Is everything alright, Ellis?" Kierra frowned in concern.

"Everything's fine, Kierra." Ellis smiled at her. "Something's come up, and I have to leave right away."

"I was looking forward to dancing with you tonight," Kierra complained, feeling out of sorts. "It's *your* own after-party. Are you sure you can't stay?" She gave him a quizzical look.

"Maybe, next time." Ellis gave her an amiable smile. Then, hunching down, he pressed a kiss to her cheek. "Thanks for coming out with me tonight!" He explored her sad eyes.

"You're welcome!" Kierra said perfunctorily.

"Goodnight, Kierra." Ellis turned to leave. He was only a few feet away, when Kierra's voice halted him.

"I'll call you later, Ellis," she called out.

Ellis turned towards the pretty Brunette. "Sure. Feel free to give me a call. Bye, now."

"Bye, Ellis." Kierra stared longingly after him.

Ellis made his way through the crowd in a guarded manner. It wasn't easy, because everyone wanted to stop him to congratulate him on the movie. He shook a few hands, issued a few smiles, and thanked his supporters. Fifteen minutes later, he drifted quietly towards the back exit of the club. It was where he'd asked Dylan to pull up in order to meet him.

Ellis ambled over to the exit doors. However, on the verge of opening them up, he was met with a fiery embrace. He recognized the young actress from a number of movies. She draped her arms around his neck amorously. Paige Clemens stood on her tiptoes, and pressed her lips to Ellis's repeatedly.

Having been pounced on, Ellis's heart still thrummed. He'd honestly believed he'd be able to leave the club without incident. However, the young and *intoxicated* actress had other ideas.

"Do you know that you're my dream guy?" she slurred, staring beguilingly at Ellis.

"That's lovely, Paige...," Ellis said delicately. He was uncertain how to react. Paige was very young, but she was a very notable up and coming actor in the industry. "I'm flattered, but I've really got to get going now." Ellis tried not to be abrasive. In a gentle manner, he wriggled out of Paige's grasp.

"Oh no, don't leave. You're so handsome! You have any idea how handsome you are?" In addition to being inebriated, she was flustered, because Ellis already had his hand on the door handle.

"Thank you for saying that. I really appreciate it, Paige." Ellis opened up the door to his right-hand side, and cautiously slipped outside.

"I love your movie!" Paige put her right hand up, as a child would in elementary school to be called by their teacher. However, the door closed shut.

"Thank you," Ellis said, hearing her muffled voice, and shaking his head humorously over the incident.

All the same, he was more than relieved to be outside the club. Just then, Dylan pulled up in the limo to meet him. For Ellis, seeing the car represented salvation. All he wanted was to be able to breathe for a minute.

"So, it's back to the mansion for now, Ellis?" Dylan asked, as Ellis slipped into the back of the automobile.

"Absolutely, Dylan. It's been a long night. Thanks for everything."

"You're welcome, sir! Anytime. What *I* wouldn't give to have women throwing themselves at me in the way they do you," Dylan admitted.

"Dylan, you have no idea. Careful what you wish for," Ellis said absently.

His mind was light years away. It was strange to be coveted by so many people. There were times it felt as if he didn't even belong to himself. Everyone seemed to want a piece of him. It was even more bizarre to have women throwing themselves at him. It wasn't unusual for women to pounce on him in the way Paige Clemens had.

As Dylan drove them away from the glitz, glam and fanfare, Ellis couldn't help pondering the irony of life. So many women were making a play for him on the set of his movies, on social media, and wherever he traveled. He had over one hundred million followers on Instagram alone. The majority of his followers were women, who vowed to do anything he wanted.

They were constantly in his DM's expressing how much they loved him, and admired his work. And then, there were the racy and inappropriate pictures they sent, trying to entice him into succumbing to their advances. However, Ellis wasn't that kind of man.

He was a Christian man, and tried to live a life pleasing to God. Even if his career seemed counterproductive to that goal, Ellis knew God had him in that milieu for a purpose. He was there to exemplify a different kind of lifestyle in a sinful and temptation-ruled climate, without falling prey to it himself.

There was something else that kept Ellis on the straight and narrow. Ellis was in love with a woman he'd never even met. At that point, he had to conclude that he was in love, because the woman consumed his thoughts. All he knew about the mystery woman was that her name was *Niecy819*.

At least, that was her name on her YouTube channel. Ellis kept up with her home and lifestyle vlogs. It didn't make any sense, but he was totally smitten! She was a plus-sized, but voluptuously striking woman!

While in the limo, being a subscriber of *Niecy819*, Ellis received a notification on his phone that she'd just uploaded a new video on YouTube. He couldn't wait to get home, change out of his dress suit, settle down, and watch the young woman's video.

The video was about twenty minutes long. For Ellis, it really didn't even matter *what* she talked about. He just loved seeing and listening to her. Ellis could hardly contain his excitement and anticipation. It was a real struggle not to watch the video in the limo on the drive back home out in Malibu Summit.

However, Ellis desisted. He wanted to wait until he was settled in for the night. Seeing *Niecy819's* face, and hearing her lilting voice, would be a lot sweeter just before he turned in. Ellis laughed ironically as he considered, "Isn't that the way life is? You can have the all of the admiration in the world. But, the admiration from the *one* you want, almost always eludes you…" He shook his head risibly over such a conundrum.

***

Later, back at home, Ellis settled in. He slipped on his PJ.'s, and was just about ready to slip into bed. However, before he turned in, he got down on his knees to say his prayers. He worshiped God wholeheartedly for his many blessings. Furthermore, he thanked God for the success of his new movie. Ellis was grateful to have the presence of God in his life. And yet, he longed for someone to share his blessings with. Being alone was tough, but he resolved to trust God to meet that need in his life.

"God, in the entertainment industry, I see thousands of pretty faces and desirable bodies. There are many glamorous women out there, but..." Ellis paused. "I *know* that it doesn't make any sense, but the only woman I have eyes for is *Niecy819*. I just can't get enough of her videos." Ellis laughed at himself. "I realize how crazy that sounds, because I don't know her at all. Still, if you're going to bring someone into my life, I hope she's a lot like *Niecy819*.

"But what do *I* know, Lord? Your word says that you look on the heart (1Samuel 16:7). As human beings, we're only capable of seeing what's on the surface. So, being attracted to someone isn't enough. It has to go a lot deeper than that. You know what's best for me. So, I'm trusting that you'll bring the right person into my life." Ellis lifted up the name of Jesus in praise and worship.

It was after one in the morning when he finally slipped into bed. No longer able to resist, he pulled out his phone and accessed YouTube. An instant smile spread over his face when he saw *Niecy819*. No other woman was capable of sparking such happiness and joy in his heart. Ellis couldn't say that *one* specific thing about her inspired celebration. It was *everything* about her. She radiated a special light. And, that light often dispelled the shadows in his own world.

"So, before we can get started making our soup, we first have to separate all of the ingredients...," *Niecy819* cheerily began her vlog.

Ellis never grew tired of looking at her and hearing her voice. She looked positively adorable in a cream-colored floral-print sweater and dark jeans. Like an impressionable schoolboy, he beamed as he listened to the young woman demonstrate the steps required to make cream of spinach soup. Ellis knew he'd probably never try the recipe for himself. However, he *would* watch the video at least three times before he finally dozed off. And, even then, *Niecy 819's* face, her voice, and grace resonated in his dreams.

***

"Evaniese, wait up... Evaniese...," someone was calling. The voice reverberated from down the hill in the employee's parking lot of the hospital.

It took a moment for Evaniese to acknowledge that someone was calling her name. Making an instinctive turn, she looked to see who it was. Evaniese saw Nicole. Nicole was one of the few *friends* Evaniese had who worked through the hospital. She'd met Nicole during orientation when they were first hired to work there. However, because they worked in different departments, it had been quite a while since Evaniese had seen her.

Evaniese stood still, and waited for Nicole to catch up. Nicole was pretty nice, but Evaniese hardly felt like socializing. Showing up for work was protocol. But, she wasn't in the best frame of mind. Her life was riddled with misalignments. Three weeks ago, she'd embarked on a journey which would inevitably lead to Bariatric surgery. It was early February, and she'd just had her second weigh-in. And, despite her best efforts, she was up by four pounds.

Evaniese had done all she could to follow Dr. Bergstrom's directive of foods to avoid. So, for all intents and purposes, she should have been four pounds *down*, but that wasn't the case. Not having things go her way seemed to be the story of her life. Dr. Bergstrom and his staff had also expressed concern. They said in no uncertain terms that her medical insurance wouldn't pay for the procedure, if she continued to gain weight. It wasn't outside the realm of possibility that the insurance company would label her as *negligent.* Moreover, they could state how she'd failed to comply with the doctor's guidelines.

Then, there was Nathan. In the past week, Evaniese had texted him a number of times. However, Nathan had failed to respond. Sadder still, she hadn't seen him around the hospital in a while. God kept reassuring her that Nathan was indeed a part of his plan for her life. Even so, *Nathan* was speaking a totally different narrative. He continued to maintain he was married. And, for that reason, he couldn't offer Evaniese anything more than friendship.

The fact that Nathan had ignored her text hurt Evaniese a great deal. She just couldn't fathom why. Returning a text only took a minute or two. So, she figured Nathan *would* have answered if he *cared* to. It stung to the core that he'd initially asked her out, but was now ignoring her. Of the three men God had said were tied into her destiny, he was the one who'd made himself the most accessible. Nonetheless, at that juncture, even *he* was deserting ship, just like Brent and Jeremy had. Evaniese was familiar with the suffering and the pain. And yet, it was difficult not to give in to self-pity, because no matter how hard she tried, she always came up empty.

Evaniese forced a smile when Nicole finally caught up. "Hey, Nicole," she tried to sound lively.

"How are you, Evaniese?" Nicole stared peculiarly at Evaniese, as she sized her up from head to toe.

Evaniese felt out of sorts under Nicole's seemingly judgmental gape. Evaniese remarked how neat and slim Nicole looked in her navy-blue hospital scrubs. Nicole had on a very thick off-white wool sweater over them. Her brown skin radiated from the brisk Indiana winds. Enviously, Evaniese imagined being able to fit into a pair of extra-large scrubs. She was bottom heavy, and-at least in her own opinion, had freakishly large legs and thighs. And, there it was again. It was the sting of envy she contended with every time she saw *anyone* who was thin, and wasn't battling their weight. It didn't matter if they were male or female.

"I'm okay," Evaniese affirmed, as she and Nicole hiked up the hill. It was a bit of a trek from the hospital's employee parking lot to the main entrance. "I can't believe how long it's been seen I've seen you." Evaniese was winded from the climb.

"Yeah, you *know* how crazy the OR gets," Nicole reminded. "But it *really* has been a while. How are things going in the ER? I've heard that it's been ridiculously busy for you guys as well." Nicole offered a hint of a smile.

Evaniese smiled back at her. "It's been even busier since the hospital implemented that new software program. So many people come through the ER now. The admissions have quadrupled," she explained.

"Are you still working by yourself?" Nicole frowned.

"Yep! They still haven't hired a second person to occupy the second desk through the registration office," Evaniese disclosed.

"So, you handle the workload on your own?" Nicole grimaced again, and shook her head mindlessly.

"There's no one else…"

"Wow! I'll tell you one thing. Here at Brookline, if they can get you to do the job of three people, and still pay you the salary for one, that's icing on their cake."

By then, Evaniese and Nicole were only feet away from the ER's back entryway doors.

"Evaniese, there's something I've been meaning to tell you." Nicole's face wrinkled in concern.

Evaniese's heart thudded in her chest in angst. "Is everything alright?" Her eyes widened in angst.

"Yes…and no." Nicole paused, and her eyes fell away from staring at Evaniese. "It's just that I've noticed how you've been continuously putting on weight. It looks as if you've gained at least sixty pounds from the first time we met…," Nicole's words trailed, when she saw the hurt expression on Evaniese's face.

Evaniese was crushed by Nicole's words, and by her observation. She couldn't believe that one of the few people she considered a friend at the hospital, had just lacerated her heart in that way. "Oh, okay…," Evaniese said, feeling bemused and mislaid.

Nicole set her hand on Evaniese's shoulder in pacification. "I'm *not* saying that to hurt your feelings. I'm just concerned. When we met seven years ago, you were nice and slim. Is everything all right?" Nicole's face twisted in compunction. "You're not sick, are you?"

Evaniese tried not to be too much in her own head. So, she forced a smile in an effort at dispelling the offense. "No, I'm fine. *I'm* not even sure how I gained all this weight either. I've been trying so hard to lose weight." Evaniese shrugged and guffawed. "I guess, I need to figure out a different plan."

"I'm sorry, Evaniese. I didn't mean to offend you. I'm just worried. You *shouldn't* gain any more weight," Nicole cautioned, "it isn't healthy. If you could *see* just how different you look from the time we first met, you'd be freaked out."

Evaniese nodded absently, even if her heart had dipped to the floor, and tears were nettling her eyes. "I appreciate your concern, Nicole," she said quickly. Suddenly, she couldn't get away from Nicole fast enough. "Would you look at the time? It's almost three. So, I've got to get in there." Evaniese pointed at the set of double doors leading into the ER.

"You're right. It's time that I got over to the OR myself," Nicole acquiesced.

Evaniese turned to walk away, but Nicole grasped her hand. "I'm so sorry if I offended you, Evaniese. I'm just concerned." Sympathy creased over her face.

"No worries. I really appreciate it, Nicole," Evaniese's voice wavered. She then turned away in haste, because tears were brimming over her eyelids.

Evaniese neared the set of motion-censored doors. Before going into the ER to face a ton of work and a busy crowd, she slipped into the breakroom bathroom. Setting her handbag on the hook behind the bathroom door, she buried her face in her hands and cried.

Evaniese tried to find comfort by reminding herself things were going to change. She would soon be submitting to the VSG surgery. That meant, she would *distance* herself from *fat* once and for all, and be a normal size. It was her only hope. Yet and still, it was difficult not to cry over the circumstances. She'd gained weight, and was up to 248 pounds.

By design, Evaniese didn't mention the upcoming procedure to Nicole. It wasn't Nicole's or anyone else's business. Only her family and best friends were privy to her plan. Because her family lived far away, Ginger and Deanna were the only ones in town that mattered. Thus, Evaniese was okay with not telling anyone else. Her first medical pre-op clearance was in a matter of days. Evaniese had the day off from work on that Friday. Her supervisor, Ann Ridges, had approved the personal day. Submitting to an Endoscopy, Evaniese would be under anesthesia for the first time.

"Did Evaniese come in yet? I haven't seen her. Wow! I really can't believe how much weight she's put on since she started working here. I guess, hospital work *does* take its toll on someone. The poor kid can't take the heat," Ted Briars deprecated. He was one of the nurses who worked through the ER.

"She's probably under a lot of pressure in her personal life," Nia said. Inwardly, she felt a sense of gratification, because Evaniese was obviously *suffering* a great deal. Evaniese was of a certain age, overweight, and all her romantic prospects had failed.

Regardless, Nia couldn't bring herself to feel too sorry for Evaniese. She had an inkling that Evaniese would come out on top. It didn't seem to matter what life threw at the woman. On the other hand, Nia had to *feign* sympathy for her beautiful, plus-sized competition.

"Ted, you need to stop talking about Evaniese that way. She's a terrific worker," Nia deceptively championed. Secretly, she could not have been more tickled to hear Ted berate Evaniese. Evaniese was very beautiful! Her one flaw was that she was at least a hundred pounds overweight.

"Ted, try to focus on your job instead of worrying about Evaniese," Grace Cooper censured. She was another one of the nurses. "Evaniese should be here any minute. And, she's much too nice for you to be talking about her that way."

"Well, it's *unnatural* for someone to gain so much weight in such a short span of time," Doctor Klein Maxwell noted. He was the head doctor working through the ER for that shift. He would be there until seven thirty in the evening. "I like Evaniese, and I think she's great, but Ted's right. All that weight gain is totally unhealthy."

Both Nia and Janice were working that afternoon. So, hearing the entire ER staff talking about Evaniese's excessive weight gain, thrilled them to no end. Nia and Janice gave each other knowing looks, and smiled deviously as they listened.

Nia and Janice were only *two* frenemies of Evaniese's who worked through the ER. They both hated her immensely. Moreover, both had employed witchcraft to perpetuate Evaniese's weight struggle. Nia had consulted with a medium to thwart all of Evaniese's weight loss efforts. While Janice had partnered with a Wiccan, who'd instructed her on how to hex the beautiful, voluptuous and spirited young woman.

There was just one annoying little glitch. It was unnerving the way Evaniese always managed to come out on top no matter what life threw at her. No doubt, her faith in God was the defining factor. All the same, they were determined to chip away at the *one* fragile area she struggled with, and that was her weight.

"I happen to like Evaniese, so I don't appreciate you all talking about her that way," Tim Bryce, defended. He was one of the PA's.

"Evaniese is great friends with Dr. Andrews. Honestly, I can tell by the way he looks at her, if he wasn't married, he'd be all over her," Meaghan Matthews, a nursing assistant remarked. "*Every* woman in this hospital wish they had that kind of connection to Dr. Andrews. You all can say anything you want about Evaniese, but she definitely has his attention." Meaghan winked at Ted. "So, props to Evaniese!"

Nathan stood at a corner of the nurse's station undetected by the ER staff. Overhearing the doctors, PA's and nurses criticizing the woman he loved, grieved him immensely. He'd been out in Colorado for the past two weeks visiting family, and it was his first day back. Nathan's work schedule was such that he was on for two weeks straight, then off for the following two.

He'd come down to the ER to admit a few critically ill patients. They were waiting to be transported to various floors of the hospital. As he stood there, he deliberated about making his presence known. He seethed in resentment, because of the way the ER team had talked about Evaniese. However, he had to set his personal feelings aside for the sake of professionalism. Pausing for a moment, he took measured steps towards the station. Clearing his throat, he made his way over to his work colleagues. Almost immediately, all eyes fastened to him.

"Dr. Andrews!" they announced in a welcoming manner.

"Good afternoon, everyone!" Nathan heralded politely. Not wanting to make small talk, he immediately addressed Dr. Maxwell, "I was told you wanted me to come down?" Nathan didn't mince words.

"Yes, absolutely! I'm glad you came down in such a timely manner. There are quite a few admissions to handle down here."

"Well, here I am." Nathan offered a faint smile. "Just point the way."

Nathan wasn't up to socializing with the ER staff. He was livid because he'd overheard them gossiping, and speaking poorly of Evaniese. Notwithstanding, he was there to do a job. He wasn't there to hob-knob with his work colleagues in the ER. As Nathan set out to consult with his patients, Evaniese permeated his thoughts. Thinking about her also brought up unpleasant thoughts of Brent Peterson. The man had warned him to stay away from her. Yet, it really matter one way or another to Nathan, because nothing would change the way he felt about Evaniese.

On Dr. Maxwell's orders, Nathan looked in on, and consulted with the patients being admitted to the hospital. As he crossed back over towards the nurse's station, Dr. Maxwell, some of the PA's and nurses invited him to use a computer desk close by.

However, with as pleasant an expression as he could muster, Nathan desisted. "Thanks…, but I prefer working through the registration area." He offered everyone an artificial smile.

In spite of the befuddled expression on the faces of his peers, Nathan turned away, and headed straight over to the registration office. He hoped against hope that Evaniese was there. Two weeks without looking into her gem brown eyes was taxing enough. Whenever he stared into her eyes, Nathan's entire world shifted into paradise. That was something he couldn't get enough of.

Evaniese was swamped with work. The ER had been busy from the outset of her shift that afternoon. After her run-in with Nicole, and hearing how *freaked out* the woman was by her extreme weight gain, Evaniese had a meltdown. However, after crying it out, and asking for God's help, she was able to pull it together. Whenever life left a bad taste in her mouth, Evaniese knew she could always go to her Heavenly Father. He was her refuge and strength, and a very present help in trouble (Psalms 46:1).

God had reminded Evaniese of Psalms 139. She was *fearfully and wonderfully* made! Although she wasn't a size two, or even a size four, she had to believe God had purpose even in that. Internalizing the truth of God's word, carried Evaniese through that afternoon.

It was almost 5 p.m. when the light knock came on the registration office door. Alerted by the knock, Evaniese's heart skipped a beat. Usually, the ER staff didn't bother knocking. They usually barged in, and made demands. Evaniese knew that one of the *few* people who bothered to knock was Nathan.

Evaniese was excited. Her heart thrummed, as she stood to her feet in expectation. "Come in," she invited.

"Hey there, stranger!" Nathan popped his head through the ajar office door.

"Nathan!" Evaniese celebrated, and rushed over to him.

"Hi there!" Nathan beamed. Automatically, slipping his arms around her waist, he crushed her to himself. "How are you?"

Evaniese was reluctant to hug Nathan back. She had no idea what to make of his display of affection. "I'm fine," she said warily. "I haven't seen *you* around here lately." She allowed her hands to rest on Nathan's flanks.

"I know. It's been a whole two weeks," Nathan admitted, relishing the feel of Evaniese so close to him. She felt so good in the folds of his arms, and she smelled like wild flowers. "I've missed *you*!" he confessed, squeezing her again.

Bewildered and somewhat apprehensive, Evaniese cautiously started pulling away. However, Nathan didn't seem to be responding in kind. He refused to remove his arms from about her waist. "I've missed you too," Evaniese replied, with a racing heart.

"You look wonderful!" Nathan finally released his hold from about her waist, but continued to gape mercilessly at her.

"Thank you," Evaniese said, bemused and pleasantly surprised. Nathan's usual malt-colored complexion was toasty. At that point, she and Nathan were facing each other only inches apart. "Did you go away again?" she asked curiously.

"As a matter of fact, I did," Nathan disclosed.

Just then, Brent's angry expression flashed in Nathan's mind, and he circumspectly pulled away. "My *wife* and I went to Colorado to visit family," Nathan fibbed about going out to Colorado with his wife. He was a divorced man. However, he was *required* to keep up the pretense. It was the only way to remain connected to Evaniese, while simultaneously keeping her at arm's length.

Hearing Nathan allude to his wife again, made Evaniese shrink back from their intimacy. "Oh...?" she questioned, as her heart crashed to the floor. "Welcome back! It must have been some trip!" she tried to sound nonchalant. Inwardly, her heart was crumbling. The circumstances were cruel, and she was losing hope by degrees.

"Yes, my wife and I had a wonderful time! We enjoyed the mountainous scenery. Colorado is beautiful this time of year!"

Evaniese forced a smile. "That *does* sound wonderful! I guess, I have to make it a point to visit one of these days." A sad smile curved over her lips, as she created a bit of distance, and began floating closer to her desk. Given the circumstances, it was the right and the wise thing to do.

"I hope you *do* get to visit one day soon. I know you'll love it!"

Nathan felt like a total heel. Hurting Evaniese was the last thing he wanted. Even if he knew he *should* let her go, he couldn't bring himself to do it. "By the way, you look amazing!" he uplifted with a wink. It was his way of reminding her of just how beautiful she was, regardless of what any of her jealous colleagues and coworkers had to say.

"Oh, thank you, Nathan!" Evaniese smiled in earnest this time around. In light of her trying day hearing those words come out of Nathan's mouth, was indeed a bright spot.

"Have you lost weight?" Nathan continued to size her up. To him, she looked positively incredible in her dark slacks, and pale-yellow dress top. Of course, it didn't really matter what she wore. She had the ability to take his breath away every single time!

Evaniese laughed, shocked by Nathan's forthrightness. She looked down, and examined her full hips. "I've been trying to..."

"Well, it shows. You look wonderful!" Nathan affirmed again. This time around, he deliberately looked over every inch of her voluptuous body.

"Well…," Evaniese started to say, but her words trailed, because her phone was ringing. "Will you excuse me for a moment, Nathan?"

"Of course," Nathan said.

He veered, and took his place at the desk next to Evaniese's. The desks were positioned side by side in cubicles. Nathan accessed the computer, while Evaniese spoke on the phone. However, he remained attuned to every word she said.

"Good afternoon, Brookline ER…Evaniese speaking," Evaniese's voice pealed over the line.

"Yes, good afternoon, Evaniese!" Paula Rivers announced.

Evaniese's heart immediately began to lash. "Yes, Paula…?" she said cursorily, already feeling flustered and out of sorts. Paula calling her down in the ER, was like overcast clouds huddling in the horizon on a sunny day.

"Ann and I would like to see you upstairs right away," Paula said directly.

"Oh, okay…" Evaniese instantly began in inward prayer vigil. "I have quite of few admissions, and some other paperwork to secure for the ER staff," she reminded.

"We're sending Gail downstairs. She will handle the ER rush until you get back."

"Should I leave right now?" Evaniese's voice wavered. *"God, please help me…"*

"As soon as Gail gets there, you're to come up to the office. Understand…?" Paula berated.

"*Yes*, I understand," Evaniese affirmed. She looked heavenward and sighed. Now more than ever, she needed God's strength.

Nathan had listened in on Evaniese's end of the conversation, while he was busy putting in admitting orders into the computer. He hated hearing Evaniese sound so stressed. If he had things his way, he would whisk her away from the unpleasantness of her job. Overhearing the opinions of the ER staff earlier on still burned him up.

Nathan was also disappointed that Evaniese was being pulled away. He hadn't seen her in over two weeks. And if she left the registration office at that point, they probably wouldn't see each other later on. Even if he couldn't get close to her *in the way* he wanted to, Nathan did look forward to their conversations. If that was the *only* way he could have her, Nathan deemed that it had to be enough.

Evaniese hung up the phone absently. There was a strained expression on her face. For the life of her, she couldn't figure out what Paula and Ann wanted. Evaniese worked hard. She also tried her best to be punctual and courteous to everyone. However, it never seemed to be enough for her two bosses. For one reason or another, those women seemed to enjoy picking her apart. Just then, Evaniese was reminded of a key truth in God's word. 2Timothy 3:12(NKJV), "Yes, and all who desire to live godly in Christ Jesus will suffer persecution."

"Is everything alright?" Nathan's rolled the armchair away from his desk to look at Evaniese. Concern wrinkled his handsome face.

Evaniese was a little distracted, but Nathan's voice perforated through her tangled thoughts. "Um, I'm fine. I've got to go upstairs for a meeting with my boss," she told Nathan, forcing a smile.

"Everything okay?" Nathan stood to his feet. Eliminating the space between them, he stood facing Evaniese. His arms crossed over his chest, as he contemplated her with involvement.

Evaniese nodded, and pasted a smile to her face. She was confused about Nathan's role in her life. So, she didn't feel comfortable dumping all of her worries on him. Her boss was interrupting her work, and asking to see her right away. Paula Rivers wasn't a very *fair* or *logical* person, so Evaniese knew that the powwow probably wouldn't be a positive one. "I'm sure everything's fine," she said, trying to sound cavalier. Evaniese guffawed, and kept the elastic smile stretched over her face.

"Hey there," Gail announced, as she stepped into the registration office.

"Hey, Gail!" Evaniese acknowledged.

"Paula and Ann are waiting for you upstairs." Gail smiled pleasantly.

"I know. I just got off the phone with Paula."

Nathan's face creased in angst for Evaniese, but he didn't want to pry, as he watched her interactions with her coworker Gail.

"I was just about to go, and get admission paperwork signed for Edward Corley in Room 7...," Evaniese tried to bring Gail up to speed on what was happening down in the ER.

"Evaniese, just go upstairs. I'll handle whatever you have going on down here. Paula's waiting." She nodded in reassurance. "I've got this." She gave Evaniese a sympathetic smile.

"Okay," Evaniese acceded. "Can't keep Paula waiting...," she said and shrugged.

Evaniese then turned towards Nathan. "It was nice to see you again."

"Likewise, Evaniese," Nathan responded, smiling.

"If I don't see you again this evening, welcome back!" Evaniese's voice faltered. She then ambled over to the office doors to leave.

"Thank you, Evaniese. Maybe, we'll catch up later." Nathan winked at her again, and offered a comforting smile.

"Maybe...," Evaniese said thoughtfully, before she drifted away.

***

Evaniese took the stairs, then opened up the door leading into the admissions office. She had kept a prayer vigil all the way up to the first floor. She trusted God to help her cope with anything Paula and Ann planned to dish out. Walking on the plush carpeting while headed over to Paula's office, Evaniese waved politely to some of her coworkers.

They all had curious expressions on their faces, and seemed confused by her presence there. However, no one stopped to talk, or asked any questions. Evaniese came to stand in front of Paula's office door, and knocked diffidently. Ann opened up the door to Evaniese.

Good afternoon, Ann!" Evaniese said cordially, with an involuntary smile.

"Come on in, Evaniese," Ann said solemnly.

The moment Evaniese stepped through the door, she saw Paula sitting at her desk with an acerbic expression on her face. Her hands were folded primly on the desk.

"Evaniese...," Paula acknowledged in a lackluster tone, and surliness written all over her face.

"Good afternoon, Paula!" Evaniese said plainly. She gulped nervously, as Ann invited her to take a seat next to hers. Both chairs were facing Paula's desk.

"How are things down the ER this afternoon, Evaniese?" Paula introduced. There was an unmistakable smirk on her face, as she inched in closer to the edge of her desk.

"Busy as usual," Evaniese said simply. Her eyes fastened intently to Paula. "Did I do something wrong?" she blurted out. The outburst was totally unplanned, but the scenario had put her in a state of angst.

"Yes, you're *always* saying it's busy." Paula glared over at Evaniese.

"That's because it *always* is," Evaniese said rather cheekily.

"I guess, it *has* gotten busier since the implementation of the *Tule Program*."

"I'm certain that *Tule* has a lot to do with the influx of new patients coming through the ER on a regular basis," Ann supported, glancing over at Evaniese, who was sitting to her left-hand side.

"Well, I'm sorry you've had to handle the load on your own for such a long time, Evaniese," Paula said *feigning* concern. "All right then. As I mentioned a few weeks ago, your work has been less than stellar. I have here," Paula looked at stacks of paperwork on her desk, "some of the mistakes you've made with the accounts you've handled." Her face warped in frustration. "Did we *not* go over the procedure with you, Evaniese?" she denigrated.

"I'm sorry…," Evaniese said shakily, realizing that her instincts were on point. Paula and Ann were only there to highlight everything they thought she was doing *wrong*. "The procedure concerning what…?"

"The procedure concerning your registrations. You continue to leave all of the necessary fields in the system empty. And, one of the most important fields, which is adding a primary care physician, is consistently left blank. If the patient doesn't have one, you need to note that. And, you haven't for at least fifty of your accounts. That is totally *unacceptable*." With an annoyed expression on her face, Paula's lower body pressed up to the edge of her desk, while her hands rested insolently on her hips.

"I've been trying really hard to include the names of primary care physicians on all of my registrations," Evaniese argued, as tears stung her eyes. She had earnestly tried, and had no idea how on earth she'd missed the mark not only for *one*, but on *fifty* of her accounts. Perhaps, Paula and Ann had fabricated those documents in order to impugn her. Quite honestly, Evaniese couldn't say that she would put it past them to do just that.

"Evaniese, we know you're working down in the ER alone, and it *does* get busy. I would imagine that it also gets overwhelming at times. That being said, there are certain aspects of patient registrations you can't afford to overlook. We are audited on a regular basis," Ann's voice was soft, like a placid wind blowing over a lake.

Evaniese wasn't sure why Ann's tone was so pacifying. Ann wasn't as abrasive as Paula. However, Evaniese realized that in spite of her sweet veneer, she was *just* as *toxic*. "I understand," Evaniese allowed, as she blinked back tears. "I will be more cautious from this point on in noting the information," she said meekly, avoiding eye contact with Paula at all costs.

However, Paula wasn't having it. "Evaniese," she alerted with glaring eyes, "you also need to remember to use your scanner to scan in the insurance information. Is that clear?" Paula asked authoritatively.

Evaniese looked up, and her eyes connected expressly to Paula's. "Yes. Was there anything else?" Evaniese asked in haste. There was an urgency to her question, because she couldn't leave that office fast enough.

"You don't get to ask that question, Evaniese," Paula said, irritated. "*I* will let you know when we're done. Just so you know, if your performance doesn't improve, we're looking at suspension, and even possible *termination* from the hospital." Paula's expression and eyes were icy.

Evaniese held both hands up in the air in a disarming manner. "Okay, I understand."

There was a storm brewing on the inside. Truth be told, she'd grown weary of her work at Brookline. In July of that year, she would celebrate, *or mourn* seven years of working there. Thus, noticing the ungrateful and deprecating looks on the faces of her superiors, Evaniese came to an epiphany. There just wasn't enough money in the world to keep working through Brookline Hospital.

She would pray, and ask God to open up a new door. Yet, she grasped how heartbreaking it would be to stop seeing Nathan once she left. On God's word, Nathan was tied into her destiny. If she quit her job, it wouldn't be *impossible* to stay connected to him. After all, she still had his phone numbers and email address. Nonetheless, working there did simplify their tenuous connection.

"Evaniese, there *are* a few other concerns Paula and I wanted to address with you before you go back down to the ER," Ann's voice was silky again, as she turned to look at Evaniese.

"All right…?" Evaniese's heart whisked, as her eyes fastened to Ann's.

However, Ann wasn't the one who addressed the next point. Paula clasped her hands primly on the desk again. Her upper body remained taut, as her eyes knifed through Evaniese's. "It has come to our attention that you've had *inappropriate* dealings with one of the hospitalists who works through the ER."

"What…?" Evaniese frowned in conflict and bewilderment.

"Yes, some of your peers from the ER have purported that you've been making unsuitable advances towards Doctor Nathan Andrews. From what I've been told, even if you're *aware* that he's a married man, you continue to make incongruous advances towards him," Paula accused.

"That's not true at all. Doctor Andrews and I are
friends. He sits at the second desk downstairs to complete his
admissions orders on the computer." Tears gleamed in
Evaniese's eyes. Her heart lashed, and she was totally
incredulous. *What on earth was this about? Now, both Paula and
Ann were censuring her over her **friendship** with Nathan?*

"That's not what some of your peers down in the ER
have alluded. They say Doctor Andrews does his work
through the office, but *you're* always hugging and touching
him improperly. That kind of thing has no place in a busy ER,
Evaniese," Paula warned, with crimson clouds whirling in her
eyes. "Don't you know Doctor Andrews *could* complain of
sexual harassment in the workplace?"

Evaniese couldn't help feeling as if this was an out of
body experience. She kept shaking her head in negation. "But
none of that is true. I *know* Dr. Andrews is married, and that's
not the kind of person I am. Neither is he the kind of man to
entertain such a thing," she argued, feeling offended. Pent up
tears brimmed over in her eyes.

"Well, it doesn't really matter what *kind* of relationship
you have with Dr. Andrews. In about a week or so, there will
be a new girl sitting at the second desk. You're *finally* going to
get the help you've been asking for," Paula said caustically.

"But, Nathan Andrews and I *don't* have that kind of a
connection," Evaniese maintained, skeptical of the matter.

"Well, if that's the case, it really shouldn't matter *who*
sits at the second desk, now will it?" Ann added insult to
injury.

"No, I guess not…," Evaniese's voice trailed.

She was stumped and dazed. No doubt, she had
enemies in the ER, but why would anyone tell straight out
lies? Evaniese was honestly rattled that she would no longer
be able to see Nathan. As it was, their relationship was
strained. So, their connection would irrefutably become even
more fragile, if someone else started to occupy the second
desk. Evaniese wanted to run away and cry.

"In the meantime, it would be wise to stay away from Doctor Andrews," Ann's lilting tone returned.

Evaniese was too baffled to offer a rejoinder.

"Is that clear, Evaniese?" Paula raised her voice, rousing Evaniese from reflection.

"Yes," Evaniese said plainly, as her eyes knifed through Paula's.

She had to ask God for the grace not to react. If she responded angrily to this injustice, she would be playing right into Paula's hands. And, Evaniese sensed that it was exactly what Paula wanted. All Paula needed was an excuse. Evaniese wanted to hold on for just a little while longer. All she needed was the approval from her medical insurance company to move forward with the surgery. That's all that mattered at this point.

"There *is* one last thing," Ann brought up during a silent lapse.

Evaniese immediately snapped to attention. It took a moment to get her bearings, because it felt as if she'd just gotten the wind knocked out of her. She wanted to speak, but had lost her strength. She didn't even bother asking *what now*? Rather, she allowed the two women to present their case in point.

"I'm afraid we're going to have to write you up," Ann's voice was honey-dripped, as she stared over at Evaniese.

"What else have I done wrong?" Evaniese finally found the strength to speak.

"Well, it has also come to our attention that you've been handing out Gospel tracts through the ER. From what we understand, you've been giving them out to the detox patients."

Anesthetized and confused, Evaniese just listened, and nodded absently.

"Are you denying that you've been sharing your religious beliefs with those who come through the ER?" Paula daunted, as her eyes widened in accusation.

"No, I'm not denying it. I didn't think I was doing anything wrong. This is after all a Catholic hospital," Evaniese pointed out.

"It may be a Catholic hospital, but there is a time and place for everything. While you're working through the ER, you have no business sharing your *religious beliefs* with anyone, especially since you're always *griping* about how *busy* it is. You need to keep your personal beliefs, and your job separate," Paula reproached.

"Okay," Evaniese acquiesced, looking from one woman to the other.

"Now, we're going to need for you to sign off on this write up. We're sorry for having to write you up for something as noble as sharing your faith, but it has no business in the workplace," Ann added, looking over at Evaniese, who sat quietly to her left-hand side.

"All right," Evaniese submitted.

As she sat there, she felt God's Holy Spirit telling her not to fight or fuss with Paula or Ann. God kept reminding her that he would open up another door of opportunity for her. Moreover, Evaniese knew that getting angry was exactly what Paula wanted. And, that was the last thing she could afford to do. She had to stay put until Brookline Bariatrics came through with the news that her medical insurance was approved for the WLS.

Once that happened, Evaniese would undoubtedly put in her two-week's notice. However, for the time being, she grudgingly signed off on paperwork, verifying her write up for sharing the gospel through the ER. Fortunately, after she signed up on that paperwork, there was very little more Paula and Ann had to say.

Soon after, Evaniese was allowed to return to the ER.
By then, Nathan was gone. Gail brought Evaniese up to speed
in respect to the most recent developments in the ER.
Evaniese smiled until her face hurt, as she listened to Gail.
The moment Gail left, there was a bit of a lull, so Evaniese
shut the office door, sat at her desk and cried. She prayed,
and hoped that no one would come in until she was able to
pull it together. God was merciful in answering that prayer,
and afforded her about half an hour of solitude.

Chapter Three

"Thank you for agreeing to come with me this morning, Dee," Evaniese told Deanna.

Evaniese stretched out on the hospital bed. She was in the pre-surgical testing area of the hospital on a Friday morning in early March of 2016. Because Evaniese would be put under anesthesia, she wouldn't be able to drive herself home after the procedure. So, Deanna had taken the morning off to be there for her. Even if Evaniese had already submitted to a number of preliminary medical appointments, the Endoscopy was a major clearance for the VSG surgery.

"You're welcome, sweetie!" Deanna said, taking Evaniese's hand in hers. "How are you feeling?"

"I'm a little nervous," Evaniese admitted, smiling hopefully. "I keep telling myself, if I can get through the Endoscopy, I'll be able to submit to having the surgery in a few months."

"Right..." Deanna offered a faint smile, in an effort at concealing her displeasure.

She was totally surprised to see how far Evaniese was taking her resolve. She'd already gone through a number of necessary medical procedures to be cleared for the surgery. It seemed, her bestie was determined to do whatever was necessary, including submitting to an Endoscopy on that morning. At first, Deanna had doubted Evaniese would follow through with her decision. But, in light of their location at the hospital that morning, Evaniese seemed to be proving her wrong.

Could Evaniese really go through with the procedure? I've seen so many videos on YouTube of those who've had WLS. Most of the time, they're totally transformed, like a butterfly emerging from its cocoon. Evaniese is already gorgeous. If this surgery works for her, she's going to be twice as stunning! When she goes out with me and Ginger, **she** *will be the one getting all of the attention…* Deanna's thoughts left her feeling unsettled, even as she smiled into Evaniese's face.

"You've been pretty brave in taking the necessary steps. Still, are you *sure* this surgery is what you want?" Deanna questioned.

Inwardly, she felt conflicted. She *did* want Evaniese to succeed. However, she couldn't bear the thought of Evaniese doing better than *her.* Deanna couldn't help feeling threatened. And yet, she realized how much she needed to pray through her feelings of jealously and resentment.

"Dee, you *know* this is exactly what I want. It's what I *need*," Evaniese affirmed, surprised that Deanna was still doubting her. Just then, her recent weight-in at the bariatric office a few days ago resonated. The sad reality was that she was up by *another* five pounds, weighing in at 253 pounds. Dr. Bergstrom promised to make an appeal to the medical insurance company. He had to find a way to appease them in respect to her weight gain. In spite of it all, Evaniese was disconcerted.

"You *know* how hard I've tried to lose weight over the years." Evaniese stared down at her full body stretched out on the bed. "Well, so far, nothing's worked. This is something I've got to do for me," she affirmed, staring unwaveringly into Deanna's eyes. "It would mean so much to me to have your total support." Evaniese gave Deanna a pleading look.

Deanna forced a smile, and squeezed Evaniese's hand. "Of course, you have my support and understanding." She gave Evaniese a sympathetic look. "You should totally do what you think is best for you," Deanna granted. "When is Dr. Bergstrom getting here?" she evaded.

Evaniese sighed. "They said he'd be here by eight. It's only a quarter to," Evaniese informed, trying not to be nervous.

What mattered most was being approved for the surgery. Once that was out of the way, she'd be free to tender a letter of resignation for her *horror-show* of a job. Aside from that, *maybe* things would change with Nathan for the better. Paula and Ann had done exactly what they said they would.

They'd hired a *twenty-something* year-old to work the second desk in the registration area of the ER. Cynthia Floyd was the new hire. And, as a result of Cynthia's new spot at the second desk, Nathan had kept his distance, working mostly inside the ER. In weeks past, he'd occasionally stopped into the registration office to say hello to Evaniese. However, being free to work side by side, and having chummy talks, was history. For Evaniese, the question remained, how would God work it out, if there was now a real rift between them? Evaniese worried that she'd lost Nathan forever.

"As soon as the procedure's complete, someone will text you, Deanna. Evaniese won't be able to drive herself home after the Endoscopy. In fact, it isn't recommended that she drive at all today or even tomorrow," Dr. Bergstrom told Deanna, when he showed up at 8 a.m. to report to the OR.

Evaniese listened to Dr. Bergstrom's directives for Deanna. She was already beginning to feel the effects of the anesthesia, which had been administered a few minutes ago. In a fog, she heard Deanna ask Dr. Bergstrom if it was all right to say goodbye.

Dr. Bergstrom agreed with a smile on his face. "Please keep it short, as Evaniese is about to be rolled out into the OR."

"Of course, Doctor," Deanna agreed.

"Hey, how are you feeling?" Deanna asked, as she took Evaniese's limp hand in hers.

"I'm feeling…," Evaniese started to say. However, she closed her eyes, and surrendered to the silent realm of slumber.

"Well, I guess the anesthesia works a lot faster than I thought. Good luck, honey," she said, and pressed a kiss to Evaniese's forehead.

Deanna turned, and began heading away.

"I will text you just as soon as the procedure's done," Dr. Bergstrom reassured Deanna before she slipped out of the room.

"Okay, thank you," Deanna said.

She drifted out of the room, and wandered down the hallway to the waiting area. Taking a seat in the expansive, nearly-empty room, she pulled out her phone, and began fiddling with it. The fact that Evaniese was taking the necessary steps in order to have WLS still nettled her. Deanna had superficially discussed Evaniese's decision with Ginger. And yet, *not even* Ginger knew how threatened she felt over the prospect. Deanna couldn't wrap her head around the fact that her beautiful-yet plus-sized friend, was about to join the *world of the thin*. Worse yet, if everything worked according to plan, it would happen in a matter of months. Deanna hated feeling that way, but the struggle was nonetheless very real.

***

"Watch your step, sweetie." Deanna helped Evaniese out of the car. They'd just pulled into Evaniese's driveway. The Endoscopy was a success, and timed as precisely as Dr. Bergstrom had indicated.

"I'm fine, Dee,"   Evaniese argued, as she trudged up the walkway leading up to her house. "I'm just a little loopy, but I can take it from here," she reassured.

"Are you sure? Dr. Bergstrom said I should monitor you for a while. This is, after all, the first time you've been under anesthesia." Deanna guided Evaniese up the stairs, and up to the front door. She then turned the key in the lock to open it up.

"I just need to lay down for a little while," Evaniese disputed, walking into the house.

It felt nice to be home in the late morning, and not have to worry about reporting to the ER later in the day. It was a much-needed respite and day off from work. "Dee, I'm good. You don't have to stick around," Evaniese emphasized, as Deanna followed her into the kitchen.

"Can I fix you some lunch or anything like that?" Deanna offered, seemingly pertained.

"No, I'm fine for now. Maybe later, I can order something through *Door Dash* or *Grub Hub*."

"Are you *sure* you can make it to your room okay? I could help you change. Dr. Bergstrom emphasized nothing strenuous today."

Evaniese nodded. "I know. I'm fine, Dee." She gave Deanna an earnest smile. "Thank you for everything you've done today, Dee! Thanks for taking the morning off just to be there for me." Evaniese threw her arms around Deanna affectionately. "It means a lot."

"Oh, you're welcome!" Deanna frowned, feeling conflicted. "So, I'm going to call you in a little while to check in, okay?" She pulled away, but pointed a liable finger at Evaniese.

"Okay," Evaniese acquiesced, "but I'll be fine. You can tell Ginger I'm okay too. What I really need right now is my bed." Evaniese felt a little dizzy.

"Okay, Niecy. If you need anything at all..."

"I won't hesitate to call you or Ginger, but I'll be fine," Evaniese reaffirmed.

"Okay… So, I'll just get going." Deanna turned to leave. In the kitchen entryway, she veered back to address Evaniese, "Get some rest, and I'll call you later."

Evaniese smiled, and nodded in agreement. "Bye, Dee. Just lock the door behind you."

"Will do. Bye."

Feeling disoriented and sleepy, Evaniese floated into her bedroom. Peeling off her clothes, she changed into a pink floral-print pair of pajamas. With the yellow hospital socks still on her feet, she pulled back the covers, slipped into bed, and was out before her head even hit the pillow.

***

"I wouldn't care if he was your uncle, Liz. He goes, and he goes today," Ellis did a great job memorizing the lines for the role of his new movie.

His character, Ryan Chase, emphasized every word that early afternoon. There must have been forty or fifty cast and crew members fulfilling their respective duties on the busy movie set. Moments earlier, there had been a number of action scenes, a car chase, and even an explosion.

Now, Ellis had to perform a love scene with actress Laura Morgan Fields. Laura was well-known in the industry. But, it was the first time Ellis had the pleasure of working with her. Laura was playing his love interest, *Elizabeth Vats* in the movie *Toxic Protocol*. Ellis's role was that of a vigilante whose wife and *only* child are murdered by a notorious mafia group, and his character is out for revenge.

"But, Ryan, we talked about this. He needs our help," Laura's character argued with Ellis's in appeal. In the movie, Elizabeth Vat's brother was in association with the people responsible for the death of Ryan Chase's family.

Ellis took Laura by the shoulders, and stared piercingly into her eyes, as he went over the scene. *"If he's tied into those people, he has to go today, and that's that,"* he said conclusively.

"All right, I will talk to him," Laura's character acceded. *"But, I can't make any promises."*

Ellis gave her shoulders an aggressive shake. *"Today, Liz, and I mean it…"*

"All right, Ryan," Laura's voice softened, as she searched his eyes. *"I will do whatever you ask, but please don't go…"*

"As long as we're clear," Ellis's character disputed. *"You know how I feel about you, but I think your brother should go back to Chicago. I really don't need him getting mixed up with that bunch of lowlifes."*

"You're right, Ryan," Laura's character agreed in a mellow tone.

Just then, Ellis was required to submit to a kissing scene. Searching Laura's eyes fondly as the role called for it, Ellis gingerly manipulated her into his arms. Then, in a gentle, yet demanding manner, his mouth melded with hers, and his lips kneaded hers affectionately. Laura responded explosively to Ellis's kiss.

"Cut…," both directors John Schaefer and Howard Biggs said in unison.

They took turns telling Ellis and Laura what they wanted.

"Ellis… Laura…, we need to go over that scene one more time? Laura, I want you to drape your arms around Ellis's neck, and clasp your hands together. It makes the kiss more intimate and relatable. Aside from the bar scene, which we'll go over again, the two of you are doing an exceptional job," John Schaefer told them.

"Where do you want us to take it from, John?" Ellis asked. He and Laura exchanged bewildered stares, because they thought they'd nailed the scene.

"Take it from the moment you walk through the door, Ellis."

"Sure," Ellis agreed.

"And *Laura*, this time around, you're going to have that sulky expression on your face when Ellis comes home. Got it?" Howard inquired.

"Got it," Laura said amenably.

Ellis was a little frustrated. This was the tenth take of the day. He'd been on the set out in Minneapolis, MN since 6 a.m. It was now almost three in the afternoon, and they'd pressed through past lunchtime. However, he wouldn't complain. How could he even think of griping, when they were paying him a cool fifteen million for the film?

Ellis was always grateful for the work. Nevertheless, he shied away from love scenes with a number of different women. Laura Morgan Fields-as with many of the other actresses he'd worked with in the past, was a stunning beauty. However, it was always awkward to act out love scenes with people he didn't love. However, it was all a part of the detail. Ellis usually got through the kissing scenes by pretending he was kissing his mystery YouTube vlogger, *Niecy819*.

It made very little sense, but he was enthralled by the young woman. He didn't even know her real name. Furthermore, privacy laws being what they were, it was impossible to know very much about her. It was frustrating to feel so strongly about someone he couldn't reach out to. Ellis considered just how off kilter his life was.

Women from every walk of life were throwing themselves at him, but the *only one* he wanted had evaded him. Sadly, with time, he found himself falling deeper and deeper in love with this person. The last thing he wanted was to leave comments in the comment section of her videos. He was determined to see if he could find her on Facebook, Instagram, Snapchat or Tik Tok. If by any chance those platforms were unavailable, he would submit to leaving her a comment or two. All the same, Ellis was hesitant to take action. The realization hit that even if he *did* tell her who he was, she probably wouldn't believe him.

"Are we ready to take that scene again?" Howard Biggs asked Ellis, stirring him from profound reflection. "You alright, El?" Howard frowned in concern, seeing the faraway expression on Ellis's face.

Ellis offered a warm smile. "I'm great! And, yes, I'm ready."

Turning, he looked over at Laura. Grinning, he winked at her. "You might want to check with Laura. She's the one who's been stuck kissing me since 6 a.m."

Laura's face turned crimson. She chuckled, and shook her head comically over Ellis's banter. "Believe *me*, Howard, I don't mind at all. It's a pleasure to work with you, Ellis!" Her entire face lit up, and her hazel eyes sparkled, as she stared at Ellis.

Ellis set both hands together in posture to say a prayer, smiled, and bowed in prostration and acknowledgement of Laura's compliment. "You've been a joy to work with as well, Laura! Anytime..." He gave her an impish wink.

"On second thought, maybe the two of you *should* take a short break. Get some air, go out and get something to eat. Then, we'll come back at around four thirty," John suggested.

Everyone on the set seemed to be in agreement, and completely relieved.

"I think that's a great idea," Ellis agreed. "Laura, are you alright with that?" Ellis turned to address the beautiful dark-haired actress.

Laura offered Ellis an earnest smile, and sighed. "I thought they'd never ask." She laughed.

Ellis chortled as well. "I know exactly what you mean. We both need a moment to regroup."

"Absolutely...as much as I've *enjoyed* our kissing scenes, we could sure use a little break."

Ellis nodded pleasantly in agreement. He was about to share a clever rejoinder. However, looking out towards the back end of the expansive set, he saw Kierra standing there.

"What on earth…?" he said silently. "Laura…, ladies, gentlemen, if you'll excuse me…?" Ellis acknowledged, as his eyes connected wildly to Kierra Spalding's.

Kierra was standing behind some of the large movie props. For a moment, Ellis could have sworn he was seeing some form of an apparition. However, Kierra wasn't fading out.

Laura followed Ellis's gaze, and her heart plunged in disappointment to see Kierra Spalding standing there. She'd hoped to ask Ellis to join her for a late lunch. Her face soured in displeasure, but she tried her best to maintain composure. "I guess, I'll see you in a bit, Ellis," she said grudgingly, as she turned, and slowly sauntered away.

"Sure, Laura. I'll be here," Ellis said absently.

Ellis's eyes fastened to Kierra's. She was smiling, and waving over at him. Ellis trudged across the set, and hauled over towards Kierra with a befuddled expression on his face. *What Kierra was doing there was anybody's guess. Why was she out in Minnesota, and how had she gotten on the movie set?* Ellis had a dozen questions.

However, Kierra pounced on him the moment he got close enough. "Ellis!" she sang, draping her arms about his neck, and crushing him in an affectionate hug.

Winded and confused, Ellis was uncertain how to react. He was annoyed, but being unkind was uncharacteristic.

"Kierra!" he announced, trying to catch his breath from her hearty embrace. Pulling away, he kept his hands on Kierra's waist. "What are you doing here?" He delved into her eyes in total incredulity.

"I spoke to Howard and John a couple of days ago. I asked if it was okay to come out here and surprise you. I was out in Michigan shooting a television special, so I wasn't too far away." Kierra reached up, and planted a kiss to Ellis's cheek. Setting her hands on his shoulders, she played seductively on his collar.

"Kierra, what's going on?" Ellis's face warped in confusion. "I mean, we *have* made a few public appearances together in the past few months, but…"

"El, don't tell me you're clueless to the fact that I'm totally *into* you?" Kierra frowned, discouraged. Short of camping out in front of his home, she'd done all she could to show Ellis how she felt, but Ellis seemed totally oblivious.

Ellis offered her an expectant smile. "Kierra, I'm flattered, and I think you're great, but…"

"Ellis, please… You're on break right now. Let's go out for lunch," she prodded. "You don't need to make any promises or lifelong commitments. Just have lunch with me…" She rubbed affectionately on Ellis's shoulders, while staring appealingly into his twinkling honey eyes.

Ellis shook his head incredulous, but offered Kierra an earnest smile. "You're something else, you know that?"

"I just know what I want," Kierra susurrated, exploring Ellis's eyes.

However, the tenor shifted completely.

"Laura breezed over to where the two were standing. "I'll see you back here at around four thirty, Ellis." Laura gave Ellis an enchanting smile.

Kierra's hands fell away from caressing Ellis's collar, and she set them cheekily on her hips, as she took a moment to scrutinize Laura. Condemnation and judgment soured Kierra's face.

"Absolutely… I'll be here," Ellis said throatily. "Oh, I'm not sure if you've been introduced." Ellis stared from Kierra and Laura.

"No, we haven't, but it's nice to meet you, Kierra!" Laura extended her hand cordially. "I'm a huge fan of your work!" She smiled amiably.

With a guarded expression on her face, Kierra grudgingly shook Laura's hand. "Thank you," she said cagily, ogling the woman, pretty much like a fox would gape at a lost rabbit out in the woods. "It's nice to meet you as well," Kierra tone was lackluster.

"Well, I will see you in a little while, Ellis," Laura said softly, staring dreamily into Ellis's eyes.

"Bye, Laura." Ellis watched her turn to leave.

"So, *she's* your love interest, huh?" Kierra asked, smirking.

"Yes, she is," Ellis said plainly, confused by Kierra's behavior.

He wasn't sure what to make of her presence on the movie set. How on earth could he tell Kierra he was only interested in being friends, in spite of how the press had painted them? Ellis knew he had to find a way to tell Kierra how he felt. The last thing he wanted was for her to keep showing up to his sets uninvited, and overstating her role in his life.

"She's pretty, I guess." Kierra watched Laura saunter off the set.

"Yes she is, and she's also *very* nice, Kierra," Ellis pointed out, critically.

"I'm sure she is, but she obviously likes you." Kierra's face twisted in annoyance and jealousy.

Ellis smiled, and shook his head in skepticism. "She's one of the most professional actresses I've ever had the pleasure of working with," he uplifted.

"That's nice, Ellis. But, are we going out to lunch, or what? I'm starved," Kierra eluded. She would undoubtedly be nauseated if Ellis went on to sing the praises of the beautiful Laura Morgan Fields.

"*Sure*, let's go out to lunch," Ellis acceded. "You and I need to have a serious talk," he said on a more urgent note.

"Whatever you say, Ellis," Kierra acquiesced, and slipped her arm through his, as they made their way off the set.

"Kierra," Ellis's eyes fastened to hers censoriously, "I'm serious."

Kierra's heart plunged in dread, but she feigned nonchalance, and smiled brightly. "I get it, Ellis. We'll talk. But right now, we're going out to lunch."

Exasperated and bewildered, Ellis led Kierra away from the studio lot. All the while, he remained prayerful. He needed God's wisdom. There had to be a delicate way to let Kierra know in no uncertain terms, he was only interested in being friends. It was a quandary only God could help him with. Even if they'd never met, there was only *one* person he was interested in. Moreover, Ellis understood that only God could help him figure out this unconventional love.

"Ellis, Kierra, are you working on a new project?"

"Turn this way. The two of you look amazing together. I guess, the romance is heating up…"

"Are the two of you planning a private trip? Wow! Please… give us a statement for *Star Style Magazine*, another tabloid reporter entreated, following Ellis and Kierra back to the set of *Toxic Protocol*.

"Sorry, I can't issue a statement at this time," Ellis called out, as he and Kierra scrambled to get back to the studio lot. Cameras flashed in their faces, and the press came pretty close to infiltrating the closed movie set. Ellis was frustrated, because the press and the media had found them. No doubt, they'd followed Kierra there. It seemed, they were just waiting for the chance to pounce. Mostly, even when Ellis felt he was evading the media, they always found a way to invade spatial boundaries.

Even so, at the moment, the press was the least of
Ellis's concerns. He had to find a way to let Kierra down easy.
At some point, he and Kierra would collaborate on a project,
or come together for some other media event. But for now, he
had to tell Kierra that her trip over to the lot was a lovey
gesture, but he had to finish work on the movie set alone.

"Are you all right?" Ellis took Kierra by the shoulders,
the moment they were back inside the studio lot. He searched
her eyes in concern.

"I'm fine, Ellis. You'd think we'd be used to all of this
by now." She shook her head humorously and smiled. "I'm
sorry I asked to go out to lunch. We should have had a few of
those cold sandwiches on the buffet table in there." She
pointed towards the far-reaching movie set, and snickered.

"That's all right, Kierra. It's not your fault. Something
tells me even if we were in Siberia, the press would manage to
find us." Ellis shook his head comically, and chortled. Kierra,
on the other hand, couldn't seem to stop laughing. "Kierra,
what's so funny?" Ellis asked, perplexed.

"El, you should have seen your face when that guy
jumped out of the car, camera and mike in hand. That
expression was priceless," she razzed.

Ellis gave Kierra a farcical look. "I'm glad I could be
your comic relief of the day," he joked, then found himself
laughing as well. "To tell you the truth, that guy did scare the
life out of me."

"I know. I could tell… Oh, Ellis…" Kierra stared
fondly into his eyes. She then reached up, and pressed her
lips to his, then strategically moved in for a deeper kiss.

Caught off guard, it took a moment for Ellis to get his
bearings. However, once he did, in a gentle yet reflexive
manner, he pulled away. "Kierra, this can't happen."

"Why not, Ellis?" Kierra asked, hurt and confused.

"We talked about this before. We're friends and work colleagues. I'm sorry I can't offer anything more," Ellis said thickly, as he explored Kierra's face and eyes. From the expression on her face, he could tell she was hurt. Hurting her was the last thing he wanted.

"Are you seeing someone else?" Kierra asked, clearly offended.

Ellis hung his head down momentarily before answering her question. *Niecy819's* face, her lilting voice, and her graceful mannerism permeated his thoughts.

Ellis's eyes then linked to Kierra's in earnest. "I'm afraid I am, Kierra. I think you're lovely, and our friendship is important to me…"

"Oh, so you have a *secret* girlfriend now? Is it that Laura Morgan Fields?" Kierra folded her arms across her chest, and demanded an answer.

"Kierra," Ellis said intently, as his eyes delved into hers, "we're not doing this right now."

"Ellis, I'm *really* into you, and if things don't work out with whomever…" Her eyes gleamed in affect.

Ellis hunched down, and pressed a kiss to her cheek. "If things don't work out, you'll be the first to know." He gave her a reassuring smile. "Are you staying out here overnight?" he asked, pertained.

"Yes, I have a hotel suite in the area." Kierra blinked back tears, as she searched Ellis's perfect face.

"Wonderful! Will you be hanging out here until later tonight?" Ellis had to know if Kierra planned on waiting it out until they wrapped up for the day.

"I don't see any reason to now," Kierra admitted. Sadness blanketed her sweet features.

"Well, my limo guy should be here in a bit. I can have him drive you over to the hotel… I'm concerned. I don't want the press hounding you. I could have him meet you right outside." Ellis pointed over to the lot's back doors.

"No, that's all right, Ellis. I'll be fine. I have *my* guy on call. He'll come get me," she glumly acquiesced.

"Are you sure?" Ellis tested, feeling like a total heel.

Kierra was obviously upset. In spite of it all, Ellis knew that he had to remain true to God and to himself. There was much he was still confused about. However, the one thing he *did* know was that Kierra Spalding wasn't his God-ordained wife. So, he had to wait for God to bring the *right* person into his life.

"Yes, I'm sure." Kierra stared yearningly at Ellis. It was difficult to stop wanting him. Ellis was perfect, and she wanted his heart more than anything else.

"All right," Ellis granted, smiling warmly at Kierra. "Thanks for coming out here to surprise me. It really means a lot."

"Sure, Ellis. Anytime." Kierra forced a smile.

Ellis glanced at his watch. It was almost four thirty, and he had to get back on the set. Setting his hands gently on Kierra's shoulders, he searched her eyes with a sense of involvement. "Are you going to be all right?"

Kierra nodded. "I'll be just fine. Go on... They're probably waiting for you...*Laura's* probably waiting for you." Kierra's smile was taut.

"Kierra...?" Ellis questioned uneasily. "I'll talk to you later. Thanks for everything! Will you text me when you get to the hotel?"

"I will. Go on, Ellis. Laura Morgan Fields is waiting on you," Kierra emphasized again, rolling her eyes in annoyance.

"Kierra," Ellis countered, shaking his head in the negation, "you're way off base."

"Whatever you say, Ellis," she said shortly. "Go on...," she prodded.

"Okay. Bye, Kierra." Ellis veered, then drifted away. However, feet away, he turned and waved at her.

Feeling totally defeated, Kierra grudgingly waved back at Ellis. As she watched him tread back over to the production area, she changed her mind. She decided not to leave just yet. She would stay and watch Ellis's interactions on set with Laura Morgan Fields. Kierra had to keep her eye on the competition. After all, if she was going to make Ellis Roman her guy, she had to know exactly what she was dealing with. Furthermore, she needed a strategy to put out any romantic fires which could possibly spark between Ellis and his leading lady.

Staying close by, Kierra watched Ellis and Laura rehearse their love scene a number of times. It got under her skin every single time she saw it. Luckily, Ellis and Laura were able to get the scene the way the directors wanted in just four takes. Kierra was relieved when they moved on to the next scene, which mercifully didn't include Laura Morgan Fields. That evening, Kierra realized just how fragile her heart was. She held it in her hands, until she could give it to Ellis. Then, she could only hope he'd handle it with care.

***

Later, back at his hotel suite, Ellis fiddled around on his laptop. Checking his Instagram account, he noticed an increase in the number of his followers. There were also a gazillion DM's. As an actor in the entertainment industry, it was the bane of his existence to keep up with social media. Needless to say, it was a necessary evil to post pictures, and event videos regularly for his fans.

"Oh, my goodness!" Ellis's cheeks flushed over some of the pictures sent to him from women who followed him on social media. He had to censor a few, as they were indecorous.

On the other hand, some of the women who followed him were sweet, and genuinely seemed to admire his work. Their uplifting and supportive messages always made Ellis's day. It was exactly what he needed after spending the entire day on a busy and loud movie site. There were scores of messages from these individuals, but Ellis deleted them right away. Some of the women-and *men*, claimed to be *Christians*, and purported to earnestly be searching for their God-ordained spouse. Ellis vowed to keep them in his prayers. However, just because they shared the same faith, didn't mean any of them were in God's perfect will for *his* life.

Ellis expressed likes for some of the comments left on his timeline. He left emoji's and brief messages where he could. He then tried to put in *Niecy819* in the search window. The desire to meet this woman intensified by the day. "God, I don't know why I feel so strongly about her. But, I'm depending on you to strengthen and guide me. I know very little.

"I can't choose someone based on appearances. Only *you* know the heart. Is there a reason why I feel such a strong connection to this woman? If she isn't in your will for my life, please take away these intense feelings. Father, God, I want your will, and your plan to prevail in my life."

Regardless of the circumstances, there was an indomitable desire to find out who this woman was. Perhaps, nothing would come of it, but Ellis was intrigued. Unable to find *Niecy819* on Instagram and Facebook, Ellis searched other social media platforms, but came up empty. He had a plan. If at all possible, he'd reach out to someone on YouTube. Maybe, they'd be able to tell him a little bit more about the young woman.

Yet and still, Ellis resolved not to rush into the matter. He would stay in prayer, until God revealed why it was that he couldn't stop thinking about *Niecy819*. Was this inexplicable attraction from God? There were times Satan created unnatural attraction between two individuals to strategically bring about a disastrous, and even deadly union. Ellis was determined to pray it out. Once he had an answer, he would move forward, or he would abandon the idea altogether.

***

Nathan stepped outside of *Greater Returns Investment Bank* on a Friday afternoon. He was on break from working a shift over at Brookline Hospital. It was a relatively mild and sunny afternoon in Amber Hills. There were just a few misguided clouds lingering in the panorama. Nathan was grateful for the chance to handle some of his banking transactions personally.

Upon glancing at his watch, he smiled irrepressibly. It was half past two. In half an hour, Evaniese would be at the hospital to start her shift. Nathan beamed, as he traipsed across the parking lot. "Oh, Evaniese, you have no idea...," Nathan susurrated.

He was only a few feet away from his Audi SUV, when Brent Peterson stepped out of a black Mercedes Benz SUV. There was an ominous expression on Brent's face.

Nathan's demeanor immediately soured, and his heart crashed to the ground. He was all too familiar with Brent Peterson. *What on earth did the man want now*? Nathan stopped dead in his tracks, as he saw Brent headed in his direction.

Brent wasn't a big or imposing guy by any stretch of the imagination. However, there was something very unnerving about the man. Nevertheless, this time around, Nathan resolved to stand his ground and not to flinch. He was tired of the man, and wary of his claim on Evaniese.

Nathan had done everything in his power to respect the boundaries with Evaniese. So, he was irate that Brent wanted to seek him out for *any* reason at all. *What on earth could Brent Peterson need from him at that point?*

Veins pulsed at Nathan's temples, as he defiantly crossed his arms over his chest. He geared up for whatever Brent decided to throw at him. "What is it that you want now?" Nathan asked, staring formidably into Brent's blue eyes the moment he got close enough.

"I thought I told you to stay away from my girl?" Brent's face puckered in displeasure.

"What are you talking about?" Nathan held up his left hand, and pointed at the ring on his finger. "I'm a married man, and I'm not making a play for Evaniese. We work together at times through Brookline's Emergency Room. That is all," Nathan said, as temperately as he could.

Brent shook his head contrarily. "You're not getting it, *Doctor*," he disparaged. "I need you to keep your distance. I know you've developed some kind of *friendship* with my girl. Well, what I need is for you to stay away from her completely," he said disdainfully.

"Evaniese is a very nice woman. I doubt, she would be happy if she knew you were going behind her back."

"That's not for you to worry about," Brent bellowed.

"It would hurt her immensely if *we* suddenly stopped talking," Nathan argued. "I mean, we've been friendly since I started working there. Do you really want to hurt her that way?" Nathan rationalized.

He hated the thought of cutting ties with Evaniese altogether. It was bad enough that he could no longer sit beside her at the second desk inside of the registration office. The department had hired someone else to help Evaniese out on her shift. Still, the thought of totally alienating Evaniese wasn't something Nathan felt prepared to do.

"Again," Brent's face turned ruddy, "don't worry about Evaniese." He pointed a liable finger at Nathan. "She's *my* girl and my concern. Just stay away from her. Please, don't make me have to tell you that again. If I have to find you and warn you about this again, I can't promise our talks will remain this friendly."

Nathan's face creased in frustration and disbelief. His eyes widened in shock, as he set his right hand on his chest. "Are you threatening me?" he asked, incredulous.

"You can call it whatever you like, *Doctor*," Brent said, edging in closer to Nathan in a daunting manner. "I don't want you talking to her, smiling at her through the ER, hugging her hello or goodbye. *Stay away* from her." Brent glared, and delved lethally into Nathan's eyes.

"You *can't* stop me from talking to her," Nathan challenged. He refused to back down this time. "If Evaniese *wants* to talk to me, that's her prerogative. I will respect the boundaries you've set, but if she wants to be friendly, I refuse to be unfriendly, nasty or rude." Nathan's already tawny complexion only reddened in resentment. "Listen, I get it. You're possessive of her. I get that, but you really need to back off."

"I don't have to do a thing, *Doctor*." Brent's eyes sparked flames. "Now, stay away from my girl," he emphasized.

Inwardly, he felt conflicted. This wasn't the person he wanted to be. He wasn't a mobster who went around threatening people. And yet, when it came to Evaniese, he was a total madman. Loving her was bringing him closer and closer to the brink.

Nathan hung his head down for a moment, and weighed his words before allowing his eyes to reconnect to Brent's. "If Evaniese *is* truly yours, and her heart belongs to *you*, why are you so insecure and afraid of losing her?" he asked throatily.

Brent's face shaded in horror and offense. For a moment, he remained completely speechless, as he watched the young doctor walk away.

Nathan sensed his words had struck a chord, that they'd possibly impaled Brent Peterson in a vulnerable place. As Nathan hopped into his SUV, tears of anger were in his eyes. He had no idea how to deal with this situation. Brent Peterson was a thorn in his side. Yet, he felt satiated knowing that he'd thrown in a few punches of his own that afternoon.

As Nathan drove back over to the hospital, tears were in his eyes. He could no longer contain the hurt and the outrage he felt. How on earth could he stay away from Evaniese, when he was in love with her? The circumstances were very cruel.

Moreover, she didn't deserve to have him snub her in any way. And yet, he couldn't tell Evaniese that Brent Peterson was pulling the strings behind the scene. Such was Nathan's conflict. Feeling both irritated and brokenhearted, it was difficult to contain the billowing storm brewing on the inside, because it threatened to carry him away.

***

"I've been sitting out in this ridiculous ER waiting room for the past three hours, and they still haven't called my name," a patient complained to Evaniese at the registration window. The thirty-something, heavy-set Caucasian man was red as a crab.

"I've already spoken to ER staff about you, Mr. Winters. It's just a little bit busy in the ER right now. Once a room becomes available, I'm sure they'll come right out and get you," Evaniese placated.

It was yet another absurdly busy day in the ER. With her coworker Cynthia on break, Evaniese was alone. Even if Paula and Ann had hired Cynthia to help out, for the most part, Evaniese was *always* the one running around. Evaniese deemed that her bosses never had it so good. She'd gotten *used* to carrying the load on her own. Her coworker helped *somewhat*, but the girl never jumped through all the hoops Evaniese was accustomed to jumping.

"Well, can you go inside and talk to them again. I'm in serious pain out here?" Mark Winters's expression was brusque, as his sharp eyes delved irately into Evaniese's.

"Sir...," Evaniese disputed.

"Please...?" he appealed with a softer tone of voice.

Evaniese offered him a temperate smile, set her paperwork aside, pushed out of her armchair and stood to her feet. "Give me a minute. I'll go in to see what the holdup is."

"Thank you," Mark told her.

Evaniese opened up the office door, and walked out into the ER. She drifted over to the nurse's station. There, she found Nia, one of the Physician's Assistants, at her desk.

"Mark Winters, came in a while ago for abdominal pain. He says he's feeling worse. Do we have a room for him yet?" Evaniese asked.

Nia was a beautiful brunette PA. She was always smiling, and cloyingly sweet to Evaniese.

God had warned Evaniese sometime ago not to trust any of her coworkers. They were backbiting and dangerous. Evaniese was aware that some of the women who worked through the ER, had engaged in witchcraft in order to ruin her relationship with Jeremy Carter.

Sadly, it seemed as if their devices had worked-at least for the time being. Jeremy had left the hospital, and had severed all ties. Ultimately, Evaniese knew that Isaiah 54:17 was more than true. The weapons would be forged against a child of God, but ultimately wouldn't prosper. Still, for one reason or another, God had seen fit to remove Jeremy from the equation.

And now, Evaniese knew without equivocation that the same women responsible for creating a rift between Jeremy and herself, were also trying to destroy her relationship with Nathan Andrews. Evaniese was constantly praying *and* fasting. However, the circumstances remained contrary. Still, she had to keep reminding herself that there was purpose for the struggle and the pain.

In any event, Evaniese set her personal biases aside. She kept a smile pasted to her face, as she addressed the beautiful, dark-haired, brown-eyed PA.

"Just let me check the board for a moment," Nia said, studying the ER's patient log. "Mrs. Murray's getting discharged in like ten minutes. So, would you kindly tell Mr. Winters we'll bring him in just as soon as she's discharged?" her voice was honey sweet.

Evaniese's smile matched Nia's. "Thank you so much. I'll go tell him now."

"No worries," Nia said.

Evaniese veered away from the nurse's station. She was about to step back out to the ER waiting room to have word with Mark Winters, when she saw Nathan. He'd just stepped out from one of the ER rooms from a consultation. Evaniese's heart skipped a beat the moment she saw him. He looked incredible in a dark gray dress suit. As always, his slick raven hair framed his winsome face perfectly. In short, he looked like something out of her fondest dreams.

Evaniese hadn't seen Nathan in quite a while, neither had they called or texted each other. And yet, she was still confident of God's promise that they'd be together one of these days. The fulfilment of God's promises was what kept Evaniese going. She had a great big smile pasted to her face, as she marched back out towards the ER waiting room.

However, before she drifted away, she took a moment to acknowledge Nathan. "Hello, there, stranger!" She threw her arms around him for a hug. She and Nathan were in habit of hugging after not seeing each other in a while.

However, this time around, Nathan brusquely pulled back. His face wrinkled in annoyance. "Evaniese, can you please not hug me anymore?" His malt complexion turned ruddy, and his eyes darted out venom. "I think it's becoming a bit awkward at this point," he raised his voice rancorously.

Evaniese flinched back in shock and offense. "Oh, I'm sorry," her voice undulated.

Her throat felt scratchy, and tears amassed in her eyes. It took tremendous restraint to stay put and not run away. "I didn't know it bothered you so much." Evaniese tried to keep smiling through the sting of Nathan's words.

Being censured in that way by Nathan was the last thing she'd expected. Evaniese remembered going through similar scenarios with Brent and Jeremy. However, she honestly believed Nathan was *different*. Nevertheless, that evening, seeing the acerbic expression on Nathan's face, and the coldness in his eyes, Evaniese realized she'd misjudged him. He wasn't different at all.

"No, no," Nathan pacified, "it isn't your fault. I should have told you it was inappropriate from the start."

Nathan felt like a monster for putting Evaniese on blasts for no reason at all. There wasn't anything he could say to take away the clear hurt on her face and in her eyes. His actions and words had wounded her deeply, and he had no idea how to fix it. "I'm a married man, Evaniese, and you're..."

"It's all right, Nathan." Evaniese baulked, crushed. "I get it. You've beat the fact that you're a married man into the ground. Believe me, I wouldn't think of coming between you and your *precious* wife," her voice broke, and tears shone in her eyes. "I was just happy to see you."

"Evaniese, I'm sorry. I didn't mean it that way," Nathan appealed. "It's just a little uncomfortable..."

Evaniese held her right hand up in a halting manner, and she frowned in conflict. "I get it. It was nice to see you, Nathan, but I've got to get back to my desk now," she said resignedly, and turned away. Evaniese took quick strides to distance herself from Nathan.

Nathan stood outside of the ER room cringing in regret over his shameful behavior. Brent Peterson browbeating him all the time had left him utterly frustrated him. So, he in turn, had taken it out on Evaniese. Tears shone in his eyes, as he internalized just how deeply he hurt her. Evaniese didn't deserve to be treated that way, and Nathan *hated* Brent for being such a selfish egomaniac. Brent obviously had no power, or control over *anything* having to do with Evaniese. So, his viewpoint was, if *he* couldn't have her, no one else would.

***

"I don't know how to feel right now, Lord," Evaniese prayed. She was in tears, as she waited in the presence of her heavenly father late Friday night after work. She trembled, and breathed spasmodically. "You told me Brent was the *one*. So, I waited over four years for something to happen at the church. I waited for Brent to say something...anything.

"You encouraged me to tell him *I* how felt, and he rejected me as if I were something vile…" Evaniese gasped, and strove to catch her breath, as she poured her heart out to God. "Then, you told me *Jeremy* was the one. Not only did Jeremy break my heart, but he left the hospital. And, just when I thought I'd caught a break with Nathan, turns out he's just as awful as the other two…"

Evaniese was both hurt and mortified over Nathan's slight. He'd asked her not to hug or touch him, because it felt awkward. Brent had denounced and humiliated her, and Jeremy had abandoned her. Evaniese truly thought Nathan was different from the other two men.

Upon meeting Nathan, God gave her revelation that he was her God-ordained spouse. So, Evaniese couldn't see Nathan hurting her as the other two men had. However, she was beginning to grasp her misapprehension. As she sobbed in the presence of God, itemizing her sorrows and misfortunes, Nathan's words resonated. His snub was the latest and greatest in her history of rejection.

At that juncture, submitting to the WLS, was the only thing she had to look forward to. Evaniese was convinced. Once she had the procedure, everything else would fall into place. Surely, the underlying reason for her suffering was because she was overweight. And, the sadder she felt, the more she self-pacified with food.

Her third weigh-in revealed that she was up three more pounds. As it stood, she'd eliminated a few of the medical clearances required to have the surgery. She'd had the Endoscopy, had consulted with a nutritionist, and had seen a pulmonologist. There was still quite a ways to go to clear for the procedure, and Evaniese was determined to check off all the boxes.

Besides being rejected by Nathan, Evaniese had noticed a shift in her relationships with Ginger and Deanna. The two had grown extremely distant. Evaniese struggled to wrap her head around how aloof they were. Earlier that night, she'd called her friends, direly needing someone to hear her out. However, they were both unreceptive, and claimed to be terribly busy. Being ignored by her best friends, made Evaniese even more grateful for her relationship with Jesus Christ.

He was the Friend who sticks closer than a brother (Proverbs 18:24). Still, it was a real struggle to stay in faith. Evaniese couldn't understand why God had allowed so much pain and suffering to come into her life. She was forty-six years old, and she'd been waiting for God to bless her with the right person since the tender age of twenty. Not only had God blatantly *not* answered with the right one, he'd sent three different people into her life. All three had broken her heart, and had killed her spirit.

In spite of the sadness and confusion, as Evaniese waited in the presence of God and opened up the bible, she was reminded of his will. She also contemplated the promises of God to flood her life with blessings. God had promised to reward her faithfulness, and her suffering-that was if she didn't give up. Moreover, God emphasized Nathan's love for her, in spite of his atrocious behavior. Thus, Evaniese had to forgive him, and keep the lines of communication open. All the same, as a result of what happened with Nathan, she had no real desire to talk to him anytime soon.

Yet, Evaniese realized she had to submit to the will of God no matter how excruciating the process. Nathan's ill treatment of her still resonated. Though, it seemed to be God's will for her to remain connected to him. The weekend had rolled around once more. And, Evaniese had nothing special on the agenda. The highlight of her Saturday would probably be to do a load of laundry. Then, go out to the local Walmart to pick up a few things.

After an emotional time of devotions, Evaniese changed for bed. Turning on the T.V. for background noise, she rummaged through her food pantry on the upstairs loft of the house. There, she found rice cakes, and a jar of *Skippy Honey Peanut Butter*. Evaniese pulled out a couple of rice cakes from the bag, and spread peanut butter on them. She also scooped a couple of tablespoons of peanut butter into her mouth in the Interim.

Soon after, she brushed her teeth, and slipped into bed. However, she sat up for a while with her back propped up by her pillows. She got her laptop, and accessed the internet. Trying to push the unpleasant account with Nathan from her thoughts, she logged into her YouTube channel, and read comments left by her viewers and subscribers. *Usually*, they were words of encouragement. Of course, there were instances where she had to deal with internet trolls. They never had *anything* positive to say. Evaniese usually deleted the comments, and blocked whoever sent them.

Some of the comments made her smile indeed. She had at least a hundred new subscribers, and she wanted to focus on that. As she went through the comments, she stumbled upon one that was quite sweet. There wasn't a name, or a face to ascribe, but it was one of the kindest comments she'd ever received since starting her vlog a few years ago.

"I look forward to watching your videos. Seeing your bright smile, and hearing your lilting voice, as you share your pearls of wisdom in respect to home and living, always makes my day."

"Aw… Someone was sweet enough to leave such an awesome comment," Evaniese susurrated, going over the comment again. The subscriber's name was *Fan4sure*. Evaniese was stirred by the words. Before long, she shut down the laptop, and put it away.

Regardless of her difficult day, *Fan4sure's* comment, managed to put a smile on her face. As Evaniese's head propped to her pillow, she thanked God for those kind words. As early morning loomed, she reread the comment on her phone. Often, the kindness of a stranger, seemed more tangible than that of a distant loved one's.

Chapter Four

"So, let me get this straight. You're worried that your friend, whom you've known for a very long time, will lose weight, and suddenly become the center of attention?" Madam Devorah, a self-proclaimed spiritualist and medium, asked Ginger early Saturday afternoon.

Ginger wasn't altogether comfortable being at *Madam Devorah's House of Spirits*. She'd read up on the woman, and about her establishment online. Thus, Ginger had driven for over an hour outside of Amber Hills to consult with the clairvoyant.

Tacitly, Ginger tried to explain, "I guess, that's *another* way of saying it. Yes, I *am* worried that she will become the center of attention. She's very beautiful!" Ginger whispered, too ashamed to raise her voice.

She also kept shifting uneasily in her chair. The chair was positioned directly across from Madam Devorah's. Even if she was miles away from Amber Hills, Ginger couldn't help thinking someone she knew would walk into the establishment at any minute. The concept created both nervous energy and angst. After all, she was a *churchgoing* person.

"So, tell me the *real* reason you're here this afternoon," Madam Devorah challenged. "What is it that you're looking for *me* to help you with?" Her wrinkled face warped in ambiguity.

Ginger cleared her throat, folded her hands, and rested them on the rim of the round table across from Devorah. With her eyes fastened to the woman's, she tried to keep her voice from wavering, "I was told that you could..." Ginger tensely cleared her throat again.

"What were you told?" Suspicion and doubt were on Madam Devorah's face.

"Well, I was told you specialize in spells, hexes and curses," Ginger uttered, with an undulating tone.

"Is *that* why you've sought me out this afternoon?" Sternness overshadowed the face of the spiritualist. "You're looking to put a curse on your *friend*?"

"Well..." Ginger hesitated. Her eyes temporarily wandered away from Devorah's piercing blue-gray ones. "Well, yes... I mean, I don't want any harm to come to her..."

"Oh, of course not," Madam Devorah said caustically, "after all she is your *friend*, right?" she derided.

"Yes... She *is* my friend," Ginger affirmed, taking offense to the woman's attitude.

"Yes, of course. That's *exactly* what friends do. They put curses and hexes on each other," Devorah scoffed. There was an unmistakable smirk on her face. "Look," her eyes lowered into Ginger's, "if we're going to do this, you've got to tell the truth. You don't love your friend at all.

"The fact is that you're jealous of her. True love isn't jealous. So, in order for a spell, hex or curse to be effective, you've got to confess your true feelings, and specify exactly what you would like to see happen to this *person*. Are we clear on that?" Her eyes speared through Ginger's.

Embarrassment shaded Ginger's face. Tears shone in her eyes, as she acknowledged just how right Devorah was. She *was* jealous of Evaniese, and had *always* been. And, with Evaniese's impending surgery, Ginger was more put out than ever. Evaniese would be thin. That meant, she would become her competition. Evaniese already had so much going for her. Ginger had consulted with a medium in the past to obstruct Evaniese's weight loss efforts. The method seemed to have worked for a while.

However, Ginger feared, with the surgery, nothing would encumber Evaniese from reaching her weight loss goals. "Yes," Ginger addressed Madame Devorah, "we're clear."

"Tell me how you *really* feel?" the medium encouraged.

"I hate that my *friend…* that the *person* in question is always *shining.* It doesn't seem to matter what life throws at her, she's like a shining star. She's bright, beautiful and blessed!" Ginger sneered in displeasure.

"So, you're envious of this woman, and you feel that her attributes are unmerited?" Devorah probed, staring at Ginger in skepticism.

"Yes, I can't stand the fact that she *always* wins." Ginger scowled. "She's always been the *fat one*, and I need for it to stay that way," she admitted, shrinking back from her own words, and startled as her eyes linked to the spiritualist's.

"Now, *that's* what I'm trying to draw out of you. A spell is only effective, if there is *true* hatred behind it. Given the level of your disdain, I think it just might work." An insidious smile spread over her face.

"But, can you ensure the *individual* doesn't lose the weight, even after she has weight loss surgery?" Ginger asked, feeling suddenly empowered.

"No, I *cannot* ensure that. There are extenuating factors to consider. This woman," introspection changed Devorah's features, "does she have faith in God?"

"Yes, she does. She's very devout in her faith," Ginger admitted.

"And *you*, do *you* attend church with her?" Doubt eclipsed Devorah's face, as she scrutinized Ginger.

Ginger felt as if the woman was literally burning a hole through her. But, for reasons unknown, she couldn't lie. "Yes, I attend church with her. I believe in God too," she added.

Devorah flung her head back, and a ripple of laughter echoed from the hollow of her throat.

"What's so funny? I *do* believe in God. I know he exists, and that he's real," Ginger disputed.

"Yes," in between spurts of laughter, "I don't doubt that you believe in God. But, the question is, in which *god* do you believe in?" Laughter now fizzled, and criticalness veiled Devorah's face again.

Ginger's expression was of confusion and frustration. "What do you mean by that? I believe in the creator of the universe?"

"All right, if you say so," Devorah said cynically.

"Look," Ginger's face wrinkled in annoyance, and her hands went cheekily to her hips, "can you help me out or not?"

"I *am* trying to help you," Devorah said, irritated, and glaring at Ginger. "I'm trying to tell you that if your friend is devout in her faith...unlike *some* others, your curse might not be as effective as you'd want."

"All right," Ginger softened, "I'm sorry. I didn't get why you were going over all that stuff. Yes, the person in question has faith, and I believe she's sincere."

"She's a *Christian* person?" Devorah prodded.

"Yes."

Devorah sighed, exasperated. "I have learned from experience over the years that trying to put a hex or a spell on a *true* Christian, is a very dangerous practice. And, whereas what you would want to see happen might prevail for a little while, eventually they emerge stronger and better from their adversities."

"So, what *are* you saying, Madam Devorah?" Ginger's tone was resentful.

"I'm saying I *can* help you conjure up your little hex, but be prepared to deal with the repercussions."

"Repercussions?" Ginger frowned in angst.

"Yes. Since *you* attend church, you should know that an attack against a *true* child of God, can only bring about misery, misfortune and ultimate destruction to those who plot against them," Devorah tried to be painfully honest. She'd seen it all too often.

Those who plotted against *true* children of God, often wound up regretting doing so in the worst ways. In some instances, some weren't even around to attest to the pitfalls of launching such an affront. Others who were, still reeled from the negative backlash, and continued nursing their wounds. Devorah had even seen the tides shift in the opposite direction. The blade had swung towards the attacker, and pierced them through with unmitigated agony.

"I just want to make sure. Is this something you really want to do?" Devorah's eyes lowered critically into Ginger's.

"Yes," Ginger affirmed, nodding. "Can you help me?"

"I need you to affirm that this is what you want," she emphasized again.

"Yes, it's what I want. I need for you to ensure that my *friend*..."

"What is her name?"

"Her name is Evaniese," Ginger said plainly.

"All right... What would you like to see befall Evaniese?"

"I want her to fail in her weight loss venture. I want her to keep being the *fat girl* in our circle."

"You don't want her to lose weight?" Devorah tested. "Anything else?"

"Yes. She's also caught the eye of a very handsome young doctor at the hospital where she works..." Ginger's eyes connected portentously to the diviner's. "I don't want that to work out either," she detailed.

"All right. *Now*, we're getting somewhere. You've got to verbalize exactly what you would want to see, or *not* see happen," Devorah said, smiling artfully.

Ginger nodded in agreement and smiled as well. "I can totally do that."

"Yes, I'm beginning to see that now. You're doing very well," Devorah encouraged.

***

Ellis took a drive out to the town of Valleyfield in L.A. on a Sunday afternoon. The plan was to see his latest movie on the big screen. The movie had hit the box office that weekend. There were times he enjoyed seeing his movies for the first time along with the audience. *Chances taken, Chances Lost,* was the film he'd worked on prior to *Deadly Roulette.* *Chances* had received glowing reviews. The numbers were definitely looking good! So far, the action-adventure flick had grossed over $90 million in the US alone that weekend.

Ellis was pleased with his work. He'd tried to go into the Valleyfield Cinema *lot* incognito. But, now that he was standing outside, blocks away from the multiplex, he realized he'd probably made a mistake by going out there alone. Halfway through the movie, someone in the theater recognized him. Needless to say, the murmurs and whispers only escalated from that point on.

Suddenly, the attention of moviegoers shifted away from the movie, and onto Ellis. At first, only a few women sitting in his row recognized him. However, it didn't take long for others to catch wind he was there. So, before long, Ellis found himself surrounded. Some of the women were screaming and in tears, as they took turns asking for autographs, and taking selfies on their phones in close proximity. Quite soon, everyone knew Ellis was there, and he was virtually ambushed. Being trapped was something he wouldn't have wished on his worst enemy.

Ellis had charmed his way through the experience. He'd tried to remain as calm, and as gracious as he could. So, after being detained out in *Valleyfield* for over two hours, he finally managed to get away. Understanding his dilemma, one of his fans stepped in to help. As Ellis made his way through the crowd on his way out of the movie house, the *twenty something* kid pulled up in his Jeep, and offered to take Ellis away from the mayhem.

Without hesitation, Ellis hopped into the Jeep. Grateful for his help, Ellis handed him a hundred-dollar bill. It was all the cash he had on hand. However, Ellis made a point to get the kid's name and number. He wanted to do something special for Tim Hines. The kid literally saved his life that afternoon.

Now, Ellis found himself standing out on Valleyfield Boulevard, waiting for his driver to come get him. By request, Tim had dropped Ellis off on the boulevard. For a number of reasons, Ellis chose not to have Tim drop him off at the mansion in Malibu Summit.

Ellis waited for Dylan near the entryway of a major strip mall. He had on a pair of jeans, a T-shirt and jacket, along with his trusty shades and baseball cap. Ellis was anxious for Dylan to find him. He couldn't risk anyone else coming along and recognizing him. His presence over at the multiplex had incited a frenzy, and Ellis couldn't go through that again.

"God, what's taking Dylan so long?" Ellis brushed through his thick, dark hair with nervous energy. His eyes scanned the area for the limo. "Okay… I get it, Lord. I shouldn't have gone to see the movie by myself. It was a mistake," he spoke to God on the matter. "I will try to be a better listener next time. I was only eager to get a feel for how the audience would receive it."

Before venturing out to see the film, Ellis had an inkling that he shouldn't risk it. If he'd heeded the warning, he wouldn't be in this predicament.

Moments later, Ellis caught sight of the limo coming from up the road. "Thank you, Lord," he said quietly, and issued a sigh of relief.

"Sir, I apologize for taking so long," Dylan said, as he hopped out of the automobile to get the door for Ellis.

"It's all right, Dylan," Ellis said. "Just get me out of here." Ellis slipped instantly into the car.

"Sir, there's something you should know." Dylan seemed disconcerted, as he took his place behind the wheel again.

"What's going on, Dylan?" Ellis saw Dylan's grimace through rearview mirror. Even if there was definitely something wrong, Ellis couldn't say he wasn't grateful they were on the move.

"Sir, Miss Kierra's at the front gate waiting for you." Dylan gulped nervously.

"Kierra...?" Ellis asked, surprised and somewhat miffed. "Did Nicholas let her in?" he asked, concerned. Nicholas oversaw the mansion gate on the weekends.

"He's waiting for *you*, Sir. He tried to call you. But, for one reason or another, he couldn't get a hold of you."

Ellis pulled his phone out of his pocket, and realized it was dead. "Well, you're right. Nick couldn't get through, because my phone's dead. *You're* the last person I was able to call." Ellis's thoughts raced. "So, Kierra's there now?" He shook his head in incredulity.

"I'm afraid she is. She's at the gate waiting, sir. If you'd like, I can call Nick, and you can speak to him directly," Dylan discreetly suggested.

Ellis' thoughts were a million miles away. Kierra's refusal to respect the boundaries *did* annoy him. When she'd dropped in on his movie set location in Minnesota months ago, Ellis had a very stern talk with her. He honestly believed Kierra understood his lack of appreciation for her constant intrusion. She always showed up to the most unexpected events, unannounced and uninvited. All things considered, Kierra just wasn't getting the message.

The last thing he wanted was to be unkind, or to hurt her feelings. Yet and still, Kierra was off on a tangent. So, Ellis had to spell it out for her. She had to respect the boundaries. "No, Dylan, I don't have to talk to Nick. Let me handle Kierra." Veins pulsed at his temples.

Kierra was beautiful, talented and sweet. However, Ellis knew without equivocation she wasn't his God-ordained person. On the other hand, Ellis found himself smiling as he thought about *Niecy819*. A little over a month ago, he'd reached out by leaving comments in the comment section of her YouTube videos. Since then, he'd left comments on her videos. Her responses were just as gracious as everything else about her. Now more than ever, Ellis wanted to make a tangible connection to the young woman.

It didn't make any sense, but it was something he'd prayed on extensively. Oddly, the more he prayed on the matter, the stronger he felt about wanting to meet her. So, taking the initiative to comment on her vlogs, had in some way pulled her into Ellis world, and vice versa. And yet, Ellis wanted so much more. However, for the moment, he had to deal with the unpleasantness of putting Kierra Spalding in her place.

***

"Kierra, you've got to stop dropping in on me like this," Ellis said, pouring her a drink from the bar in his private den.

"I remember all too well what you told me, Ellis," Kierra said, in a hushed tone, flinching that he'd raised his voice at her. She stared idly at the plush carpeting to avoid eye contact with him.

"Kierra, look at me." Ellis handed her the club soda she'd requested. "Hey, look at me," he urged in a gentler tone. Inwardly, he realized he was being a bit too hard on her.

Kierra's face wrinkled in remorse, and her culpable eyes finally connected to Ellis's. "What is it, Ellis? I *know* you're upset with me. I get that you're mad, but please hear me out." She pouted.

Ellis sighed, and his expression tempered. "All right," he waved his hand in approval, "what is it, *Key*. Talk to me."

Kierra's eyes fastened furtively to Ellis's. Setting her free hand on his shoulder, she tried to capture his complete attention. "I'm really sorry for coming out here unannounced and unexpected." Her eyes veered in awkwardness. "Look, I get it. You're only interested in being friends, but I have a favor to ask." Her eyes delved into his in petition.

"Just spell it out, Kierra," Ellis prodded, exploring her big hazel eyes. They shimmered in the sunlight filtering through the expansive room. "You don't have to mince words. We *are* after all friends." He nodded approvingly.

"Well, there are actually two things I'd like to ask..." Kierra frowned in uncertainty, as her eyes searched Ellis's in entreaty.

"Key, *just* tell me. I can't stand all of this deliberation." Ellis's face flushed red, and his eyes sparked in exasperation.

"So, okay... I was over at the Palisades Studio yesterday morning. There was talk of a new movie due to come out in November," Kierra began to explain. "It's a collaborative effort of Morgan Lester and Todd Hanley."

"Okay... Morgan and Todd usually work in collaboration on *lots* of movies at that studio." Ellis shrugged with a puzzled expression on his face.

Kierra nodded quickly. "In a matter of months, they're going to start work on their new movie, *Symmetry*." Kierra smiled excitedly. "I overheard them talking about offering *you* the lead role."

Ellis's expression changed, and a smile broke across his face. Shaking his head nonsensically, he tested, "Are you sure?"

"I'm positive, Ellis. Morgan Lester said there's no one else they're interested in casting for the part of Tanner Mane. Word has it, it's going to be one of those *John Wick, Mission Impossible* type films. So, you might need to brush up on stunt work. You might also want to focus on spending a little bit more time at the gym..."

Kierra stopped short to scrutinize Ellis's toned and rugged body. She reached up, and set her right hand on his chest, and issued an alluring smile. "Not that you need to go crazy. I happen to think you're perfect just the way you are."

Ellis shook his head comically, and gently took hold of Kierra's hand. "Key, *focus*... What are you getting at?" he asked straightforwardly.

"Well, there's talk that they're going to contact you *this* week, probably first thing tomorrow morning," Kierra went on to explain, winded.

"Okay...," Ellis doubted, "where do *you* factor in in all of this? You're *not* getting to the point." There was a cagey expression on his face.

"Todd and Morgan said they'd leave it up to *you* to select the actor you want as your love interest...," Kierra said, and closed her eyes with a sense of uncertainty. She recoiled in angst that Ellis would put her on blasts.

Ellis shook his head humorously, and chuckled. "So, you're here this afternoon, because you want me to tell them *you're* my pick?" He laughed comically over Kierra's calculating set of actions.

"Yes. The role *would* mean a lot to me. Besides, I would get to play opposite to someone I *really* like." Kierra stepped away, and went to rest her drink over at the bar. She then sauntered back over to Ellis, and draped her arms about his neck. "Please, El... Do it for me?" she pleaded with a velvety tone, suppliant eyes and pouty lips.

"Key, that's asking a lot. First and foremost, *if* Morgan and Todd approach *me* for this role, I would have to first accept it right?" Ellis stared at Kierra in skepticism.

"Please, accept the role, Ellis. It'll do wonders for both of our careers. I've been dying to work with you. I can see it now. You and I will step out on the red carpet for all kinds of parties and promotional events." Kierra stared fondly into Ellis' jewel amber eyes. He was so handsome he was making her forget how to breathe. No doubt, she wanted Ellis to be her guy. "Please, El...?" Kierra reached up, and pressed a kiss to his cheek.

Kierra was obviously using her feminine wiles to manipulate him. So, Ellis gently pulled away. He wasn't upset. However, as a Christian man, he still had to remain guarded.

Putting some distance between them, he gave her a pleasant smile. "First and foremost, they would have to call and offer me the role. Still, Kierra, even if you heard them allude to *me* choosing a love interest in the movie, they would still need to be in agreement with my pick," Ellis pointed out. "It *is* after all *their* movie."

"I get that, Ellis." Kierra inched in close to Ellis again, but refrained from touching him. She realized she might be moving a little bit too fast. She knew Ellis's core beliefs, and his reserved stance. It wasn't very popular in Hollywood, but she respected him for it, nonetheless.

"That's why I want *you* to drop my name, so that I can audition for the part. My job will be to blow them away. They'll have no choice but to cast me. Can you do that for me?" Kierra set her hand on Ellis's cheek, and caressed it fondly.

Ellis surrendered to a slow nod in grudging agreement. "*If* and *when* they reach out to me, and I agree to work on the film, I will definitely drop your name. I can't promise anything else though," he said wisely.

"Oh, Ellis!" Kierra celebrated. Throwing her arms about his neck, she crushed him to herself. "You won't regret this. I promise."

"Whoa there! Don't thank me just yet." Ellis set his arms about her waist, and squeezed her affectionately. As much as he wanted to stay angry at Kierra, he couldn't bring himself to. She was a very sweet girl. Though, he knew he had to set the record straight in respect to their friendship.

Ellis had to delineate they could *only* be friends. Even if he was currently unattached, his heart *did* belong to someone. Ellis had no idea what would come of his infatuation with the mystery YouTube vlogger. Nevertheless, he knew without equivocation, Kierra Spalding *wasn't* the one.

"Thank you so much, Ellis," Kierra said, beaming as she pulled away.

"You said there were *two* things…?" Ellis grilled, realizing nothing was ever cut and dried with Kierra.

"Yes. I want you to come out with me for the premier of, *Roses are dead.*" Kierra's face wrinkled in appeal. "I had a date with Garland Stanton, but he'll be out of town next week. Will you grace me with your presence yet again for the premier and after party?"

Ellis found himself nodding in agreement. He and Kierra had danced this two-step before. For the past few months, according to the tabloids and entertainment news, they were dating.

"Sure, Kierra." Ellis didn't want to say no, neither did he want to alienate Kierra. His affiliation with her was good for their careers, and their statuses in Hollywood.

"Thank you." Kierra reached up, and pressed a quick kiss to Ellis's cheek again. "I appreciate that you took the time this afternoon."

"Did I have a choice?" Ellis chortled, and shook his head farcically.

"I'm sorry again for just dropping by. I thought you should hear about the impending movie offer news from me," she said wispily, staring devoted into Ellis's eyes.

"Yes, of course, you were thinking *only* of me…," Ellis said comically, and winked at her.

"Of course…," Kierra rose to the occasion. "So, I guess, I'll get right out of your way. You *do* have that commitment later." Kierra seemed glum.

"Yes, I do, Kierra. Thanks a lot for coming by with such favorable news." Ellis gave her a heartening smile. "Are you good? Do you need a ride? I noticed you sent Victor home." Victor was one of Kierra's limo guys.

"I'll just call him, and ask him to come get me," she told Ellis.

"Not at all. I'll have Dylan take you wherever you need to go," Ellis offered generously.

"Are you sure?"

"Positive."

Ellis crossed the room to access the phone. It was on a charging port at his desk. He then autodialed Dylan. About ten minutes later, Dylan was all set to drive Kierra home.

Ellis lingered in his den for a while after Kierra left. He sat at his desk trying to unwind. He had another premier party to attend that night. This time around, he'd be walking the red-carpet solo, because he didn't have a date. Kierra had thrown all kinds of hints of wanting to be his date, but Ellis resolved to attend the function alone.

As he sat there in the stillness and the solitude, he prayed for God's will and direction for his life. God had blessed him with wealth and status. All of his blessings were primarily to help those less fortunate. Giving back was more than just his duty. It was a ministry. Through a number of philanthropic organizations, Ellis subsidized, and lent aid wherever it was needed.

Such endeavors were indeed fulfilling. Nevertheless, Ellis realized there was a missing link. He longed for a partner to share the ups and downs of life. He had a few friends, but no one close enough to *truly* know him inside and out. Thus, only that special someone could fill the profound longing he had in his heart for love.

Reflexively, he checked his phone and accessed YouTube. There was a notification that *Niecy819* had responded to a comment he'd left on her latest vlog. Ellis's smile was as impressionable as a schoolboy's upon seeing her message.

It read; *"To my latest and greatest inspiration! Fan4sure, I just wanted to highlight how you've given me the motivation, and the strength not to give up. It means so much knowing something I'm doing is positively impacting lives. And for this much, I thank you."*

Totally stirred and more smitten than ever, Ellis enjoyed the little stint of privacy before having to attend the pompous premier party for his latest movie. Mulling over the young woman's words made him indescribably happy, and offered so much hope. Ellis prayed that he'd come to know *Niecey819* in some way, shape or form. At that juncture, their paths had in some way intersected. She was now a part of his world, and in his personal space. It was something Ellis wanted to build on, because he certainly wanted to be a part of her world, and share in *her* personal space.

***

In the middle of May, Evaniese sat in an armchair in Dr. Bergstrom's office inside the bariatric office at Brookline Hospital. It was her *fifth* weigh-in appointment, and she was now a hefty 262 pounds. Moments earlier, she'd submitted to getting on the scale. Adding insult to injury, there was an $80 copay for every appointment. So, essentially, Evaniese was paying the office $80 just to hear them validate just how fat she was.

She already knew she was fat. Hence, the reason why she'd sought them out for help. The circumstances were discouraging. It didn't matter what she ate, or how much she exercised, her body seemed to be working against all of her efforts. Truth be told, she was *relying* heavily on the surgery to see the numbers move in the opposite direction on the scale.

Evaniese had a very long day ahead, and it was only 10 a.m. Later in the day, at about a quarter to one in the afternoon, she had an appointment with a psychologist. It was to fulfill yet another clearance for the surgery. Ensuing, she'd return to Brookline Hospital at three. Most of the authorizations needed to have the surgery were out of the way.

According to Dr. Bergstrom, if everything worked according to plan, the surgery was scheduled for July of that year. Still, Evaniese worried that her medical insurance carrier would opt out of paying for the procedure. She feared they'd say she was liable for not holding up her end of the bargain. Her part of the bargain was to actually lose weight. However, instead of losing, she'd gained close to twenty pounds since the initial consult with the bariatric team at the hospital.

Sadly, she *was* doing everything in her power to shed the pounds. Evaniese had to conclude that something was off. Perhaps it was her age. She was after all forty-six years old. So, maybe a slow metabolism was to blame. Earlier on, she'd tested negative for Hypothyroidism. According to tests, her thyroid was functioning just fine, but Evaniese couldn't lose weight to save her life. Nevertheless, she trusted God to make a way for her. Praying extensively on the matter, she had God's word that the surgery would be a beneficial measure.

On the other hand, at that very moment, as she waited for Dr. Bergstrom in his office, Evaniese was in tears. *What if Wellbeing Plus, her medical insurance, wouldn't cover the surgery, because she'd gained so much weight?*

Evaniese sniffled, and tried to meter out her breathing before Dr. Bergstrom returned. Reaching into her pocketbook, she found tissues. She then quickly dried her teary eyes and blew her nose. Dr. Bergstrom didn't need to see her sniveling like a child.

"Evaniese!" Dr. Bergstrom announced amiably, striding back into the office. There was a very encouraging smile on his face. The older Caucasian gentleman with pepper-colored hair, seemed to be in great spirits. Taking his place behind the desk, he settled into the armchair, clasped his hands together, and stared curiously at Evaniese.

Evaniese strove to pull it together. Staring hopefully into Dr. Bergstrom's eyes, she forced a smile.

"Are you all right?" Dr. Bergstrom asked, frowning in concern.

"I'm all right," Evaniese's voice undulated, as the rubber smile melded into her features.

Dr. Bergstrom gave her a pertained, but questioning look. "Were you crying?" His face wrinkled in perplexity, as he moved closer to the edge of the desk to examine her.

"I'm okay," Evaniese reassured, trying to perk up. The smile on her face was cemented at that point.

"You don't have to worry, Evaniese. Everything's going fine. In fact, everything's right on schedule."

"But I've gained weight," Evaniese groused, ashamed.

"Oh, dear," he said, grimacing. Dr. Bergstrom then redirected, "That's all right." He offered a good-natured smile, and held his right hand up in a halting manner. "You don't have to worry about that, dear. It's fine. We will work with your insurance company." His eyes lowered intuitively into hers.

"Are you sure?" Evaniese tested, still shaky on the matter. "I've been trying so hard…"

"Yes, dear, I'm sure you have. You're doing great. Many people who come here do so, because of their struggle to maintain a healthy weight. So far," Dr. Bergstrom quickly glanced over Evaniese's chart, "you've managed to knock out most of the medical clearances. So, in about three months or so, you and I will meet up in the OR again. This time around, it will be for your surgery." He smiled, and winked at Evaniese.

Evaniese laughed lightly and guffawed. "Thanks so much for all your help, and for being so understanding." She felt better at that point.

"So, let's see here," Dr. Bergstrom reviewed, "you're seeing the psychologist this afternoon?"

"Yes, my appointment's scheduled for 12:45 p.m.," Evaniese said plainly, feeling a lot more at ease. "Is it too soon to schedule the sleep study?" she asked. Her sleep study would be done through the hospital as well. And, from what she'd been told, there was a waiting list.

"No, it isn't too soon. Hopefully, we can get that done weeks prior to the surgery. Your final clearance will be for an overall physical with your primary care physician, Dr. Keith West."

Evaniese nodded. "I've already scheduled *that* appointment." She smiled. "The more clearances I get out of the way, the more excited I get about having the procedure."

"It *is* a pretty exciting event. I'm sure you've watched your share of videos, especially on YouTube of those who've submitted to the VSG. Their entire lives have changed-for the better."

"Yes, I *have* seen a lot of YouTube videos from the WLS community." Evaniese sighed. "I hope I can do half as well as some of the people I've seen." Her eyes sparkled in affect.

"I'm sure you will do just fine," Dr. Bergstrom encouraged, smiling into her eyes.

"Thank you for being so positive, Dr. B," Evaniese praised.

"I've been around the block enough times for me to know everything's *going* to work out. You'll be surprised to see how well things will work out." He winked at her again.

"Thank you," Evaniese said, enlivened.

She felt empowered. Dr. Bergstrom's encouragement helped her focus on the positive things in her life. Even if very little had changed with Nathan, Evaniese had a new friend. *Fan4sure*, one of her subscribers, always left uplifting and kind words in the comment section of her YouTube videos.

The grim reality was that Evaniese was still waiting for God to step in. She still had faith that God would manifest his power by establishing a relationship with the men he'd said were tied into her destiny. Though, according to what she believed, she was supposed to be linked to Brent, Jeremy or Nathan. However, Evaniese wasn't any closer to any of them than she'd been from day one. The circumstances were cruel. Evaniese often felt as if God had dangled all three good-looking and successful men in her face, only to say, "Well… Guess what? You can't be with any of them."

Fan4sure's comments on her YouTube videos were bright spots in her life. Lately, Evaniese had noticed odd behavior from Ginger and Deanna. Since telling them about the surgery, her besties had changed. Of course, Ginger and Deanna still called her often enough, and Evaniese occasionally hung out with them. However, something indefinable had shifted in their friendship.

Evaniese adhered to her faith, and to her relationship with Jesus Christ. Apart from that, this *Fan4sure* person seemed extremely devoted, and scarily consistent in uplifting all of videos. From what she perceived, it was a man, perhaps a *secret admirer*.

At least, it made her feel better to believe that. And yet, as mordant as her love life was, Evaniese knew she couldn't go outside of God's will. Her focus had to be on the three men God had delineated. It didn't even matter if none of *them* wanted to be with *her* at that juncture. Even so, it felt good to be noticed and appreciated by someone else-virtual or otherwise, even if the appreciation wasn't coming from the people she wanted.

"So, should I give you guys a call as soon as I schedule the sleep study?" Evaniese tried to stay in the moment, because her thoughts had drifted.

"Definitely give us a call. The sooner that's out the way, the sooner we can come up with a tentative date for the surgery," Dr. Bergstrom happily announced.

"All right, then. I will try to schedule that as soon as possible. Is there anything else I need to have done today?"

"Did you take care of your copay?"

"Not yet," Evaniese answered.

"Well, pay Deidra at the desk, and I will see you next month," Dr. Bergstrom said.

"Will do," Evaniese said, standing to her feet. She offered Dr. Bergstrom a warm smile just before she slipped out of the office.

She had a few errands to run before her appointment with the psychologist in the early afternoon. Evaniese would unquestionably be exhausted by the time she showed up for work later in the day. Usually, she had a little window of time to rest prior to going into the hospital. However, there would be no such luxury on that day. Yet, it was all good, because every medical clearance was bringing her one step closer to her goal. That was to have the surgery, and finally distance herself from being fat.

***

The skies were shadowy and grim, and the clouds held an ominous summit overhead, as Evaniese pulled into her driveway in the late morning. No doubt, the heavens threatened a downpour on Indiana residents. Evaniese was back from the local strip mall in downtown Amber Hills. She'd wanted to purchase a new blouse at the *Queen's Boutique Unlimited*. Nonetheless, she was put out about purchasing any new clothes. The stylish cranberry-colored blouse she liked that *actually* fit was in a size 2X.

Wanting something new to wear to work, Evaniese grudgingly gave in and bought the blouse. She had to keep reminding herself that she'd soon be giving most of her clothes away to charity. Needless to say, a few weeks post-op, the new blouse would no longer fit. The fact that the top was forty percent off also encouraged the sale. So, even if she felt like a *tent*, she realized she still had to make the most of her appearance. Before stepping out of the SUV, Evaniese checked her phone again. She'd texted Nathan a few days ago, but there was still no response.

Such a scenario wasn't at all unusual in the ongoing saga with Nathan. To Evaniese, it seemed God's promise of a solid relationship with Nathan, was quickly slipping through her fingers. In fact, she hardly saw Nathan at all. And, whereas God had asked her to keep reaching out to him via texting, it was always *hit* or *miss*. Furthermore, because her coworker Cynthia occupied the second desk inside the registration area in the ER, it was mostly *miss*.

Evaniese sat in the car for a moment trying to keep a stiff upper lip. In July of that year, she'd be turning forty-seven, and she was *still* waiting on the Lord to bless her with her person. Tears flooded her eyes to reminisce about how hopeful she'd initially felt upon meeting Nathan. Though, two years had passed, and she was no closer to being his girlfriend now, than on the day he breezed into her office in September of 2014.

As she sat there with a broken heart, she received an impression from God's Holy Spirit. She was reminded of God's faithfulness, and the immutability of his promises. *Still, how much more could she take?* Nathan had put on her blasts for *touching* him. His censure regarding the awkwardness of her PDA's, was extremely mortifying. His reaction made Evaniese feel like a needy and desperate woman. Of course, Nathan intermittently stopped by the registration office to say hello, but it was nowhere near with the frequency he'd displayed at the beginning.

They seldom got to talk in the way they used to. But, that was neither here nor there. At the end of the day, her connection to Nathan was virtually nonexistent. So, Evaniese wasn't surprised that he'd ignored her text. It wasn't the first time, and probably wouldn't be the last. There were instances where Nathan would wait weeks before answering *one* text message. Though, at other times, he answered right away. Of course, the dialogue was always impassive.

Things being what they were, and pressed for time, Evaniese wiped tears away from her eyes. She hopped out of her SUV, grabbed her shopping bag, and rushed into the house. She *had* to keep her appointment with Dr. Sylvia Lester. Doctor Lester would be conducting the psychological evaluation she needed in order to move forward with the surgery. The goal was to see if Evaniese was mentally prepared to handle the stressors, which came along with the lifestyle changes in the aftermath of the procedure.

Taking a quick shower, Evaniese rushed to get ready for her appointment. From the counseling center, she had to go into work. It was sad that she purposefully avoided looking into the full-length mirror in her bedroom as she dressed. After putting on her black dress slacks, she slipped on the new blouse. Unable to avoid looking at herself in the mirror completely, she was both stunned and horrified to see how much wider her hips were.

Working past feelings of shame, she tried to focus on her beautiful face. Evaniese assessed her face as a gift from God. And, as she preened and applied makeup, there was a sense of pride about how gorgeous she was. People told her she was pretty all the time, and there were a few times where she could actually attest to the fact.

With matching cranberry-colored accessories, makeup and lipstick, Evaniese deemed she looked quite lovely. She perked up, smiled and praised God. In spite of her ongoing battle with her weight, she was relatively in good health, and she *was* beautiful. Slipping on stylish boots, Evaniese threw on a chic black jacket. The skies were overcast, and the temperature had dipped down to 53 degrees. Indiana weather in May was usually a lot warmer.

It was 12:15 p.m. when Evaniese picked up her phone from off her nightstand. Something instantly brought a smile to her face before she left the house. There was a notification on YouTube. *Fan4Sure* had left a comment on her most recent vlog. Evaniese's face radiated sheer joy, as she rushed out of the house. Settling back into the driver's seat and securing her seatbelt, she took a moment to read the comment.

It read: *"Thank you so much for putting a new spin on something as mundane as grocery shopping. You actually make me look forward to my next trip to the supermarket. Lol. Then, again, you have that quality that brings life and color to **all** things black and white."* Fan4sure left a smiley face emoji right next to the comment.

Hope melted in Evaniese's heart like chocolate. She considered that *Fan4sure*-and she assumed it was a gentleman, admired her. It was a lot more than she could say for Brent, Jeremy or Nathan, even if they were God's *promised* beloveds.

"Lord, I thank you for using this individual to encourage and uplift me, even on my worst days," Evaniese whispered a prayer just before pulling out of the driveway. Then, off she went. She had to get over to the town of *Rolling Hills* for her appointment with Dr. Lester.

***

"Let me get this straight, Evaniese. You're saying that you seldom go out on the weekends...even with your friends?" Dr. Lester's face wrinkled in reflection, as Evaniese sat in her office.

"Well, I *do* go out from time to time," Evaniese disputed, trying to make her life sound a bit more fulfilling. The reality was that both Deanna and Ginger had boyfriends, but she didn't. And, most weekends, her besties were busy spending time with their boyfriends.

"You mentioned your two closest friends...?" Dr. Lester brought up, making notes in a chart. She looked up, and her eyes linked to Evaniese's in query. "You don't go out with them?"

"I *do* go out with them often enough, but both have significant others, so..." Evaniese's face warped in mortification. No doubt, she sounded like a total *loser*. Her lifestyle made perfect sense to *her*, but brought under scrutiny, Dr. Lester was shedding light on all that was wrong.

"You've already told me you're not seeing anyone right now. Being a person of faith, you honestly believe God has brought *three* different men of purpose into your life?" Dr. Lester verified, staring at Evaniese as if she had three heads.

"Yes..." Evaniese said thickly, embarrassed. She realized how bizarre it all sounded, but she had to be truthful.

"So, *neither* of these men have asked you out, and they've all rejected you to one capacity or another?" Dr. Lester continued to take notes.

Tears formed in Evaniese's eyes, as she internalized the matter. Hearing her circumstances highlighted by someone else, made them sound all the more deplorable. "Yes…, but God promises to fix it. He's told me all three of the men are tied into my destiny," she argued, sounding as if she were trying to convince Dr. Lester she was a chicken from Mars.

"Evaniese, in light of all you've just explained, you *do* realize you're suffering from some form of dysthymia? You're living with underlying symptoms of depression."

Evaniese nodded in agreement, as tears pooled in her eyes. "I do realize that I've been sad," she admitted, as her eyes scantily connected to Dr. Lester's.

"Evaniese, is it alright if I point something out?" Shadows hung over Dr. Lester's face, as she leaned in closer to the edge of her desk.

"Of course…," Evaniese encouraged, with a wavering voice.

"Holding out hope for these three men, who've treated you so poorly, is extremely unhealthy. Granted, *I* have faith too. I believe when God make promises, he keeps them. Still, Evaniese, in the interim, you've got to live *your* life. You *will* know when the time is right. If these men are meant to be in your life, they will come around, and catch up with you on *your* journey." Dr. Lester pointed a liable finger at Evaniese. "However, in the meantime, you've got to move on and live your life.

"You've talked about your lifestyle vlog. I think that's an amazing hobby. That said, you've got to develop some others. You're a very beautiful young woman-full of life, and here you are slowly dying…" She guffawed.

Evaniese was stunned to hear Dr. Lester's assessment. In her opinion, she *was* making the *most* of her life, but the reality was that she was living *depressed*. She'd perceived her life to be lackluster in comparison to the lives of others. Undoubtedly, she was ready to admit she lacked the spark and joy others seem to have. It was something she'd prayed about. So, Evaniese couldn't help thinking God was using Dr. Lester to offer a bit more clarity on the matter. "I never realized how dire my circumstances were."

"Nothing's too dire, if we're willing to put in the work."

Evaniese nodded in agreement.

Dr. Lester went on to say, "Evaniese, you talked about your job at the hospital. You're obviously being bullied by both the director of the department and by your supervisor..."

"Yes, I agree. They've taken advantage of me from day one."

"Do you see yourself staying on at the hospital?" Dr. Lester frowned in concern.

Evaniese weighed her words before speaking. Then, her eyes fastened to Dr. Lester's. "No. I honestly can't see myself continuing to work there. I've been praying for God to open up another door of opportunity for me."

"So, while you're praying and waiting, you *should* probably start looking for another place of employment." Dr. Lester gave Evaniese an affirming nod.

Evaniese thought about how horribly she was treated at the hospital, and how mean-spirited and distrustful her coworkers and colleagues were. Essentially, it was almost like working through a landmine. However, the concept of separation from Nathan, made her hesitant to follow through with quitting her job. And yet, the lack of viability between them, seem to be pushing her closer to the brink of that awful choice. "Yes, I am prayerfully exploring other options," she admitted shakily.

"Don't allow *anyone* to treat you in the way you described. There are labor laws, and if you wanted to, you could bring a lawsuit against them for the way they've abused you in the past..."

Evaniese shook her head in negation. "It isn't even worth the trouble. Once I'm approved for the surgery by my medical insurance, I will put in for resignation." Evaniese's gaze remained affixed to Dr. Lester's this time.

"Will you go back to teaching?" Dr. Lester asked, pertained.

"I'm not sure. I know God has a plan, but it's difficult to know if going back to teaching is the end goal."

"Well, I'm sure you'll be amazing in whatever it is you decide to do." Dr. Lester offered Evaniese an amiable smile.

"Thank you." Evaniese smiled back.

"Now, Evaniese, does mental illness run in your family?" Dr. Lester addressed, taking even more notes.

Hearing those words set off an alarm. Evaniese worried Dr. Lester would call the bariatric office over at Brookline, and tell them she was psychologically unfit to have the surgery. The notion bothered her. Nevertheless, she tried to be honest. "Yes, I have a brother who suffers from Schizophrenia. He was diagnosed when he was about seventeen." Tears gathered in Evaniese's eyes, and her throat felt scratchy.

"Okay, that makes sense. And what about *you*, Evaniese?" Dr. Lester's face was stern, as her eyes delved critically into Evaniese's.

Evaniese deliberated, and fiddled nervously with her fingers. Her eyes had dipped down to staring at the carpeting. "Yes, I had an episode of MDD (Major Depressive Disorder) in my early twenties." Evaniese finally looked up. Dr. Lester's eyes speared through hers like lasers.

"Okay. So, tell me about that...," the doctor encouraged.

"Well, it was around the time I was with my first boyfriend…well actually he was my fiancé. I'd just moved from Bridge Manor to Amber Hills. Back then, I was going to school full time."

"So, all of the changes, and the pressure put a strain on your relationship?" Dr. Lester explored. "I'm sure it didn't help that you'd just moved to a new town, and had a full load of courses."

Evaniese nodded. "Well, along with all of *those* changes, my fiancé was cheating on me with a mutual friend. Our *mutual* friend lived out in Bridge Manor. So, he thought it was a lot easier to hook up with her." Pain permeated inwardly for Evaniese to relive that dark time. "Apparently, my move to another part of town proved to be too much for him. He said he'd love me forever." Evaniese shrugged in perplexity.

"No doubt, that experience was absolutely gut-wrenching," Dr. Lester commiserated. "So, that's when you succumbed to your bout with depression?"

"I'd been sick for a while before I succumbed to MDD," Evaniese admitted.

"And, what was that like?" Dr. Lester stared at Evaniese sympathetically.

"Oh…?" Evaniese's entire demeanor changed, and she straightened up in the armchair. "It was awful. What I *can* say is that I wouldn't wish anxiety and depression on my worst enemy. I felt like a walking corpse. And, since *you* mentioned having faith, I can only try to describe what being in that state was like."

"All right…," Dr. Lester gestured for Evaniese to go on.

"In that state of mind, the spiritual realm-whether good or bad, becomes more tangible. Spiritual warfare is intensified. At one point, while in that frame of mind, it felt as if an entity had physically entered into my body.

"There was a constant sense of unrest and persecution. At every given turn, demonic forces were telling me that I needed to end it all. The voices weren't audible, but the narrative in my head was constant. 'You're never going to get better, Evaniese, so you might as well end it now. You're going to be this miserable for the rest of your life...,' that storyline played in my head like a horrible recording," Evaniese tearfully explained.

"And did you listen...?" Dr. Lester goaded.

"Yes, I *did* at one point," Evaniese's voice broke, and her face warped in sadness. "I did try to commit suicide. I tried to take a handful of painkillers. Luckily, my mom came into my bedroom at the very moment I was about to put them into my mouth. She slapped them out of my hand. God sent her to check in on me in the nick of time."

Dr. Lester nodded compassionately. "What about medication and hospitalization?" Dr. Lester explored.

"I was diagnosed with *clinical depression*-what we call Major Depressive Disorder nowadays, and hospitalized for a month. The doctors put me on 20 milligrams of Prozac (Fluoxetine) at the time."

"Did you keep up with your meds after you were discharged from the hospital?" Dr. Lester shifted closer to the edge of her desk, and scrutinized Evaniese.

Evaniese wasn't altogether comfortable sharing the details of that dark chapter of her life with Dr. Lester. However, there was an inward prompting not to hold back. "I took the Prozac for about eight to nine months then stopped."

"Is there a reason why you stopped taking the medication?"

"Yes. I was determined not to be dependent on any kind of medication. As far *I* was concerned, I didn't need medication prior to that episode. So, I prayerfully weaned myself off of it," Evaniese admitted, baulking in shock. It dawned on her that such an admission was counterproductive to being approved for the surgery.

"And, you've managed without medication all this time?"

"Yes. That episode was almost twenty-seven years ago," Evaniese said uncertainly, surprised by that tidbit. "Wow, I can't believe that horrible time was so long ago...," she reflected.

"But you're over that now, Evaniese. You made it through that dark season. You were able to finish school, get your degree and teach for a while." Dr. Lester offered an encouraging smile. "You've also established a good life for yourself in Amber Hills."

Striving to pull herself together, Evaniese wiped tears away from her eyes. "Yes, but only by the grace of God. God brought me out of that horrible place of despair."

"And, God has a lot more for you, Evaniese," Dr. Lester affirmed. "But, you've got to start believing you're worth it." She smiled, as she added to her notes. "Are you all right?" She stopped short to look at Evaniese.

"I'm fine," Evaniese asserted.

Dr. Lester nodded agreeably. "You've come a long way. And, one sure indication you're in recovery is that you're here this afternoon." Her smile brightened, as she met Evaniese's melancholic expression.

"Really?" Evaniese perked up and smiled.

"Yes, you *are* making strides to improve the quality of your life. The very fact that you're taking the necessary steps to be approved for the VSG, means you *want* to live."

"I *do* want to live, Dr. Lester, but I *don't* want to live overweight," Evaniese admitted.

"I realize that. Taking stock of your appearance, is a sure sign you're coming out of depression. In my opinion, WLS is a step in the right direction." She nodded again in the affirmative.

Evaniese's smile revivified. "I *need* to have the procedure. Something tells me that my life will change for the better once I do."

"Evaniese, in my professional opinion, you should continue with counseling, even *after* you have the surgery. You've suffered tremendous emotional trauma. So, it'd be a good idea for you to continue to unpack some of the issues we've touched on today." Dr. Lester's expression was of both sympathy and concern.

Evaniese nodded compliantly. "I certainly wouldn't be opposed to talking to a counselor on a regular basis."

Evaniese had her own opinion. The only counselor she needed was her Lord and Savior Jesus Christ (Isaiah 9:6). He was the counselor of counselors! She trusted God to heal her, and to guide her through the miasma of all the hurt and pain she'd endured.

In her estimation, God had allowed the suffering. Therefore, he alone had the antidote and the cure. That afternoon, while in Dr. Lester's office, Evaniese *verbally* complied with whatever the woman prescribed. Dr. Lester had *her* opinion about Evaniese's connections to Brent, Jeremy and Nathan. However, Evaniese knew what God wanted, and what he'd asked of her.

And even if the circumstances were excruciating, she knew God would make it good in the end. As far as Evaniese was concerned, Dr. Lester's approval and clearance for the surgery, was a means to an end. Moreover, she *did* respect humanistic viewpoints, but Evaniese knew God's ways were often a mystery to those who adhered to secular perspectives.

Chapter Five

"Lula says if I blend these herbs and spices together, I should be able to effectively cast a spell on someone," Deanna gave herself a pep-talk on a Saturday morning. She'd used a wooden spice-crusher to blend the aromatic plants. In a little while, she'd be meeting Evaniese and Ginger for lunch. Shortly after, they'd go out to The *Vista Multiplex* to see the latest Ellis Roman movie, *Toxic Protocol*. All three were huge fans of Ellis Roman! Evaniese had been *crushing* on the Hollywood A-lister since his first movie back in the 90's.

However, that morning, Deanna read from a Grimoire off of the Internet. She had seen a number of YouTube videos in respect to casting spells and hexes. She shut the blinds, and turned off all the house lights. The fact that Amber Hills was blanketed by a sheet of rain, added to the shadowy backdrop and the arcane theme.

Deanna lit candles in various places, and created a pentagram in the center of her living room floor. She sat cross-legged on the hardwood flooring and chanted. The fact that she was dabbling in such practices was baffling. It was unlike anything she'd ever done before. After thinking the matter through, she realized such practices were *evil*. She was-for all intents and purposes, a churchgoing person. And yet, as the days neared for Evaniese to have the WLS, the more threatened she felt. The prospect of her *bestie* losing a ridiculous amount of weight tormented her.

Deanna couldn't see Evaniese becoming thin, and leveling the playing field, so of speak. Evaniese was already too beautiful for her own good, and Deanna couldn't help thinking where *she* would stand if Evaniese got skinny.

"Dee, I'm so upset. I haven't been able to lose an ounce since I signed up for the procedure. Dr. Bergstrom outlined a special diet plan, and I've tried my best to adhere to it. But, instead of losing weight, I've been gaining…," Evaniese had recently admitted to Deanna.

"Evaniese, you've got to give the diet a chance to work. It will eventually… Maybe, your age is a factor in all of this. Your metabolism is probably a little slow," Deanna tried to placate. "You *did* get your Thyroid checked, right?" She'd feigned concern.

"Yes, the tests all came back normal. I don't have thyroid issues. For the life of me, I can't figure out why I've been steadily putting on weight."

"You *will* lose it all, Evaniese. You'll see." Deanna gave her a phony smile. "One way or another, the weight will come off…"

Now, as she made incantations for the sole purpose of cursing Evaniese's weight loss efforts, Deanna allowed the jealousy and resentment she felt to come through.

She hated the fact that Evaniese was trying to better her circumstances. "Not if *I* can help it, Evaniese. You're going to *stay* in your place. You *will* stay fat. We're not having all that drama. You're not going to lose the weight. Then, you'll get the *big head*, and start thinking you're better than me and Ginger. Oh, no… We're not having that at all," she said disdainfully.

Deanna intoned a spell for Evaniese's WLS to fail. Taking things a step further, she also delineated for Evaniese to remain single and lonely. Both she and Ginger had boyfriends. That was yet another thing they had over Evaniese. And, Deanna didn't want any of it to change. She wanted Evaniese to hold the status of the *fat one*, the *eldest and* the *man-less* one in their circle. Deanna was resolved to keep *Ginger* in her place as well-that was, if *she* got too big for *her* britches.

"Hi, honey!" Deanna greeted Evaniese at the front door a few hours later. She pressed a kiss to Evaniese's cheek, as they hugged.

"Hey, Dee," Evaniese said, crushing Deanna affectionately in her arms. "Are you all set?" Evaniese beamed. She was genuinely excited over the prospect of seeing the new Ellis Roman movie. She *loved* Ellis Roman, and had a fan-to-actor's crush on him. He was one of the biggest names in the entertainment industry. Not to mention the fact that that he was one of the most handsome men-not only in Hollywood, but in the entire world.

And, in Evaniese's fondest dreams, she'd be with someone like Ellis. He would be kind to her-totally *unlike* the other men she'd dealt with, who'd treated her atrociously. So, at least for one afternoon, she could set her troubles aside. Seeing Ellis Roman's new movie, *Toxic Protocol*, would help her to temporarily lose herself in his world.

"I'm all set, sweetie." Deanna gently pulled out of Evaniese's arms. "I just have to grab my phone and pocketbook." Deanna's face crinkled, nonplused, as she stared curiously at Evaniese. "Are you losing weight, Niecy?"

Suspicion veiled Evaniese's face. Sizing herself up in her black jeans, she was unnerved. Of course, she realized black was always slimming. However, the reality of the matter was that she hadn't lost any weight. She was actually up by a few pounds, and biding her time until the surgery.

Shaking her head mindlessly, she chortled. "Oh, Dee, I only *wish* that were the case." Evaniese held her pointer finger up as a philosopher would. "But, it probably will be in a few months." She winked and smiled at Dee.

"Of course." Deanna grinned. "I'll be right back, honey. I'm just going to grab my things."

"I'm not going anywhere," Evaniese reassured.

Evaniese stood at the front door, and waited for Deanna to return. She passively stared up at the overcast skies. She disliked that it had been raining incessantly in Amber Hills lately. However, she was grateful the rain was finally abating. There was a haze of sunlight trying to push through a wad of spectral clouds.

"Okay, let's go." Deanna ambled back over to the front door. Shutting it closed, she draped her arms affectionately around Evaniese. "I'm so happy to see you, girl! You look amazing!" she said, and gave Evaniese a loving squeeze.

"Thanks, Dee. I've missed you too!" Evaniese affirmed, as she and Deanna made their way down the house walkway, and hopped into her SUV.

"You *know* I'm proud of you right?" Deanna was all smiles, as she stared over at Evaniese, who was already behind the wheel.

Evaniese set her hand on her heart, stirred by Deanna's words. "*You're* proud of me?" Her face warped sappily.

"Yes, I *am*. I'm so proud you've taken such a courageous initiative, and in a few months…" She winked. "You'll be *skinny-Minnie*."

"Go on, Dee… Stop…," Evaniese said, with reddened cheeks.

"Watch out world, here comes the new Evaniese!" Deanna feigned encouragement. Inwardly, she stewed in jealousy over Evaniese's opportunity, and anticipated her downfall once she did submit to the procedure.

***

"I'm sorry, sir, but the ER's just extremely busy today. There isn't an available room or bed for anyone at this time," Evaniese tried to appeal to an irate patient. The man had been sitting out in the ER waiting room for quite a while.

"So, I'm *not* going inside? And, you're only calling me *now* for registration? I saw you chatting it up with that nurse just a moment ago," the angry man recriminated.

Evaniese's face warped in bewilderment. "Sir, not that I need to justify my conversation, but that nurse and I were discussing a patient."

"Well, you looked like you were talking about *nothing*, while I sat out there in the waiting room in pain. Talking about that patient must have been very hilarious, because the two of you were laughing."

"Sir, what is your name?" Evaniese evaded the man's allegation. "Have you been to Brookline before?" Evaniese stared into his face with a bewildered expression. Her coworker Cynthia wasn't on that evening. So, Evaniese had to face the madness of a packed emergency room all by herself. The balancing act of working the shift alone, was something she hadn't experienced in a while.

"I'm not interested in *registration* right now. I want to know why you were ignoring me ten minutes ago, and chatting it up with that nurse." The irate Caucasian man's face flushed red. "Who's your supervisor?" he demanded irascibly.

Evaniese sighed, and stared heavenward in frustration. The ER was overcrowded, the waiting room was packed, and she had a gazillion new admissions to sign into the hospital. She was being pulled in a hundred directions. Trying not to give into tears, Evaniese whispered a prayer for God's help.

"The name of your supervisor?" the irritated patient exacted.

"All right… If that's what you want, I will call her for you myself," Evaniese said freely. In her estimation, she'd done absolutely nothing wrong. She was only guilty of answering questions for one of the nurses in the ER concerning an admission that took place the day before. So, Evaniese *couldn't see* Paula Rivers, or Ann Ridges *not* siding with her. After all, she *was* doing her job, and upholding ER protocol.

"Yes, that's *exactly* what I want," the man bellowed.

Evaniese picked up the phone, and dialed the admissions office. One of her coworkers answered the phone, and Evaniese asked to be connected to Paula's office.

Moments later, Paula came over the line. "Is there a problem down in the ER, Evaniese?" she jumped in right away.

In a calm and levelheaded way, Evaniese tried to explain the situation. In her heart and mind, she surmised that even someone *like* Paula Rivers would be *reasonable* enough to grasp that the man harassing her down in the ER was a troublemaker. However, Evaniese could not have been more wrong.

"Evaniese, you need to understand that the gentleman feels as if you were neglecting him. I realize it's a busy ER, but he felt totally ignored. And, furthermore, you had your back to the registration desk, while talking to the nurse," Paula censured.

Incredulous, Evaniese tried to reason, "Paula, there's only one reason why the gentleman's so angry. He came into the ER complaining of chest pain. He was brought in for an EKG. His EKG must have been normal, because they sent him back out to the waiting room. He certainly thought they'd rush him right in, and give him a room inside the ER. Because he's had to wait, he's taking it out on me."

"Evaniese, you need to do your job, regardless of the circumstances. You were supposed to call him in for registration, but you didn't."

"I didn't get the chance to, Paula," Evaniese argued, befuddled. "I had paperwork to finish up. Once I completed the work, I returned to my desk to call him over for registration. However, it was at that moment the nurse came into the office, asking me about a previous admission," she explained.

"Evaniese, you're not paid to make excuses. When someone comes into the ER, it's your *job* to make them feel like they're a priority. Do you understand?" Paula hissed.

Evaniese was completely floored, and incredulous over what was happening. She'd been left alone and defenseless on that horrendous Wednesday afternoon in the middle of May. She had no idea what to say, or how to appeal to this incorrigible, unreasonable and inexorable woman.

Evaniese blinked back tears. As far as she knew, she'd done everything right. Notwithstanding, she'd worked through the hospital for close to seven years. So, in spite of their differences, Evaniese honestly believed Paula would have her back. Surely, Paula would take her word over some infuriated man, who didn't want to wait his turn to be seen inside a congested ER.

However, that afternoon, Evaniese realized nothing she said mattered. For Paula, it was personal. Evaniese had no idea why Paula and Ann hated her so much, but the lines of demarcation were no longer blurred. "I understand," Evaniese acceded. "I will apologize to the gentleman."

"Is he still at your desk?" Paula exacted.

"Yes," Evaniese admitted. "All right then, apologize to him."

"I will. Can I get back to work now?" Evaniese asked abruptly.

"What...?" Paula's voice was shrill. "You will get back to work when I say, Evaniese. Is that clear?" she berated.

"Yes, it's clear," Evaniese's voice broke. Her fingers brushed nervously through her hair, as she glared at the man facing her.

"Finish up the registration, and do your paperwork," Paula demanded in a degrading tone.

"Yes," Evaniese said, defeated. The last thing she wanted was for the horrible man at her desk to see her falling apart.

"Well..., I *still* want to talk to your supervisor," he adamantly maintained, lowering at Evaniese.

"You can speak to her on your own time, sir. But, right now I'm required to take your information. If you're not registered, you won't be seen in the ER," she said temperately.

"You'd *better* believe I'm going to contact your supervisor on my own time," he threatened.

Evaniese was confused. She had absolutely no idea why this man was so hateful. She'd been kind, and had tried to help him. However, at that moment, Evaniese remembered scripture. There was an ongoing battle between God's children, and the dark and evil forces of this world.

"For we wrestle not against flesh and blood, but against principalities, against powers, against the rulers of the darkness of his world, against spiritual wickedness in high places." Ephesians 6:12 (KJV). Thus, the dark spirits indwelling this man, were at war with the Holy Spirit of God residing within her.

So, Evaniese tried to remain as calm as possible, as she sat there and took the man's information. Long after he was brought into the ER to be seen, the man continued to give Evaniese the death stare when their paths crossed. Nonetheless, Evaniese tried to put the entire episode out of her mind.

That evening, she longed to see a friendly face, and Nathan came to mind. He was clearly *not* romantically interested in her. Nevertheless, Evaniese was confident she could talk to him, and that Nathan would commiserate with her. However, on that fateful afternoon in May, that grace wasn't extended. She had to bear the brunt of the misery alone, and things went from bad to worse.

"Where's Mr. Hammond's paperwork," Janice demanded, later on in that same evening. She was one of the nurses who worked through the ER.

"Mr. Hammond was admitted at 10 a.m. this morning, Janice," Evaniese informed. "Dinah should have had that paperwork in the admissions bin at that time." Dinah was Evaniese's coworker. Her shift started at seven in the morning, until Evaniese relieved her at three. Dinah also had Cynthia for *part* of her shift, in the same way Evaniese did. Though Cynthia was available for Dinah's shift, Evaniese couldn't say the same. For personal reasons, Cynthia had left earlier than usual.

"Well, I checked the admissions paperwork bin, and it isn't there. Mr. Hammond is about to be taken up to his room," Janice disputed.

"I don't know what to tell you. That paperwork was Dinah and Cynthia's responsibility, not mine," Evaniese argued, frustrated. *Could things get any worse?* She was already having one of the most challenging shifts ever, threatened by a patient, and censured by her boss. So, she really didn't need some nurse yelling at her about paperwork, which should have been done by her coworkers on the previous shift.

"Well, what can I tell *you*?" Janice retorted. "The paperwork wasn't done this morning. Regardless of the shift, I'm asking *you* to get it done right now." Janice glared at Evaniese, with hands insolently set on her hips.

"Janice, I'm sorry. I honestly can't right now. I've got a gazillion other admission to handle on *this* shift. So, Mr. Hammond will just have to go up to the seventh floor without paperwork." Evaniese tried to soften her approach. "I will try to handle it later."

"He's going up right *now*, Evaniese," Janice contended, rolling her eyes. "That's all I'm saying. It's *your* department. Even if Dinah or Cynthia didn't do the work, *you* need to handle it." Her face reddened just before she turned, and walked away in a huff.

Evaniese felt like pulling her hairs out. Trying not to lose it, she prayed, and asked God for calmness and peace. Taking deep breaths, she sauntered away from the nurse's station, and returned to her desk. Once there, she set aside paperwork required for *her* shift, and started working on a set of forms for Mr. Herbert Hammond's admission. The man was being admitted to the hospital for elevated enzyme levels in his liver.

It took some doing and scrambling, but Evaniese completed six admissions, while simultaneously minding her desk, with an ongoing stream of registrations into the ER.

Moments later, she crossed back over into the nurse's station, and handed Janice the paperwork for Mr. Hammond. "It's done," Evaniese said, and stared expectantly into the woman's eyes.

However, Janice snatched up the packet, and gave Evaniese a disdainful glower. Janice's glower reminded Evaniese of the disgruntle patient's scowl she had to deal with earlier on. The rude nurse didn't even bother to say *thank you*. Evaniese didn't say a word. She shook her head in incredulity, and crossed back over to her desk in the registration area. She hardly got a moment to sigh, when a frantic knock came to her office door.

Bursting in, the young man rushed over to the registration desk window. "Miss, can you please tell someone inside my dad is having chest pain?" he entreated. Feet away, there was a young lady sustaining an older man, whom Evaniese assumed was the dad.

Without hesitation, Evaniese rushed over to the Triage Area to look for the nurse. But, the nurse wasn't there. So, she dashed into the ER to alert the staff someone was having chest pain. This was the protocol in such cases, especially when she couldn't get a hold of the triage nurse.

"There's a man standing in the waiting room with chest pain," Evaniese addressed Nurse Margaret. By then, she was winded from rushing around. Margaret Downs was on as the head nurse that evening.

"Evaniese, how many times do I have to tell you to address the triage nurse, before you come running in here like some lunatic?" the older Caucasian nurse chided.

"Deborah isn't out there," Evaniese said, grated by the circumstances, still trying to move past all of the other annoying issues which had transpired earlier on.

Nurse Margaret's eyes flashed in outrage, as they knifed through Evaniese's. "Well, you need to go find her before you come in here," she censured, clearly peeved.

"If I knew *where* to find her, I wouldn't have come in here," Evaniese said. "I'll let the nursing staff work that one out. Look, I've told you someone's having chest pain." Evaniese walked away dismissively, and traversed back over to her desk.

Inches away from her desk, the young man came up to the registration window again to remind Evaniese, "My dad's having chest pain. Did you tell them?" His cheeks were flushed.

"Yes, they're aware. Someone should be right out to you," Evaniese informed.

"Okay, thank you," the young guy told her. Moving away from her window, he drifted back over to the waiting area.

Evaniese sighed, and tried to get her bearings. It was only 6 p.m. She still had a few more hours to endure before her shift ended. Truth be told, she was falling apart. As much as she needed a job, she didn't need the disrespect, the lack of consideration for her feelings, and the poor working conditions. Evaniese wanted a moment alone to talk to her Heavenly Father. He alone had the answers she needed.

That evening, Evaniese resolved to quit her job. She'd taken the abuse for close to seven years. Evaniese had faith that God had better things in store for her. Still, there was very little time to reflect. She peaked out into the waiting area, and counted at least fifteen new patients. They'd just signed in to be seen in the ER. So, she had to be in the right frame of mind to register each and every one of them.

Moments later, in the middle of a registration, the office door opened. Nathan stood to the side of the door with a pining expression on his face. He offered Evaniese one of his signature smiles. Dressed to the nines in a caramel-colored dress suit, he looked like a dream! The color accentuated his pumpkin-pie colored skin, and golden-brown eyes.

From the look on Nathan's face, Evaniese perceived that he wanted to come into the office to chat. Nevertheless, he seemed conflicted, because he clearly saw how busy she was. For Evaniese, Nathan's presence there was like a balm over a throbbing wound. She'd longed to see him earlier on when all hell had begun to break loose. So, even if she didn't get her wish then, seeing him at that juncture, was better late than never.

Evaniese stared yearningly over at him, and smiled back at him. It was the best she could do after all she'd endured on that shift. She wanted to reach out, but was much too busy. Besides, the bustle showed no signs of stopping. Evaniese and Nathan exchanged pining look, but neither spoke. Nathan smiled again, and nodded understandingly. He knew that it was just a bad time. So, he held his right hand up in a hello gesture.

Just as mysteriously as Nathan appeared, he drifted away. Evaniese felt such a sense of emptiness and isolation when he was gone. In spite of it all, she tried to focus on work. A woman had just settled across from her, and set her insurance card on the desk. However, Evaniese had temporarily tuned everything out, because Nathan was in close proximity.

"This is my new information," the woman told Evaniese for the umpteenth time.

"I'm so sorry," she told the woman, still a bit distracted.

"You asked for my insurance card...?" The woman frowned in uncertainty.

"Right..." Evaniese forced a smile, picked up the insurance card, and positioned in into the scanner on her desk.

***

On Saturday afternoon, Evaniese was at the beauty salon for a perm. Her stylish had just applied the relaxer, and would return once the chemical processed. Evaniese couldn't stop reliving the horror show that took place at the hospital during her shift on Wednesday. She'd prayed on the matter, and felt reassured that God had a plan.

Furthermore, God promised to bring her out of that minefield, so to speak. In fact, God affirmed that it wouldn't be too long before she could kiss her job over at Brookline Hospital goodbye. For Evaniese, that day couldn't come fast enough. Even if the hospital was the only place whereby she could see Nathan, Evaniese figured, if she and Nathan were to stay in touch, they could do so through texts and emails. As it was, their connection was tenuous. So, Evaniese couldn't see quitting her job making much of a difference.

After Nathan dropped in to see her in the office on Wednesday evening, he went MIA for the remainder of the week. Evaniese had texted him a few times since then. She wanted to apologize for being too busy to take a moment. However, it was Saturday, and there was still no response. As Evaniese sat on the huge black chair at the salon, she checked her messages.

However, this time around, she didn't come up empty. There *was* indeed a text message, but it *wasn't* from Nathan. The text was from Doctor Jeremy Carter. As per God's instruction, Evaniese had continued texting him, even if he no longer worked through the hospital. Against her own better judgment, Evaniese had texted him off and on for the past four years.

A smile curved over Evaniese's lips. *Dare she believe Jeremy was finally responding to her messages after all this time?* Maybe, this was the beginning of something new. After all she'd endured, Evaniese considered that perhaps it was time for God to create a lasting connection between Jeremy and herself. She honestly didn't care with whom he got the ball rolling with, Brent, Jeremy or Nathan. What Evaniese cared about was having someone to share her life with. After all, she'd waited for such a long time. So, it really didn't matter which of the men reached out first. Excited, she instantly accessed Jeremy's text.

*"Listen, you psycho, whoever you are, Eva...Evan, Denise... I'm tired of you sending text messages to **my** man. You're pathetic, and you need to find another hobby. My guy Jeremy has allowed me to answer all of your sick and sad texts, because he can't be bothered with you.*

*"You're so **sad** talking about how you think it's **God's** will for you to be with him. Well, you need to leave him alone, because he doesn't want you. In fact, he left Brookline Hospital because of you. He says you were following him around like a lost puppy. Says you're some kind of **cougar** who won't leave him alone. Well, I'm warning you. You'd better stop texting him."*

Stunned and traumatized, Evaniese began to quaver. Tears gathered in her eyes. Reading such horrible words from Jeremy's phone number, was the last thing she'd expected. Evaniese always thought very highly of Jeremy. He always *seemed* to be so kind. So, she couldn't wrap her head around Jeremy giving this *person* carte blanche to humiliate her in such a way. She couldn't stop trembling, as tears snaked down her cheeks.

Evaniese was devastated. With unsteady hands, she set out to respond. *"I can't imagine Jeremy putting you up to this-whoever you are. For the record, I never followed Jeremy around the hospital. It was the other way around. He followed me, and we became good friends-at least that's what I* **thought**.

"I can't even imagine him telling you to say such horrible things to me. If he did put you up to this, he isn't the person I thought he was at all." Evaniese's fingers tremored, as she accessed the keypad, while simultaneously blinking back even more tears.

At that point, the relaxer stung on her scalp, but the emotional trauma seared a lot more. Her heart jumped when the notification bell went off on her phone again.

"Listen, I don't care how you feel about Jeremy, or who you **thought** *he was. The fact remains, he's not the person you thought, because he doesn't want you. I saw your pictures on Facebook and on Instagram by the way. You're fat and disgusting. Jeremy also says you're super old too. Maybe,* **Ourtime.com** *or* **Christian Mingle** *might be a way to meet a man more your age-that is if anyone will take a* **second** *look at you."*

Evaniese felt emotionally maimed, as she tremored and cried unrelentingly. Her heart had taken a huge hit as a result of Jeremy's betrayal. And yet, she decided to text this *person* back, even if her heart lashed, and it felt as if someone had taken a hammer to it.

"*I've never met you, and I've never done anything to you. There's no need for you to come at me in this way. Not to mention the fact that I've never been anything but kind to Jeremy, while we worked through the ER together. I was never anything but respectful. So, I don't understand why he would have **you** launch this attack, and say all of these horrible things...*"

"*Well, it's because you were shameless in the way you went after him. And, let me tell you something, lady, he's not available. So, please stop texting my man. If you don't stop, both Jeremy and I are going to report you to the authorities for phone stalking,*" the woman responded.

"*I've been texting Jeremy for a while now, and if he **really** wanted me to stop, he would have blocked my number. In fact, I encourage you to have him block my number...*" Evaniese's face warped in anguish, as she tried to express herself.

She went on to say, "*As a person of faith, I prayed about it. And, God told me to keep the lines of communication open with Jeremy. Texting him wasn't **my** idea. As a Christian person, I do whatever God asks of me. But, honestly, you and Jeremy would be doing me a huge favor if you blocked me.*"

Evaniese baulked in misery. She wept silently, and kept wiping tears away from her eyes. Helene, her stylish, would be back any minute to wash the relaxer out of her hair. And, she'd be mortified if the woman returned, and found her an emotional wreck.

However, the affront from Jeremy's *significant other* wasn't over yet. The individual just kept going. "*Jeremy laughs about it. He thinks it's funny you thought there could be a romantic connection. He told me you said you were in love with him. Ha, ha... What a joke! Did you really think a man-a doctor of Jeremy's caliber, could ever want someone like you?*"

"*I don't know what Jeremy told you, but I've never tried to force him to pay attention to me. Jeremy showed me in so many ways that he was interested,*" Evaniese disputed. But inwardly, she was so crush she felt completely inept. There was very little fight left in her.

Not only was she skeptical, she was brokenhearted and disillusioned. *What had she done wrong to deserve the kind of pain and suffering she was going through?* Jeremy was the last person on the planet Evaniese would have imagined hurting her. And yet, there he was doing exactly that.

"Well, when you told Jeremy you love him, and he said he had someone in his life, you should have listened... In fact, Jeremy told me to reach out to the director of the admissions department through Brookline, and to your supervisor to let them know what's been going on. And, that's exactly what I did.

"It was Jeremy's idea. But, we both agreed, because we knew how embarrassed you'd be by the matter. Were you? Now, listen, I won't tell you again to stop texting Jeremy. He says that you're physically disgusting, and that you're poor. Aren't you some registration clerk or something like that...?"

"Tell Jeremy thank you very much for the kind words. I truly thought he was a gentleman, but I guess I was wrong about a lot of things. I was totally wrong to think he was a decent human being. And, for the record, I am a teacher working through the ER."

*"I don't care anything about your moral standing. Leave my fiancé alone. He's made it clear he doesn't want you. And, thank you for clarifying that you're more than just an ER clerk. You're probably even poorer than we thought, **because** you're a teacher."*

Evaniese was about to rejoinder, but the Holy Spirit of God told her not to. Shattered, she found herself shuddering, and her head was throbbing. Disillusioned, her thoughts were racing. God had revealed Jeremy as her God-ordained spouse. Nevertheless, at that point, it was becoming a real struggle for Evaniese not to hate Jeremy. The agony and humiliation of her past experiences overwhelmed. Thus, there was a brand-new wave of pain as the cherry on top.

How could something so awful happen? She'd been obedient to God every step of the way. Taking God at his word, and at his request, she did tell Jeremy she loved him years ago. Now, he'd insulted and debased her in the worst way. The cruelest aspect was having his *girlfriend* or *fiancée* inflict the wound. Evaniese was dazed and completely unsettled. For a while, it felt as if she was having an out of body experience.

"Are you burning, honey?" Helene sauntered back over to finish up Evaniese's hair.

The perm had been stinging Evaniese's scalp for quite a while. However, she'd been numbed by a *different* kind of pain.

"Is the perm stinging, Evaniese?" Helene asked again, rousing Evaniese from her stupor.

Evaniese nodded absently, but her face contorted in misery the moment Helene looked away. Evaniese strove not to fall apart right then and there. And yet, she didn't think she was doing a very good job. Following Helene to the back of the salon over to the sink, she mechanically settled down in the small, black chair. Evaniese was totally dazed, as she cautiously tilted her head back, and surrendered to the warm stream of water. She barely felt Helene powering through her hair, and washing the chemical out.

Her scalp *had* sustained a few burns. Nevertheless, the pain was nowhere near the scalding of betrayal, and the affront she'd just sustained. Realizing she'd been attacked by someone she honestly thought cared about her, made the matter even more acerbic. God had said Jeremy was *her* guy. So, the circumstances felt utterly surreal. Evaniese was having a difficult time processing what had just transpired.

Going through the motions at the hair salon, she acceded to the reality of the wound. Worse yet, she still heard the texting notification bell going off on her phone. Irrefutably, Jeremy's significant other wasn't quite done picking her apart. Evaniese's heartstrings unraveled with every alert. She imagined the new ways her enemies were coming up with to degrade her. Remembering how kind, sweet and attentive Jeremy *seemed*, made Evaniese feel miffed and disenchanted. More than anything else, she wanted to run away, and find a safe place to fall apart.

***

"Is there another appointment on the calendar, Brenda?" Doctor Jeremy Carter spoke on his office phone to his receptionist at his medical practice.

"I don't see another appointment on the calendar until later this afternoon. However, there is a walk-in. I don't think the gentleman's here to be seen…*medically*," Brenda said uneasily.

There was a very good-looking and distinguished Caucasian man standing at her desk, asking to see Doctor Carter. Under different circumstances, she would have welcomed such a handsome guy, but there was a very chilling quality about the dark haired, blue-eyed man.

"What is the gentleman's name?" Jeremy asked, perturbed.

"He says he's an *associate* of yours," Brenda said warily, shifting uncomfortably in her armchair under the man's glower.

"All right, Brenda," Jeremy acceded, "send him in."

"All right, Dr. Carter," Brenda complied. She then looked up at the man standing in front of her unwaveringly. "Dr. Carter says he'll see you."

"Great!" the man told Brenda, with a widening grin.

Brenda flinched to see a smile on the gentleman's face. At first blush, he seemed totally unapproachable and incapable of smiling.

Sitting in his comfortable leather armchair, Jeremy anxiously awaited the visitor. Agitated, he played with his ballpoint pen, flicking the tip in and out. Staring at the phone, he deliberated about calling Brenda to say he'd changed his mind about seeing the guest. Jeremy was just about to get up out of the chair, when the knock came to his office door.

"Yes…?" Jeremy said in anticipation.

However, his heart dipped to the floor, when the door opened deliberately, and he saw the person standing beyond it.

Jeremy immediately got on the defensive. "I thought I asked you not to contact me in person?" Veins pulsed at his temples, and his caramel skin fused with blood.

"I *wanted* to see you in person. I had to make sure you got my message loud and clear," Brent said, edging closer to Jeremy's desk.

Jeremy stood to his feet, and walked around the desk to face Brent. His eyes sparked flames of irritation and resentment, as they delved into Brent's. "Just so you know, going behind Evaniese's back, and trying to keep other men out of her life, will only alienate her. She's going to find out what you've been doing, and she'll hate you for it," Jeremy said incensed.

Brent smiled temperately. However, inwardly, he stewed over Jeremy's recrimination. His tan skin turned crimson. "You let *me* worry about Evaniese. She's no longer your concern, Doctor," Brent berated, staring dauntingly into Jeremy's eyes. "You let me worry about how things turn out with her. Did you, or did you *not* do what I asked?" Brent exacted, gesturing with his hand.

"Yes, I did exactly what you asked," Jeremy said, through gritted teeth. "I insulted Evaniese in every way, just like you wanted me to." Jeremy shrugged with a sense of resignation.

"Are you happy? I'm sure she hates *my* guts now, and she'll probably never speak to me again," his voice wavered. Jeremy grimaced in regret, as recounted the nasty things he and his girlfriend said to Evaniese through a barrage of text messages.

"I'll be *happy* when you, and all of those cretins over at the hospital stay as far away from my girl as possible. I don't care about anything else."

"It's obvious you don't care," Jeremy indicted. He shook his head senselessly over Brent's callousness. "You're hurting this woman by trying to manipulate matters in her life. You say you love her, and yet you'd do anything to own her-and *not* in a good way." Jeremy's glower condemned Brent.

Brent's face turned even ruddier, and he pointed an accusatory finger at Jeremy. "You know nothing about me, or how I feel about Evaniese. Furthermore, *who* do you think she'll hate more, after all the horrible things you and your girlfriend told her?"

"You *asked* me to say those horrible things," Jeremy argued.

"Yes, but it was your *choice* to take a hundred thousand dollars from me. You put a higher premium on the money than on a relationship with her. So, you see, *Doctor*," Brent denigrated, "if you tell Evaniese the truth about *our* deal, you'll only wind up hurting yourself. If you try to take me down, I will take you down even harder." Brent smirked.

"I need for you to leave my office now," Jeremy said, miffed. "We've concluded our deal. I've agreed to stay away from Evaniese. So, there's really nothing left for us to discuss." Jeremy scowled in resentment.

"You're right, Doctor Carter, our deal *is* settled for the time being. I've already transferred the money into the account you specified. Now," Brent hesitated for a moment, "stay away from Evaniese for good."

Jeremy inched away, as he continued to glare at Brent. "I gave you my word." He walked back around to take his place behind the desk. However, he didn't sit in the armchair. Rather, he stood at the desk on his guard, warily watching every move Brent made.

"Good... I'm glad we understand each other, Doctor Carter." Brent grinned with a sense of satisfaction.

Jeremy kept shaking his head in skepticism over the man's smugness and audacity. "She'll hate you, you know?" Jeremy strove to keep his antipathy for Brent under wraps.

Brent arched his head back, and allowed a ripple of laughter to resonate from his throat. "Yes, I'm sure she will. Still, if *I* can't have her, no one else will." Brent's eyes delved irately into Jeremy's.

"Well, good luck with that," Jeremy said sardonically

"Enjoy that extra hundred thousand," Brent's tone was judgmental.

"Get out of my office," Jeremy said heatedly.

"Pleasure doing business with you, Doctor Carter," Brent derided, before turning away. Shifting over to the office door, he twisted the doorknob. However, before he stepped out of Jeremy's office, he turned and smiled insidiously. "Get off of your moral high horse."

Jeremy was incensed, as he continued to glower at Brent. The moment Brent stepped out of the office, he settled back in his armchair. Burying his face in his hands, he sobbed. The last thing he'd wanted was to hurt Evaniese.

Humiliating her was the *only* way he knew to discourage her from continually reaching out. Furthermore, Brent Peterson would stop at nothing to make sure no one else had a chance with Evaniese. Brent himself had messed things up with her, and had no idea how to set things straight. So, he'd made it his life's mission to keep all other men at bay.

It was extremely selfish of Brent to trash every man who came into Evaniese's life, when he himself refused to step up, and become the man she needed. Jeremy hated himself for taking Brent's offer. Still, from the outset, he'd perceived that Evaniese Spencer would always be just beyond his reach. For that very reason he'd agreed to Brent's offer. Jeremy resigned, if he *had* to live without Evaniese, gaining one hundred thousand dollars was by no means a consolation prize. But, it was better than nothing.

***

"Hello, Ellis!" Laura Morgan Fields greeted. She was all smiles to see Ellis seated at the table hosted by celebrity charities on a Saturday morning. Uncertain Ellis had heard her, she drifted across the jam-packed area to connect to him.

The Zenith Center was packed. And, its arenas, and fields were equally crowded with celebrities playing spirited games of lacrosse, tennis, volleyball, hockey and basketball. This was an all-day sports charity event for the benefit of underprivileged children around the world.

Having participated in everything from tennis, to lacrosse, Ellis felt a sense of fulfilment to be a part of such an amazing organization. The proceeds were to benefit several charities. The Zenith Center in L.A. was overcrowded with patrons and fans, who regularly showed up to support the fundraiser.

Surrounded by security, Ellis, along with a number of his colleagues, took turns signing paraphernalia for their supporters. So far, Ellis had signed basketball, T-shirts, Mugs, Jerseys and a number of other items.

"Mr. Roman, I'm a huge fan of your work!" a young lady announced. She was blonde, had fair skin and gray eyes. Obviously nervous and awestruck, her eyes wandered away from Ellis's intent stare, and her cheeks reddened. "Will you please sign my T-shirt?" she asked diffidently.

Ellis was about to answer, when Laura singled him out. An earnest smile stretched across his face to see her. "Hey, there, Laura!" he greeted enthusiastically, as his eyes fastened to hers.

"Hello, Ellis." Laura smiled amiably. "It's nice to see you again!"

"It's nice to see *you*!" Ellis beamed.

"Not that any of us can complain, but I can see your hands full." Laura noticed the extended line of fans waiting to connect to Ellis.

"Just a little..." Ellis chuckled. The crowd was such, he could no longer see the last person standing on line.

"I guess, we'll catch up later." Laura waved silently at him.

Ellis nodded with a smile, and watched Laura saunter away.

He then redirected towards his bashful fan. But, the moment his eyes met hers, she issued a nervous smile, and looked away. However, Ellis strove to get her attention. "You have such a lovely smile!" he complimented. "You really shouldn't hide it."

"What...?" The young woman's jaw dropped, but she urged herself to hold Ellis's stare. "Are you talking to me?" she asked quietly.

"Yes, I am. What is your name?"

"I'm Stephanie," she muttered uneasily, doing all she could not to look away.

"Well, *Stephanie*, I said you have a lovely smile!"

"Thank you, Mr. Roman," Stephanie stammered, with florid cheeks.

"Please...," he encouraged, "call me *Ellis*."

"Oh...all right, *Ellis*," Stephanie said, cheerily. "I think you're amazing!" she added.

"Aw... That really means a lot to me! Thank you for coming out here to support this event. And, it would be an *honor* for me to sign your T-shirt," Ellis affirmed, with a winning smile.

"Thank you, *Ellis*." Stephanie smiled bashfully. "And, after today, I can add *nice* to all of the wonderful qualities I think you have."

Ellis stopped signing the shirt midway, and stared earnestly into Stephanie's eyes. He was moved beyond words by her kindness. "Thank you so much!" he stated emphatically.

Ellis knew he probably shouldn't, but there were promotional tickets to his movie, which was due to come out in June, and he had just a handful of them to give out on that day.

The passes would be for the premier of his movie, *Disoriented*. He himself would be gracing the red carpet for the event. "Stephanie, don't tell anyone, but I'm giving you a pass to come out to the opening of *Disoriented* in a few weeks. It's for you and your plus one," he said and winked.

Stephanie cupped her mouth in shock, as she stood there staring at Ellis. "What...? Are you serious? I get to see *you* on the opening night of your movie?" she asked, stunned.

Ellis set his finger over his lips, indicating that Stephanie not make his gesture public. His eyes lowered urgently into hers, urging her to keep the matter a secret.

"All right, all right...," Stephanie said softly, both agitated and excited.

Ellis shook his head humorously, as he reached into a box under the table. He then slipped a red envelope over to Stephanie at the table, tickled by her reaction. Ellis could tell she wanted to react, but she was doing everything in her power not to give him away. The fans standing behind Stephanie on line were rubbernecking to see why she was so stoked. Regardless, Ellis couldn't be rude to the rest of his devotees, and had to keep it moving.

"Thank you so much, Ellis...," Stephanie said, on cloud nine.

"You're welcome! I look forward to seeing you on the red carpet." His eyes linked kindly to hers.

"I wouldn't miss it for the world!" Stephanie said, still trying to subdue her joy.

Laura stood at a corner, watching Ellis interact with his fans. The last time she and Ellis were together was on the opening night of *Toxic Protocol*. She'd longed to spend the night on his arm, but Kierra Spalding was there. And, Kierra had stuck to Ellis's side like glue. Laura knew that Ellis and Kierra were only dating *promotionally*. The publicity stunt was to build momentum for their careers. Yet, Kierra was extremely possessive and territorial of Ellis, and treated him like property.

Laura hoped Ellis was *Kierra-free* that morning. She was dying to ask him out on a date. *A date* with Ellis Roman, was a coveted event by *most* women in America. Thus, that morning, because Kierra Spalding was nowhere in sight, Laura decided to take a chance. Ellis was so worth it. Not only was he incredibly good-looking, but he was also a standup guy. Laura wanted to know so much more about him.

"Hey, there, stranger!" Ellis took Laura's hand in his, and pressed a kiss to it. "I'm sorry I couldn't chat a little while ago," he told her with a sincere smile. Laura was someone he truly liked. Since working together on the set of *Toxic Protocol*, they'd seen each other at a few promotional events, and were now great friends.

Laura blushed, because of Ellis's fond kiss on her hand. "That's all right. You had your hands full for a while. You must have signed a gazillion items for your fans just now," she commented.

Laura was totally pumped to have Ellis in such close proximity. She assessed just how perfect he truly was. His coffee skin and honey eyes gleamed in the sunlight filtering through the windows of the expansive center.

"Well, I would be nothing without my fans. So, it's always nice to spend a little quality time with them," Ellis expressed in earnest. "I didn't know you were going to be here today." He explored Laura's pretty face and eyes. She was a lovely person in his estimation!

"Yes, I signed up a little while ago. I've only been to this event twice since it was spearheaded." Laura's expression was alluring. "If I knew *you* subsidized this fundraiser, I would be here *every* year." She winked.

Ellis chortled, with reddened cheeks. "Well, it's truly nice to have you here today! How have you been? I believe the last time we saw each other was..."

"Was at the premier a while back," Laura filled in, searching Ellis's eyes.

Ellis nodded in affirmation. "That's right. That *was* a great night!"

"Yeah, it *was* pretty wonderful! I would have spent more time with you, but..."

"But what, Laura?" Bewilderment shaded Ellis's face.

"Well, where's your better half today?" Laura's gape was cheeky.

"Oh...?" Ellis laughed, somewhat taken aback by Laura's question. He set his right hand on his heart. "I didn't know I had one."

"Well, what I *meant* to ask is, where's *Kierra*?" Laura brazenly crossed her arms over her chest.

"Kierra...right," Ellis said, and shook his head in negation. "Well, she obviously didn't sign up for the benefit this year. If I'm not mistaken, she's in France promoting a film," Ellis explained. "Is that the way everyone sees it? They're all under the impression Kierra and I are an item?" His face creased in perplexity.

"Well, yeah... Pretty much everyone thinks you're dating," Laura informed. "*Are* you?" she quizzed.

Ellis worked past feelings of awkwardness, and tried to weigh his words before speaking. "Kierra and I are great friends," he admitted.

"Are you sure? I don't think *she* knows that." Laura gave him a knowing wink.

"Well, it is what is it is. We're friends," Ellis said plainly.

"Is that so?" Laura tilted her head, and her fingers brushed through her dark curls in a flirtatious manner. "I was thinking..."

Even if he perceived what was coming next, Ellis's smile was cavalier. No doubt, Laura was about to ask him out. In spite of the fact that he liked Laura, and he refused to offend her, Ellis couldn't tell anyone he was in love with someone he'd never met. *Niecy819* consumed his thoughts. In fact, he couldn't wait to be home. Lately, he'd been on the fence about direct messaging her on Instagram.

Niece819 had recently started going live on Instagram. Ellis had prayed extensively on the matter, and felt led to message the young woman anonymously as *Fan4Ever*. Instead of using his current Instagram account, he wanted to create a new account and profile.

Quite soon, he'd be flying out to the Virgin Islands to start work on a new project, and he looked forward to unwinding every night by chatting with *Niecy819.* There wasn't anything he didn't want to know about her. However, at present, he had to find a way to navigate out of a very delicate situation with a very kind colleague and friend.

"Yes, Kierra and I are *friends,*" Ellis cautiously highlighted. He stopped short for a moment, and desisted in saying anything more.

"How is it that the most eligible bachelor in Hollywood isn't spoken for?" Laura explored Ellis's eyes beguilingly.

"Well, to be perfectly honest, there hasn't been very much time for romance," Ellis openly confessed. "When you're working on seven films in the span of a year, it *does* take its toll."

"Tell me about it. You're certainly right about that. It does get overwhelming at times," Laura acceded.

"Seems to be the story of my life," Ellis agreed.

"Ellis, my friends and I are getting together later for drinks over at my place. You know I live out in Crestview Valley, right?"

Ellis nodded. "So, I've heard."

"Would you like to come over for drinks?" Laura asked plainly.

Ellis's face wrinkled in uncertainty. "Tonight, huh? Well, it all depends. I have to make a flight at nine."

"You can come over at six," Laura encouraged, exploring Ellis's sparkling amber eyes.

"Sure," Ellis said kindly. "But, I probably won't be able to stay for long," he specified.

"That's fine. Maybe, we can do a raincheck for another time."

"Maybe…," Ellis said generically, smiling into Laura's eyes.

The last thing he wanted was to be disrespectful. He also didn't want to alienate any of his associates. In the industry, there was always the possibility of a collaborative future project. So, it was unwise to burn any bridges.

"Okay, so great! I'll be expecting you at six. Give me your phone, Ellis," Laura prodded.

"Sure," Ellis acceded. He took the phone out of the pocket of his jeans, unlocked, and handed it over to Laura.

"So, I'm adding my name in your list of contacts." She gave him a come-hither look, as she put her number into his phone. "Feel free to give me a call...anytime."

"Okay..." Ellis smiled timorously.

"So, I guess I will see you a little later." Laura handed the phone back to Ellis.

Ellis took the phone from Laura, but said nothing. It was difficult to be in his position. Just because he wasn't going around with someone, didn't mean he was free. Ellis resolved to pray all the more diligently about his circumstances. It was gut-wrenching to feel so strongly about someone he didn't know. It was even more difficult not to have her by his side. Categorically, only God had the solution to his problem.

"I'm looking forward to seeing you later." Laura added, winking at him.

Ellis smiled and nodded. "Me too."

"Ellis, Ellis, they're waiting on you. Some of the kids from your *personal fan club* in the community are asking for pictures and autographs," Jane Morgenstern, Ellis's publicist, frenziedly announced, as she gripped his arm.

"I'm sorry, Laura." Ellis frowned apologetically. "Will you please excuse me?" He hated being rude.

"Sure, of course. I know all too well. Duty calls," Laura granted.

"Thanks for understanding," Ellis said kindly.

"Ellis, come on. They're waiting," Jane said shortly, with an annoyed expression on her face.

"Bye, Laura," Ellis said, as Jane tugged on his arm.

"Bye, Ellis," Laura said solemnly, as she watched him dash away with his publicist.

Chapter Six

Hearing Paula's voice over the phone, made Evaniese's heart dip down to the floor. In the past few weeks, things had gone from bad to worse working through the hospital. And, for reasons unknown, that particular Wednesday afternoon in May, seemed to be the day of reckoning.

Paula had called, and asked Evaniese to meet her down in HR. Since the incident with the irate man in the ER some time ago, Paula had been on a warpath. Not taking Evaniese's word on anything, Paula called Cynthia frequently behind Evaniese's back to get a feel for the climate down in the ER.

Then, there were the two nurses who'd falsely and unfairly accused Evaniese of not doing her job on the day in question. Adding fuel to the fire, emails were sent to Evaniese by Paula and Ann, highlighting errors made on her registrations. Evaniese *herself* hadn't made the errors. The discrepancies were made by some of her work colleagues, who'd previously worked on the accounts. Certain fields on the registration grid were left empty. So, Paula and Ann maintained Evaniese was at fault, even if the initials underlined in the accounts were clearly those of others.

Evaniese tried to appeal to Paula and Ann's sense of fairness, disputing any wrongdoing. But, apparently-Paula *more* so than Ann, had no sense of impartiality, and refused to hear Evaniese out. And now, Evaniese walked the long stretch of hallway on the ground floor of the hospital headed over to Human Resources. She'd barely put in one hour on her shift when the phone call came in. So, Evaniese had to leave the ER, and allow Cynthia to hold down the fort for the time being.

With her heart trouncing like jungle drums, Evaniese kept an inward prayer vigil, as she strode over to the department. Stepping through the set of doors, the receptionist asked why she was there. "Paula Rivers, the director of admitting is here," Evaniese's voice wavered.

"Oh, right, Paula...," the pretty, young dark-haired Caucasian receptionist said, with a faint smile. "She's in boardroom four waiting for you." She gave Evaniese an amiable smile, but Evaniese could hardly bring herself to establish eye contact, let alone offer her a smile in return.

"Thank you," Evaniese said plainly, as she proceeded to walk past the reception area. She wandered down another stretch of hallway, and looked for the boardroom door with the number four posted on it. Evaniese whispered one final prayer, as she stood in front of the boardroom. She trusted God to guide her through whatever was waiting on the other side.

She then diffidently pushed opened the door.

"Come on in, Evaniese," one of the directors of HR, whom Evaniese had never seen or met before, encouraged.

Evaniese walked warily into the room, and saw Paula. As it would seem, Paula had been in the conference room waiting for her for quite a while. Paula didn't say anything. Rather, she stared disdainfully over at Evaniese.

Evaniese was unaware of the glower on her own face. It was uncharacteristic, but everything about Paula Rivers got under her skin. Hindsight was twenty-twenty. And, so Evaniese acquiesced to the fact that-at the time, she'd failed to show Christ-like attributes of longsuffering and forgiveness. Rather, because she was frustrated, her response was guttural.

Paula held a sizable file in her hand, as she simultaneously stewed in resentment, and held her tongue.

"Good afternoon, Evaniese! I'm Marcia Hollman. I'm one of the directors of HR for the hospital," the woman introduced.

Evaniese stood in front of the conference table trying not to glare at her boss. She was hesitant to entertain what this ambush was all about. From what she gathered, Paula had been there for at least an hour or two, and had probably fed this *Marcia Hollman* a bunch of lies.

"Have a seat, Evaniese," Marcia encouraged.

Evaniese deliberately pulled out a chair across from the two women, and slipped into it. The fact that she'd been called to HR by Paula, made her both mistrustful and disillusioned.

"You *do* know why you're here, don't you?" Marcia asked, staring intently over at Evaniese.

It suddenly occurred to Evaniese why Paula had preceded her to HR. It was undoubtedly to play damage control. In light of the abuse Evaniese had endured in the past seven years, Paula had to keep her from airing out the admissions department's dirty laundry. Just then, Evaniese felt a twinge of regret for not initially reporting of their exploitation and maltreatment beforehand. And now, Paula had beat her to the punch.

"No, I'm *not* sure why I'm here at all," Evaniese said plainly. "I came in to work this afternoon like always, and I was asked to come here," her tone was rueful.

"Well, Paula has cited a *number* of concerns regarding your overall work performance."

"What have I done?" Evaniese asked, immediately on the defensive. The last thing she wanted was to get emotional, but she was already triggered by the injustice of the circumstances.

"She's claiming insubordination. She says you've argued with her on a number of occasions," Marcia went on to say.

"What?" Evaniese questioned, with a bewildered expression.

"Hold on just a minute…" Marcia held her right hand up haltingly. "Before you say anything, Evaniese…," she admonished.

Evaniese took a deep breath. However, she kept shaking her head in denial over what was happening. In spite of the contention brewing interiorly, she was doing her best to remain calm. Crossing her arms over her chest, she remained silent, as she listened to the charges brought against her. Occasionally, she caught Paula's eye and lowered at her. Evaniese was beyond incensed and incredulous.

Still, in the back of her mind, she feared losing her job. It was May, and only one clearance remained for the approval of her WLS. And, given the circumstances, checking it off couldn't come fast enough. She'd gained so much weight from her *initial* consultation with Dr. Bergstrom at the bariatric center.

Undergoing a sleep study through the hospital, was the final requirement to move forward with the surgery. If she lost her job, she would also lose her medical insurance. After being bullied and abused for the past seven years working through Brookline, Evaniese considered the surgery as her compensation and severance pay.

"Your boss claims your attitude is challenging, and that your behavior in the ER has been unprofessional and combative. Some of your coworkers down in the ER have also complained how difficult you are to work with, and how you refuse to do your job. A couple of the nurses have personally emailed me stating that your work ethic is inappropriate and unacceptable."

"What...?" Shocked and offended, Evaniese kept shaking her head in renunciation. "That isn't true." Her eyes knifed through Paula's. "No one's been more hardworking, or conscientious..."

"So, you're saying that you *didn't* send several emails to me *challenging* errors I noted on your work? Also, you're denying highlighting your arguments in capital letters in order to emphasis your point?" Paula finally spoke up, and stared disdainfully at Evaniese.

"None of that is true, and you know it," Evaniese retorted on the defensive. "I was simply trying to explain that the mistakes noted weren't mine. Those errors were clearly made by some of my colleagues who'd previously worked on the accounts."

"And, I've explained *you* were responsible for making the necessary changes in those accounts, and you failed to. Moreover, you went back and forth with me and Ann on the matter," Paula recriminated, grimacing at Evaniese.

"The initials are at the bottom of every registration grid. Anyone can see that *I* wasn't the one who neglected to put in the information," Evaniese disputed.

"Ladies…," Marcia intervened. "Evaniese," she addressed, "allow me to finish, and then you'll be given a chance to speak," she settled.

Evaniese tried to compose herself, but the entire scenario was a nightmare. She was stunned and totally miffed. Even if she tried to remain composed, she couldn't help getting emotional about what was happening. She'd endured many inequities at the hospital, but this was by far the worst.

"Are we calm now?" Marcia looked from Paula to Evaniese.

Evaniese didn't answer. Rather, she remained quiet. It was an exercise in self-control not to give in to the strong feelings of resentment over Paula's lies and allegations. Evaniese now understood why she'd been asked to come to HR. She was there for Paula, and this *Marcia woman*, to gaslight and waylay her.

"Now, Evaniese, your boss says you've also been written up for falsifying your timesheets, coming into work late, excessive and unexcused absenteeism." Marcia Hollman held up the documents in her hands.

"What…?" Evaniese's face warped in mystification. "Those are straight up lies. None of that's true–"

"Evaniese, I'm going to need for you to remain quiet for a moment," Marcia stated in an irate tone, and giving Evaniese the death stare.

Evaniese shrank back in shock and intimidation. She wanted to react, remonstrate and rail against the false indictments. However, she held her tongue, rather than saying anything that could potentially get her fired right then and there.

Yet, that afternoon, she realized only God could deliver her from this brood of vipers. Working through the hospital was no longer worth it. For sure, it was the only place she occasionally got to see Nathan. However, at this juncture, she was ready to assent to the fact that the relationship wasn't going anywhere.

Her entire world was caving in. The WLS scheduled for June was all she had to look forward to. Dr. Bergstrom had tentatively scheduled her surgery for Wednesday June 15th. The procedure had to be pushed back a bit, because she had to repeat her sleep study. The first one had gleaned inconclusive results.

Regardless of how upsetting this powwow was with her boss, Evaniese couldn't afford to rock the boat until the insurance company paid for the surgery. So, she tried not to react, as Paula and Marcia Hollman read off indictments, which were for the most part blatant lies. Evaniese couldn't believe how these supposed *professional women*, were such bullies and bold-faced liars.

Paula had *doctored* emails. She'd used bits and pieces of conversations past to make Evaniese look dishonest and disrespectful to her bosses. The woman had actually taken time to falsify documents to make her look bad. Evaniese was flabbergasted, as she tried to wrap her head around how conniving and downright *evil* her *boss* was.

Even more bizarre was Marcia Hollman's behavior. The woman had never met Evaniese, but had jumped on the bandwagon along with Paula. Irrefutably, Marcia had access to Evaniese's work history, and her satisfactory evaluations of the past seven years.

Marcia went on to say, "Paula states you've falsified your time sheets for the sake of receiving unearned pay. Then, there was the matter of sharing your religious beliefs with patients you register through the ER. You were written up for *that*," she added.

"I handed out gospel tracts at my desk to the detox patients. Paula, my supervisor Ann and I discussed that in Paula's office. They made me aware of the infraction, and the subject was never revisited," Evaniese blurted out

"One more outburst from you…," Marcia said angrily, shaking her head in in rebuff.

"You're forgetting her inappropriate relationships with-not only *one*, but *two* of the ER doctors. Of course, Jeremy Carter no longer works through the hospital," Paula said, staring derisively over at Evaniese.

"Ms. Spencer here intimidated Doctor Carter to such an extent, he had no other choice but to resign from the hospital. Furthermore, Doctor Carter and his fiancée have put in several complaints that Evaniese has been phone-stalking them," Paula said scathingly.

Evaniese's heart sank to the floor. Tears stung her eyes, as she listened to Paula and Marcia compound lies, misapprehensions and fabrications about her. "None of that is true," her voice broke.

"Well, the documentation Paula has brought to my attention, verifies that *all* of it is," Marcia hissed.

"If I was such a horrible employee, why has the hospital kept me on? Why would the hospital ever give me seven years of consecutive satisfactory ratings? I haven't done anything wrong," Evaniese defended, staring disdainfully from one angry, scorned woman, to the other.

"What...? Are you calling me a *liar*?" Paula now challenged, with dart issuing from her eyes in Evaniese's direction.

"I'm saying that the things you have accused me of..."

"So, you *are* calling your boss a liar?" Fire sparked in Marcia's eyes, and her tan skin turned crimson. "I had my doubts when Paula first came to me to express her concerns and her dissatisfaction with your work. However, after meeting you this afternoon, I have to conclude she's absolutely right. You are extremely belligerent. And, according to Paula's recommendation, you *are* in need of anger management."

"I can't believe any of this. Is this even for real?" Evaniese asked, chagrinned and confused. "I've done nothing but give the hospital *two* hundred percent of my services for the past seven years ago. *Now*, I need anger management?" She frowned in hurt.

"Yes. You have argued with *me*, you argued with the *gentleman* in the ER that afternoon. He called me sometime after the incident to emphasize just how much you ignored him. He said you were too busy to pay any attention to him, because you were engaged in banter with a nurse down in the ED," Paula went on to impugn.

"What...?" Shock veiled Evaniese's face. "None of that is true...," she susurrated.

"Now, Evaniese... You might not like Paula, but you're sure going to respect her authority and experience as your superior. Are we clear on that?" Marcia's face warped in sternness, and her death stare targeted Evaniese. Things only worsened from that point on.

"Yeah, totally clear...," Evaniese said passively, as her thoughts whizzed. She was still in denial over the matter. She'd walked straight into Paula's trap.

"Now, I have some paperwork for you to fill out. Paula and I have prearranged for you to attend four sessions of anger management," Marcia informed. "I wanted to give you a chance to come down here this afternoon, and hear *your* side of the story. However, having met with you, I *see* why Paula has recommended anger management," Marcia settled.

Just then, it occurred to Evaniese how the two had planned everything out beforehand. Paula had fabricated documents, and had told outright lies about to the director of HR. Paula had already filled Marcia's head with horrible preconceived ideas.

Before Evaniese stepped foot into that boardroom, the two had predetermined how things were going to play out. They'd even drafted out the paperwork for Evaniese to sign. What was happening was a very bad look for the hospital, as both of these Caucasian *authority figures* had bushwhacked an African American woman, who'd tried to uphold nothing but integrity in the seven years she'd worked through the hospital. The racial implications were underscored.

"You are to attend four sessions of anger management with a private counselor outside of the hospital. The hospital will pay for these sessions, as part of our employee wellbeing program."

"And, if I choose *not* to attend these 'counseling sessions…?'" Evaniese asked, doing all she could to uphold aplomb and discretion in the presence of the two serpents.

"Well, the counseling sessions are mandatory. Noncompliance will result in termination," Paula said, with a satisfied expression on her face.

"I see," Evaniese said quietly and meditatively. She was dazed.

It now resonated just how much she was reviled in that environment. She was hated by a number of nurses, and other professionals in the ER. Moreover, she was loathed by her boss, and her supervisor. Now, she was despised by Marcia Hollman, who knew absolutely nothing about her, except for the lies Paula Rivers had fed her.

Evaniese didn't want to compile her misery. But, in addition to this new crisis, it also didn't help that her relationships with Ginger and Deanna was strained. The two had changed towards Evaniese, and not in a good way. Yet, Evaniese resolved to cling to the side of her Lord and Savior. Jesus alone was the same yesterday, today and forever (Hebrews 13:8). Even ones closest and most trustworthy loved ones were mutable. But, God never changed. And, Evaniese leaned into his breast for refuge on that awful afternoon.

All the fight was drained out of her. So, she stopped trying to state her side of the story, and assented to their desire. Apparently, she had to sign off on paperwork that she'd both *heard* and was in *agreement* with her superiors. Moreover, she had to submit to anger management sessions. After she was coerced into signing the paperwork, Paula and Marcia asked if she felt *okay* to return to her desk down in the ER to finish out her shift.

"We do realize how the things discussed in this meeting could have upset you," Marcia said with a soothing voice, *feigning* concern. "So, we'd understand if you wanted to leave work early tonight."

"Are you all right to finish out your shift?" Paula tested.

Evaniese deliberated. If she left-and they seemed to want her to-they would have even more ammunition to use against her. The scheming pair would say, she was so *angry* she couldn't finish out her shift.

So, instead of giving them the satisfaction, Evaniese desisted. "No, I'm fine to finish out my shift," she said courageously. Standing to her feet, she set out to leave the boardroom. Though, she remarked the fact that Paula wasn't budging from her place at the table.

It was then Evaniese perceived that Paula had been there hours before launching her attack. So, it followed, she and Marcia Hollman would remain joined at the hip, long after she left the HR that evening. After all, they needed time to finalize their wicked plan. Recognizing she was fighting a losing battle, Evaniese walked out of the boardroom feeling angry, stunned and unsettled.

As if heavily medicated, she walked deliberately out of the HR office, and hauled through the hospital corridors to get to the elevator. There were tears in her eyes, and she couldn't help trembling. Evaniese was outraged, hurt and completely disillusioned over what had just occurred. Adding insult to injury, she had to attend four counseling sessions with a psychologist. Slipping into the empty elevator, she finally buried her face in her hands, and surrendered to weeping.

"Are you all right, Evaniese?" Cynthia asked, the moment Evaniese returned to the ER's registration area.

Evaniese tried to conceal how shaken up, and traumatized she was in the aftermath of her powwow with Paula and Marcia at HR. "I'm fine," she said forcing a smile, and shifting back over to her desk.

Cynthia pushed back in her rolling armchair to get a better look at Evaniese. Evaniese seemed poised to get back to work. "Paula said you were going home for the day," Cynthia informed with a puzzled expression on her face.

"No, I'm not," Evaniese affirmed. "I'll be here until eleven," she added, staring warily over at Cynthia.

"Oh, okay," Cynthia said, looking away from Evaniese's piercing stare. "You mind if I go on break?" Cynthia asked, trying to finalize paperwork.

Evaniese was about to answer Cynthia, when a gentle knock came to the registration office door. Neither she nor Cynthia said a word.

However, Nathan popped his head through the door. Evaniese was startled, and immediately roused from catatonia. "Nathan...," she muttered, surprised.

"Hello, Evaniese...," Nathan greeted, smiling.

He then turned towards Cynthia. "Hello," he said cursorily.

"Hello," Cynthia said, warily eyeing Nathan.

She then stared over at Evaniese. "I'm going on break, okay?" She gave Evaniese a knowing look. It was to convey that Evaniese *not* allow Nathan to take her seat at the second desk. There were times Nathan came in, and sat at his old spot, while Cynthia was on break.

"Yeah, sure," Evaniese told Cynthia dismissively, but her eyes remained fastened to Nathan.

She and Nathan were in sync, because his eyes didn't waver from her, as he radiated his special light.

With Nathan there, the horror show Evaniese had endured, had to take a back seat. Nathan had a way of making her temporarily forget her woes. She smiled in earnest at him, and the taut heartstrings in her chest began to unwind. Although she felt the weight of Cynthia's curious stare on her and Nathan, Evaniese refused to give the girl any credence.

Cynthia had conveyed, in no uncertain terms, *she* was the one Nathan should have befriended, not Evaniese. After all, she was the one in her twenties, had blonde hair and blue eyes. In short, the complete antithesis of Evaniese. In fact, Cynthia had blatantly told Evaniese that Nathan was only *being nice* to her, whenever he stopped in to chat. In other words, it wasn't possible for a man like Nathan Andrews to be interested in anything but friendship with Evaniese.

Regardless, Evaniese refused to care what Cynthia thought. She had God's word that Nathan was *her* guy. It was gratifying to know that Nathan had proven time and again that he genuinely liked being around her, in spite of what any of her work colleagues had to say. Evaniese was aware that some of the medical staff working through the ER, spoke ill of her. Hence, they'd plotted and schemed to destroy her relationship with Jeremy Carter. Now, they were all trying to undermine her connection to Nathan as well.

"Mind if I come in?" Nathan asked, all smiles. He hadn't budged an inch from his spot in the doorway.

"No, not at all," Evaniese welcomed, relieved to see him. She sensed Nathan's visit as a gift from God. Certainly, God knew how much she'd needed to see a friendly face. Even if her relationship with Nathan left a lot to be desired, he was fundamentally a *friend*.

"I'm going now," Cynthia announced, staring nosily between Evaniese and Nathan.

"Okay, bye," Evaniese said quickly, not once looking in Cynthia's direction.

As Cynthia gathered up her things to go on break, Evaniese tangibly felt her disapproving frown on her and on Nathan. It seemed, her egress from the office was happening in slow motion.

Evaniese and Nathan exchanged befuddled looks. Both wondered what Cynthia's problem was.

The moment Cynthia left, Evaniese stood to her feet, and Nathan stepped fully into the office.

At that time, Evaniese could completely size up how dashing he looked in his navy-blue dress suit. Nathan looked as cool as a February morning in New York City. The color enhanced his caramel complexion, and his golden-brown eyes. Evaniese's heart lurched, and butterflies danced in the hollow of her stomach. It'd been a while since she'd seen him.

"You can come in, and have a seat, Nathan," Evaniese welcomed, unable to contain her joy.

Nathan closed the door after himself. "How are you?" he asked, turning to face Evaniese.

Evaniese closed the gap between them. At that point, the two were standing only inches apart. "I've been better," she admitted, shrugging nonchalantly.

"Everything all right?" Nathan's face wrinkled in concern, as he inched in even closer.

Evaniese nodded. "I'm okay," she evaded, and smiled with as much strength as she could muster. The last thing she wanted was Nathan's pity. She didn't want him getting sucked into her sob story. His presence there was enough. Their connection certainly lacked definition, but Evaniese was just happy to have him close by.

"Are you sure?" Nathan eyes delved into hers, gripping her left arm in concern. "We talked about this before, Evaniese. Don't allow any of these nut jobs around here to give you a hard time. It's not even worth it," Nathan affirmed, searching her eyes. "Do you hear me?" he tested.

Evaniese nodded, with a faint smile curving over her lips. "I hear you. And, how have *you* been?" she sidestepped, changing the subject.

"Me...? I'm great!" Nathan's smile brightened, as his eyes continued to explore Evaniese's.

"Did something happen?" Evaniese asked, curious. Suddenly, she was completely engaged in conversation with Nathan, and felt encouraged to remain in the moment.

"As a matter of fact, something *did*." Nathan's cheeks flustered, and his eyes sparkled like champagne.

"Care to share?" Evaniese baited, hopeful of good news.

"Well, you *know* how much I love Brookline, and how living out in Marble Terrace is a distance from here...?

"Yes, I remember. We talked about the inconvenient commute, when you first started working here," Evaniese granted.

"Well, guess what?"

"What...?" Evaniese's heart whisked in angst, hoping against hope Nathan *wouldn't* bring up his wife again. From the time he'd told her he was married, it was always a nail-biter whenever Nathan said he had an announcement to make. Evaniese prayed Nathan's declaration pertained to something other than his *mysterious* and *elusive* wife.

"I just moved out to Amber Hills!" Nathan excitedly proclaimed.

"Nathan, I'm so happy for you!" Evaniese genuinely perked up, elated to hear the news.

Her thoughts were whizzing. Had Nathan moved out to Amber Hills just to be closer to her? God had shown Evaniese Nathan did love her, in spite of the way he behaved, and the things he said. Just then, Evaniese chose not to ask Nathan about *his wife*.

Hearing Nathan speak, Evaniese surmised that *he'd* rented out an apartment in the area. That conclusion made sense. In the past, during times of inclement weather, Nathan had spent the night at the hospital, or at a nearby hotel just to make a morning shift.

Evaniese felt encouraged. Perchance, God was *finally* answering her prayer. *Was it possible that God was ready to establish a relationship between Nathan and herself?*

"You're renting a place out in Amber Fields Commons?" Evaniese doubled-checked. She had to make sure she'd heard Nathan correctly.

Amber Fields Commons was ten minutes away from where *she* lived. Evaniese wondered if Nathan would finish what he started two years ago when he asked her out.

"Yes, I love the area, and I love my new place!" Nathan avowed, beaming. "We're not too far away from each other now," he emphasized, searching Evaniese's eyes.

"No, not at all," Evaniese said, uncertainly. She didn't know what to make of Nathan's observation. *Did he have it in mind to move closer to her all along?*

"I'm so happy for you, Nathan!" Evaniese celebrated along with him.

Regardless, she refused to get her hopes up. She and Nathan had been going around in circles for the past two years. There had been times Evaniese was convinced of a positive change, that they could even possibly get their relationship off the ground. However, circumstances had degenerated, and created an even bigger rift between them.

"Thanks, Evaniese!" Nathan smiled, and searched her eyes intimately. "Maybe, we can finally grab that coffee one of these days?"

At that moment, Nathan had a twinge of regret. He'd inadvertently asked Evaniese out again. Brent Peterson's angry face flashed in his thoughts. The man was insanely jealous and possessive of Evaniese.

So, Nathan had to backpedal. "Maybe, you can double date with me…and with my *wife*," he quickly added.

Evaniese offered Nathan a generic smile. She wasn't as hurt as she *should* have been hearing him allude to a double date. She was all too familiar with the jargon…and the *suffering*.

After all, she'd been through the mill for two years. "Right…," she said, smiling. Irrespective of the nature of their conversation, it *was* nice having Nathan there. He was a welcome distraction, after being browbeaten by her boss and the director of HR.

Evaniese was excited to hear Nathan rave about his new place. It was curious indeed that he didn't bring up his *nameless* wife again during the course of that conversation. Even so, she tried to accept the sad set of circumstances.

For a while, she'd waited for something momentous to take place. And, something life-altering *had*. By his own admission, Nathan now lived in Amber Hills. The irony of it all was that Evaniese would soon be putting in her two-week's notice to the hospital. There was no way she'd continue working for an institution where she was bullied and exploited by angry, jealous and conniving women.

Unfortunately, the circumstances never seemed quite right to move forward with Nathan. Nathan had taken the leap, and finally moved out to Amber Hills. However, *Evaniese* was ready to cut her losses, and move on from Brookline Hospital.

As soon as her insurance carrier approved the surgery, she'd be out of there. In the interim, she'd grudgingly acquiesce to sessions of anger management with a counselor. The very concept made her blood boil. Evaniese considered, if becoming incensed over being undermined, demoralized, and ill-treated warranted anger management, she was definitely guilty as charged.

***

One Saturday morning at the end of May, Ginger walked through the lobby of the extensive Orange Valley Hotel. Having just registered for the Wiccan Conference, she turned her head in the opposite direction of the registration desk to avoid being seen. Her eyes weren't deceiving her. Deanna was standing on line as well. Ginger was beyond shocked! Yet, she had no idea how she was going to remain incognito during the colloquium.

Orange Valley was at least twenty miles away from Amber Hills. One of the reasons why Ginger had signed up for the seminar was *because* it was so far away from town. *But what on earth was Deanna doing there?* Ginger had *her* reasons, but couldn't imagine what Deanna's were.

Taking quick strides through the lobby, Ginger slipped on sunglasses, and tried not to look behind her. Deanna, along with the other registered patrons, were hot on her heels. That weekend, those who practiced Wicca and other spiritualists, would be sharing their pearls of wisdom on effectively casting spells.

Ginger was all in. In a matter of weeks, Evaniese would have Bariatric surgery. So, Ginger's job was to ensure Evaniese's weight loss efforts failed. That was *her* story, but Ginger could hardly wrap her head around why Deanna was at the conference. That was neither here nor there, her goal at the moment, was to avoid Deanna at all costs. So, Ginger picked up the pace.

"Ginger...? Ginger...," Deanna called out from feet away. She couldn't be sure, but from the back, the woman looked exactly like her bestie.

"Oh no...," Ginger muttered, and pretended not to hear Deanna. Her worst nightmare was now a reality. Deanna recognized her. *What on earth was she going to tell her bestie? They were both* **churchgoing** *people. Why on earth was Deanna there anyway?* Ginger was frustrated.

Deanna sprinted down the hallway. She had to be sure her eyes weren't deceiving her. *Was the woman she just saw Ginger? Had Ginger come all the way from Amber Hills to come out to the Wiccan Conference?* Deanna was ready to explain away *her* reasons for being there. Already, she was mentally rehearsing what to tell Ginger. She would tell her bestie she was there to garner information for a thesis paper in her cultural studies course. Part of her Master's program was to learn all about Wicca.

Her thesis would compare and contrast the Christian faith, to those who practice paganism and Wicca. Yes, that's exactly how she would explain it. That was her story, and she was sticking to it. Yet, for the life of her, Deanna couldn't figure out what Ginger's excuse might be. "Ginger, Ginger…," Deanna hollered, as she closed the gap between them.

Realizing it was a losing battle, Ginger rethought trying to keep her presence there a secret. Once everyone took their seats, Deanna would certainly see her sitting out in the lobby meeting hall. There was no way of hiding. Having spent over four hundred dollars to be there, Ginger refused to be sidetracked. She would learn how to successfully cast spells on whomever she willed to. So, she sucked it up, and geared up for the performance of a lifetime.

Making a startled turn, her face widened in the most superficial smile. "Deedee," she exclaimed, feigning a surprised expression, "what are *you* doing here?"

Deanna rushed over, and threw her arms affectionately around Ginger. Pulling back, she pointed at Ginger. "I *thought* that was you. Wow! Funny bumping into you here. I had no idea you planned on being here this weekend." Deanna marveled, smiling openly. Anticipating Ginger's questions, Deanna planned to strike while it was hot.

"Yeah, well, I was invited by someone from work." Ginger's face strained in uneasiness. "My supervisor wants everyone around the office to learn more about Wicca. Apparently, quite a few people practice the religion in the workplace," Ginger tried to sound credible.

"The thing is, my supervisor, wants us to be more tolerant, and even sensitive to the beliefs of others, even if it's Wicca. Essentially, it's considered a religion." Ginger laughed nervously. Her expression conveyed awkwardness. "It's all about religious tolerance and sensitivity."

Deanna examined Ginger with a perturbed expression on her face. She kept nodding in agreement to the *story* Ginger was trying to sell her.

She couldn't help thinking it would have been much easier for Ginger to try and sell her the Brooklyn Bridge. "Oh, okay...," Deanna said inquiringly. "So, did your job pay for both the conference, and the overnight stay at the hotel?" she prodded, staring skeptically into Ginger's eyes.

"Yeah, yeah... Of course, they covered the entire seminar. I signed off on paperwork that I would attend the conference this weekend... And what about you?" Ginger evaded.

Deanna's heart thrummed, as her face stretched out in a rubber smile. Setting her hand on her heart, poised to recite a pledge, she began building her argument, "Me...? I'm here this weekend, because I'm writing a paper on the subject of Wiccan practices." She tried to exude confidence in those words.

"Oh, really...?" Ginger stared at her peculiarly. "Is that right?" she fished.

"Yeah, it's a twenty plus page paper. So, I've got a lot of notetaking to do this morning." Deanna strove to steady her gaze under Ginger's analytical stare.

"Wow! Look at *you* being a great student and all! You really get *into* your subject."

"Of course...," Deanna said agitatedly. "You *have* to, if you want an A," she continued to fib.

"You want to sit together?" Ginger invited.

At that point, Ginger could care less why Deanna was there. With the workshop starting in a few, she only had one goal in mind.

"Sure," Deanna said, surprised.

She was there to learn how to effectively put a hex on Evaniese. The date for Evaniese's WLS was approaching. Deanna couldn't say she wasn't surprised by how staunchly Evaniese had powered through obtaining her medical clearances. Even more astounding was the fact that she refused to give up, even if she never stopped putting on weight.

It really didn't matter. To one capacity or another, Evaniese had fulfilled the requirements to secure the procedure. There seemed to be nothing standing in the way at that point. And, that's precisely why Deanna was there. She *had* to come up with a way to sabotage her. Evaniese was extremely beautiful, intelligent and strong.

However, there was one intrinsic difference between. *She* was a size four, and Evaniese was probably a size eighteen. Thus, Deanna wanted to make sure that never changed.

"You lead the way, Ginger," Deanna said, feeling empowered, and excited to be a part of the symposium.

"You have no idea how happy I am that we've bumped into each other this weekend!" Ginger draped her arm about Deanna's shoulders. The two continued down the stretch of hallway, leading up to the hotel lobby.

"Yeah, I'm glad we ran into each other too, Ginny!" Deanna said spiritedly.

They came to the entryway of the extensive room, and remarked how quickly the empty seats were filling up.

"I think up there might be a good spot." Ginger pointed to the left-hand side of the room. There were available seats in the third and fourth rows.

"I wouldn't mind sitting in the third row," Deanna agreed.

Deanna and Ginger hiked over to eagerly take their seats. They were looking forward to learning all they could about Wicca. Their aim was to discover how they could utilize the practice to serve their purpose. The end goal was to obstruct Evaniese's weight loss efforts. Additionally, they had to sabotage her chance with Brent Peterson, Jeremy Carter and Nathan Andrews. Even if the women were at the forum for the same reason, neither had the courage to admit it.

"We've all had to deal with that pesky coworker, or that cheating husband or boyfriend. Oh, and don't forget those insufferable and condescending bosses..." Chandy Walters introduced, as the first keynote speaker.

The woman appeared to be in her late twenties, and clothes were Goth-themed. Her raven hair, her jewelry and makeup were esoteric, and her black-painted fingernails gleamed like chrome in the sunlight streaming through the hotel lobby.

"Have you ever wished you could get revenge on those who've hurt you? Have you ever wanted to make that competitive and backbiting coworker disappear? Ever wish you could do that to your boss, or to a cheating spouse? Well, that's exactly what we're going to talk about this morning." A smile curved over her full, onyx-tinted lips.

Ginger and Deanna whipped out their notebooks, and instantly began taking copious notes, as Chandy shared her knowledge. The ladies felt privileged to be under the tutelage of such renowned witches. They were also eager to absorb as much as information at they could. Perhaps, they too would excel in the craft, and become enchantresses. And, so began the symposium on a very promising note!

***

"Oh, how are you doing dear?" Nora Peterson, Brent's mom, gave Evaniese a loving squeeze on a Sunday morning at the end of May at church.

"I'm doing well," Evaniese affirmed, smiling earnestly at the woman. Evaniese sat in the front row of pews, towards the right-hand side of the assembly. Making a point to get to church earlier than usual, she'd taken a moment to pray, and to meditate quietly in the presence of God.

"You have such a beautiful face!" Brent's mom praised, and patted Evaniese endearingly on the cheek.

Evaniese issued a fond smile at the woman. Nora Peterson just wasn't any good at mincing words. No doubt, it was by design that she didn't tell Evaniese was *overall* beautiful, but had highlighted her *face*. Evaniese couldn't say she blamed the woman for failing to compliment her body. Since her initial consult with the bariatric center at Brookline, she'd gained about twenty pounds. So, there was absolutely nothing praiseworthy about that.

Equally, Evaniese was on her guard with Nora Peterson. God had exposed the woman as a frenemy. From what Evaniese understood, the older Caucasian woman had engaged in witchcraft in order to discourage a relationship between Evaniese and her son Brent.

Evaniese couldn't help thinking how hypocritical people were. She couldn't say that about *all* Caucasian people. However, she now realized it didn't matter how much love they expressed at church. It also didn't matter how lovingly they crushed her in their arms with hugs. When it came right down to it, anyone who didn't look the way they did was repudiated.

Come hell or high water, they were determined to do anything in their power to keep the *wrong* people at bay. Evaniese's packaging was all wrong. Not only was she African American, but she was overweight to boot! So, it was a given. Nora Peterson didn't want Evaniese anywhere near her successful *white* son.

Evaniese perceived the opposition and the hypocrisy. That morning, Evaniese's eyes were opened as to how treacherous the woman could be.

"Thank you. That's very kind of you to say," Evaniese said modestly, over Nora's *backhanded* compliment. Nonetheless, she was distrustful of the woman.

"Mind if I sit with you for a minute before service?" Nora asked, with the same insincere smile.

"Not at all." Evaniese gestured for the woman to have a seat.

Knowing how much Nora Peterson hated her, in spite of the pleasant façade, Evaniese was cagey. Yet, she had no way of knowing the woman was about to release an arsenal.

"So, how have you been?" Nora's voice was soft as silk.

"I've been good," Evaniese said generically.

"I've missed you at church these past few Sundays."

"Honestly, I've been a little preoccupied with work and other things," Evaniese admitted.

The truth was, because of the extreme weight gain, Evaniese had had reservations attending church. She wasn't ignorant of her duplicitous *church family.* They pretended to like her, while they continued to backbite and plot against her. It also didn't help that none of her clothes fit anymore. Perhaps, her feelings were superficial and even vain. All the same, Evaniese hadn't found the courage to face the crowd. She knew she'd feel empowered again, once the weight began to come off.

"That's too bad, because we sure miss your smiling face around here." Nora cupped Evaniese's chin, and squeezed her face endearingly.

"I miss you all too," Evaniese enlivened, smiling.

"Speaking of missing... I've been waiting on my son, and his *girlfriend* to show up," Nora announced. "You *do* remember my son Brent, don't you?" Nora asked deviously.

Evaniese's heart crashed to the floor, when Nora mentioned Brent in the same breath as a *girlfriend*. The other shoe had dropped. Evaniese shrank back in shock over Nora's words. However, she tried to keep her poker face on.

How on earth could the woman ask *if* she remembered Brent? *Everyone* at the church knew of the scandal that took place between Brent and herself. Brent had made Evaniese's declaration of love a public debacle for everyone to pick apart, and to criticize. So, how on earth was Nora asking her whether, or not she *remembered* Brent?

How could Evaniese *ever* forget such humiliation and degradation? Also, not much time had elapsed since Brent had publicly shamed her and put her on blasts. Even if a hundred years had passed, Evaniese couldn't forget who Brent Peterson was. Brent was the man whom God had said was her ordained spouse, even if the circumstances said otherwise.

Nora Peterson's transparent ploy to discourage Evaniese was shocking! It seemed to be the only reason why she'd brought up *Brent and his girlfriend*. It was a direct affront to Evaniese's heart.

However, Evaniese courageously played along. "Of course, I remember Brent," she said offhandedly with equal finesse.

"Well, he and his *girlfriend* are running late. I've been checking the lobby for them for the past forty minutes," Nora emphasized.

"I'm sure they'll get here just fine," Evaniese said, sounding unaffected.

Even if things had played out badly for Brent and herself years ago, it still struck a chord to hear his mom allude to him having a significant other. The pain was real, even if God had consistently affirmed to Evaniese how much Brent loved her, in spite of his conflicting behavior. But, the question remained, if Brent *truly* loved her, why was the man entertaining other women?

In spite of it all, Evaniese refused to get sucked into a miasma of pain. She'd moved on since Brent. Even if nothing was happening with Nathan, Evaniese was encouraged something eventually would. After all, she had God's promise. Instinctively, she wanted to put Nora Peterson in her place. Surely, the woman had to know Brent wasn't the *only* eligible, good-looking successful bachelor in the world. She was tempted to tell Nora, "Since your son, Brent publicly repudiated me, God brought *two* equally good-looking and dynamic men into my life."

On the other hand, Evaniese desisted from acting on impulse. In theory, she knew Nora Peterson wasn't *really* on her side. Hence, Evaniese finally got a handle on that reality that Sunday morning. Nora Peterson had thrown shade, but Evaniese refused to remain in the shadows. Rather, she daunted to take her place out in the sun, even if there wasn't one hopeful ray of sunlight shining in the horizon.

"I sure hope they get here soon. The service's about to start," Nora stressed again, with a plaster smile.

"Maybe, there's a traffic issue," Evaniese tried to sound cavalier. "So, I wouldn't worry too much about it," she uplifted, even if her heart had sunk to the bottom of her feet, as a result of the woman's clear snub. Still, Evaniese dared to trust God no matter what.

"Thank you, dear. I'm going back out to the lobby to look for them again," Nora settled.

"I hope they make it. In a few minutes, the service will start," Evaniese championed.

Nora smiled again. "Well, I will see you in a bit, dear," she said, standing to her feet.

"Sure," Evaniese told her.

Evaniese sat there in the church pew trying to hold it together. She wanted to have an *in-your-face* moment with Nora. However, she found it difficult to keep a stiff upper lip. None of the men God had highlighted as her kingdom spouses, were actually within her grasp.

Worse yet, neither had given her the slightest indication they would ever be. *Faith* told her that in spite of the circumstances, it *had* to happen, because God was incapable of lying (Numbers 23: 19. Hebrews 6: 11-20). So, Evaniese took heart, and did all she could to remain optimistic as the sanctuary filled up. She cheerily greeted other church members, and gave them hearty hugs.

Moments later, the praise and worship segment began. The worship song, "All in for Jesus," was posted on two projection screens on either side of the assembly. As Evaniese began to sing, Ginger and Deanna walked up the church aisle, and slipped into seats next to her. Truly encouraged to see her friends, Evaniese beamed, as they exchanged hugs and kisses. She was honestly happy to see her besties. It was the first time they'd been together in quite some time.

The three silently celebrated coming together, and sang the chorus of the song with verve. The chorus went as follows: *"The only way to win, the only way to win is to be all in, be all in… the only way to win, and to gain victory over sin, is to be all in for Jesus…"*

Evaniese felt enabled, because her friends were there. Shortly after the praise and worship segment, Pastor Templeton asked everyone to take a moment to welcome those around them to the service. Evaniese bypassed everyone she'd formerly greeted. Making a sudden turn, she caught sight of Brent sitting next to a dark-haired, blue-eyed Caucasian girl. She forced a smile, though inwardly, she was falling apart. The woman looked to be about 5'7." She was slender, had a small waist, and was curvy in all the right places.

In spite of the hurt, Evaniese still felt stirred to say hello to Brent. However, she quickly redirected. The scowl on Brent's face said it all. Evaniese refused to venture out, and take that chance. She had absolutely no idea why Brent was glaring at her. As she'd moved in to say hello, Brent's face was ruddier than a crab's. Notwithstanding, he'd viciously turned away. Doing all she could not to allow Brent's erratic behavior to affect her, Evaniese drifted back up the church aisle, and slipped back into her seat.

Ginger grasped Evaniese's left hand the moment she settled back into her seat. "Are you okay?" She frowned in concern.

"I have the same question as Ginger. Are you alright?" Deanna's face warped in commiseration. She set her hand lovingly on Evaniese's back, and brushed caringly on it. "That was brutal," she remarked, and just plain rude. I can't believe he-"

"I'm fine," Evaniese said quickly, forcing a smile. She really didn't want to dwell on what had just occurred with Brent. "I'm okay," she emphasized. "Besides, we need to be quiet. Pastor Templeton's about to read scripture." Evaniese looked straight out in front of her, and kept her eyes on the screen projector.

"Are you sure, Niecy?" Ginger tested, unsettled by the matter.

"He isn't even worth your time or energy," Deanna added, rubbing on Evaniese's back in a pacifying manner.

"Guys, seriously… I'm okay. Hush… Here comes Pastor Templeton," Evaniese dodged.

She was so grateful when Pastor Templeton took his place behind the pulpit, and began reading from the word of God. The last thing she wanted was pity from her thin and beautiful friends. Both Ginger and Deanna had good-looking boyfriends. It was difficult for Evaniese to process Brent's slight. What on earth had she done to him?

It was true. She'd moved on emotionally from Brent to Jeremy, then from Jeremy to Nathan. However, Brent's hurtful behavior broke her heart. At the end of the day, someone she'd once felt very strongly about, had treated her with disdain. Yet, Evaniese resolved not to allow Brent's rejection to maim her. She was already facing so many other challenges.

In the suffering, it was difficult to understand God's plan. Even so, Evaniese had to believe there was purpose in all the pain. Her heart was broken, and everything seemed awry, but she had to stand on her faith. She *had* to believe God knew exactly where she was. Furthermore, he had a plan of love for her life (Jeremiah 29:11).

At some point, why she'd cried so much would become clear. In spite of the heartache, the still small voice of God's Spirit kept reminding her of Isaiah 61:7 (NKJV); "Instead of your shame *you shall have double honor*, And *instead* of confusion they shall rejoice in their portion. Therefore, in their land they shall possess double; Everlasting joy shall be theirs."

Chapter Seven

The 85th annual *Diamond Destiny Awards* ceremony was
finally here! Usually, Ellis didn't look forward to attending.
However, this year he was nominated for best actor in a movie
he was cast in at the end of last year, *Lead Horizon*. The film
depicted the true-life story of a man wrongfully incarcerated.
It chronicles his life prior to, and after he's falsely accused. It
also follows his experiences in prison, fighting the justice
system, and finally his release. All are depicted beautifully in
the film!

It wasn't a role Ellis would have usually gone for.
However, his agent convinced him it was exactly the role he
needed. Being typecast only as an action/adventure actor in
the industry wasn't something Ellis wanted. The role had
undoubtedly stretched his range as a thespian. And, tonight,
surrounded by the glitz and fanfare of the red carpet, he was
grateful for having met the challenge.

Ellis chose to attend the awards ceremony unescorted.
Laura Morgan Fields had wanted to be his plus one. That was
something she made no qualms about. However, Knowing
Kierra Spalding would be there, Ellis had respectfully
declined. And, the last thing Ellis needed on his special night
was Kierra's territorial tendencies to douse the flame of his
excitement. Kierra was making it almost impossible for him
to breathe. Much to his chagrin, Kierra had even *called* Laura,
warning her to keep her distance from him.

Ellis's resolve was to distance himself from Kierra. Moreover, he refused to string Laura along. As unconventional as the circumstances were, his heart belonged solely to *Niecy819*. After seeking God extensively on the matter, Ellis was compelled to reach out to her in a more tangible manner. The strong inclination he felt towards the young woman still baffled him. And yet, Ellis couldn't say for sure she was in the will of God for his life. Discovering God's will required much prayer, patience and waiting, as God's ways were past finding out. (Isaiah 55:8-9).

Still, Ellis knew he had to explore the possibility. That night, as he sat inside the extravagant and expansive Crystal Coliseum, waiting to hear his name called along with the other nominees for best actor, Ellis determined it was high time to get a dialogue started with the woman. Short of gushing, there was only so much he could say about her lifestyle vlogs. Hence, he had to take his admiration to the next level.

The awards ceremony was coming to an end. Only two categories remained; best actor and the best picture of the year. Ellis sat on the edge of his seat, and held his breath. The moment had arrived. He loosened his tie, and wriggled uncomfortably in his Armani tux.

"Here are tonight's nominees for best actor in a dramatic role...," Lisa Calderon, a former *Diamond Destiny* winner announced. She was on stage with a former nominee, Kent Dillon. Lisa went on to announce, "Jared Matta for *Sunset Follows*. Matthew Palmar for *Native Dance*, "Ellis Roman for *Lead Horizon*..."

Ellis's contemporaries who sat close by, shouted all the more boldly, when his name was announced. Ellis smiled, and his cheeks reddened in embarrassment over their accolades. Still, his heart remained lodged in his throat, as Lisa continued to say the names of the remaining two nominees. "Grant Trident for *Forwarded Mail*, and Lester Mason for *Small Running Stream.*"

Lisa looked out into the audience with a spirited smile. She then proceeded to cautiously open up the envelope. "And the award goes to...'" She looked out into the vastness again, with an excited smile. "Ellis Roman..., *Lead Horizon*!" she breathlessly announced.

At first, Ellis was convinced he'd heard wrong. So, he found himself momentarily dazed. His friends and peers patted him on the back, and on his arm to congratulate him on the win. Still a bit shocked and disoriented, Ellis stood to his feet, and stepped out into the aisle. He was about to start making his way up to the stage, when Kierra rushed down the aisle, threw her arms around his neck, and pressed a kiss to his mouth.

"Congratulations, Ellis!" Kierra heralded. She cradled his head in her hands, and planted another kiss to his lips.

Ellis was dumbfounded over the win, but Kierra's display left him stunned. The audience went completely ballistic, but Ellis tried not to react right then and there. No doubt, the media was poised to have a field day with Kierra's little publicity stunt. Nonetheless, at that very moment, Ellis brushed past it, and headed for the stage. He would address Kierra's impulsive behavior later.

The smile on Ellis's face couldn't be contained, as he made his way up to receive the award. There were fellow actors, patrons and friends cheering him on every step of the way. The screeches and the howls were also notable.

"Ellis...," everyone celebrated, as Lisa handed him the coveted diamond-shaped, lead crystal structure with the golden base and stand.

"Congratulations, Ellis! You deserve this!" Lisa shouted, and pressed a kiss to his cheek.

"You surely do," Kent agreed, heartily shaking Ellis's hand.

"Thank you so much!" Ellis said, humbled by their kindness.

"Wow!" Ellis exclaimed looking out into the infinite sea of familiar faces. "I'm stunned. What can I say?" He held up the award in his right hand. "I want to thank a number of people..." Ellis went on to read a list of names from a small cue card. He tried in earnest not to forget anyone who'd worked in collaboration on the film *Lead Horizon*, and those who'd subsidized it.

"And, I know this isn't popular in Hollywood, but Hollywood doesn't determine anyone's *destiny*, so to speak. God does. So, I want to thank God for blessing me with so much! I know that without Jesus Christ, I could do absolutely nothing...," Ellis stated boldly.

At first, the audience seemed flabbergasted over hearing his words. But, then a rousing and thunderous applause resonated throughout the assembly. Fellow actors, actresses and supporters stood to their feet, and gave Ellis a standing ovation. Ellis was even more graced by their tribute.

It didn't matter if he was in Hollywood, or out in Houston, he would *always* lift up the name of Jesus! Jesus had given him his status, and had blessed him beyond his wildest dreams. And, that was something he would never be ashamed of. No matter how it was perceived by his peers, he'd said his peace. So, it really didn't matter what Hollywood thought.

The final award of the night for best picture went to *Small Running Stream*. Ellis wasn't fazed that *Lead Horizon* didn't win the best picture of the year award. He was terribly proud of his first *Diamond Destiny Award* for best actor. The night was just getting started. Reporters, paparazzi and the media took turns taking Ellis's picture, and congratulating him on his success.

For Ellis, winning his first *Diamond Destiny Award* in some way felt like a dream. It was taking a moment to process the reality of the matter. Regardless, he'd already made up his mind not to attend any of the after parties. Having fame and fortune meant absolutely nothing without love. More than anything else, he longed to share the moment with someone he truly loved.

The night stretched out into eternity, as Ellis entertained his colleagues and friends. It was almost midnight when he stepped out into the lobby of the Crystal Coliseum. There were still a few of his peers and patrons socializing in the area. Some were waiting on rides to drive over to one after party or another. Ellis was about to step out fully into the open space, but pulled back when he saw Kierra and Laura having words. Both seemed terribly upset. Their faces warped in irritation.

Even with angry scowls, it was difficult to escape how stunning both women looked in their designer gowns. Kierra's gown was Kelly green with a plunging V-neck. The bodice revealed her shapely hips and small waist. Laura's gown was classic and more reserved. The powder blue sequined fanned out skirt and diamond crusted neckline, made her look like a Disney princess. And yet, no matter how classy they *looked*, classy was the last word Ellis would have used to describe their behavior.

"I don't know what's so difficult to understand, Laura. I'm *not* trying to sound like the wicked witch of the west, but Ellis is *my* guy." Kierra pointed a liable finger in Laura's face. "So, I'm telling you to back off," she censured.

Laura shook her head nonsensically, and her hands went sassily to her hips. "Get out of my face, Kierra. Ellis *himself* told me the two of you are just friends," she retorted.

"Well, Ellis feels sorry for you. So, he would say anything. Not only will Ellis and I play love interests in our new movie, but we *are* certainly more than friends," Kierra argued.

"Sounds like *you're* the one Ellis feels sorry for, and would say *anything* to, Kierra. You look and sound so desperate right now," Laura disparaged, as her lethal eyes gunned into Kierra's. "I'll bet anything Ellis goes to the after party with *me* tonight," Laura said superciliously.

"He isn't going anywhere with you tonight, Laura dear. He's going with *me*."

"*You're* the one who needs to back off, Kierra. Oops, your *desperate* is showing, dear," Laura shaded. "And, that kiss you planted on Ellis tonight during the ceremony, is exactly when *you* dropped the ball."

"Listen, you little has been…," Kierra hissed, as darts shot out from her eyes. Pointing an accusatory finger at Laura, she went on to say, "if you think you're the one who will be on Ellis's arm tonight, or any other, you've got another thing coming…"

"I was *never* a fan of your work anyway, Kierra," Laura said icily. "Not only is your *desperate* showing, sweetheart, but your *amateur* is also on display. I have nothing more to say to you." Laura crossed her arms defiantly over her chest. She then drifted over to a corner in order to distance herself from Kierra. "We'll just see what Ellis has to say," she muttered.

"You might want to try a little Botox for your *crow's feet*, Laura," Kierra susurrated. "And, I agree, we'll wait for Ellis. You'd better put in a call to your limo driver. Ellis and I are definitely leaving *together*," Kierra established. She also moved away to a corner of her own.

As it was, Ellis detested attending huge celebrity events and after parties. However, that morning, he'd made up his mind. No one would bulldoze him into going to an after party. No doubt, he'd run into trouble if he did. Ellis stood to the side, took out his phone, and called his limo guy. Dylan had the night off this time around. So, Ellis asked Bernard, another one of his drivers, to meet him on the other side of the coliseum.

Ellis waited a few minutes, and tried to avoid the hoopla of press and media. Irrefutably, he'd be chided for not showing up to any of the after parties. As if Kierra's impromptu kiss at the award's ceremony wasn't enough, Ellis knew the paparazzi would also have a field day criticizing him for his disappearance act. But just then, Ellis could care less. He'd already put in his obligatory few hours. He'd received the best actor award, and had thanked all of the necessary parties. Now, he just wanted to find a nice, quiet spot away from it all.

The limo pulled up, and Ellis slipped in faster than anyone could blink.

"Are we going to the after party in West Hollywood, Sir?" Bernard checked.

"No, we're not. If you wouldn't mind, I'd like to go home," Ellis told him categorically.

"Of course, sir," Bernard's tone was compliant, as he cautiously navigated away from the pomp, and fanfare that early morning, following the awards ceremony.

***

Ellis alighted from off his knees from having devotions later that morning. Even if he'd prayed on the matter, he was still unsettled about his resolve. The plan was to create a private Instagram account in the hopes of reaching out to *Niecy819*. He would still use his alias *Fan4ever*, but without a profile picture. For a number of reasons, he felt it best to uphold anonymity. Needless to say, he had to see how things were going to play out, before he revealed his true identity to the young woman.

He couldn't help smiling, as he caught sight of the *Diamond Destiny Award* on his nightstand. Ellis felt totally empowered! Slipping into bed, he accessed his phone.

"Lord, I'm about to try and connect to this beautiful and clearly special woman. Please, guide me in the matter. I'm only testing the waters here, because I've never done anything like this before." Ellis sighed, and stared heavenward.

Taking deep breaths to still his drubbing heart, he created the private Instagram page under the name *Fan4ever*. So, *Fan4ever* officially started following *Niecy819* on Instagram. Ellis smiled, and sighed with a sense of satisfaction after direct messaging her a request to talk. His heart skipped a beat, as he anticipated an answer. Nevertheless, he realized he had to talk himself down, because the young woman first had to notice that he'd reached out.

Ellis skimmed over comments made by fans on a few of his posts that week. Suddenly, he received notification that *Niecy819* started following *Fan4ever on* Instagram.

Ellis's heart somersaulted in his chest, and he felt shaky typing words on the keypad of his phone. "Hi. I saw your profile on Instagram, and decided to reach out."

"Wow! Is it really you?" *Niecy819* replied.

"Yes, it's me. I'm like your biggest fan. Your vlogs are absolutely amazing! Then, again, I think I've conveyed that a number of times in my comments on your YouTube channel." Ellis's face radiated like the sun! He couldn't believe he was personally connecting to the young woman.

"Yes, I've seen your comments. They're extremely encouraging. Having your support means a lot to me," *Niecy819* shared. "On some of my worst days, seeing your kind words have made all the difference in the world!"

Ellis commiserated, but his smile was irrepressible. For months, he'd longed to reach out, but seemed to lose his nerve every time. The experience of connecting to *Niecy819* felt surreal. "Well, I'm glad to hear something I've said encouraged you."

"It's a lot more than *one* thing. It's all of the inspiration, and support you've given me. Thank you," *Niecy819* uplifted.

"You're welcome! I truly love your style. You have a way of making the most mundane chores and events sound exciting. I also *love* your smile!" Ellis put it out there with a smiley face emoji. It didn't seem to make sense, but *he* found himself blushing after sharing his heart.

"Thank you so much for saying that," *Niecy819* exclaimed, with a praying hands emoji.

"You're welcome! If I may ask, what is your name?" Ellis asked directly. There was a sense of angst as he awaited an answer. Maybe, she wasn't ready to tell him her name. Though, he realized he might have put his foot in his mouth by being intrusive.

"My name is *Evaniese*," *Niecy819* shared plainly.

"Wow, such a beautiful name for such a beautiful woman!" Ellis declared. *Evaniese*, he susurrated. Hence, *Niecy819*. Ellis was already in love with Evaniese's vlog, and now he was falling for everything else.

"Thank you so much! What might I ask is *your* name *Fan4ever*?" *Niecy819* asked.

"My name is El," Ellis wrote out. There was a sense he should come clean, but he couldn't just yet.

"Just El?" *Niecy* asked.

"Actually, *El* is short for Elbert," Ellis fabricated. He had to know he could confide his true identity to Evaniese.

"Oh, that's nice... So, everyone calls you El?"

"Yes..."

"I like it."

"Well, Evaniese, I like *you*," Ellis wrote out brazenly.

"Wow! Okay... You don't mince any words, El," *Niecy819* responded, adding a shocked-expression emoji.

"Are you seeing anyone right now?" Ellis explored.

"I am...and I'm not. It's complicated," *Niecy819* answered.

"Well, just putting it out there. I think you're beautiful, and I love your work!" Ellis expressed, unabashedly. He couldn't believe how brave he sounded. In all honestly, he couldn't say he was surprised over his own transparency.

He'd yearned to connect to *Evaniese* for quite a while. So, he'd fantasied about all the things he would say when he finally *did*. His impressions gushed like a fountain. Ellis realized that he would have been a lot more reserved, if he was looking into Evaniese's eyes. So, in that respect, *chatting* on Instagram was liberating.

"Thank you, El. I'm very flattered by the appreciation and attention. What about you? Are you married, seeing anyone...?"

"No, I'm not, actually," Ellis admitted without hesitation. "The truth is that I've been anticipating a connection with you. I would *love* to take you out..." Ellis wasn't particularly proud of his approach. The last thing he wanted was to come off as some guy using pickup lines.

"Wow! I'm surprised, and a little bit taken aback," *Niecy* disclosed.

"I'm sorry for the way that sounded. I wasn't trying to sound *smooth*. Believe me, I'm *not* that kind of guy. I happen to think you're quite beautiful, talented and amazing…," Ellis redirected.

And from that point on, he invited Evaniese to chat with him using the *Chat Channel*, a private chatting app. She agreed, and the two spent close to two hours chatting that first time.

As Ellis rested his head on his pillow in the wee hours of the morning, he was so excited about his new friendship with *Evaniese*, it was difficult to fall asleep. He hadn't estimated things going so well. It took all of the self-control in the world not to message her again. Based on first impressions, Ellis deemed Evaniese to be shy and reserved.

Furthermore, he sensed her misgivings. How on earth could she tell if he was on the level? He resolved to prove to her that he wasn't the kind of man who played games. When he wanted something, he went after it wholeheartedly. And before drifting off to sleep, Ellis acknowledged that he *wanted* Evaniese…and in the worst way.

***

"So, what are your plans moving forward, Evaniese? It's obvious Paula Rivers, along with the director of HR at Brookline, are complicit in destroying your reputation and your stellar work ethic," Alicia Bergen, assessed. She was the psychologist Evaniese had submitted to seeing for anger management. It was clear to Dr. Bergen that Evaniese's boss had used gas-lighting tactics.

Grateful it was her final session with the doctor, Evaniese deliberated. She sat in the comfortable armchair inside the walk-in basement of Dr. Bergen's home. The basement had been converted into her private counseling office. Evaniese thought on the woman's question. But, at the moment, she only cared about fulfilling the obligatory sessions, which her boss and the director of HR had mandated, in lieu of facing termination.

Evaniese had submitted to their mandate. She'd done so in order to bide her time, until her medical insurance through the hospital approved the surgery. On that particular Thursday afternoon, Evaniese felt as if a tremendous weight had been lifted from off her shoulders. She'd had her consult with the bariatric center at the beginning of the year. Inconclusive results with her sleep study had pushed back the date of the surgery. However, it was now the middle of June, and she'd finally been cleared to have the procedure. In fact, her WLS was scheduled in two weeks.

Her medical insurance company had shelled out in excess of 40,000 to pay for the Vertical Sleeve Gastrectomy. So, Evaniese was all smiles. On that very day, she would tender her two-week's notice to the hospital. Evaniese was excited for other reasons. Just a few days ago, she started chatting via the *Chat Channel* with one of her YouTube subscribers. His name was *Fan4ever*. This man had created a private Instagram page for the sole purpose of reaching out to her.

As far as Evaniese knew, his real name was *Elbert*. But, his friends called him *El* for short. El had not minced any words. He'd openly told her how beautiful and special he thought she was. In fact, *El* had made his *romantic* interest in her abundantly clear. Never had anyone ever spoken to Evaniese in the way this man had. He called her *Love* and *Beautiful*, as if they were her name.

It was strange to be falling for someone she'd never met, or even seen. And yet, that's exactly what was happening. In just a few days, Evaniese had undeniably developed real feelings for El. However, she still struggled with guilt and shame. God hadn't changed his mind about Brent, Jeremy or Nathan as her potential spouses. So, Evaniese couldn't figure out where El factored into the equation. The uncertainty left her feeling unsettled.

All the same, just thinking about stopping the chats with El, threatened Evaniese's sanity. El spoke a furtive language to her heart she'd only dreamed and prayed about all her life. The man had touched her in an unprecedented way. El knew how to uplift her in a way none of the other *three* men had ever daunted.

Evaniese reasoned, as long as her relationship with El remained platonic, she didn't have to feel guilty. While sitting in Dr. Bergen's office, Evaniese was unaware that she'd slipped into fantasy mode again. Daydreaming about El, what he was like, how he looked, and the sound of his voice, consumed her.

"Evaniese...?" Dr. Bergen tried to get her attention.

"Yes, Dr. Bergen," Evaniese replied, finally snapping to attention. Somewhat embarrassed, her cheeks turned scarlet. "I'm sorry. I guess, I have a lot on my mind."

"What's going on with you?" Dr. Bergen stared curiously at her.

"Oh, nothing," Evaniese evaded.

She wasn't ready to talk about her special connection to El with anyone. In fact, it was a secret she hadn't yet shared with her best friends. Neither Ginger, nor Deanna knew she was chatting with the mystery man.

"I was just thinking how excited I am to finally be able to hand in my two-week's notice to my boss this evening," Evaniese told Dr. Bergen, with a satisfied grin.

"Wow!" Dr. Bergen gasped in shock, and set her right hand on her chest. "You've decided?" A deliberate smile curved over her lips.

"Yes, I have. It's high time I left that awful place," Evaniese added, perking up.

"Good for you!" Dr. Bergen nodded in endorsement. "I'm so happy you've made up your mind. What your boss and that *awful* woman from HR did was only the beginning. And, as much as I've *enjoyed* our sessions, they were totally unwarranted.

"Based on all you've told me, and looking over your history at Brookline, you're one of the most longsuffering people I've ever met. You did nothing to deserve the abuse and misrepresentation on your job. Something tells me, Paula Rivers has done this before-and more than just a few times."

"There's no doubt in my mind she has," Evaniese assented. "But, I refuse to go on being her punching bag." There was a reflective expression on her face.

"Well, I'm really happy for you, Evaniese! You've gone above and beyond for Brookline Hospital these past seven years. Sounds to me as if administration has enjoyed taking advantage of you."

"You *would* be right in making that judgement call," Evaniese echoed.

"Do you have the letter all ready?" Dr. Bergen asked

"I've had it all written out from a month ago," Evaniese admitted. Feeling enabled, she settled more comfortably into the armchair. "In fact, I started looking for new employment a while ago."

"Have you found anything yet?" Dr. Bergen leaned in closer from across the desk. She seemed equally excited for Evaniese.

"I've decided to hold off on looking for another job," Evaniese informed. "I'm going to need a little time off after the surgery."

Dr. Bergen knew of her plan to submit to the VSG Surgery. The woman had undergone the procedure herself. So, she was overjoyed to hear that Evaniese was a candidate for the same operation.

Dr. Bergen smiled. "Yes, that's right. I'm so happy you're doing something *completely* for yourself. It seems, in the past, you've always tried to please others."

Evaniese had a rueful expression on her face, and she nodded reflectively. "Yeah, that's been the story of my life."

At that moment, Nathan came to mind. Evaniese had real feelings for him. So, the thought of no longer being able to see him at the hospital saddened her.

However, she wasn't as brokenhearted about it as she thought she'd be. Nathan had had *two years* to make a move, but had failed to. Additionally, even his recent move to Amber Hills had done very little to change the dynamics of their relationship. Nathan continued to bring up his *elusive* and *nameless* wife, whom Evaniese had never seen or met.

For all intents and purposes, Nathan was *still* living across town. The fact that he lived only ten minutes away from her was of no consequence. Evaniese hadn't seen him *once* outside the hospital. As per God's edict, she continued to text him. However, whether or not Nathan responded, reminded her of a sad game of roulette. Sometimes Nathan answered, while at other times, he left her hanging. Even when he *did* answer, his answers were supercilious and extremely concise.

"What are you thinking about now?" Dr. Bergen asked, smiling.

"I was thinking about Nathan. Leaving the hospital means I won't get to see him anymore."

Dr. Bergen sat back in her armchair, and clasped her hands together, as her eyes explored Evaniese's. "Well, Evaniese, in light of all you've told me about Nathan Andrews, it won't make much of a difference at all." Her face warped in commiseration. "I know you *think* this man is God's will for your life. That very well may be, but the timing's off.

"Maybe, he will play a part in your future, but he hardly seems ready to make a move. I understand you're trying to uphold faith. However, holding on to that faith, also means putting your life on hold. You get what I'm trying to say?" Her eyes narrowed into Evaniese's.

Feeling as if she'd just received an epiphany, Evaniese acquiesced. She had to consider maybe Dr. Bergen was right. Perhaps, the timing *was* off for her and Nathan. Because God's ways were higher than man's, it was often difficult to decipher the times and seasons he'd set in his will.

So, reviewing the circumstances through new eyes, Evaniese made a decision. She resolved to enjoy her chats with the suave, sweet and charming El. Dr. Bergen's words had loosened the noose of culpability from about her neck. As it stood, her relationship with Nathan was virtually nonexistent. So, Evaniese doubted that resigning from the hospital would in any way alter its course.

Sometime later, Evaniese slipped into her SUV, which was parked across the street from Dr. Bergen's home. She and Dr. Bergen had said their obligatory goodbyes. And, regardless of the fact that Paula Rivers and her minions had used the anger management sessions to undermine her, Evaniese could attest that the sessions had in some way worked out for her good (Romans 8:28). Being able to talk to Dr. Bergen, had proven to be very insightful. Through the sessions, Evaniese had received clarity, and felt emboldened to move forward.

Evaniese beamed, as she imagined the shocked expression on Paula's face when she handed in her resignation letter later on. However, as she turned the key in the ignition, her smile brightened all the more, because the notification bell for the *Chat Channel* had just gone off. El was calling…

"Hey, *beautiful*, how are you?" El wrote with all kinds of heart and admiration emoji's.

Evaniese's face was all aglow, as she began texting her response. "I'm good, El. How are you?"

"Fine, *beautiful*. How is your day going?"

"Well, I just finished up my last session with Dr. Bergen," Evaniese shared.

"How did that go?" El inquired.

"I'm honestly glad I got to meet her, and had those sessions. I thought they were going to be a lot worse. But, as it turns out, I might have actually needed them," Evaniese explained.

"I guess so, *sweetie*. What people often mean for evil, God always makes good for his children," El shared his heart. "Are you okay?"

"I'm fine. I missed hearing from you earlier on," Evaniese admitted.

"Aww… I'm so sorry. I actually had a lot going on earlier. And, I don't like to chat, unless I can give *you* my *undivided* attention," El wrote out, sounding extremely considerate.

"Aww… You're so sweet," Evaniese expressed, filling the page with heart emoji's.

"*You* bring out the sweetness in me, *Love*. Are you going to be all right? You told me last night about handing in your letter of resignation to the hospital today."

"Yes, definitely. But, I'm okay. It's a hard decision, but I honestly think it's the right one. Besides, I haven't been able to think of much else. I want to hand that letter *personally* to that horrible Paula Rivers," she admitted.

"Lol," El wrote out, with laugh out loud emoji's. "I'm happy for you too, baby! I'm also happy about the surgery…"

There was a pause after El wrote out those words, and Evaniese frowned in uncertainty. "Is anything wrong, El?"

"No, baby, I was just wondering if you were going to be okay… I mean, with the surgery. The truth is, I think you're *perfect* just as you are…"

Evaniese's heart melted to see El's words. Tears shone in her eyes. It was the first time a man had seen her in all of her *fullness*, so to speak, and still wanted to uplift her. El called her *beautiful* on the regular. "El, you're melting my heart. You're so sweet."

"Evaniese, I know we haven't been chatting for long, but I like you a lot more than you probably realize. In fact, please message me with the information about the surgery as soon as you can."

Evaniese gasped in shock, and set her right hand on her chest, stunned. "You want to be there on the morning of the procedure?"

"I would love to be there to support you. Will your family and friends be there?" El asked, concerned.

"My parents and siblings don't live out in Indiana, but my best friends will be there."

"That's wonderful, sweetheart! If it's not asking too much, I would also like to be there with you," El emphasized.

Tears rolled down Evaniese's cheeks, and she was all choked up. She and El had only been chatting for a few days, and she could already perceive how vested he was in her. What was even more sobering was that she was beginning to feel just as strongly for him. It was the most bizarre thing which had ever happened to her, but also one of the greatest blessings.

"Evaniese…are you there?" El tested, worried that he'd lost her.

"I'm here, El."

"I'm sorry, baby. I know it's a bit soon to want to see each other, but it would mean a lot to me if you'd let me come out to the hospital on that morning," he highlighted again.

"El, I promise to message you with the information just as soon as I have all of the details. Thank you so much for wanting to be there."

"Of course... But, can I tell you something?"

"Absolutely..."

"You're the most beautiful woman I've ever laid eyes on, and you're absolutely perfect! Nevertheless, you have my total support whatever you decide."

"Oh, El...," Evaniese wrote out.

Her heart melted like chocolates in the palm of her hand. She found herself stunned and speechless. Never had anyone spoken to her in this way. And, her heart was stirred beyond all comprehension. With a thrumming heart, and a stomach full of butterflies, Evaniese chatted with El for a few more minutes. It was always difficult to stop their chats, but duty called. She had to go home, and get ready for work.

"I'll message you to check in a little later, baby," El wrote out.

"Thank you, El. I'll let you know how things go just as soon as I hand in the letter."

"Please, let me know how it goes, baby."

"So, we'll talk later, okay?"

"All right, baby. Be safe," El said with a ton of love and heart emoji's

"I will, only if you promise to do the same," Evaniese texted. She added a number of love and admiration emoji's to her page as well. "Bye, El..." She posted a dozen kiss emoji's.

"Bye, baby," El wrote out again, inundating his page with decorative *like* and *love* symbols.

Evaniese was overwhelmed, and tears flooded her eyes, as she shut down her phone. El was a *different* kind of man. Brent, Jeremy and Nathan had broken her heart, humiliated her, and had judged her to be unworthy. But, El spoke a totally foreign language-one only her soul could comprehend. Evaniese brushed tears away from her eyes, as she drove away from the area.

She lifted up her hands in praise to God! Dare she believe that love was finally materializing in her life? Sure, the circumstances weren't perfect, and it was a long-distance connection. Yet and still, in her estimation, it was a lot better to have someone love her from afar, than to have them ignore her in closeness and intimacy.

***

Evaniese was virtually on cloud nine, as she climbed up the steps leading up to the admissions office. She had the letter of resignation in hand. Earlier on, she'd called Ann Ridges, and told she had a pressing matter to discuss. Since the powwow over at HR, where Paula had prevaricated and contrived falsehoods to tarnish her reputation through the hospital, Evaniese had had no contact with the woman. However, Evaniese was *looking forward* to having word with both women on that notable Thursday afternoon in June.

A bright smile stretched across Evaniese's face, as she opened up the set of doors, and walked down the hallway leading up to the work area. As she breezed through the office, she greeted some of her coworkers, who were busy at their desks.

"Hi, Evaniese," some of her colleagues hailed, with open smiles.

Evaniese smiled back, and waved at her peers from a distance.

She ambled into the main office area, and checked to see if Paula was there. Her heart dipped down to the floor upon seeing Paula's office door closed. Not only was it closed, but the lights were off.

"Are you looking for Paula?" Ann stepped out of her office, with an inquisitive expression on her face.

Startled, Evaniese clutched her heart, and smiled awkwardly. "Yes, I was hoping to have word with both of you," she told Ann.

"Well, Paula's away on a business-related seminar. She won't be back until next week," Ann disclosed, frowning. "Is everything all right?" she asked, seeing the envelope in Evaniese's hand.

"Everything's okay," Evaniese reassured. "I just wanted to discuss a very important matter with both of you," Evaniese said, disappointed to hear Paula was out of town.

"Well, is it something that can wait until Paula gets back?" Ann asked, taking steps towards Evaniese.

Evaniese shook her head in negation. She was at an impasse. For weeks, she'd imagined Paula being there when she handed in her resignation. She'd wanted that *in-your-face lady* moment. Nevertheless, she didn't want to wait another week to tell them she was quitting.

So, she addressed Ann's question, "Actually, it can't. So, can we have a moment in your office?" Evaniese asked straightforwardly. Evaniese figured Paula would get hit with the news soon enough.

Even if Evaniese wouldn't see Paula's face when she got wind of the news, it was satisfaction enough to *imagine* the look on the woman's face, once she heard of Evaniese's resolve to leave the hospital. For a narcissist like Paula, losing Evaniese as a punching bag, would definitely put her into a tailspin.

"Are you *sure* you don't want to wait until Paula gets back?" Ann's face crinkled in perplexity.

Evaniese nodded. "I'm sure."

"All right," Ann said, turning towards her office.

White envelope in hand, Evaniese followed behind her. Stepping inside Ann's office, Evaniese sat adjacent to Ann's desk. She deliberated before staring squarely into Ann's eyes.

"What's the pressing matter you wanted to discuss, Evaniese?" Ann seemed impatient.

"Well, I wanted to let you and Paula know that I'm leaving Brookline Hospital!" Evaniese announced. A slow smile curved over her lips, as she verbalized the words. "I came up here this afternoon to give you my two-week's notice." Evaniese held up the letter in her right hand.

"What...?" Ann questioned, taken aback. "You're leaving the hospital?" Stunned was the only way to describe the expression on her face.

"Yes," Evaniese said, feeling gratified. "I've decided it's time to move on."

"Is there a specific reason why you want to leave *now*?" Ann asked, apparently affected by the news.

"Well, I *can't* say what Paula did at HR *hasn't* affected my decision," Evaniese admitted. Inwardly, she wanted to tell Ann that *both* she and Paula had been unfair and abusive from the outset. However, she refrained from doing so. Evaniese grasped that in spite of Ann's horrible behavior, the woman was just Paula's patsy. She too was a victim of Paula's reign of terror through that office.

Furthermore, Evaniese didn't want to leave the department starting little fires, and with even more bad blood than she had with Paula.

"Well, I'm sorry about what happened. I can't say that I *condoned* that, neither did I choose to be a party to it," Ann said.

Evaniese stared curiously at Ann. Just then, it dawned on her that Ann probably wouldn't have used Paula's tactics. Still, that in no way made the woman innocent. Ann too had pulled her share of stunts, and had made harsh and unfair demands of Evaniese during Evaniese's seven-year stint at Brookline.

However, Evaniese saw no point in telling the woman, "I don't know why you're acting as if *you* have nothing to do with why I came to this decision. You're sitting there condemning Paula, but you went along with every offensive thing she ever did and said concerning me."

But, that was neither here nor there. Evaniese had to let go. It was time to let it *all* go. Her time at the hospital was up. There was no point holding on to the anger and resentment. So, with a smile pasted to her face, she went on to say, "Thank you for taking a chance on me, and hiring me to work through the hospital. I'm grateful for the job I've had these past seven years."

"You're welcome, Evaniese! It's going to be *different* not having you around-and not in a good way. You will surely be missed," Ann acquiesced.

Surprise veiled Evaniese's face, and she nodded with a sense of satisfaction. "Thank you for saying that. It means more than you know."

"So, in two weeks...?" Ann held up the resignation letter Evaniese had handed her.

"Yes, in just two weeks," Evaniese affirmed. "Please, see to it that Paula gets a copy of the letter?" Evaniese frowned in uncertainty.

"I definitely will," Ann reassured, holding the envelope up again.

"Honestly, Ann, I was looking forward to handing that letter to Paula personally." Mischief played on Evaniese's face. "But, I can't hold out until next week." She shook her head in irony. "Still, seeing the impression on Paula's face was the *one* thing I was looking forward to doing."

Ann chuckled. She realized how much Evaniese had longed to tell Paula herself. "I'm sorry she isn't here for you to hand it to her *personally*. No doubt, you would have wanted to see the expression on her face." She shook her head humorously.

Evaniese chortled. Irrefutably, Ann knew what a horrible *person* and *boss* Paula was. So, the woman was able to commiserate.

"You have no idea. I've only imagined the moment I'd give it to her a hundred times. But, I guess it wasn't God's will. Maybe, this is God's way of limiting my interactions with Paula before I leave the hospital," Evaniese concluded. She felt free to share her faith and personal beliefs with Ann, because the woman had also confessed faith in God through Jesus Christ.

In spite of her questionable behaviors and brownnosing when it came to Paula, Evaniese perceived Ann was sincere in her faith. After all, who was *she* to judge? All believers had flaws and shortcomings, which they were trying to overcoming with God's help.

"I honestly wouldn't be *brokenhearted*, if I didn't cross paths with Paula for the next two weeks," Evaniese told Ann.

"I totally understand." Ann nodded and laughed. "So, do you have another job opportunity lined up?" she asked.

"I was thinking about going back to teaching," Evaniese informed. "But, I'll probably take the next few months off," she added.

"All right," Ann said softly, "I'm in receipt of your letter, and will pass the news along to Paula." She smiled at Evaniese.

Evaniese stared into Ann's eyes and smiled as well. "Thank you for passing the news along. Also, thanks again for taking a chance on me seven years ago." Evaniese gave Ann a genuine smile.

Just then, it occurred to her that Ann wasn't a *terrible* person. Evaniese assessed that Ann was doing all she could to cover *herself* in a toxic work environment. So, Evaniese resolved to keep Ann in her prayers.

"You're welcome! Thank you for being such a wonderful employee these past seven years!"

Taken aback by Ann's words, Evaniese was rendered momentarily speechless. Her eyes then fastened to Ann's. "Thank you so much for saying that!"

Standing to her feet, Evaniese considered what a huge difference it would have made if Ann had *acknowledged* that in the past. All things considered, Evaniese wouldn't sweat the matter. A while back, God had mandated her to resign from Brookline Hospital, and that's exactly what she was doing.

Ann stood to her feet, and guided Evaniese back towards the office door. Evaniese turned the doorknob, and stepped out. "Have a good night, Ann." She began drifting away from the office.

"Good luck with everything, Evaniese!" Ann called out, as Evaniese sauntered away.

Evaniese turned back to look at Ann. Ann was still standing in her office doorway. Evaniese gave her a faint smile. "Thank you."

That said, Evaniese stepped out of the admissions office. She had to return to the ER. As she traveled back downstairs, she was overjoyed for more reasons than one. The mission was accomplished! In the past, she'd doubted having the courage to tell her bosses she was quitting her job. However, God had strengthened her to do what she'd once considered impossible!

Evaniese was giddy over the victory, but even more so, because she was falling in love with El. Evaniese couldn't wait to get back to her desk. Once there, she'd be able to send him a quick message. She had to tell him it was done. She'd handed in her resignation.

Also factoring into Evaniese's lighthearted and lightheadedness, was because she was on her pre-surgical two-week liquid diet. She had a cup of Jell-O in the ER breakroom's fridge, and she couldn't get to it fast enough. All those undergoing VSG Surgery, had to submit to a liquid diet. It consisted of things like water, tea, soups, broth, protein shakes, Jell-O and light puddings. Shrinking the liver of all fatty composition, would ensure no complications on the day of the surgery.

At her highest, Evaniese had weighed in at 272 pounds. However, she was no longer heartbroken over failing to lose weight. What mattered was that she'd gotten through all of the preoperational clearances. The surgery was just about two weeks away. And, if all went according to plan, the weight would come off as easily as butter melts off of hot corn on the cob.

Rushing back down to the ER, Evaniese made detour for the breakroom. She grabbed her lemon Jell-O and woofed it down. It was only day two of her liquid diet, and she wondered if she'd make it through for the next twelve days. In addition to the Jell-O, Evaniese made herself a cup of hot tea with lemon.

"Hey, you're back!" Cynthia announced, when Evaniese coasted back into the registration office.

"Yep," Evaniese said vaguely, crossing back over to her desk.

Cynthia pushed back in her rolling chair to look at Evaniese.

Evaniese had just set the cup of hot tea on her desk.

"Everything okay?" Cynthia asked nosily, feigning concern.

Evaniese couldn't help smiling. "Everything's great! I just gave Ann my letter of resignation!" she gladly announced.

"What...?" Cynthia's mouth gaped in shock. "You're leaving Brookline?"

"Oh, yeah. After what happened with Paula at HR, I couldn't see myself staying on here," Evaniese admitted, though she was fully aware Cynthia *wasn't* someone she could trust. But, Evaniese hardly cared about coming clean to Cynthia on that particular afternoon.

"Wow! I totally get that. What she did was completely messed up," Cynthia tried to sound supportive. "So, in just two weeks, huh?"

"Yep." Evaniese nodded. "In just two weeks." She smiled at Cynthia.

"Wow, Evaniese... Things sure won't be the same around here without you!" Cynthia's mien was melancholic. "You like *run* this ER," she uplifted.

"Well, thank you for saying that, Cynthia. That's really nice of you, but it's high time for me to move on."

"Did you find another job?" the girl pried.

"Yes...," Evaniese said, and didn't go into any details. "I'm going to miss you guys around here!" Evaniese eluded.

"We're going to miss you too." Cynthia's face puckered in sadness.

"You're going to do just fine." Evaniese gave a disarming wave of the hand and guffawed. "But, shouldn't you be going on your break?" she reminded, direly wanting a moment to herself.

"Yes, but I'm just a little sad about your news," Cynthia confessed.

"We can talk about it a little more when you get back," Evaniese heartened.

"Okay," Cynthia agreed.

"Has it been really busy since I went upstairs?" Evaniese asked, watching Cynthia push out of the armchair, and stand to her feet.

"For the moment, we're pretty much caught up. So, you might actually be able to breathe for a few minutes." Cynthia smiled.

Evaniese nodded gratifyingly. "That's good to know. So, I'll see you in a bit?" she said pleasantly.

"Sure. I'll be right back," Cynthia said.

"Enjoy your dinner!" Evaniese observed Cynthia step through the office door.

Relieved for the brief moment of silence, Evaniese whispered a prayer of thanks to God, and gave him the glory. At last, he was removing her from the den of thieves she'd had to work through for the past seven years.

Soon after, she took her phone out from the desk drawer. "I did it, El! I just handed in my resignation!" she texted through the *Chat Channel* app.

There was a lapse, and El didn't answer right away. So, Evaniese was a bit disappointed. The ER was unusually quiet, so Evaniese continued fiddling with her phone.

About ten minutes later, the notification bell for *Chat Channel* went off. "Hi, baby!" El responded. "I'm so proud of you, honey! I'm so happy to hear how brave you were in doing exactly what you set out to. Are you all right?"

"I'm just fine, El. I had to give the letter to my supervisor," Evaniese shared. "Paula Rivers wasn't there. Can you imagine? I've only imagined handing her that letter personally a hundred times. I've wanted to say *in your face* for the longest…"

"I know, baby, but it really doesn't matter if you saw her or not. There will still be shockwaves throughout that office when she gets wind of the news. So, don't even worry about it. But, I'm *so* proud of you, baby. You were so brave. Maybe, the Lord didn't want you to cross paths with that woman again. Sometimes, God allows you to see the face of your enemy *one* last time. I can only surmise that God didn't want you seeing *that woman's* face again," El wisely assessed.

"How did you get to be so smart?" Evaniese wrote out.

"Well, about a week ago, I started chatting with an angel," El responded.

"An angel, huh?" Evaniese flirted with an irrepressible smile.

"She's the most beautiful woman I've ever laid eyes on! And, I think I might be falling for this angel," El admitted.

"Does the angel have a name?" Evaniese trifled. Even if *she* was beginning to fall for El, she felt it to be much too soon to tell him so. And yet, El wasn't holding back. Maybe, the entire situation was too good to be true. So, Evaniese resolved to tread cautiously.

"Yes... My angel's name is *Niecy819*." El added a wink emoji.

Tears shone in Evaniese's eyes, and she remained temporarily speechless. It was the first time in her entire life a man had spoken so lovingly to her. El had seen her vlogs, and knew she was plus-sized. However, he still told her on the regular how stunning, and breathtakingly beautiful she was to him.

"Baby..., are you there?" El asked, perplexed by the lull. Hearts and other romantic emoji's littered the chatting app's page.

"Yes, El, I'm here," Evaniese reassured him, with tears in her eyes. She couldn't stay on her phone for the obvious reasons. However, she took advantage of the rare quiet moment through the ER to speak to the *first* man who'd communicated such warmth and unconditional love.

Chapter Eight

"You've already made up your mind, huh?" Nathan asked, with a perturbed expression on his face. Finding a minute between hospital admissions, he sat inside the hospital café. Evaniese was on her break, and the two had bumped into each other.

"Yeah, I'm leaving this Friday," Evaniese told him.

She was drunk with joy. In light of the way she was beginning to feel about El, it felt strange to interact with Nathan. It was an uncanny experience! Even if she and El had never met, Evaniese was enamored. In spite of it all, she couldn't say that her feelings for Nathan had altogether evanesced. Yet, she knew all too well that a flame could only grow if properly fanned. And, Nathan had stopped fanning the fire over two years ago.

"I'm sorry you and I never talked about your decision. My wife and I were on vacation for two weeks. I had no idea you'd made up your mind to leave Brookline."

"I *did* text you to let you know that I'd completed my anger management sessions with Dr. Bergen," Evaniese reminded him. "You *know* how devastated I was after what happened with HR."

"I knew you were unhappy, Evaniese. Honestly, I had no idea you planned on leaving so soon." Nathan's face warped in both sadness and conflict.

What on earth was he going to do? Brent Peterson had made his life a living hell from day one. The man had warned him to stay away from Evaniese. Nathan had done his best to comply, and had kept Evaniese at bay. But, she never stopped being a part of his life. Now, she was going away *indefinitely*. The thought of never seeing her again broke his heart.

Evaniese's face wrinkled in sympathy. She was stirred by Nathan's reaction. He was obviously grieved about her impending departure. "Well, you of all people know all that I've been through since I started working here."

Evaniese was tempted to reach across the table, and cover Nathan's hand with hers. But, she desisted. Remembering his reaction to her displays of affection a while back, kept her from acting on her impulse. "I wish it hadn't come to this," she said softly, finding his sad eyes. "But, I can't continue to work here."

"I do know how much you've endured in this horrible place. So, I can't say that I blame you," Nathan's voice undulated, as he searched Evaniese's eyes. He issued a sad smile. "I *had* hoped we could see more of each other, since my recent move out to Amber Hills..." Nathan shrugged, and guffawed with a sense of resignation.

"We can always *call* and text," Evaniese said, not truly hopeful of that scenario. She and Nathan had *only* texted sporadically since exchanging phone numbers. Notwithstanding, they'd never had a *real* phone conversation. So, Evaniese doubted her absence from the hospital would make much of a difference in that regard.

Rather, Evaniese suspected, out of sight-at least for Nathan, would definitely mean out of mind. And, Evaniese was prepared to deal with that. Even if God had shown her Nathan was tied into her destiny, it was unclear as to how. Perhaps, Evaniese considered, they would meet again somewhere down the road. For now, she was encouraged, and excited about her blossoming relationship with El.

"Calling and texting sounds like a plan," Nathan said generically. "So, your last day is *this* upcoming Friday?" he quizzed, searching Evaniese's eyes from across the small table.

"Yes...," Evaniese said deliberately, giving Nathan an empathetic look. It was difficult to tell, but it seemed her resignation from the hospital affected him. "Will you come by the office on Friday to say goodbye?" Evaniese explored his honey eyes.

Nathan nodded and offered a faint smile. "Of course. I'll stop in on Friday," he affirmed. "I wish you nothing but the best in all of your future endeavors, Evaniese!"

"Thank you," Evaniese said quietly, fiddling with the straw in her iced coffee cup.

"Wow!" Nathan glanced at his watch. "I have to get back to the third floor. I'm admitting a patient on the east wing of the hospital."

"Oh, okay." Evaniese gave him an understanding look. "So, I guess I'll see you a little later," she said glumly. Evaniese wasn't sure why her impending disconnect from Nathan bothered her. After all, she'd held out hope for him to make a move for a very long time. Her dream hadn't panned out, so she had to let it go.

"Sure… Hopefully, we will see each other later. If not, we will catch up soon." Nathan stood to his feet.

"I'm sure we will," Evaniese agreed quickly. She figured he was pressed for time.

"Bye, Evaniese," Nathan said thickly, turning away.

"Bye, Nathan." Evaniese watched him rush out of the café.

Evaniese remained seated at the table, feeling conflicted. In spite of the sorrow and the misery she'd known in the past, God had given her a little chunk of happiness. El had a way of speaking to her heart, and lifting her up more than anyone else ever had. However, El was still a mystery man.

She and El had never actually seen each other. Thus, it was probably much too soon to contemplate a meeting. It was so ironic. The man who'd *seemed* accessible, turned out not to be, while the one who wasn't, actually was. That was the story of her life. She always seemed to have all of the ingredients, but could never quite bake the cake.

***

"I've been keeping a close eye on you since you were bold enough to move out to Amber Hills, Doctor Andrews," Brent told Nathan.

They were both at a medical seminar in downtown Amber Hills one late morning in June. The seminar was also a luncheon fundraiser.

Nathan was fixing himself a plate from the buffet table, when he heard Brent's voice. Brent was standing behind him, so Nathan made a startled turn. Sure enough, Brent Peterson was standing in close proximity. Brent was all decked out in a gray business dress suit. So, Nathan could only assume *he* was a benefactor or subsidizer of the event.

Nathan closed his eyes meditatively, and tried to temper his words before speaking to the irritating man. "And, good morning to you too, Mr. Peterson!" he said through gritted teeth, and forced a smile.

"Good *afternoon*, Doctor Andrews!" A cunning smile curved over Brent's lips. "It's a lovely day for such a worthy event, isn't it?" Brent stared all about at the beautiful well-manicured lawns, the floral gardens, and the ornately set tables.

"What is it that you want from me *now*?" Nathan set his plate on the buffet table, and turned around completely to face Brent.

"Why is it that you always *think* I want something?" Brent patronized, with a contrived expression on his face.

"You never just pop up without an agenda." Nathan sighed, frustrated. "Look, I'm through with your games. I've done everything you've asked." He held both hands up in a disarming manner. "I've stayed away from *your* girl."

"No, you haven't, Doctor Andrews." Brent was suddenly flustered. "You've been hanging around her, and trying to be *friends*. I happen to know you were all up in her face the other day at the hospital café. What part of *leave her alone* are you having trouble understanding?" Brent crossed his arms over his ample chest.

"I *have* left her alone. You really can't expect me to be rude to her." Nathan shook his head contrarily. "I *won't* hurt her no matter how much you've threatened me. Evaniese has been under the impression that *we're* friends from the very beginning.

"So, I refuse to rock the boat." Nathan's expression was solemn, and his eyes fell away from Brent's penetrating stare. "What difference does it make at this point? She's leaving Brookline in a couple of days."

"I know she's leaving the hospital. She expects you to come by her office on Friday to say goodbye, but that's *not* going to happen. Once Evaniese leaves the hospital, your connection to her ends."

Brent glowered condescendingly at Nathan. "That's precisely what I came here to tell you this afternoon. You and Evaniese have *already* said your goodbyes. So, please don't bother going by her office on Friday. In fact, stay away from her on her last day working through the hospital."

"I've already told her I would stop in to say goodbye," Nathan argued, incensed.

"Well, she's just going to have to think you're a no show," Brent exacted, unwaveringly.

"I don't know what your problem is, but Evaniese doesn't deserve to be treated this way," Nathan retorted. "And, from what *I* understand, *you've* been dating other women. How is it fair that you're still trying control everything in *her* life?" Daggers issued from Nathan's eyes, and aimed at Brent.

Brent's face turned ruddy. "What I do is *my* business. All you need to know is that Evaniese *belongs* to me."

"I'm not out for a war with you, but you need to make up your mind. Step up and tell Evaniese you love her, or leave her alone," Nathan delineated. "And, for the sake of all things sane, leave *me* alone as well. I'm not after your girl. I've made it clear to her that I'm a married man," his voice broke and tears shone in his eyes. "I've crushed Evaniese's heart in every way possible. And yet, that's not enough for you." Nathan shook his head, incredulous over the matter.

Brent was momentarily silent. Nathan's words had struck a chord. However, even if he knew Nathan Andrew's words were absolutely on point, he would never admit to it.

"Just as long as we're clear, Dr. Andrews," Brent said offhandedly. "Stay away from her," he emphasized. Picking up a glass of champagne from off the buffet table, he sipped from it. "What a beautiful day!" he declared, taking in the backdrop.

Nathan stared hard after Brent, as he watched the man turn and walk away. It was difficult to control his urge to tear into the man. Nonetheless, it occurred to Nathan that the days of having to deal with Brent Peterson were quickly coming to an end. What a dichotomy it was to be in such a serene setting, and yet feel so rattled and out of sorts.

***

"Ellis, wait...," Kierra called out. She was trying to catch up with him before he left the premier of their movie, *Inside Out*. It was a movie he and Kierra had worked on together last year. The premier was being held out at the grandiose Blue Shale Theater in West Hollywood. Celebrities were scattered throughout the entire locale, which was decked out for the opening night of the film. A sea of red carpet adorned the walkways. Kierra took to sprinting in order to catch up, because Ellis's gait towards the waiting limo was swift. "Ellis...," Kierra called out again.

Ellis made a sudden turn, and saw Kierra rushing toward him. His limo guy held the car door open. However, Ellis asked him to hang tight, because he didn't want to be rude to Kierra. She'd played his love interest in the movie. And, as predicted, the opening night was amazing! The film had scored an impressive 95% on *Rotten Tomatoes*. Moreover, critics had hailed it as a *must see*, giving it four stars. Ellis was both excited, and humbled that the movie had done so well on its opening weekend.

Ellis stood in front of the limo, and watched Kierra saunter over to him. The last thing he wanted was to lose his composure. For the past few weeks Kierra and Laura Morgan Fields had engaged in mortal combat in the battle to win his heart. What *they* and all of Hollywood didn't know was that his heart already belonged to someone else. Ellis was in love with *Evaniese Spencer*, who lived out in Amber Hills, Indiana.

He and Evaniese had never met. However, they'd been consistently chatting through the *Chat Channel* app for the past month or so. Ellis was properly in love for the very first time in his life, and it was something he wanted to protect. For that very reason, he refused to reveal the details of his new love interest to anyone. As it was, his life was already under a great deal of scrutiny. So, the last thing he needed was even more intrusion. What he and Evaniese shared was a clandestine love, and Ellis wanted to keep it that way, at least for a while.

"Whoa, there," Ellis said, as Kierra rushed into him.

She draped her arms about neck, and stared dreamily up into his eyes. "Are you all right, Kierra?" He gently maneuvered out of her potent grasp. Taking her by the shoulders, he searched her eyes intuitively.

"El, I thought you were going to hang out with me at the after party," Kierra reproached, frowning in displeasure.

"I'm afraid I really can't tonight, *Key*. I have a flight scheduled like…," Ellis glanced at his watch, "right now."

"El, this is *our* movie. We're supposed to be promoting it together," Kierra groused, staring at Ellis in skepticism. "This is the last night for you to pull a no show. Do you know you're *notorious* for not showing up to after parties, *Mr. Diamond Destiny Award winner*?" Kierra said scathingly, and rolled her eyes. Setting her hands on Ellis's shoulders, she massaged them seductively. "Ellis, why do you have to make everything so difficult?"

"Believe me, I'm *really* not doing it on purpose. By the way, at some point, I knew that I'd gain a reputation for *something*," Ellis said nonchalantly.

"Kierra, listen to me," he appealed seemingly conflicted, "this *has* to stop, honey. We've gone over it a million times. We're friends and colleagues in the industry." Ellis looked away for a moment, before finishing his train of thought. "I like you, *Key*. And, don't get me wrong... It means a lot that you care so much, but..."

"It isn't that way for you?" Kierra said densely, with glistening eyes. "You haven't even given us a chance, El." She shook her head, perplexed and hurt.

Ellis's face warped in compassion. "I care a lot about you, Kierra, you know that. But, I'm sorry I can't offer you my heart."

"Is it because of Laura Morgan Fields?" Kierra asked, cagily.

"No, not at all. Laura and I are also just friends. Well, at least I *thought* we were. She hasn't really spoken to me since the *Diamond awards*." Ellis gave Kierra a knowing look. "I *did* overhear your little powwow with her that night."

Kierra pulled back, and gasped in shock. "You heard us talking?" Embarrassment veiled her pretty face, and her cheeks flushed red.

Ellis nodded and guffawed. "I did. But, I can hardly describe what I saw that night as *talking*. Sadly, I'm not the only one who heard you. That's why I didn't bother going to *that* after party, in spite of my glowing win." Ellis's face wrinkled in urgency.

"El, I'm sorry about that night. I know I probably came off as some…"

"Crazed jealous girlfriend?" Ellis inserted humorously.

Kierra nodded. "Yeah, something like that… I'm really sorry, Ellis." Her eyes connected earnestly to his. "Now, you know just how much I like you," she admitted.

Ellis set his hands gently on Kierra's shoulders again, and explored her glistening eyes. "I like you a whole lot, Kierra, but that's as far as it goes. I think you're great, but-"

"Just not for you…?" Tears teemed over Kierra's eyelids.

"Not in that way, sweetheart," Ellis said, and tenderly caught a stray tear rolling down her cheek.

Kierra's face twisted in hurt, but she surrendered to a slow nod. "I get it… Still, Ellis, please come out to the party tonight?" She pursed her lips suppliantly.

Ellis shook his head contrarily, and offered her a genuine smile. Hunching down, he pressed a kiss to her cheek. "I'm afraid I've got to make that flight in just a few hours. So, I have to respectfully decline." Ellis cradled her face in his hand.

"Kierra, Ellis…," the press and the media gathered around the bustling red-carpet area. "Please, face this way. We want a good angle for these pictures," they entreated.

Ellis and Kierra posed for a number of pictures for the media. However, just then, one of their colleagues, A-list actor, Taggart Lane found them.

"Congratulations, Ellis!" Taggart said, and extended his hand to shake Ellis's.

"Thanks, Taggart!" Ellis said spiritedly, and heartily shook the man's hand. In Ellis's opinion, Taggart was an unpretentious actor and a standup guy.

"Kierra...," Taggart acknowledged, with reddened cheeks and wandering eyes.

"Hey, Taggart," Kierra said offhandedly, with her eyes fastened to Ellis the entire time.

"You were great as Reva North!" Taggart complimented Kierra, doing all he could to get her attention.

"You think so?" Kierra finally turned to address him.

"Ellis smiled sentimentally, seeing the way Taggart gawked at Kierra.

"Ellis, Taggart, Kierra, look this way...." The press and media hounded.

"You were absolutely amazing!" Taggart told Kierra, in an undulating tone of voice. In an unobtrusive manner, he searched her eyes.

"Thank you for saying that, Taggart! That means a lot coming from you," Kierra said sweetly, and offered him a sincere smile.

While chatting, the three simultaneously posed for pictures.

"Well, that's *my* cue," Ellis said minutes later.

"El...?" Kierra queried with an expressive look. "The party...?" she made a silent inquiry.

"Maybe, next time, *Key*," Ellis told her.

"Are you headed over to the after party?" Taggart asked Kierra, as he unabashedly sized up how breathtaking she looked in her sage-green sequined gown.

"What...?" Kierra questioned, startled by Taggart's direct question.

"The after party...?" Taggart cleared his throat, and steadied his gaze into Kierra's beautiful eyes. "Would you like to go with me?" He sighed, relieved to have gotten the words out.

"You want to go to the after party together?" Kierra asked, surprised.

"I would very much like to go together," Taggart emphasized.

Ellis smiled, and gave Kierra and approving nod.

"I guess, I will see you guys later," he affirmed, overjoyed to see the admiration on Taggart's face. The man was obviously smitten!

"Oh, all right...," Kierra acquiesced, still bewildered.

Taggart looped his arm through Kierra's, and led her away. However, Kierra kept looking back at Ellis. Ellis stood in front of the limo watching the pair walk off together. As soon as Taggart secured Kierra into a limo, Ellis slipped into his, and asked Bernard to take him home.

Ellis had taken the initiative to purchase a smaller house in Atlanta, Georgia in upscale area of Misty Morning. The decision was made for the sole purpose of entertaining Evaniese-that was whenever he revealed his true identity. Ellis planned on going down to Misty Morning that weekend to oversee the care of the new fifteen-room house.

Ellis already had a room designed for Evaniese, if and when she decided to visit. There was a gym, a home theater, a personal office and other perks. Everything Ellis did was with Evaniese in mind. He was head-over-heels in love! Evaniese only knew him as El. However, the more Ellis prayed on the matter, the more confirmation he gleaned that she could quite possibly be his person.

Ellis took a moment to access his phone on the way home that night. He wanted to tell Evaniese how excited he was about a certain project in his life which had paid off. The project of course was the opening night of his new movie *Inside Out*. Evaniese had no idea he was *Ellis Roman*, Hollywood actor. Ellis wanted to wait a while before filling her in on the ins and outs of his highly publicized life. However, at the moment, he just wanted to share the excitement of one of his projects gone right.

"Hello, my love. I miss you so much! I just wanted to share how excited I am about the business venture we talked about. Guess what, beautiful? It worked out, and I'm so happy! It feels so good to be able to share things with you..."

Tears shone in Ellis's eyes, as he expressed his feelings. As he sat in the back of the limo, he summed up the depths of his loneliness for such a very long time. Essentially, love was a concept foreign to him, but familiar to everyone else. However, at that point, Ellis felt as if love was almost within his grasp.

"I miss you so much, baby! Are you there?" Ellis wrote out through the app. "I miss you! I hope you're all right. I'm sorry your procedure was rescheduled again, but you did promise to fill me in on the details. It would mean so much to me..."

"El...?" Evaniese wrote out, excited. El's first set of messages had found her on the road, but she'd just pulled into her driveway. "Hi, my sweetie pie!" She littered the page with love and heart emoji's. "I'm so happy about your project! I told you it'd be great!

"I'm so happy for you, baby!" Evaniese gushed. Her heart inundated with appreciation and fondness for El. She was afraid to admit she was in love with him. It still seemed to be much too soon. However, Evaniese *felt* it. "I wish I could be there with you!" She filled up the page with kiss emoji's, as her heart swelled in affection.

"I wish you could be here too, baby. Thank you so much for always supporting me! I feel so blessed to have you in my life!" Tears escaped Ellis's eyes. "I love you, Evaniese!" Ellis wrote out, directly, shrinking back in shock over his own sense of vulnerability.

Tears were in Evaniese's eyes, as she read and contemplated El's words. She was momentarily speechless, as tears meandered down her cheeks. Remembering the humiliating moments she'd endured with Brent, Jeremy, and even with Nathan, Evaniese couldn't stop crying.

"Evaniese, are you there, baby? Are you okay, my love?" Ellis wrote out, frantic that she'd suddenly grown quiet. "I love you, baby!" he emphasized, posting a hundred love emoji's to the chatting page.

"I'm here, El," Evaniese texted. She paused for a moment, but then decidedly wrote out, "I love you too, El!" She filled up the page with hearts and kisses. Breathing spasmodically, she smiled through the tears.

Ellis surrendered to tears, as the limo's drone infiltrated the silent drive back over to the mansion. "I love you so much, baby!" he highlighted, and celebrated the fact that love had finally found him. God had been so good! There were still some missing puzzle pieces. However, without a doubt, Ellis knew he'd finally found the one his soul had longed for.

"I love you too, El!" Evaniese boldly stated.

"I love you more, baby!" Ellis inscribed emphatically. There was a hopeless smile on his face, and yet he was fighting back tears, because he was so in love. At last, his heart had found a safe haven!

***

"Yum...!" Evaniese declared, biting heartily into her I-Hop buttermilk pancakes. She, along with Ginger and Deanna, were having breakfast at the I-Hop located within the strip mall. They'd made plans to do a bit of shopping later. Then, they would see Ellis Roman's latest movie, *Inside Out*. Along with most women in America, all three were huge fans of Ellis Roman's. Ginger and Deanna decided to treat Evaniese as a sort of last hoorah, before she had to *fast* I-hop and some other goodies for a while.

It was a Saturday in the middle of July, two days before Evaniese submitted to the VSG surgery. Her first liquid diet had been cut short, because the procedure was pushed back a few times. This time around, Evaniese had fasted for twelve days, even Dr. Bergstrom and his staff had specified two full weeks. Evaniese *had* complied…at least for the most part.

However, on day twelve, she heeded God's directive to eat solid food. Having been instructed to eat, after twelve long days of drinking water, protein shakes, soup, and slurping Jell-O, Evaniese refused to argue with her heavenly father. The liquid diet had certainly taken its toll on her body. So, she was extremely grateful to be able to break the fast. She was also confident that the VSG would be a complete success.

As she sat there, she remembered her last shift at Brookline about a month ago. Sadly, no one from the admissions department even bothered giving her a thank you card, neither did they take a moment to acknowledge she was leaving. Essentially, she felt as if she'd been a ghost for the duration of her seven-year stint at the hospital.

Undoubtedly, there was bad blood with Paula…and probably even with Ann. Still, after suffering their abuse, Evaniese had expected a greater level of professionalism and grace. However, neither woman had risen to the occasion, or had tried to be the bigger person, so to speak. Evaniese didn't receive so much as a phone call from anyone from the department after her faithful service. There wasn't even one card in her mailbox, wishing her well in her future endeavors. No such courtesies were extended.

Even more puzzling, was that her *coworkers* in the *ER*, took the initiative to honor her. They were gracious enough to plan a surprise going away party, with catered food and presents for Evaniese. Evaniese found their accolade bizarre. For the most part, the nurses and the physician's assistants who worked through the ER, were hypocrites. They always smiled in her face, and talked horribly behind her back. But, no matter how backbiting the ER staff was, they'd exemplified a greater level of grace than those in her *own* department.

However, nothing shocked Evaniese more than Nathan failing to keep his word. He'd promised to stop in on her last day to say goodbye, but hadn't. In fact, Evaniese hadn't heard from him at all, not one phone call or text. Evaniese was indeed hurt and disappointed by Nathan's behavior, but she wasn't shattered. To the contrary, she was ready to chalk Nathan off as a learning experience, and to move on.

In fact, she wanted to put the past behind her altogether. And yet, Evaniese couldn't ignore what God had revealed about Nathan. He'd told her that the man was tied into her destiny. Evaniese knew, without equivocation, if God said it, it was true. He's not like men who often changed their minds. (Numbers 23:19)

Even so, at that juncture, Nathan Andrews was out of sight, and out of mind as far as she was concerned. Evaniese resolved not to think about him anymore. All she cared about was the impending surgery, and her blossoming relationship with El. He was still the mystery guy whom she talked to all the time through the *Chat Channel* app.

The situation was unconventional, but they'd both professed their love. Evaniese was in love with him. However, she had yet to discuss the details of her newfound love with Ginger and Deanna. Evaniese had no idea how her love for El radiated on her face. She beamed as she drizzled more blueberry syrup on her pancakes. Recounting the loving messages she exchanged with El, kept her heart and her countenance aglow.

"Evaniese, what's going on with you?" Ginger teased, playfully slapping Evaniese's hand from across the table. There was a curious expression on Ginger's face. "I get it. Those pancakes are *really* good, but I honestly can't see them being the reason for that smile on your face. Something's definitely up." Ginger scrutinized Evaniese peculiarly.

"Nothing's going on with me," Evaniese muttered unconvincingly, with reddened cheeks and wandering eyes.

"I didn't see it before, Ginger, but I do now. What's going on, Niecy?" Deanna crossed her arms cheekily over her chest, and stared inquisitively at Evaniese.

"What gives, girlfriend?" Ginger goaded mercilessly.

"You'd better tell us," Deanna prodded. "Is it the surgery? I know how exciting that is," Deanna commented, feigning excitement for Evaniese. Inwardly, she'd condemned, and had hexed Evaniese's impending surgery from the outset. In fact, she'd celebrated that the procedure had to be rescheduled twice.

Evaniese's looked from Ginger to Deanna with flushed cheeks. "I *am* excited about the surgery," she admitted, as she reflexively poked the pancakes on the plate with her fork.

"Well, it's normal to feel excited about the surgery! It's what you've always wanted, right?" Ginger established, forcing a smile. The very concept of Evaniese losing weight threatened her sanity. Ginger had taken measures to ensure that the WLS failed. So, she'd be microscopically monitoring Evaniese's progress, or *lack* thereof.

"Of course, it's exactly what I want," Evaniese spoke up. "It seems like I've been waiting an eternity to have the VSG. The months have certainly dragged on. Not to mention the fact that the date has been pushed back more than once." She shook her head inanely. "Having to repeat that horrible sleep study, then having Dr. Bergstrom cancel a few weeks ago, almost broke my spirit. I'm *so* glad God brought me through all of that." She smiled.

"'I'm happy that worked out for you too, Evaniese," Deanna affirmed. "Speaking of which, I'm also sorry about what happened with Nathan. I thought for sure he'd at least have the decency to say goodbye." She frowned in disapproval over Nathan's course of actions.

"Yeah, I thought he would too. Honestly, I'm not worried about Nathan right now." Evaniese stared passively down at her plate, trying to conceal her blush, and the joy bubbling up on the inside.

"What's going on, Niecy?" Ginger demanded this time. "You haven't stopped smiling since we've gotten here, and your cheeks are all *red*." Ginger's eyes fastened inquisitively on Evaniese.

"Something's definitely up with you, girlfriend, and you'd better start talking." Deanna gave Evaniese a daunting look.

Evaniese moved food around on her plate deliberately. However, she looked up from the task, and stared from Ginger to Deanna. "I think I might have met someone," she announced timorously, grinning.

"What...?" Ginger and Deanna questioned, stunned by the revelation.

"Evaniese Spencer, dish... Who is he? Do we know him?" Deanna jumped right in.

"How long have you been seeing this guy?" Ginger asked, sounding a bit hurt. "And, why is this the first time we're hearing about it?" She set her plate aside, and placed her hands insolently on her hips.

"Whoa, just a minute there." Evaniese held her right hand up haltingly. "I will answer your questions one at a time. And, Ginger," she addressed, "we've only been talking for a short while."

"Well, what are you waiting for?" Both Deanna and Ginger gave Evaniese expectant looks. "Spill..."

Transported and overwhelmed by love, Evaniese opened up about her relationship with El. She shared the ins and outs of chatting with *Elbert* through the *Chat Channel*. However, midway, Evaniese stopped sharing, and her heart dipped down to the floor. From the looks on her friends' faces, she perceived disapproval. "What's wrong?"

Ginger and Deanna gave each other befuddled stares. Inwardly, they hated to see Evaniese so happy. After all, *they* were the ones with cute boyfriends, who *always* represented for them. Evaniese was the one who yearned for companionship, but it always eluded her. She was always *close* but never quite there. Ginger and Deanna rather liked the fact that she was the fat and lonely one in their circle.

"Evaniese, do you even hear yourself?" Ginger asked, lowering at her.

"What?" Evaniese questioned, shaking her head in bafflement, as her heart crashed to the floor.

"This *El guy* sounds like a fake and a fraud. I'm sure you've heard of *catfishing*. It happens all the time on Instagram. Scammers create a personal pages, impersonate other people, and target lonely women," Ginger detailed, staring at Evaniese with a fake pertained expression on her face.

"Niece, I'm afraid Ginger's right. You just said you've only spoken to this El guy through *Chat Channel*. You've never met him, and have absolutely no idea what he looks like. Not to mention the fact that he hasn't even expressed a desire to come out here to meet you," Deanna criticized.

Bewildered and shocked, Evaniese kept shaking her head in denial, as tears streamed down her cheeks. Moments earlier, she was so excited to share her precious and *sacred* love story with her friends. However, she couldn't have predicted their adverse reaction. "He has a very demanding job," she defended.

"Well, do you *know* what he does for a living?" Ginger asked, frowning warily.

"He's in sales…," Evaniese said generically. By then, her thoughts were racing. "And, what you said isn't true, Deedee. El wants to be here on the morning of the surgery. We both agreed to have the day of the procedure be the first time we see each other in person," she disputed.

"Evaniese, I don't know what's going on here, but this *doesn't* sound good. It sounds as if this guy has an angle. Has he asked you for money? Usually, these scammers play women. They make them think they're in love just before asking for their bank account details," Deanna lectured. "Evaniese, can't you see it's a setup?" She grimaced in irritation.

"No, that's not right. El has *never* asked me for anything…" Fresh tears shone in Evaniese's eyes.

"Yet…," Ginger filled in. "He hasn't asked you for anything *yet*, Evaniese. That's because he's stringing you along. When he gets you exactly where he wants, you'd better believe he's going to ask… I think you should delete that app, and never chat with this guy again.

"He hasn't even shown you a *picture* of himself. He's asked you to call him El-as if that's not obscure enough." Ginger shook her head in skepticism. "Honestly, he sounds dangerous. There's no way he can be on the level. If a guy's keeping secrets, that's definitely a red flag. He's a scammer, and it's all just one big game. So, I think you should remove yourself from that equation."

"I hate to say this, but Ginger's right, Niecy." Deanna glowered in disquietude. "You really fell for him, didn't you?" she softened.

Even if she kept blinking them back, Evaniese's eyes brimmed over with tears. She nodded in the affirmative to Deanna's question. She was struggling with feelings of uncertainty, confusion but mostly hurt. The wound ran deep, because she'd never fallen so deeply for anyone. Opening up about her relationship with El, made her realize the level of her naiveté.

"Does this *El* guy know where you live?" Ginger asked, panicked.

"No, but I'm sure he knows her name, and that she lives out here in Amber Hills," Deanna pointed out.

"You can't honestly believe he'll come out here, and try to hurt me?" Evaniese asked, feeling even more befuddled.

"Let's hope for the best, honey. We're going to make sure that doesn't happen, because you're *shutting* it all down today." Ginger set her hand on Evaniese's from across the table. Her eyes flickered intently. "Do you hear me? It ends today. In fact, give me your phone," she demanded.

Startled, Evaniese pulled back. "That's not necessary, Ginger. I will take care of it," she avowed.

It killed her to hear so many negative reports about someone who'd come to mean the world to her. Evaniese found herself trembling. If she *had* to delete the app and cut ties with El, it was a loss she had to process all on her own.

"Promise me you'll stay away from this person," Deanna censured, staring intently into Evaniese's eyes. "I say *person* loosely. For all we know, it could be a woman. And, that woman could be pulling all of those strings. The aim for someone like that is to make unsuspecting people fall in love, and let their guard down," she formulated.

"I promise," Evaniese said, feeling totally lost.

"It's going to be okay, Niecy," Ginger reassured.

"Yeah, I know that." Evaniese forced a smile.

"Are you sure you're going to be okay?" Deanna tested.

"Fine...," Evaniese asserted.

"You want to take the rest of your breakfast home? We still have to hit the mall, and see the new Ellis Roman flick," Deanna inspirited.

"Suddenly, I'm not feeling very well," Evaniese said. "I just want to go home, and lay down for a while," she glumly announced.

"Evaniese, this is supposed to be *your* day, dedicated solely to *you*," Ginger argued.

"I know, but I just need to be by myself right now. The two of you should go ahead to the mall, and enjoy the movie for me." Evaniese issued a sad smile.

"Evaniese, I don't want you sad. That, *El person*, whoever, or *whatever* he is, is a real jerk! God has the perfect guy for you. You should forget about all of them; Brent, Jeremy and Nathan. But, as far as this El guy is concerned, he's definitely not the one." Ginger stroked Evaniese's hand from across the table.

"Yeah, sweetie. Trust me. You're going to find someone who gets you, and who loves everything about you," Deanna heartened.

"Sure...," Evaniese said, with very little animation.

"Are you sure about the movie...?" Ginger quizzed. "I mean, it is after all, *Ellis Roman*," she enticed.

"I'm sure... Thanks for breakfast, guys." Evaniese instantly stood to her feet. "I'll call you a little later." She slipped out of the booth.

"Okay, honey." Deanna's face was veiled in commiseration.

Evaniese had only walked a few feet away from the table.

But, Ginger called out to her, "He's a *fake*, Niecy, but God's got the *real* hookup for you." Her face warped in sympathy. "And, it probably won't be long before you meet him."

Evaniese nodded quietly, doing all she could not to bolt. All she wanted was to take off. She wanted to run away where no one would find her. However, with as much composure as she could muster, she deliberately walked out of the I-Hop.

***

Later, back at home, Evaniese alighted from off her knees. She'd spent the entire afternoon in prayer, crying out to God for help and strength. Sharing her secret with Ginger and Deanna earlier on, had left her with a splintered heart. She was still reeling, hurt by their reaction as a result of her professed connection to El. Evaniese had no idea what do to. She trusted God to give her direction. Though, she was unsure of God's will on the matter.

What she *did* know was that her heart was shattered, and she couldn't stop crying. Her surgery was scheduled for that upcoming Monday. And, by all accounts, it should have been one of the happiest times of her life. She was finally going to have a tool set in place to help her manage her weight.

However, what she felt was brokenhearted. As it would seem, the man she'd fallen for on Instagram, whom she'd chatted with regularly, was some kind of scammer. From the outset, El had been secretive about a number of things. Even if he said he loved her, there was very little she knew about his work, his family or his friends.

It resonated that perhaps El was keeping her in the dark by design. Evaniese felt torn, because it really didn't matter all of the strikes against El. She was head-over-heels in love! Nevertheless, she had to be wise, and give credence to the things her friends had pointed out. And yet, Evaniese had no idea how to cut ties with him. She couldn't even bring herself to delete the app from off her phone.

Dejected, she drifted into the adjourning bathroom in her bedroom, and turned on the water faucet. Massaging a wash cloth over her face, she gently brushed away the caked-on tears. Breathing spasmodically, she tried to reign in the emotions to no avail. Pulling her lengthy hair back into a ponytail, she stared into the bathroom mirror, and her face warped in misery again.

Plunging deeper into a private world of despair, Evaniese's heart jumped, when the notification bell for the *Chat Channel* went off. The phone was in the bedroom on the bed. Evaniese shuddered, and her heart lashed, as she stepped out of the bathroom.

The notification bell resonated, as she took steps closer to the phone. It seemed as if El had a lot to say that afternoon. As if the phone had a life all its own, and was capable of jumping at her and causing pain, Evaniese inspected it warily. The bell just kept going off, and notifications from El littered her lock screen. Fresh tears teemed over in her eyes, as she picked up the phone. Evaniese set down on the bed. With trembling fingers, she put in her password.

Shakily clicking on the icon for the *Chat Channel* app, her heart throbbed to read all of the things EL had to say that afternoon.

"Hi, beautiful! I just wanted to say hello this afternoon, and to let you know I'm thinking about you. I miss you so much, baby! I know we spoke just this morning, but even if we spent the entire day talking, I would still miss you the moment we said goodbye.

"How are you doing, baby? I can only imagine how excited you are about the surgery on Monday morning! I'm excited too, but only because I know it's what you've always wanted. I love you so much! It doesn't matter if you're a size two or a size twelve.

You're so damn beautiful, I will *always* be in love with you, Evaniese Spencer! Baby, are you there? Can't you hear the bell going off? I miss you, baby! I miss you so much! When we don't connect, there are times it feels as if I just can't breathe…" EL filled the page with hearts, and other love-themed emoji's.

"Alright, my love, I guess we'll catch up a little bit later. I hope you're safe and smiling wherever you are. You're always on my mind. I love you, Evaniese-more and more every day!" More loving emoji's followed.

Evaniese trembled keenly, and her face warped in sadness. With the phone cradled in her hand, she was all set to respond to EL. After all, this had been the routine from the beginning. Fundamentally, she was an addict trying to resist her drug of choice. It was sheer torture.

"God, please help me. You never told me that EL was *one* of the men tied into my destiny." Tears continued to brim over her eyelids. "Maybe, I went on this little adventure on my own, and this is your way of pulling the reigns back, and helping me come to my senses."

She kept shaking her head in denial. "Lord, this hurts. I feel so strongly for this man…*whoever* he might be. Please, strengthen me in this situation. Help me forget all about him. Even if we've never met, it still hurts so badly. I doubt it would hurt any less, if we had a conventional relationship. Please, help me, Lord…"

Evaniese set the phone on silent mode, and set it to the right-hand side of her pillow. Slinking underneath her comforter, she allowed herself to cry without intermission. She still didn't have the strength to delete the app. Doing away with the app, would also mean doing away with El, and Evaniese couldn't bring herself to do that.

However, she silenced the phone, so that she'd be deaf to the notification bell for El's messages. It was also a way to temporarily silence the internal drone of pain searing like forceful winds. Contrarily, Evaniese considered, if her *boyfriend* was only an app on her phone, maybe Ginger and Deanna were right. It wasn't something worth holding on to, even if she was *in love with the app.*

***

"This is going to hurt just a little, but it should be fairly quick," the nurse told Evaniese early Monday morning on July 18th.

Ginger had taken the day off from work to be there on the morning of Evaniese's surgery. Having only secured half a day off from work, Deanna would be along sometime in the afternoon. Evaniese and Ginger had gotten to the hospital super early.

Evaniese had registered through the pre-surgical unit. So, she already had an ID band on her wrist. Now, this was the part she hated. The nurse was trying to put in the IV. A few veins surfaced on her left hand. The nurse pricked each one she saw to find the right one. Before long, the needle when through a vein on her left hand. Soon after, a piece of adhesive tape covered the throbbing area. Evaniese closed her eyes in order to process the pain.

Ginger flinched, seeing the look of discomfort on Evaniese's face. "Are you okay, sweetie?" She reached over, set her hand on Evaniese's right hand, and stroked soothingly on it. "That *had* to hurt."

"I think I was dreading that part of the process more than the actual surgery," Evaniese admitted. Everything else was a distraction at this point. She'd spent the entire weekend in tears, because she hadn't connected to EL. It took all of the courage she had not to respond to his messages.

Feigning nonchalance was challenging, because EL had left over a hundred messages. He'd unabashedly reminded her over and again how much he loved and missed her. Just last night, Evaniese finally found the courage to delete the app from her phone. Moreover, she'd deleted her Instagram account, and had blocked *Fan4ever* from the comment section of her YouTube channel.

As far as she was concerned, taking those drastic measures, was the only way she could let go of *this person* completely. Since cutting El off, Evaniese had felt like someone only going through the motions. She was conditioned to keep moving and breathing. It didn't matter how heartbroken she was at that juncture, this was a day she'd anticipated for close to a year. She'd moved along from one medical clearance to the next for the sake of the surgery. Furthermore, she'd watched so many YouTube videos on people who've sworn by the VSG. For the most part, they all had one thing in common. They'd all morphed from a caterpillar to a butterfly.

Evaniese hoped to enjoy the same kind of success. So, in spite of the brokenness and the emptiness she felt over losing someone she truly loved, she had to find the strength to bask in this moment. After all, it was her reward after working seven long years through the ER of Brookline Hospital. The consolation prize was using their medical insurance to do something for herself, and to improve her quality of life.

"You okay, Niece?" Ginger's eyes narrowed into Evaniese's in concern.

Evaniese pasted a smile to her face. "I'm okay." Her face wrinkled in discomfort. "If only I can take my mind off of how much the IV hurts." She stared down at her left hand.

"You should tell the nurse when she comes back. It won't be too much longer before Dr. Bergstrom comes in. Then, you'll be under anesthesia," Ginger detailed, rubbing affectionately on Evaniese's arm. "So, you should definitely tell the nurse before then." Ginger's rubber smile returned. She had to at least *pretend* to be happy for Evaniese. "Are you excited?"

Evaniese nodded, grinning. "I *am* excited, Ginny. Not that I'm excited about eighty percent of my stomach being cut out, but I am excited for what's to follow."

Evaniese's eyes were sad, as she *attempted* to convince herself that the surgery was the epitome of all that mattered in her life. Regardless, EL still remained on the forefront of her mind. It was impossible to forget about him.

She couldn't help thinking that, as he'd promised, he would have come out to Indiana. EL had expressed enthusiasm over being there with her that morning. Regret overwhelmed Evaniese, as she wondered if he would have shown up. Her lifelong dream of being able to manage her weight was about to come true. And yet, her heart was fractured, because she was disconnected from El.

"Yeah, before long you're going to be *Skinny Minnie.*" Ginger laughed nervously, and stared all about the room.

The very thought of Evaniese becoming thin created inner angst for Ginger. Just a few days ago, she'd revisited the spiritualist at the occult store off of Route 28. Ginger had to reinforce the hex she put on Evaniese months ago. It wasn't something she could risk.

Evaniese guffawed and chortled. "I seriously doubt I'll be skinny. I just want to feel comfortable in my own skin, and be able to wear a nice pair of jeans. Do you know what I mean?" Evaniese's face furrowed in earnestness.

"Yeah, I totally get that. But, you're gorgeous, Evaniese! You've always been gorgeous!" Ginger's hand brushed sensitively over Evaniese's arm.

"Thank you for saying that, Ginger, and thanks for being here with me this morning."

"Of course..." Ginger gave a dismissive wave of the hand. "Where else would I be? By the way, have you heard from that guy?" Ginger did a total one eighty.

"Oh, the guy we talked about on Saturday?" Evaniese momentarily looked away. She kept her eyes on the IV on her hand just to avoid eye contact with Ginger. Ginger didn't need to know how brokenhearted she truly was.

"Yeah, Niece...*that EL guy*." Suspicion shaded over Ginger's face, and she stared cagily at Evaniese. "Have you heard from, or chatted with him?"

Evaniese looked up and forced a smile. "He did message me quite a few times last week, but I deleted the *Chat Channel* app. I blocked him on the comment section of my YouTube, and I deleted my Instagram," Evaniese said with a wavering voice, in spite of trying to sound brave.

"That's great, honey! Good job! Trust me, it's for the best." Ginger nodded in approval. "If he never showed you a picture of himself, and kept you in the dark about the important things, he's a total fake."

Evaniese nodded absently in concurrence, even if her heart hurt even more than the IV on her hand. She swallowed the chunk lodged in her throat. "Yeah, I get it. You're right, Ginny." Evaniese shrugged and guffawed. "I don't know what I was thinking. I guess, I just *wanted* it to be true." Her eyes wandered away from Ginger's intent stare.

"That's all right, honey." Ginger gave Evaniese a sympathetic look. "He sounds like a real charmer that one. There are people out there who know how to hit where it hurts." She set her left hand on her heart.

"Yeah, I guess so," Evaniese dodged, trying to keep a stiff upper lip.

What she really wanted was for Ginger to drop the subject. Evaniese looked over at her phone. "Why haven't they texted me yet?" she eluded, bringing up her mom and her sister.

"What time did they say they'd be here?" Ginger asked, puzzled.

"My mom said she and Bethany would be here by noon."

Her mom and sister were coming from Pennsylvania. Evaniese figured they'd be in Amber Hills, after the procedure, when she was wheeled into the recovery room. Seeing them again would definitely lift her spirits.

Evaniese hadn't visited her family out in Pennsylvania in months. Her mom and sister decided to surprise her at the last minute. In spite of her crumbling heart, because so much was going on, Evaniese was grateful for less time to obsess about El.

"Niece, are you scared?" Ginger asked, on a more serious note.

Evaniese shook her head contrarily. "I'm not. I've prayed about this for close to a year, and God has promised to walk me through it. Besides," Evaniese smiled, "I'll be under anesthesia, so that *alone* makes me feel *brave*."

Ginger laughed. "That's right. In a little while, you're going to wake up, and realize *something's* different," she added humorously.

"I'm *so* ready to get this over with." Evaniese sighed.

Just then, through the glass slot of her hospital room door, Evaniese saw Dr. Bergstrom. He'd arrived just in time to perform the procedure. "Dr. B's here!" she announced cheerily. "Yay!"

Ginger laughed. "Yay! The man who's going to perform the surgery is here," she teased. "He's going to cut my stomach out. That's definitely worth cheering about!" She winked at Evaniese.

Evaniese laughed earnestly. "As a matter of fact, it *is*," she rose to the occasion.

For the first time in days, she felt hopeful. Since stopping the chats with El, she'd felt an extreme sense of disconnect to everything. It was unnatural to fall in love, only to sever all ties with the object of affection. Nevertheless, this was the day she'd prayed about, and had waited on for such a long time. So, Evaniese resolved to relish in the victory of this dream come true, even if it was with a splintered heart.

Moments later, Evaniese was wheeled over to the OR on a gurney. It was time to prep for the procedure. She quivered on the rolling bed, because the expansive room was chilly.

"Are you all right, honey?" one of the nurses asked Evaniese. The PA, who'd be helping Dr. Bergstrom, had just administered the anesthesia.

"I *am* a little cold," Evaniese admitted, trembling. Suddenly, fear and panic wanted to set in. However, Evaniese had already committed the surgery to God. Ultimately, her life was in his hands, and she was under his care. But then again, Evaniese didn't have a chance to reevaluate her decision. Before long, she slipped into another realm, a dimension of utter solitude and silence. Even in her subconscious mind, she trusted God with her whole heart, and had faith he would carry her through the process unscathed. After all, he'd promised to do just that.

Chapter Nine

In the new house out in Misty Morning, Ellis retreated to his private den. It had taken quite a few trips out to the town, but the house was completely furnished. Contractors and Interior designers had worked for months to bring Ellis's vision for the house to life. And, he was pleased with the way in which they'd honored his wishes.

It was a chilly night in October. The menacing onyx skies drizzled angrily on the terrain. Thunder clapped ominously, and lighting flashed in the vista, as Ellis stared out of the expansive picture window. His tenor matched perfectly with the weather. He found it difficult to stop the flow of tears streaming down his cheeks.

Essentially, the walls were closing in. Evaniese had pulled away close to four months ago. She'd removed any trace of their connection from the *Chat Channel*. Moreover, she'd either blocked, or deleted much of her social media platforms. Ellis had hoped to be there for Evaniese on the morning of her surgery. However, just one day before her procedure, Ellis's mom called to share sad news. Omar Ellis Roman, Ellis's dad, was diagnosed with pancreatic cancer.

Ellis had flown immediately out to Connecticut to be there with his family. And, he'd supported them until the very end. Ellis was there during the months in which his dad battled the disease. However, just days ago, Omar Roman had succumbed to the illness, compelling his family to say goodbye. Now, Ellis was back at the house he'd bought with Evaniese in mind.

In his absence, the laborers had done everything to specification. In fact, they'd exceeded his expectations. The house was totally live-in ready. However, none of it mattered. Evaniese was no longer a part of his life. Ellis received an outpour of support from his Hollywood affiliates. They sent flowers, cards and financial gifts to his family. Furthermore, they'd inundated his social media platforms with their condolences over the loss of his father.

Regardless, Evaniese was the *one* person Ellis hoped would have reached out. The woman he loved had pulled away, and removed herself from the equation. It was the very first time in his life where he had absolutely no idea what to do next. He'd texted Evaniese for months, to no avail. Ellis was still trying to figure out what he did wrong. The notion that he'd in some way offended her troubled him.

Evaniese had turned away months ago. Yet for Ellis, it felt just like yesterday. Tears snaked down his cheeks, and created lonely tracks. The way he longed for and missed Evaniese was indescribable. Through the picture window, lightening flashed. Thunder also crashed so loudly it reverberated. The turbulence impaled his tender and bleeding heart.

"God, I don't know where I went wrong, but I've lost her," Ellis shared his heart. "I love her so much, Lord! I thought I'd be able to move on, but I've been frozen. I haven't been able to function since she pulled away."

Ellis buried his face in his hands. "I got this house for *her*. I wanted to provide a safe place for us to be together. I didn't want to expose her to the craziness of my life out in L.A.

"What am I supposed to do, Lord? I've never felt this way about anyone."

On impulse, Ellis reached for his phone, and messaged Evaniese through the *Chat Channel* app. Realistically, he knew it was a losing battle, but texting her made him feel in some way still connected to her.

"Baby, where are you? Please, don't shut me out. Talk to me...," Ellis entreated for the umpteenth time. "Baby, please..." Ellis filled the page with sad-faced emoji's.

"Lord, she won't answer me. You told me she's the one. I wouldn't feel so strongly if she wasn't *my* person. I was lonely for such a long time, and you promised to answer..."

Ellis remained silent for a moment. There was an impression from God's Holy Spirit. *"I know how strongly you feel about Evaniese. You're just going to have to go after her. Right now, she's struggling with a great deal of fear and insecurity. Do everything in your power to find her, and let her know everything's all right."* Those words resonated for Ellis.

"But how do I reconnect to her?" Ellis questioned. "She's shut me out of her life completely."

However, this time around, the answer came in loud and clear. Ellis was suddenly inundated with ideas of how to bridge the gap with Evaniese. Reaching out to her on Instagram was a dead end. So, Ellis thought about changing his profile name on YouTube in order to access her channel again. But, Evaniese hadn't uploaded a video quite in a while. Ellis was eager to contact her, even on that very night.

Then, something occurred to him. He could fly out to Amber Hills, Indiana in disguise. He was connected to a number of makeup artists, and they had the wherewithal to make him look totally unrecognizable. Upholding anonymity whenever he traveled was paramount. Ellis had Evaniese's full name, and knew that she lived in the town of Amber Hills. Moreover, he knew she was a former employee of Brookline Hospital. One way or another, he was determined to find her. Love was such a rare gift! So, if fighting to keep it was something he had to do, he would do so staunchly. There was no way he could give up, because he loved Evaniese with all of his heart.

***

Evaniese sat at a table at the Blue Papaya Restaurant in downtown Amber Hills. Perusing the menu, she sipped water from a glass, as she waited on Nathan. The restaurant was about a mile away from Brookline Hospital. Nathan was currently there finishing up a shift. He and Evaniese agreed to meet at the restaurant when his shift was over. It was the first week in 2017, and Evaniese felt like a brand-new person! She was six months post-op, and had already lost in excess of one hundred pounds.

The first few days after the VSG Surgery were the hardest. Evaniese had felt displaced, and wondered what on earth she'd done to her body. Essentially, she felt like an experiment gone wrong in some madman's laboratory. It took some time to finally be able to hold down any food, even foods as soft as scrambled eggs. In the beginning, anything with a texture was too abrasive for her new stomach.

She also had to get used to not drinking half an hour prior to, or after meals. Nevertheless, now she was finally getting the hang of how to manage the Gastric Sleeve and her new body. For Evaniese, smiling whenever she looked in the mirror was bittersweet. Her heart was still in shards, because she was forced to relinquish the illusive love she shared with El.

Even if there was a sense that the entire thing was a fantasy, and nothing good could have come from their connection, Evaniese couldn't stop wanting to hear from him. There was a constant desire to chat with him. No one had ever been as loving, and Evaniese missed that. Getting through the holiday season without him was brutal. But, by the grace of God, Evaniese had taken one day at a time. She'd shed so many tears, but God had kept her alive.

It was all so cruel. She was finally looking the way she'd always wanted to. However, the great love of her life wasn't around to see her come to this epiphany. There was just one ray of sunlight in her overcast skies. After over six months of no communication, Nathan had finally texted. Alluding to missing her, he asked to meet for lunch.

Once again, Evaniese dared to believe God was answering her prayer. She forgave Nathan for not stopping in to say goodbye on the last day she worked through the hospital. Although she couldn't say for sure, perchance Nathan was ready to start dating after all. He'd told Evaniese how everything had changed-and not in a good way, since she left the hospital. It seemed, Nathan was speaking a totally different dialectal. So, Evaniese was enlivened of getting their relationship off the ground.

"Evaniese..?" Nathan had a questioning look on his face, when he breezed into the restaurant. His eyes dilated to the size of mini pancakes, as he sized her up.

Evaniese's thoughts were a million miles away. So, Nathan's sudden appearance had startled her. She stood reflexively to her feet, and grinned excitedly to see him again. "Nathan!" she exclaimed.

Nathan set his hands on Evaniese's waist, and scrutinized her. "Wow! Look at you!" he raved, unable to stop gawking. He kept shaking his in disbelief. "You look amazing!" His eyes remained distended.

"Thank you," Evaniese said modestly.

She had no idea why her eyes kept wandering from Nathan's intent stare. Evaniese momentarily sized herself up in her jeans, her powder blue sweater and stylish blue UGG Boots, concluded how nice she looked. Evaniese had the hems of her jeans tucked into the boots. Also, her freshly washed and set hair, tumbled gracefully over her shoulders and back.

Nathan took Evaniese's hands in his, and continued gaping mercilessly at her. "You are even more beautiful than I remember! How much weight have you lost?" he inquired, trying to move past his initial shock.

"What I *didn't* tell you before I quit my job at the hospital, was that I had planned on having weight loss surgery," Evaniese told Nathan, as he guided her back over to her seat.

She couldn't help noticing that Nathan himself had taken off a few pounds. Upon meeting him, Evaniese always thought he was a dreamboat. Nevertheless, she was surprised to see him nursing a full-on beard and moustache. Even so, she couldn't say that the look didn't suit him. She snickered because of Nathan's reaction over seeing her again. The same shocked expression remained on his face, as he continued gawking at her. Irrefutably, he was surprised to see how much she'd changed.

"I had no idea you wanted to have weight loss surgery. I mean, don't get me wrong. I'm glad you did, because it's definitely working for you!" Nathan gestured, showcasing Evaniese's new look. "You took a huge risk, and it paid off bigtime."

"Thanks," Evaniese said unassumingly, and forced a smile.

Up until that moment, she and Nathan hadn't been in close enough proximity for her to see the *stupid* platinum wedding band on his finger. Seeing the ring again, made her heart dip down to the floor. Yet and still, she resolved to remain cavalier.

When Nathan had asked to meet for lunch, Evaniese was sincerely hopeful of a shift in their relationship. However, that didn't seem to be the case after all.

"How have you been?" Evaniese asked, with a taut smile pasted to her face. Even if it killed her, she resolved to make the best of their lunch date. She refused to give Nathan the satisfaction of hurting her again

"I'm good, Evaniese," Nathan affirmed. "I'm obviously not as good as *you* are." He kept shaking his head dubiously. "You're like a completely different person!" he uplifted.

"I *feel* like a completely different person," Evaniese echoed. She pushed back into her chair, and brushed her fingers through her lengthy curly mane. "Honestly, it's been quite a journey to get here," she admitted.

"I can only imagine. Care to share what your journey has been like?" Nathan propped his face with his right palm.

"Wow," Evaniese laughed and guffawed, "how much time do you have?"

"We actually have the rest of the afternoon to talk if you'd like. My shift just ended, and I'm in no rush to get home," Nathan said, openly admiring everything about Evaniese.

Truth be told, he was completely stunned to see how beautiful she looked! The way he'd behaved before, had absolutely nothing to do with a lack of interest or desire for Evaniese. Brent Peterson was-and probably still remained the culprit.

"Well, what about your wife...?" Evaniese brought up, beating Nathan to the punch. "I'm sure she's probably waiting for you."

It was Evaniese's way of playing damage control. Dropping the hatchet on her own heart by bringing up Nathan's mysterious wife, was a lot better than waiting for Nathan to do it.

"Oh, my wife? Right...," Nathan said, hesitantly, as he simultaneously studied the platinum band on his finger. He then stared Evaniese directly in the eyes. "She's fine. I gave her a call a little while ago. By the way, we're expecting our first child," he announced, sounding melancholic for one reason or another.

Evaniese flinched in shock, but she tried her best to cover it up. On impulse, she wanted to run away, but rather kept a controlled smile on her face.

"That's nice. How far along is she?" she dared to ask, staring brazenly into Nathan's eyes, while concurrently blinking back tears.

"She's about sixteen weeks," Nathan said without skipping a beat.

Inwardly, he felt like a total heel for continuing the charade. However, it was the only way he could *see* Evaniese without running into complications with Brent Peterson. Nathan had already come to terms with the fact that Evaniese was never going to be his. He *had* indeed recently met, and had started *dating* someone else. Nevertheless, he'd asked Evaniese to lunch for the sake of closing the chapter on their story once and for all.

"That's amazing!" Evaniese pretended to be happy. "Do you know if it's a girl or a boy?" she asked offhandedly.

"We're expecting a little girl," Nathan said without batting an eyelash.

"Wow! You're having a little girl," Evaniese affirmed. She mulled over the prospect, as she nervously played with the rim of her water glass.

The waiter strolled back over to their table just then. "Are you ready to order drinks?" he asked with a cordial smile.

"Evaniese, what would you like to drink?" Nathan asked.

Evaniese frowned in conflict. However, she kept trying to get her face to agree with her perky performance. "Raspberry iced tea," she said plainly.

"I'll have the same," Nathan looked up, and addressed the waiter.

"Very good." The young man set menus on their table before walking away.

Evaniese's smile was so artificial, it was a wonder her cheeks hadn't fallen off, as Nathan continued to gush about his pregnant wife. Supposedly, he and wife had already picked out a name for their baby girl. They'd chosen the name, *Ava Joy*. Evaniese refused to allow Nathan's words to break her heart.

Because she'd felt coerced to say goodbye to El, Evaniese had thought that God was on the cusp of fulfilling his promise to her with Nathan. Nevertheless, just then while sitting at the restaurant, she realized her misapprehension. It was just another closed door, and a dead end. Nathan continued to maintain he was a married man. Worse yet, he and his wife were expecting a baby. Evaniese measured, even if she *looked* and *felt* like a brand-new person, some of the former miseries had remained unaltered.

Hence, she was no longer considered obese. In as far as her clothes, she wore between a size six and eight. For the first time in a while, she actually felt good about herself. Her self-esteem was up, but her spirits were extremely low. And, in light of all she'd endured with Nathan, Evaniese recognized that there was still one thing she wanted more than a slim body. That one missing puzzle piece was love. For a while-or so it seemed, she'd found it with El, only to have it swept away. The sad part was that she was still in love with him.

And yet, she was beginning to understand that their connection had been one big illusion. Something unprecedented had occurred. Nathan had *finally* asked her out. Evaniese had earnestly hoped it was a turning point, but that was clearly not the case. As Evaniese sat there with Nathan, they talked like old friends. All the same, she couldn't help thinking that the scenario was the story of her life. She was always dressed up with no place to go.

***

The mall was mobbed with patrons early one Saturday afternoon. The smell of Cinnabons and other mouth-watering confections, wafted in the air, as Evaniese, Ginger and Deanna bustled through the crowd.

"Hey, there, beautiful!" a very handsome, but rather young Caucasian kid gave Evaniese the once over, openly flirting with her.

"Hi," Evaniese said demurely, with reddened cheeks.

Her heart fluttered in apprehension and uncertainty. It was weird having such a young guy ogling, but Evaniese was getting used to it. It was the kind of attention she'd gotten since taking off the weight.

"Did you see that cutie flirting with Niecy?" Deanna asked Ginger, with a quizzical expression on her face.

"Yeah, I know," Ginger said plainly. "Evaniese has been getting that a lot lately," she said, sizing Evaniese up with a cynical expression.

"Why didn't you talk to him?" Ginger asked Evaniese. "It seems, they *all* want to talk to *you* nowadays," she said sardonically. The acerbity in her tone was subtle, but nonetheless present.

Ginger was tired of Evaniese getting all the attention. It was exactly as she'd predicted. Now that Evaniese was thin just like her and Deanna, she was the frontrunner. Men seldom looked at her and Deanna anymore. It was *all* about Evaniese.

"He's like half my age," Evaniese argued, with flushed cheeks.

Getting so much attention from men-even painfully younger ones, was something Evaniese still had trouble processing. Although she was flattered, her heart and mind were elsewhere. She still thought about, and yearned for the kind of relationship she'd had with El. Her brief association with him, made her forget the misery she'd known with Brent, Jeremy and Nathan. During her brief relationship with El, Evaniese hardly thought about the other three.

That morning, Evaniese was at the mall to buy some new outfits. Because her old clothes no longer fit, she was constantly buying new things. Even if she was a bit distracted, she wanted to remain in the moment with her friends. Because of their initial reaction, Evaniese never brought up El to Ginger and Deanna again. They had no idea how much she still cried over losing the only man who'd found a unique way of touching her heart.

"Well, you need to step it up, and talk to some of these guys. They're totally into you," Deanna told Evaniese.

Inwardly, Deanna stewed in jealously and resentment, because Evaniese was actually slightly smaller than she was at that point. She wondered why the curses she'd intoned had failed.

The weight loss surgery was working wonderfully for Evaniese! She'd lost over one hundred pounds. Deanna hated the fact that things were working out. Nevertheless, she wouldn't stop trying to bring Evaniese down until she accomplished her end goal. There was no way Evaniese was going to get more *play* than her and Ginger.

"Well, I can't talk to *everyone* I see, guys. That special someone *has* to be in the will of God," Evaniese reasoned, as they all walked into "Fringes," a department store for trendy fashion.

"It's high time you put all three of those *losers* behind you," Ginger said, drifting over to peruse dresses on a clothes rack.

"Yeah, well, I'm waiting to see what God does next," Evaniese affirmed, as she browsed the store's selection of jeans.

As Evaniese inspected the items on sale, Ginger checked out tops at the other end of the shop. All the while, she kept iterating incantations. The curse was for the sole purpose of making Evaniese regain all her weight. For Ginger, it was crushing to see Evaniese so thin. Evaniese was so beautiful it was unsettling! The success of the WLS was extremely unnerving.

At the Wiccan conference she and Deanna attended last year, they'd learned how to cite invocations in order to put curses on people. Moreover, they were taught how to invoke dark forces to cast spells. So, Ginger was practicing that now. She seethed in jealousy and bitterness, watching Evaniese pick out her skinny jeans. Evaniese definitely had a glow of joy about her. She seemed to be in a very good place, and had a new sense of confidence about her. Contrariwise, Ginger was there to ensure that the tides shifted again.

"What do you think about these?" Evaniese strolled over to find Ginger, holding up three different pairs of jeans.

"Why don't you try them all on? I'll have a better idea once I see you in them," Ginger said with a pretentious smile glued to her face.

"Okay," Evaniese acceded. She drifted away in order to find the dressing rooms.

"Ginny, I'll be right back." Deanna drifted back over to Ginger. She'd just browsed over the shoe selections.

"Where are you going, Dee?" Ginger frowned.

"I'm going to call Scott," Deanna said, referring to her boyfriend. "We're going out later."

However, Deanna lied to Ginger. She wasn't going to call Scott. On the first-floor level of the mall, she'd seen a spiritual reading booth. She wanted to drop in to see if they could help out with her current dilemma. The conundrum was called, *former fat friend syndrome.* Evaniese was no longer fat, and she was getting the *big head,* so to speak. Deanna considered it *her responsibility* to play damage control.

"All right," Ginger acceded. "We'll text you to let you know when we're leaving the store," she told Deanna.

"No worries. I'll see you guys in a bit." Deanna dashed out of the shop.

Ginger was both impatient and annoyed, as she waited for Evaniese to come out of the dressing room. Irritated, she tried to busy herself by checking out the store's formal attire.

"What do you thing, Ginny?" Evaniese floated out of the dressing room, wearing a pair of black designer jeans, stylish boots, and a beautiful cranberry-colored cardigan.

Ginger flinched. Her heart fell in discontent, as she contemplated Evaniese. Evaniese looked amazing! And, Ginger felt nauseated. It was disconcerting to see how Evaniese had morphed into an exquisite butterfly. With her lengthy highlighted brown hair, her creamy butterscotch skin, she looked like an angel! Ginger's heart knotted in envy. "You look amazing!" she said through gritted teeth, and a phony smile.

"You like it?" Evaniese brushed her hands self-consciously over her clothes. "I really didn't think I'd be able to get into the jeans, but they fit perfectly." Evaniese postulated with a sense of both insecurity and *dignity*.

"No, you look great!" Ginger emphasized, staring at her phone. "Would you look at that? I just got a text from Aaron." A pseudo apologetic expression warped her face. "I can't hang out with you and Dee like we planned. I forgot. Aaron has something going on over at his parents' today," she lied.

At that moment, the number on Ginger's *jealousy meter* had reached an all-time high. Never had she felt such envy and resentment towards Evaniese. Suddenly, she couldn't leave the mall fast enough.

"Oh, no," Evaniese said, disappointed. "I thought you and Dee would hang out with me for the entire afternoon," she complained. "Where's Deedee by the way?" Her eyes skimmed over the area in search of Deanna.

"She stepped out to talk on the phone with Scott," Ginger said.

"*Please* stay, Ginny," Evaniese coaxed, feeling out of sorts. Since losing the weight, she'd noticed a shift in the way Ginger and Deanna treated her. Evaniese perceived that it was taking a minute for her besties to get used to her new body. Even so, it was hurtful to have them treat her like an alien from another planet.

"Oh, honey, I really wish I *could*, but Aaron will kill me if I don't show up. As it *is*, his parents aren't the most welcoming people in the world," Ginger prevaricated.

"I get it, Ginger." Evaniese acceded, frowning.

"I've got to go, guys," Deanna announced, piloting back into the shop. Her face wrinkled in urgency.

"What...?" Evaniese asked, surprised. "You're leaving me too, Dee?" She set her hand on her heart, clearly put out.

"What do you mean *too*? Ginny, where are *you* going?" Confused, Deanna gave Ginger a questioning look.

"I've got this family thing with Aaron, and he just texted to remind me. I've got to get home to shower and change," Ginger continued to fabricate.

"Oh, okay...," Deanna acquiesced, staring curiously at Ginger.

"So, both of you are leaving me out here all by myself?" Evaniese shook her head, incredulous.

"Sorry, Niecy..." Deanna's face warped apologetically. "Scott fell at home. I'm not sure how badly he's hurt, so I told him I'd be right over," Deanna fibbed.

She *was* going over to her boyfriend's, but only because she couldn't stand being around Evaniese for a minute longer. Evaniese was too beautiful! Nowadays, she got all the attention from both men...*and* women.

"It's all right," Evaniese reassured, gesturing with her hands. "I'll be okay. Go on, the two of you. It's a good thing *my* car's parked out in the lot." Evaniese smiled, trying to move past hurt feeling.

"*I'll* give you a ride over to Scott's," Ginger told Deanna.

"Sure. Thanks, Ginny."

"We're so sorry, Niecy," both women said in concert.

"It's fine. Raincheck?" Evaniese said spiritedly.

As offended as she felt over her friend's snubs, she sensed that she shouldn't fight them. Rather, she felt prompted to let them go.

"Promise to make it up to you," Ginger assuaged. She threw her arms around Evaniese, and gave her a hearty squeeze.

"I promise you a redo," Deanna echoed, and pressed a kiss to Evaniese's face. "You should keep shopping here. That outfit looks phenomenal on you!" she uplifted.

"Thanks." A sad smile curved over Evaniese's lips, as she watched her friends saunter away. "All right then...," she said, resigned. Then, staring heavenward, she prayed, "Lord, help me pick out the right clothes."

Evaniese resolved not to get *in her feelings* about Ginger and Deanna's behavior. She couldn't say for sure, but they'd seemed eager to distance themselves from her. Evaniese honestly thought they were having a great time. Nonetheless, she'd waited for such a long time to fit into *normal* sized clothes, and God had made that a reality. So, in spite of the setback of losing El and the odd behavior of her closest friends, Evaniese wanted to enjoy every minute of obtaining such a victory. She just had to praise God for his many blessings!

Later, Evaniese was on the lower level of the mall, carrying the spoils of her successful shopping venture. She had at least three bags in each hand. As she made her way outside on that crisp, yet sunny February afternoon, she suddenly froze in her steps. Were her eyes deceiving her? She thought she saw Brent Peterson with someone. However, before long, Brent and his *girlfriend* Denise came into focus. In fact, they were headed for the mall's main entrance.

Momentarily, Evaniese remained stationary, as she stared at Brent. Essentially, it felt as if she'd lost the ability to move or speak. Similarly, it seemed Brent was suffering from the same affliction. His eyes morphed to the size of saucers as he ogled. For a lapse, Evaniese's eyes connected furtively to his. She wanted to say something, but found it difficult to escape Denise's glower. Darts were shooting out from the woman's eyes.

Sometime after the incident at church last year, Evaniese found out who Brent's girlfriend was. Her name was Denise Hart. Denise had accompanied Brent to church on the Sunday Nora Peterson had proudly announced to Evaniese that Brent was dating someone new. That day, Evaniese got to see the extremely antisocial and mean side of Brent.

After a brief pause, Evaniese said nothing. Rather, she stared right past Brent and Denise, and kept it moving. She sauntered in the direction of the busy parking lot. As she strolled away, she could still feel Brent's gaze hot on her. In fact, the intensity of his gape could have burned a hole right through her. However, Evaniese didn't bother looking back.

Brent had had so many chances to do the right thing. He'd had countless opportunities to show kindness, and to come clean. God had revealed to Evaniese that Brent *did* love her. However, she didn't have the strength, or the time to keep trying to draw the feelings out of him. It was an arduous upkeep.

It was either Brent stepped up, or he stepped off. Besides, Brent was dating someone else. So, Evaniese judged that it was high time for her to do the same. In light of that encounter with Brent and Denise, Evaniese was determined to do what Ginger and Deanna had advised earlier on. She would open up herself to the possibility of dating other men.

***

Ginger had been kind enough to offer Deanna a ride over to Scott's house. Scott was Deanna's boyfriend of two years. The two were totally in love, and Deanna was actively anticipating a marriage proposal. Deanna had chosen to leave the Kaleidoscope Mall just to get away from Evaniese. She no longer felt comfortable around her. Evaniese shone like a jewel, and eclipsed her and Ginger. Deanna couldn't tell, but she perceived Ginger felt the same way.

They were a few miles away from Scott's, when Deanna decided to speak out. "Ginny, is it *me*, or is Evaniese just the slightest bit conceited nowadays? In my opinion, losing all that weight has gotten to her head," she said in a hushed tone.

"You noticed that too?" Ginger queried, surprised over Deanna's observation.

Ginger slipped into the expressway. "Dee, I swear… Since Evaniese got the surgery, and lost all that weight, she's been in her own head." Ginger rolled her eyes in annoyance. "It's all about *her*," she said caustically.

"I didn't want to say anything, but she's gotten to be so self-centered, and even a little *vain*." Deanna made a face. "Don't get me wrong, I'm happy for her. But, she needs to take it down a notch or two. She went from being our sweet, quiet little Evaniese, to this diva on steroids," she criticized.

Ginger gave Deanna a quick glance, while simultaneously trying to keep her eyes on the road. She shook her head in irony. "I *know*. She's a completely different person. It's like she's a darker, more evil version of herself. A *deadly double*… There's the quiet, nice and meek Evaniese. And then, there's the one who's all up in your face." Ginger nodded in affirmation. "Well, Dee, guess what? *Now* we have the evil twin. Evaniese is no longer quiet, nice or meek."

"You think we should have a talk with her next time?" Deanna asked generically. She could care less about having a heart to heart with Evaniese. Truth be told, Evaniese had done absolutely nothing wrong. Deanna's only concern was to guarantee that her weight loss stalled. It didn't matter what she had to do to make that happen. Deanna couldn't see herself living in a world where Evaniese Spencer *looked better* and *got better* than she did.

"What are we going to say to her, Dee?" Ginger asked. "Evaniese, you're getting way too big for your britches, and you really need to tone it down?" she postulated.

Inwardly, she hated that Evaniese was so beautiful, healthy, strong and confident. Ginger plotted her downfall by any means necessary. "No, just leave her alone. Honestly, being that thin has made her temporarily insane. Just let her have her moment, then she'll calm down," Ginger berated.

Ginger and Deanna had nothing positive to say about Evaniese. How wrong and unsupportive they were being didn't factor in at all. On the contrary, they'd both chosen the petty and jealous route. In their hearts they knew the truth. Evaniese hadn't changed at all. Her crime was being a lot more confident in her new body. Both women refused to admit their resentment over Evaniese's transformation. They were embittered that she was becoming a better version of herself.

About a mile away from Scott's place, Ginger exited the highway, and followed the route for Overhill Avenue. The avenue was populated with storefronts and restaurants. Ginger came to a full stop at a red light. However, as they halted, from a distance, Deanna saw something that rocked her entire world. She baulked, her eyes widened in shock, and her jaw dropped. Just then, stepping out of Breeze's Bar and Grill, was her boyfriend Scott. But he wasn't alone. A beautiful, dark-haired girl clung to his side. Scott pulled the woman into his arms, and lavished her with hugs and kisses.

Deanna watched her boyfriend's PDA's with another woman. She trembled in affect, and tears teemed over her eyelids.

Ginger had tried to rush through a red light, because she'd seen Scott with the girl, before they stepped out of the pub. But to no avail. Scott shamelessly had his hands all over her. Ginger had hoped to spare Deanna from seeing the pair. However, seeing Deanna so distraught and in tears, Ginger realized it was too late. "I'm so sorry, Deedee." Her face warped in sympathy.

"Just keep driving, Ginger. Please, let's just get away from this area," Deanna's voice undulated, and fresh tears brimmed over in her eyes.

"Are we still going over to his place?" Ginger's eyes sparkled with tears in commiseration.

"No, please...," Deanna muttered, "please just take me home." Burying her face in her hands, she wept with a sense of abandon.

Deanna allowed herself to look at Scott again. He was still carousing with the strange girl. "Ginger, please drive," she ordered, turning her head in the opposite direction.

The last thing Deanna had expected was for Scott to cheat on her. As Ginger rushed away from the bar and grill, Deanna found it difficult to breathe, and just couldn't seem to get enough air in her lungs.

How on earth could this be happening? Scott said he loved her. In fact, they talked about getting married. Deanna's heart was totally vested in him, so his duplicitous behavior baffled her. *How could he deceive her that way?* **She had done absolutely nothing wrong.** No sooner than that thought crossed her mind, Deanna realized she *might* have done a *few* things wrong.

Dabbling in witchcraft with the intent of destroying someone who considered her a dear friend, was reprehensible. Deanna had plotted, and had schemed against someone who truly loved her. Certainly, what was happening with Scott, was *divine* payback for her evil set of actions. Deanna couldn't help thinking God was punishing her for being underhanded and disloyal to Evaniese.

Maybe, *God* had absolutely nothing to do with was happening. She'd invoked evil spirits to bring harm to someone else. Instead, *harm* had found *her* address, and had hit hard. Now more than ever, Deanna resented Evaniese. Essentially unremorseful, Deanna blamed Evaniese for Scott's infidelity. So, come hell or high water, Deanna avowed a counterattack.

***

"Ellis, Ellis, how does it feel to be vindicated today? You've been absolved of all charges brought against you. Turns out, Nina Tyson fabricated the entire story. You never behaved inappropriately towards her on the set *Live Wire?*" one of the reporters surrounding the courthouse, asked Ellis as Ellis quickly dismounted the steps.

The media delimited Ellis like buzzards surrounding a carcass out in the wilderness. Nina Tyson, an actress and a high-profile model in the industry, had stalked Ellis for months. So, because Ellis had turned down her advances, she'd made a public statement accusing him of sexual harassment on the set of the movie *Live Wire*. It was a film they'd worked on together a while back.

Regardless of the disillusionment Ellis felt over being falsely accused by a peer, he strove not to rail angrily in the public eye. He knew the truth would eventually come out, and that he'd be cleared of any wrongdoing. And, God had secured his victory on that day.

Unable to get away from the mayhem outside, Ellis deemed he did owe his fans a statement. They'd stood staunchly by his side, and had never doubted his innocence. "My vindication this morning feels absolutely liberating! As I've maintained from the start, inappropriate behavior on a professional set is-not only uncharacteristic, but something I personally condemn. Anyone who's worked with me in the past can attest to that."

"That's absolutely right," Kierra boldly attested, as she hurriedly dismounted the court steps. She rushed over to take her place beside Ellis, and set her arm about his shoulder in support. "Not only is this man one of the finest actors in the world, but he's also one of the best humans I know! I'm so happy that the truth has prevailed. The world now sees that this *woman*-and I use that term loosely-lied, and plotted to cast a shadow on Ellis's good name..."

Ellis set his arm about Kierra's waist, and squeezed her affectionately. "Thank you for coming out here for me this morning, Key. I feel blessed to have you standing with me. It means more than you even realize," his voice broke, and tears gleamed in his eyes.

Kierra's eyes connected sentimentally to Ellis. "I couldn't stand by, and let anyone lie on my *friend*," her voice wavered with emotion. "You've been such a great friend to me, Ellis!" Kierra smiled mawkishly.

"Thank you," Ellis said throatily. "This entire situation has been a nightmare."

"But, it's over now, Ellis. I'm so sorry it happened to *you*. You're the last person in the world anyone should *ever* accuse."

"Kierra, Ellis…, please give us your official statements…," the press exacted.

Ellis and Kierra zeroed in on the media.

Ellis spoke up, "I'm just grateful justice was served today. In this day and age where it's easy for predators to cast a shadow on someone's name for *personal* reasons… Well, I'm just glad the truth prevailed over the lies."

"Ellis, with the 'Me Too' movement so prevalent in the industry, were you concerned about being blackballed, or labeled a predator?" one of the entertainment news reporters asked.

"I'm a firm believer that if you live a life of honesty and integrity, that will speak for itself." Ellis smiled through the tears in his eyes. "And, living a life of honesty and personal integrity, is what I strive for every single day. That would be my MO, wherever life takes me."

"There was never any doubt in *my* mind Ellis would be found innocent," Kierra unabashedly gave her statement to the press.

She then turned towards Ellis, and offered him a clement smile. "I can take it from here, Ellis. Your limo guy's waiting. Go on… Get out of here," she encouraged, then protectively took her place between Ellis, the press and a sea of spectators.

"Thank you, Kierra." Ellis gave her an earnest smile. "Say hello to Taggart for me," he said. Kierra and Taggart Lane were now an item. The two had been dating for months, and were surprisingly happy.

"You're welcome, Ellis! Go on… I've got this." Kierra winked at him.

Ellis took the escape clause Kierra offered, and made a dash for the limo. Sliding into the car, the driver instantaneously shut the door. As they pulled away from the area, reporters and media people followed. Nevertheless, Ellis was grateful that his driver was skillful at navigating through a crowd, and leaving the commotion behind. Even from a distance, Ellis could hear Kierra's voice. She was poised, and totally in control of the situation. He shook his head humorously, as he thought about Kierra's way of subduing the press. At the end of the day, she always had them eating from the palm of her hand.

"Are we still scheduled for the airstrip later, Mr. Roman?" Greg, Ellis's new limo guy inquired.

"Absolutely, Greg. I've already made arrangements to utilize the jet. The pilot will be meeting me there. Now that this horrendous media circus is behind me, I'm moving forward with plans to go out to Indiana," he detailed.

Several months had passed since Ellis had lost connection with Evaniese Spencer, through the *Chat Channel*. Shortly after his father passed away, Ellis resolved to go out to *Amber Hills* to find her. Wanting to find Evaniese was a priority, but one event after the next had impinged on his plan. After his father's death, Ellis was called to return to the set of a movie he'd worked on months earlier. Some of the scenes had needed revamping.

Ellis tried to get around dealing with the trivialities, but was unsuccessful. The changes had to be made on the film, and as stipulated in his contract, such matters were nonnegotiable. Notwithstanding, he was paid a hefty twenty million for the lead role in the movie, *Black Boots and Waterfalls*.

So, Ellis had spent three weeks in Vancouver British Columbia, reshooting a number of scenes for the movie. At that juncture, he'd gotten used to going through the motions with a broken heart. And yet, it was strange. The months he'd spent separated from Evaniese, had only strengthened his love for her. His love for her deepened with every passing day. Nothing could make him waver. Ellis no longer had any doubt she was the *one*, his God-*chosen* wife. The past few months had indeed been challenging, but Ellis assented to the fact that nothing worth having ever came easy.

Because he was so in love, Ellis resigned to do whatever was necessary to get her back. Nina Tyson's lies, the court fiasco, and revamping the movie were all distractions. Now, Ellis was more than ready to find the woman he loved. After praying extensively on the matter, he was confident God would help him in his quest to bridge the gap to his lost love.

Evaniese had deleted most of her social media connections, and had blocked him from commenting on her vlogs. So, Ellis had no other choice, but to find her in person. She had to know the truth without any games, cover-ups or pretenses. He was ready to come clean about his identity. Still, he realized that he had to proceed with caution. It was the first time he was going out of town completely on his own. An entourage of security people, body guards, or publicists were not a part of the equation. Ellis knew a few tricks of the trade. One of those was how to make himself unrecognizable. He already had the perfect disguise in mind.

By the time he put on the salt and pepper-colored wig, added the fake wrinkles, the full-on beard and moustache, and put on his trusty Fedora, not even the members of his own family would be able to recognize him. So, that part was covered. What he didn't have figured out was how he'd approach the beautiful young woman without isolating her. But then again, Ellis was hopeful of God's help and wisdom. His love for Evaniese was such, he had to find a way back into her life.

***

Later, out on the airbase, Ellis took a seat in his private jet, and awaited instruction from his pilot Howard Moss.

"We're all set to leave, sir," Howard told Ellis, stepping out from the cockpit. "We should be in Indiana at approximately 12:30 a.m. Eastern Standard Time."

Ellis still watched Evaniese's YouTube videos. She had uploaded a few in the past few months. Seeing her again took his breath away! In light of her dramatic weight loss, Ellis concluded she'd submitted to the VSG. And, it turned out to be a complete success! Angelic was the only way he could describe how beautiful she looked! Of course, Ellis was biased, because that was the way he'd felt the very first time he laid eyes on her. Even so, he was overjoyed to see how much confidence she exuded. He was fiercely proud of her courage and resolve!

"Sounds great, Howard," Ellis said absently to the pilot, consumed by thoughts of Evaniese.

"Is there anything else before we take off, sir?" Howard tested.

"No, not at all," Ellis affirmed with an earnest smile. "Let's get this thing off the ground."

"Absolutely, sir!" Howard nodded in agreement, and gave Ellis a hearty thumbs up.

***

Tears of frustration were in Evaniese's eyes, as she tried to zip up her jeans. She'd gotten them only a few weeks ago at the mall, but now they were hardly making it past her hips. She found herself bemused. She'd not only remained consistent with exercise, but she'd cautiously watched what she ate. Nowadays, she could only ingest four to six ounces during any given meal. The Gastric Sleeve only allowed her to eat but so much. And yet, Evaniese had *mysteriously* gained twelve pounds.

How was it possible to watch what she ate, exercise for an hour four to five times a week, and still gain weight? Worse yet, the weight gain didn't show any sign of stopping. Evaniese couldn't process what was happening. Those days- as it would seem, if she breathed, she gained another pound. Her jeans no longer fit. But, it was a lot more than just one pair of jeans. All of her clothes were fitting snugly.

Evaniese stepped away from the mirror, and toppled onto her bed. Burying her face in her hands, she wept. "God, what's going on? Why am I gaining weight? I'm twelve pounds up. The clothes I bought just a few weeks ago no longer fit.

"Not to mention the fact that none of my coats fit. Why is this happening?" she muttered and slid down to her knees. "I don't understand, Lord. You promised to walk me through this surgery. You kept your word, and carried me through the procedure. You said you would honor my obedience in this area of my life. I started out so well. But now, not only am I stalled, I'm inexplicably regaining the weight. It's like a landslide, and I'm powerless to stop it."

Distressed, Evaniese breathed spasmodically. Whenever she was confused or overwhelmed, the Lord always had the answers. Why was this happening? She'd done everything in her power to distance herself from being fat. However, it seemed *fat* had never stopped stalking, and had found her address again. Her greatest fear was being mocked by those who knew she had the WLS. She imagined their derision. No doubt, they'd say she had the surgery, only to regain the weight. It was a no brainer. If this trajectory continued, she'd soon be back to where she was before the surgery.

First things first. Evaniese realized she had to make an appointment with Dr. Bergstrom. He was probably the only one who could help her figure out why she was steadily gaining. At the foot of her bed in the presence of her heavenly father, she prayed for help. God was the only one who could help her make sense of any of it.

After a while, Evaniese managed to pull it together. Searching the scriptures, the Spirit of God highlighted Isaiah 54:17 (NKJV) "No weapon formed against you shall prosper, And every tongue *which* rises against you in judgment You shall condemn. This *is* the heritage of the servants of the LORD, And their righteousness is from Me," Says the Lord."

The longer she remained in the presence of God, the more clarity she received. The Lord brought several passages of scripture having to do with divination and witchcraft to her attention. In the stillness, Evaniese received even more revelation. She remembered all of the catty and hateful women she'd worked with over at Brookline Hospital.

As it would seem, because she'd had the attention of doctors Jeremey Carter and Nathan Andrews, those jealous and backbiting women were hating on her. Furthermore, even some of the women at church hated her because of Brent. Sadly, what these women didn't know was that she was no closer to Brent at that point in time, than on the day she met him. Maybe, Brent *did* love her, but he was obviously more enamored with his status and reputation.

Evaniese was *certain* that these evil women had employed witchcraft to frustrate her relationships with all three men. However, an attack on her weight wasn't what she'd foreseen or anticipated. Evaniese recounted the laborious efforts of her weight loss journey prior to WLS. No matter the sacrifices made, she'd been unable to take off a single ounce. Just then, an internal alarm went off. *Had these atrocious people cursed her weight loss efforts? Was it even possible put a hex on someone's weight loss efforts?*

Evaniese bounded to her feet, and drifted over to the mirror again. Examining her distended stomach, burgeoning hips and widening buttocks, she came to a conclusion. Evil forces in the spiritual realm, *were* indeed capable of impacting the physical world.

In short, the hatred of jealous women wasn't in itself *tangible,* and yet their wickedness had *palpably* impacted her life. Just then, God dropped a word of advice into Evaniese's spirit. She was reminded of Matthew 17:21 (NKJV) "However, this kind does not go out except by prayer and fasting."

That passage of scripture was the confirmation she'd needed. What was happening to her body was a *spiritual* attack. Moreover, prayer alone couldn't destroy this malicious yoke. She would need to submit to fasting. Evaniese acquiesced to God's revelation. Isaiah 58:6 was also brought to mind. "*Is* this not the fast that I have chosen: To loose the bonds of wickedness, To undo the heaven burdens, To let the oppressed go free, And that you break every yoke?" (NKJV)

As Evaniese scrutinized herself in the mirror, she decided to take off the jeans. Honestly, she felt like a *Ball Park frankfurter* in them. Grudgingly, she slipped on a pair of tights and a blue floral-print top. She still blinked back tears over the circumstances. But, at least, she was now aware that the bizarre weight gain was indeed a satanic attack.

The spiritual realm had impacted the physical, and had left her distended. It was like a disease. Nevertheless, God promised to help, so she couldn't give in to despair. And yet, it was excruciating to come to terms with what was happening. She'd made so many sacrifices. With the VSG surgery, most of her stomach had been cut out. And, in light of that, weight regain wasn't only a nightmare, but a tragedy. What was even more frustrating was that it was through no fault of her own. Failing WLS was indeed a catastrophic blow to Evaniese's heart!

As Evaniese mulled over the injustice of the matter, Ginger and Deanna came to mind. They'd been different with her since her dramatic weight loss. Both were extremely distant and withdrawn. Evaniese wondered if Ginger and Deanna were also lumped in with her enemies. *Had they engaged in witchcraft against her too?* Evaniese hated entertaining the thought. Perhaps, she was being paranoid.

For the past few weeks, Ginger had brought her a smoothie every morning. It was one of Evaniese's favorite fruit smoothies. Because Evaniese was still unemployed, Ginger had swung by every morning before going off to work. Ginger seemed all too thrilled to do it, stating that her job wasn't too far away from Evaniese's house.

Were Ginger and Deanna in on the plot? Tears brimmed over in Evaniese's eyes, as she considered such an atrocity. Just then, she received an impression from the Holy Spirit of God. The impression told her to stop accepting the smoothies from Ginger.

Ellis's heart lashed, as he made his way up Evaniese's walkway. He loved the cute little starter home! The little brick house was quaint! Daffodils, Cherry Blossoms, and an array of spring flowers adorned the front yard. His legs wobbled, as he neared the front door. So far, things were going as planned. In his disguise, in as far as being recognized, no one was the wiser.

That afternoon, he had a package to deliver to Evaniese's door. The package included a letter from his alter ego, *El*. In it, Ellis expressed how much she meant to him, and how much he'd missed their chats. Ellis had also enclosed a roundtrip plane ticket, extending an invitation to his home out in Misty Morning, Georgia.

Ellis wanted Evaniese to understand that he was on the level. Furthermore, if she took him up on his invite, he would explain everything. *Why was his hand trembling upon ringing her doorbell?* Sunlight spilled over in the horizon on that beautiful May afternoon! However, it was still a bit nippy out in Amber Hills. So, Ellis didn't feel out of sorts wearing his gray and black designer fedora. He *did* however feel ridiculous wearing brown delivery overalls. But, if it meant having Evaniese in his arms in the end, he would jump through the necessary hoops.

"Yes...?" Evaniese opened up the front door to the delivery guy.

Her thoughts were racing, as she tried to process everything God had just revealed to her. Angry and jealous people were employing witchcraft to overturn her weight loss efforts. The doorbell was an added source of irritation, but the last thing she wanted was to take her frustration out on a stranger. Evaniese brushed the tears away from her eyes, but doubted she could conceal the under-eye puffiness. Hopefully, the delivery guy wouldn't remark how horrible she looked.

"Good afternoon...," Ellis stammered. However, he found himself temporarily frozen. He found himself winded and mesmerized seeing Evaniese in person for the first time! She was even more beautiful than she appeared in her videos. In her navy-blue stretch pants, dark blue floral print top, she looked like an angel! Her beautiful hair was pinned up in a barrette, but a few tendrils cascaded over her shoulders and back.

He assessed how *sweet* she looked in flip flops. Her wine-colored painted toes were *too cute*! Ellis smiled contemplatively, as he took her in. If he'd been in love before, he was completely smitten at that point! His heart hammered all the more to be in such close proximity to the woman he loved. It took tremendous restraint not to act on the impulse to take her in his arms, and cover her in kisses.

Upon closer investigation, Ellis noticed the red, puffy eyes. He deduced she'd been crying, and he direly wanted to know why. Ellis frowned in commiseration.

He wanted to address the sadness in her eyes, but first had to find the courage to speak. "I have a deliver for Ms. Evaniese Spencer!" he said, clearing his throat. Ellis found himself even more entranced, as he continued to scrutinize every inch of her.

"You have a package for me?" Evaniese set her right hand on her heart, staring curiously at the strange looking man at the door. There was something totally off about him, but she perceived no real danger. Warily, she examined his face. He reminded her of someone. But, that was neither here nor there. "I didn't order anything." She stared cagily at the gentleman.

"Well, this package is definitely for you," Ellis pleasantly disputed. Hearing Evaniese's voice stirred his heart. "See?" He pointed out with a welcoming smile. There was a twinkle in his eye, and his heart inundated with joy, because he was close to her. He'd only dreamed about this moment for what seemed like an eternity. "It has *your* name on it." He held up the box, in order to show the name written on it.

Evaniese smiled, and guffawed over the stranger's amiable jesting. "Well, I can't argue with that. It *does* have my name on it," she acquiesced.

"Will you sign for it?" Ellis asked thickly, delving into her striking garnet eyes. They gleamed like jewels as sunlight assaulted them.

"Sure," Evaniese said, nodding.

Ellis extended the writing pad for her to sign. Their hands brushed lightly, as she took the pen from his hand. Ellis got butterflies.

There was a curious expression on Evaniese's face, as she absently signed the sheet. Her eyes fastened to the interesting stranger. "Has anyone ever told you that you look like an older, more distinguished Ellis Roman?" She smiled openly. Evaniese's thoughts had temporarily drifted away from her current struggle.

"No way," Ellis dispelled, and chortled. "I could be his grandfather."

"Well, you remind me of him," Evaniese said, and took the package he extended.

Evaniese's hand brushed Ellis's again, and created havoc inside him. His heart flagellated, and he felt flustered. "Thank you for saying that." He swallowed hard. "Given he's a celebrity and all, that's actually very flattering," he said modestly.

"You're welcome! Ellis Roman is actually one of my favorite actors. Not only is he an amazing actor, he seems really kind and down-to-earth," Evaniese uplifted.

Ellis's cheeks turned cerise, and his eyes shimmered in affect hearing those words from the woman he loved. However, he had to veer away from the subject, because he wasn't yet ready to disclose his identity. "I will say this... Ellis Roman is so lucky to have a fan like you!" he praised, looking away timidly from the intensity of Evaniese's stare.

"Well, I'm like his number *one* fan," Evaniese admitted, smiling.

Ellis's smiled brightened, and he allowed himself to quietly contemplate the beautiful woman.

"Thank you for the package," Evaniese said kindly. The fact that she'd gained twelve pounds through no fault of her own, resonated again, and she blinked back tears. Parenthetically, something about the kind stranger made her feel a little better.

"You're welcome!" Ellis said, momentarily stalled at her front door. Truth be told, he was totally awestruck. However, he had to remind himself he was just the delivery guy for now. Right then and there, he *couldn't* be Ellis Roman, who was entirely lost in love with Evaniese Spencer.

Ellis offered Evaniese a pleasant smile. "Well, have a nice Saturday!" He stared yearningly at her. That said, he hesitantly began taking steps backward.

"You as well." Evaniese's eyes affixed inquisitively to the stranger's.

Ellis forced himself to turn away. But, before he got too far, he turned back to face Evaniese, who was still standing at the front door. "Can I tell you something?" he asked from feet away.

"Sure," Evaniese acceded.

"You're much too beautiful to be sad!" He winked at her.

Evaniese flinched, completely taken aback by the stranger's kind words. She offered him a genuine smile. "Thank you for saying that. I think I actually *needed* to hear that today," she admitted.

"You're welcome! Bye," Ellis said shakily, before he involuntary turned away from his dream girl. The image of Evaniese smiling in the doorway stayed with him long after he slipped into his car rental.

As he drove away, he whispered a prayer. Ellis prayed that God would stir Evaniese's heart to accept his invitation. "Lord, I've done my part. Now, I'm counting on you to do yours. Thank you for the gift of meeting Evaniese in person, and looking into her amazing eyes..."

Evaniese stepped back into the house, and shut the front door. Her face wrinkled in perplexity, as she crossed back over into her bedroom with the package in hand. "That was strange," she said mutedly.

Her troubles temporarily took a backseat, as she contemplated the box in front of her. Sitting down on the bed, she cautiously opened it up. Evaniese then ventured inside the package, and saw two envelopes enclosed. One was bulky, and the other thin. "Lord, what is this?" She frowned in uncertainty.

Taking up the bulkier envelope, she undid the clasp, and removed first-class, round-trip tickets to Atlanta, Georgia.

Confused, Evaniese set the tickets aside, and picked up the other envelope. Her heart somersaulted in her chest when she began reading the letter inside.

"Dear Evaniese: I hope you're not angry with me for doing everything in my power to reconnect to you. Since we've stopped chatting, I've been trying to figure out what I did wrong.

"I've been retracing every word exchanged, hoping to understand what it was that I did to alienate you. I'm sorry if I've been a little secretive. I'm now ready to share *everything* with you. All the same, you must realize that the one thing I *wasn't* secretive about is how much I love you. I love you, Evaniese, and that's never going to change!

"Please, give me a chance to prove that I am an on the level guy. Our connection on Instagram, and on the *Chat Channel*, wasn't a game to me. In fact, everything we shared has left an indelible impression on my heart. I am enclosing round trip tickets to my home out in Atlanta. It would mean a lot to me if you came out, and we met in person. If you're not altogether comfortable with that idea, we can meet in a public setting. Please, allow me the chance to prove just how real I am, and that my intentions are pure.

"I am so in love with you, Evaniese! I know I said that a hundred times before I lost you. Honestly, things have been at a standstill in my life, because you haven't been a part of it. All I want is to meet in person. After which, you can decide if you'd be willing to be my girl. We don't have to reconnect on IG, YouTube, or via the *Chat Channel*. I've also written out my phone number. Please, just send me a text, or leave a voicemail to let me know if you've accepted my invitation for the upcoming week. Love, El."

Evaniese was both stunned and dazed. *Was this a dream? Had El truly sent her an invite to his home in Georgia?* She was having difficulty processing it all, and kept pouring over every word. *What on earth?* She'd severed ties with El. So, their relationship had ended-or so she'd believed. But, according to his letter, the story wasn't over for El. Tears were in Evaniese's eyes, but they were tears of joy! She was stirred beyond words to see the lengths El had gone through just to find her. He'd reaffirmed his love for her, and Evaniese was *certainly* still in love with him.

"God, I can't believe this. El wants me to fly out to Georgia to meet him. I guess, Ginger and Deanna were wrong about him." Evaniese frowned, as her frenemies came to mind. Now that her eyes were opened, she realized how fake they were. Therefore, she refused to waste time thinking about them at this juncture. Her life had just taken an unexpected twist. The only man who knew how to speak to her heart had found a way to do it again. El had moved heaven and earth to reach out.

"Lord, what should I do? I made a huge mistake by listening to my frenemies... Should I go out to Georgia to meet El?" Evaniese inquired, still trembling. Just then, Psalm 32:8-9 (KJV) resonated. 8. "I will instruct thee and teach thee in the way which thou shalt go: I will guide thee with mine eye. 9. Be ye not as the horse or like the mule, which have no understanding: whose mouth must be held in with bit and bridle, lest they come near unto thee."

Chapter Ten

The church's parking area remained jammed pack, even if the service had ended. Evaniese meandered through the busy lot to find her car. She'd just sat through the early morning service at church. As she powered through to find her car, she tried to ignore the fact that Brent was staring at her from across the lot. He seemed oblivious to the fact that his girlfriend, Denise, was somewhere nearby. Although, for the moment, Evaniese didn't see her.

Evaniese was feet away from her car, when Brent jutted out from his spot to have a word with her. "Evaniese, Evaniese...," Brent called out.

Startled, Evaniese made a sudden turn, and saw Brent closing in. She frowned in perplexity. However, she didn't want to be rude, even if Brent had been notoriously rude to *her* in the past. Evaniese stopped short of her car, and waited to see what he wanted. Her eyes remained affixed to the ground, and her arms crossed over her chest, as she paused for Brent to approach.

"Evaniese," Brent said breathily, finally in close enough proximity to face her.

"What is it, Brent?" Evaniese looked up at him.

She was leery and apprehensive, because of Brent's past actions. He'd seen her so many times, and in various settings, and yet he'd ignored her every single time. She wondered what on earth he wanted now. Evaniese tried not to cop an attitude, but she looked heavenward, and rolled her eyes.

"I, uh... I, uh...," Brent said nervously, as his eyes searched Evaniese's. "I just wanted to tell you how amazing I think you look!" Brent's heart hammered, and he smiled awkwardly.

Surprised, Evaniese softened, as she searched Brent's cool blue eyes. "Thank you for saying that, Brent. I really appreciate it!"

"You're welcome!" Brent remained frozen.

One thing he knew for sure was that he would always be in love with her. However, he didn't have the courage to defy society or his family. For the moment, it was safe for him not to rock the boat. There were times in life where sacrifices had to be made. Brent had already resolved to let his heart take the hit.

"I really appreciate your words, Brent," Evaniese admitted. "Strange that we should talk today." She smiled musingly. "We used to talk all the time before...," Evaniese began to say.

Yet, in the distance, Evaniese saw Denise scampering over. No doubt, she was coming to stake her claim on Brent.

"Brent, Brent...," Denise called out, literally sprinting over to find him.

Evaniese closed her eyes in resignation, and offered Brent a taut smile. "Well, it was nice talking to you," she said quickly.

"Nice talking to you too," Brent said, gaping mercilessly at her.

"There you are, baby!" Denise instantly slipped her arm through Brent's. "Hello," she said cursorily, staring guardedly over at Evaniese.

"Hi," Evaniese said cheerily, then redirected over to Brent. "It was nice seeing you again, Brent!" That said, she turned and jetted away.

Opening up her car door, she slipped quietly inside. With her back pressed up to the car seat, Evaniese sighed. "Please, help me, Lord. I am more than ready to put Brent, Jeremy and Nathan behind me." A bright and hopeful smile curved over her lips, and tears gleamed in her eyes. "And, I'm so ready to move on with El. I can't wait to meet him!" She then shifted out of her parking space, and began to roll away from the lot.

As she did, she saw Brent and Denise walking back over to Brent's SUV. Evaniese shook her head nonsensically. She felt a certain level of dignity and gratification, because of the way she'd handled things with Brent. Seeing him with Denise no longer hurt in the way it had before, and Evaniese was grateful. Even if gaining weight unexpectedly still dampened her spirits, she felt hopeful and happy for the first time in a while. She was totally in love with El. That very afternoon she'd call him to let him know she'd decided to take him up on his invite.

In the past, she would have run to Ginger and Deanna for advice. However, her eyes were now opened, and she knew the truth. God had exposed both women as adversaries, and Evaniese was told to steer clear of them. She still struggled with the notion of severing ties. For such a long time, Ginger and Deanna had played a vital role in her life. Nevertheless, God had told her to *find* a way to distance herself from them. From what Evaniese understood, the two had-and probably were still, dabbling in witchcraft with the end goal of destroying her.

In that regard, Evaniese considered, the offer to fly out to Georgia couldn't have come at a better time. Once she had an indication of where her relationship with El was headed, she'd have time to deal with her former besties. The cold truth was that they were witches, dedicated to her downfall. Evaniese stood firm on God's word (Isaiah 54:17). No weapon formed against her would prosper. Evil weapons would always be formed, but would never prevail against a true child of God.

***

Once home from church, Evaniese fixed a salad for lunch. Attending the earlier service had been by design. She knew Ginger and Deanna usually attended the second. Avoiding them that morning was a blessing. So, Evaniese thanked God for small favors. She set the salad on a tray, along with a bottle of water, and crossed back over to her bedroom. Setting her lunch on the nightstand, Evaniese took deep breaths before accessing her phone.

Toppling over on the bed, she closed her eyes meditatively, and whispered a prayer to God. The time had come. She would call El, and leave a voicemail, only to be followed by a text in confirmation of their appointment later in the week. El was already in her list of contacts, so she accessed the number. Her heart raced in angst as the phone rang. She wasn't sure why El didn't answer, but she trusted God's leading. He'd approved the trip, so she wanted to be obedient.

"Yes, hi, El. It's Evaniese...," Evaniese introduced over the phone. "First of all, I just wanted to say thank you for reaching out, and sending me such an elaborate invite. I honestly didn't expect to hear from you, but I'm so glad I did. Just wanted to let you know that I am taking you up on your offer. I will be coming out to *Misty Morning, Georgia*. The flight from Indiana leaves Tuesday morning. I'm really looking forward to finally meeting you!"

Tears of affect shone in Evaniese's eyes, because she'd just confirmed the reservation. "God, you don't make mistakes, and you've asked me to go. So, I'm trusting you wholeheartedly for a positive outcome."

Evaniese also texted El to let him know she'd be flying out to meet him. She wanted a return text in order to get a dialogue going again. But, she was okay if it didn't happen that afternoon. If all went according to plan, she'd meet him in person on Tuesday. Then, all of her questions and concerns would finally be addressed.

Later, in the early evening, Evaniese uploaded a video to her YouTube Channel. This time around, the vlog was about weight gain after VSG Surgery. Of course, she couldn't tell 140K plus subscribers how she'd *supernaturally* gained weight, as a result of witchcraft from jealous and angry women.

Nevertheless, she decided to make lemonade out of lemons, and use such a sore subject in her life to advance her cause. Aside from money she'd saved from years of working through the hospital, her status on YouTube was keeping her financially afloat during her stint of unemployment.

So, even if it was a painful topic, Evaniese was determined to use her trial as a springboard for something positive. She was hopeful of taking off the weight again, as she publicly showcased her challenges to the viewers. Furthermore, as she faithfully fasted and prayed, she was encouraged that God would move on her behalf. Evaniese set aside her camera and recording equipment. Her laptop light blinked off just as the doorbell rang.

Not expecting anyone on a Sunday evening, Evaniese baulked in both surprise and dread. Nonetheless, curious to see who was calling, she rushed out of her home office, and crossed over to the front door. Through the front window, she noticed the radiant harvest moon in the panorama. Nevertheless, dusky shadows were waging a war against the ebullient light.

The doorbell chimed once again. "Hold on a minute," Evaniese said, confused, and a little annoyed by the impatience of her caller.

Evaniese opened up the front door, only to find Ginger and Deanna standing beyond it. Her heartstrings immediately tightened in her chest, and she felt malaise. However, an elastic smile instinctively stretched across her face. "Hey, Guys," she guardedly addressed, with a wavering voice.

"Hey, girl!" Ginger and Deanna said in concert, smiling at Evaniese.

Evaniese stood in the doorway scrutinizing them. Both looked incredible! Ginger had on a pretty wine-colored dress, matching heels and accessories, and her hair was out in curls. Ginger was also holding a bag from the smoothie shop. Evaniese saw the large Styrofoam cup within the bag, and knew instinctively Ginger had brought yet another smoothie for *her*.

Signature of Deanna's style, she had on dark jeans, a stylish sage-colored top with matching heels, and swanky accessories. Her hair was up in a fancy ponytail, and her coffee skin radiated in the glow of the orange moon. Both ladies were all dolled up, and ready to paint the town red.

"Hey, what's going on?" Evaniese tried to sound perky. "I had no idea you guys were coming over. You didn't call or text." The pliant smile returned. Inwardly, Evaniese felt unsettled. Now that she knew who Ginger and Deanna *really* were, she no longer felt at ease around them.

"Well, we just decided at the last minute. Dee and I are going to see that play, *Both Feet Planted* at the Montrose Theater. We want you to come with us," Ginger told Evaniese, with a welcoming smile.

"Originally, *Scott* and *I* were supposed to go." Deanna rolled her eyes cynically, because she and Scott had recently broken up. "I got the tickets before I found out he was a cheating sleaze." Deanna shook her head nonsensically. "Whatever… I *did* manage to get an extra ticket. So, do you want to come out with Ginger and me? We're going to Cotton Candy after the play. We know how much you love to eat there. We can make a girl's night of it," Deanna cajoled.

For reasons unknown, Evaniese began to feel physically sick. It was the strangest thing in the world. Suddenly, she was picking up negative vibes from the two women she'd once considered her closest friends. The air around them felt stifling and oppressive. Furthermore, dark shadows loomed, and threatened to suffocate Evaniese at her front door. What was even more disturbing was that Ginger and Deanna were morphing before her very eyes.

Their pretty faces, bright smiles, and attractive outfits, instantaneously changed. Evaniese couldn't be sure, but she perceived she was having some form of vision. Her former besties had on jet black bodysuits, their eyes were dark, and their faces were pallid. Fundamentally, they looked like the *walking dead*. Evaniese guardedly took steps back, and kept her distance. No matter how many times she blinked, the way she saw Ginger and Deanna remained the same. Hence, the air grew even stuffier, and the tone all the more obscure.

Evaniese tried not to give in to fear, as the two *witches* transmuted right before her eyes. This revelation was both alarming and quite frightening. "Dee, Ginny, I'm so sorry. I can't go out tonight." Evaniese looked away agitatedly from their intent gazes. She kept thinking, if she turned her eyes away a few times, they would look like themselves again. However, that wasn't the case.

"Evaniese, come on. It's a beautiful night!" Deanna argued.

"Yeah, come on," Ginger encouraged. "What else are you doing but staying home anyway?"

"I would love to go, but I'm not feeling great right now." Evaniese frowned in ambiguity. She chose her words carefully, because she didn't want to be dishonest. It *was* true. She *was* suddenly feeling sick.

"What's the matter, honey?" Deanna asked, with a pertained expression on her face.

However, Evaniese couldn't escape Deanna's pale white face and dark demonic eyes. "I'll be fine," she evaded, "I just need a little rest." This time around, Evaniese didn't look away in angst. She refused to give in to fear, as this supernatural manifestation continued to unfold.

"Are you sure you can't come out with us tonight, Niecy?" Ginger sulked. "Dee *did* go out of her way to get that extra ticket. That wasn't easy."

"Yeah, I know. I'm sorry about that, Dee. I really wish I could go." Evaniese feigned disappointment. Regardless, she wasn't budging. And, she certainly wasn't going *anywhere* with Ginger or Deanna...not ever. "I wish you'd told me in advance."

"You're right. We should have texted, or called before coming over," Deanna agreed, giving Evaniese her best sad face. "Are you sure?"

"I'm sure." Evaniese nodded, and gave them a sympathetic look.

"We're going to miss you tonight," Deanna said glumly.

"Yeah, I'm going to miss you guys too," Evaniese said robotically.

"But guess what?" Ginger chimed. "Dee and I picked up your favorite smoothie before we came over!" Ginger took the ginormous cup out of the bag. "Kale, mango, and raspberry!" she cheerily announced.

"Wow!" Evaniese feigned excitement. "That's super nice and so thoughtful. Thank you!"

"You're welcome, honey!" Ginger handed the cup over to Evaniese.

Evaniese wanted to say no to the gesture, but found herself absently taking the cup from Ginger's hand.

"Well, we *really* need to get going," Deanna told Evaniese. "Sorry you're not coming out tonight, but I hope you feel better. Get some rest." Deanna gave Evaniese an understanding smile.

"I'll be just fine. Thanks, Dee," Evaniese said quickly. "Raincheck for another girl's night out?" she evaded.

"You certainly *do* owe us a raincheck." Ginger examined Evaniese curiously. "But, I'm not mad at you." She stepped into the foyer, and wrapped her arms around Evaniese. "I'll call you later. Feel better."

"Thanks...," Evaniese coughed out with a nervous smile, as she mechanically hugged Ginger back.

Soon after, Ginger and Deanna turned away. They sauntered back out to the driveway. Taking a moment, they hopped back into Ginger's SUV.

Evaniese stood in the doorway, smiling until her face hurt. Coming into contact with her former besties was nauseating. It felt as if she'd just been touched by pure evil. There was a sudden and strong urge to peel off her clothes, and jump into the shower. Nevertheless, Evaniese knew the stains of wickedness ran a lot deeper than what could be superficially discerned.

She waved at Ginger and Deanna, as Ginger pulled out of the driveway. Evaniese then shut the front door, went straight into the kitchen, and tossed the smoothie into the garbage. She prayed and pled the blood of Jesus over herself and her home. She had started a fast that morning. So, there was no doubt in her mind that seeing Ginger and Deanna morph into demons, was God's way of showing her their true nature. Such was the power of fasting! Evaniese resolved to keep fasting until she, through the power of God's Holy Spirit, destroyed the yoke of the enemy.

***

"I really had a great time tonight, Ginny," Deanna celebrated, as she and Ginger were driving home from the Cotton Candy Restaurant.

"Yeah, dinner was great, and I personally loved the show! What'd *you* think about the show?" Ginger asked excitedly.

"Are you kidding me? It was awesome! I'm so glad those tickets didn't go to waste. I'm even happier Scott didn't get to go. That play's way too good for him. He didn't *deserve* to see it tonight," Deanna said acerbically. "I can't believe that loser actually cheated on me." Deanna shook her head in skepticism. "I trusted him so much..."

"Dee, you're just going to have to get over it. Besides, Scott doesn't deserve *you*. Let him stay with that Sabrina girl." Ginger turned to glance at Deanna for a split second on the one-way street. "I always say, what goes around, comes back around..."

"Ginger, look out!" Deanna yelped in fear and shock.

Ginger looked straight on, but she stalled in slamming on the brakes. Another SUV headed in the wrong direction at about 50 mph, slammed right into hers. There was very little reaction time. Upon impact, Ginger shrieked in horror. Suddenly, she found herself immersed in a realm of fogginess and obscurity.

***

"Is the main guestroom all set up with fresh linen and flowers?" Ellis asked Maureen Bridges. She was the head housekeeper of his small staff for the house out in Misty Morning. It was late Tuesday morning, and Ellis had a few errands to run before he welcomed Evaniese into his home.

Essentially, he was just like a child on Christmas morning. He was beaming, and could hardly keep his wits about him. Hearing Evaniese's voicemail, and receiving her text on Sunday evening, had stirred him to tears. Ellis praised God for the opportunity to meet the woman of his dreams. He hadn't stopped thanking God since finding a way to reconnect to Evaniese.

"Yes, sir. The main guestroom is ready. I've done everything according to your specification," Maureen told Ellis. The highly coveted job of working for Ellis Roman was fairly new, and Maureen was eager to please. Although she was a happily married woman, it was hard not to have the slightest crush on her new boss. Not only was the man incredibly good-looking, but he was also surprisingly kind.

"Thanks, Maureen!" Ellis gave her an affable smile. "Please, remind Calvin and the rest of the staff to refer to me as *El*, once my guest arrives-at least for a little while." His face creased in earnestness. "I have a few errands to run, but I should be back by lunchtime.

"Absolutely, sir. Your name is *El* once your guest arrives," Maureen affirmed spiritedly. "Sir," she introduced with reddened cheeks, "may I ask something?"

"Of course..." Ellis veered back to look at Maureen. It seemed odd for Maureen to want to introduce a brand-new subject, when he was obviously pressed for time.

"Should I serve champagne, or wine at dinnertime?" Maureen asked uneasily. She had pursed her lips a number of times before asking Ellis that question. The truth was that she was chomping at the bit to find out if his *guest* was a significant other. Nevertheless, she desisted from prying into his personal affairs.

"Both would be nice, Maureen. I like to give my guests options." He smiled clemently. "Perhaps, my guest and I will enjoy a glass of wine *or* champagne later."

"Of course, sir," Maureen said perfunctorily.

"Thanks, Maureen. I appreciate it," Ellis emphasized.

Turning away, he crossed over to the front door, dashed over to his car and drove off. There were a few last-minute things he wanted to handle, before Evaniese got there. In light of Evaniese's text messages, she'd be there by lunchtime. Ellis was on a cloud, as he drove out to the main road. He tried to keep his wits about him, but it was difficult to contain his excitement. Once he got back, he'd be meeting the love of his life.

The thought of staring into Evaniese's gem brown eyes again, gave Ellis butterflies. This time around, he wouldn't be in disguise, neither would he be incognito using the *Chat Channel*. Rather, he'd be one hundred percent Ellis Roman, the man who'd fallen head-over-heels in love with her.

***

Evaniese's eyes were everywhere, as the limousine drove through the beautiful town of Misty Morning. She was bordering delirium, because she couldn't wait to meet El. Now more than ever, she was anxious to find out who he *really* was. A luxurious stretch limo had met her at the airport, and now they were driving through a gorgeous affluent town. Every mile covered revealed bigger and bigger houses, and more lavish properties.

The flight out from Indiana to Georgia was for the most part uneventful. A lot more tired than she realized, she'd fallen asleep on the plane. Because excitement and anticipation had gotten the better of her the night before, sleep was a real challenge.

Was this really happening? Was she finally going to meet this wonderful man? Even if she and El hadn't chatted in a long while, her feelings for him were stronger than ever. The words and impressions they'd shared perpetually resonated in her heart. There was nothing she *could* forget about the way El had made her feel. Now, more than ever she was in love.

"We should be there shortly, Ms. Spencer," David, the limo driver told Evaniese.

"*Misty Morning* is so beautiful and majestic! All I've seen are mansions and estates. Are there any regular houses?" Evaniese inquired.

David chuckled. "Well, Misty Morning, for the most part, is an affluent area. There are a few houses, but mostly mansions and estates. There are also a number of landmark manors and castles," he informed.

"Wow!" Evaniese marveled. "It's incredible out here!" She loved the way the sunlight dripped like liquid gold over every stretch of the landscape. At that point, there were only mansions and manors up ahead in the pristine area. The immaculately manicured lawns, and beautiful spring flowers embellished the luxurious grounds. Evaniese kept looking through the tinted window like a little girl at her favorite popstar's concert.

"Yes, it is quite lovely!" David agreed.

"Will Mr. El be home when we arrive?" she asked hesitantly. Evaniese wasn't afraid or intimidated over the prospect of meeting El. Having prayed on the matter, she felt a sense of affirmation that she was indeed in the will of God. And, God was incapable of steering her in the wrong direction.

"Mr. El is currently out, but should be back in time for lunch," David informed.

"Lunch...? Right...," Evaniese said pensively.

Her heart raced over the thought of meeting El. However, she refused to keep pestering David with questions. Furthermore, she would try to hold it together until lunchtime. As her thoughts whizzed, the notification bell for the text feature on her phone went off. There was a text from El. Evaniese's smile brightened instantly.

"Welcome to Misty Morning, Evaniese! So sorry I won't be there to see you step over the hearth, so to speak. There were a few last-minute things I had to take care of. I should be back fairly soon. Please, make yourself at home. If you need anything at all, don't hesitate to alert the staff." El posted a smiley face emoji to the text.

Evaniese's heart plunged to the floor. She was ecstatic over El's text message. It totally put her mind at ease. Still, she couldn't help wondering who on earth this man was. She was in a limo headed over to a mansion or a manor, and he had a *staff.* She definitely felt intimidated to consider the *kind* of man she was about to meet. Her heart thrummed all the more, when the limo pulled up in front of a beautiful lavish mansion.

Going through the main gate, David parked on the grounds. He then proceeded to help Evaniese out of the car. She was stunned and speechless to see the ginormous property with gushing fountains, manicured stretches of buoyant greenery and a front gate. Evaniese followed behind David, and daintily climbed up the stairs. Once inside the mansion, her jaw dropped, as she took in how expansive and extravagant the house was.

"Good afternoon, Ms. Spencer!" a middle-aged, Caucasian woman greeted Evaniese at the set of doors. True to form, she was wearing a black housekeeper's dress, and a white apron. Two gentlemen stood on either side of her.

"Good afternoon," Evaniese stammered, overwhelmed.

"We're here to assist you in any way we can, until Mr. El returns," the woman informed.

Evaniese swallowed hard, but tried not to falter. "Thank you."

"My name is Maureen! I'm the head of staff for Mr. El's residence here." She offered a faint smile. Just then, Maureen realized why Ellis had gushed and beamed all that morning. A sentimental smile curved over her lips to size up Ellis Roman's *beautiful* houseguest.

"This is Brady!" Maureen gestured. "He's the chef. Lunch should be ready in about an hour."

"Hello," Brady said timidly. He was a tall, slender, dark-haired, hazel-eyed Caucasian gentleman, who appeared to be in his mid-thirties.

Evaniese offered a faint smile. "It's nice to meet you, Brady!"

"It's nice to meet you too, Ms. Spencer," Brady replied.

"No, please... Call me *Evaniese*," Evaniese said diffidently.

"Okay, *Evaniese*. That's a beautiful name by the way! I should have lunch ready in exactly one hour. Mr. El wanted to know if you were okay having lunch in his private quarters..."

Dazed, Evaniese just nodded. "That sounds nice."

"Hi, Evaniese! I'm Calvin. I'll be taking your bags up to the guestroom. If you'll follow me...?" the other man told her. Calvin was African American. He was a little on the heavy side, had light brown eyes, and skin the color of sand.

"Oh, okay...," Evaniese acceded.

"So, if you will...?" Calvin invited. "Come this way..."

Evaniese finally got her legs to work, and started following behind Calvin. Apparently, Calvin was taking her over to the guest's quarters.

"It was nice meeting you, Maureen, Brady...!" Evaniese turned to address the two.

"Welcome to our home, Evaniese!" Maureen said.

"It's nice to meet you too, Evaniese!" Brady echoed.

Evaniese explored the extensive guestroom. It was decadently furnished with the most excessive trappings. The closet was already full of exquisite designer clothing. And oddly enough, the dresses, tops and slacks were in her size. There was a dazzling mauve-colored gown, which Evaniese was especially fond of. She wondered if she'd get the chance to wear it during her visit. The entire experience felt surreal. Nevertheless, the question still remained. *Who on earth was El?*

Evaniese drifted into the spendthrift custard-colored bathroom. The spacious room was highlighted with gold accents, and had columns. The gorgeous claw-foot tub looked more like a piece from a museum. Evaniese couldn't wait to try it out as soon as she got the chance. Drifting past the bathroom, she stepped into a private powder room to freshen up. She was already showered, and had on a blue and white floral-print wrap dress, with stylish opened-toe heels. In spite of the weight gain, this was one of the few outfits that still fit, and Evaniese thought she looked pretty nice in it.

Meeting El when she was up by a few pounds, felt counterproductive. Evaniese wished she could have met him when she got down to her ideal weight. But, her hopes of that were dashed. She'd suffered a setback, and had regained a total of fifteen pounds. Evaniese prayerfully and cautiously strove not to put on another pound. Thankfully, she had God's reassurance that she wouldn't. Her enemies had indeed set her up for failure, but the weapon would not prosper (Isaiah 54:17).

Thinking about Ginger and Deanna brought tears to her eyes. The sting of their betrayal was a knife to the heart. Nevertheless, Evaniese refused to grieve. She refused to give in to depression and despair. She was about to meet the man of her dreams, and there was *no time* to cry.

When she got back to Indiana, she'd deal with her frenemies. However, for the moment, she pasted a bright smile to her face, as she freshened up, and brushed out her lengthy bangs. Tears indeed sparkled in her eyes, but they were tears of joy. Elation overwhelmed in anticipation of meeting El.

Ellis stalled in front of the set of doors leading into his private dining quarters. His heart whipped so palpably, he was convinced everyone in the house could hear it. Now, only those doors were separating him from Evaniese. She was already inside waiting on him. Ellis took deep breaths in order to control his racing heart. As planned, he was back from running his errands just in time for lunch. He'd showered, changed, and had groomed extensively for the encounter. Ellis had also prayed a great deal, but he was still a little nervous.

"God, please help me to calm down. My heart is still drubbing. I've prayed about this, and I'm confident everything's going to be all right. All I'm asking is that you help me pull it together. Evaniese means the world to me! So, I really want to make a good first impression." With as much fortitude as he could muster, Ellis was poised to open up the set of doors.

Evaniese sat at the ornately set dining table. Brady had ushered her into the dining room, and had told her lunch would be served shortly. However, for the moment, she admired the mansion grounds through a beautiful picture window. The view displayed a majestic fountain, trimmed lawns, and breathtaking flower gardens. The backdrop was so serene. However, hearing stirring at the set of doors, her heart instantly took to hammering. Evaniese pushed back her chair, stood to her feet, and deliberately began taking steps towards the doors.

Her heart twanged in expectation. *Was El about to make his entrance? Was this the moment she'd been waiting for?* If so, she was finally about to find out who El was. She'd finally have clarity about their connection. Only a few feet away from the doors, they suddenly sprang open. Evaniese's eyes widened to the size of saucers. She gulped, and her mouth gaped in shock just before her legs gave way, and she dropped to the floor.

"Oh, no," Ellis cried out, panicked.

He dashed over to break Evaniese's fall, but didn't get to her fast enough. Ellis stooped down, and collected the young woman in his arms. His eyes shone with tears of affect. Having her in his arms made him indescribably happy. It felt good to be so close.

Ellis gently brushed hairs away from her eyes, and stared yearningly at her. "You're even more beautiful up close and personal! Are you all right?" he pacified, and delicately caressed her face.

Even if he knew Evaniese would eventually come to, Ellis was a bit apprehensive. So, he lingered there holding her securely in his arms. He also kept her body propped to his chest. Tears were in his eyes just to contemplate her. Now that he had her near, he never wanted to let go. Hunching down, he pressed a loving kiss to her forehead. What he wanted was to kiss her sweet pouty lips, but desisted. If he *was* going to kiss her for the first time, they both had to be lucid.

"It's okay, sweetheart… You're going to be okay," Ellis mitigated, brushing the sides of her face and stroking her hair.

Coming to, Evaniese's head rocked from side to side. Ellis prayed that seeing him again wouldn't startle her. So, in order to keep her from hurting herself, he held her protectively in his arms.

Evaniese eyelids fluttered, as she strove to open up her eyes. She was anxious about what to expect. Now, everything made sense. Coming out to *Misty Morning, Georgia* to a luxury mansion, being received by El's staff, had been one big fantasy. Worse yet, she'd imagined El as her favorite movie star, Ellis Roman. So, at some point, Evaniese perceived she'd wake up in her bedroom back in Amber Hills.

Evaniese's eyes reflexively sprung open. Shrinking back, she instinctively shoved away from Ellis's arms, and bounded to her feet.

Ellis impulsively jumped to his feet as well. "It's alright… It's alright…," he placated, both hands held out in a halting manner.

"What…?" Evaniese kept shaking her head in disbelief. Terrified, she began to retreat away from the man. "This isn't real… *You're* not real," she concluded, shaking her head in denial. "You *can't* be Ellis Roman," she said, troubled. "I must be dreaming…"

"This isn't a dream, *Evaniese*," Ellis said throatily, taking measured steps to close the gap between them.

"What? You know my name?" Evaniese asked, even more unsettled. "You're *really* Ellis Roman?" Tears of bewilderment shone in her eyes.

"I *am* Ellis Roman, Evaniese. But, to you, I'm just El," he said humbly, and edged in even closer to her. Ellis moved in, and tenderly cradled her face in his hands. "I'm *just* El to you, baby," he emphasized.

"You're…, you're EL…?" Evaniese questioned shakily, with tears snaking down her cheeks.

Ellis smiled lovingly at Evaniese, and explored her eyes. "I *am* El," he told her again. "Evaniese, why did you pull away? Why did you shut me out of your life?" he asked thickly, as tears brimmed over in his eyes.

Evaniese was still expecting to wake up from a dream, as she stared into Ellis's beautiful face and eyes. Taking in how perfect he looked in his dark slacks, midnight blue shirt and cream-colored cardigan, Evaniese doubted that it *could* be a dream. Ellis had a stalwart build, and his butterscotch skin was as flawless as his dark wavy hair. Sunlight filtering through the extensive room, blazed in his honey eyes.

Evaniese was stunned, but still tried to enunciate words. There was a lot she wanted to say. Mostly, she tussled with feelings of guilt, because she *had* shut him out of her life. "I'm sorry that I pulled away. I didn't think you were real. When I told my friends about you, they convinced me you were just out for a scam." Her face warped in penitence.

"No, sweetheart. What we had was *very* real." Ellis's eyes delved intuitively into hers. "It killed me not being able to connect to you." He brushed her face caringly with his thumbs. "I've been in love with you since I saw your first video," he confessed, staring at her as if seeing a shooting start dart out from the sky.

"I can't believe *you're Fan4ever*," Evaniese said, trembling. "You kept leaving all of those encouraging comments for me." She smiled through the tears.

"Yes," Ellis fondly brushed her tears away, "I had to find a way to get close. So, I created that Instagram page, and told you my name was *Elbert*, just so we could talk. Do you have any idea how much I love you?" he asked gutturally. Ellis hunched down, and covered her face with tender kisses.

"I love you too," Evaniese whispered, still trying to process what was happening.

"So, you thought I was a scammer, huh?" Ellis smiled, with twinkling eyes full of love.

Evaniese nodded, dazed. She had only seen him on the big screen, but it honestly had failed to do him justice. He was much more beautiful in person! "My friends made me feel ridiculous, and said I was being naïve and trusting. I listened to them, and deleted the app and most of my social media," Evaniese explained. She closed her eyes meditatively, as Ellis delicately toured her face with kisses.

"I'm so sorry, honey. I guess, I wasn't very forthcoming about a lot of things," Ellis admitted, cradling Evaniese's head gently in his hands. "There were *things* I couldn't disclose. If I told you the truth from the start, I would have lost you for sure."

"And, *I* pulled away... I'm so sorry, El... Ellis," Evaniese enunciated.

"It's all right, baby. I understand," Ellis's voice broke. "That's why I couldn't get into too many details. I hope you understand." He searched her eyes.

Evaniese nodded, mesmerized. "I do now." She guffawed, and shook her head contrarily. "I can't believe *you're* El." She marveled.

"El in the flesh! I'm the man you shared so much with," Ellis said hoarsely. "I'm the man who fell in love with every word you said. I love you, Evaniese!" Ellis stated emphatically, gazing into her shimmering eyes. "I have waited for such a long time to look into your eyes, and to tell you that." His face bridged to Evaniese's, and he pressed a fond kiss to her nose.

"Oh, El, it really *is* you!" Evaniese acclaimed. Just then, all her fears and insecurities melted away. Evaniese realized Ellis wasn't a stranger at all, because of all they'd shared. So, she *did* know him. She draped her arms about his neck, and crushed devotedly in her arms. "I love *you*, Ellis!" she declared.

"I love you too, baby!" Ellis held her acquisitively, and relished the moment.

Evaniese pulled slightly away to stare into the eyes of one of the biggest celebrities in the world. She kept shaking her head in incredulity. "El is Ellis Roman," she said wonderingly, unable to stop smiling. She tiptoed, and pressed a kiss to his cheek. "Do you know that I'm one of your *biggest* fans?" she asked, bewildered.

"And, do *you* know that I'm one of *yours*...?" Ellis beamed, more in love than ever.

Evaniese laughed, overwhelmed and overjoyed. Surely, this was the most wonderful dream she'd ever had, and she never wanted to wake up. "You *don't* say...," she flirted.

"I *do*...." Ellis smiled lovingly into her eyes.

Bending down, his mouth fused affectionately to Evaniese's, and he kneaded every corner of her mouth with his. Ellis took his time to taste the sweet nectar, and drank ardently from the pleasant stream. He realized that he could have drunk from this agreeable brook all day, and his thirst still wouldn't be quenched. There was no way he'd *ever* be able to get enough to drink. So, he had to pull back. If he didn't, he knew he'd be unable to stop. Also, taking time to get to know his God-ordained spouse, wasn't something he wanted to rush.

***

"Are you cold, baby?" Ellis rubbed on Evaniese's arms in order to create friction. He and Evaniese had taken a walk down the lane, and through the surrounding meadows beyond the expansive property. But, they'd stopped short in front of Misty Lake.

"I am a little cold, but this is breathtaking, Ellis!" Evaniese praised, as she took in the serene backdrop. She felt happier, and safer with Ellis than she'd ever felt with anyone else.

Ellis slipped his arms about her waist from behind, and propped his chin to her right shoulder. "Is this a little better?" he asked throatily, enjoying their closeness.

Ellis's croaky voice and soft breath on her shoulder, gave Evaniese chills. It was such a wonderful feeling, she never wanted him to let go. "Much better," she said, turning to look at him. "I love it out here!"

"It *is* pretty nice...and so quiet," Ellis agreed. "You *know*, I purchased this property with you in mind," he said softly, urging her to turn around fully. Ellis kept his arms around her waist, and stared meaningfully into her eyes.

"*Really*?" Evaniese asked, stunned. The dream just kept getting better and better, and she had yet to wake up in her room back out in Amber Hills.

"Uh-huh... Last spring, I wanted to find a safe place for us to meet." Ellis shook his head emphatically. "I didn't want to pull you into the mayhem of my crazy world out in L.A."

"So, you bought this house in Misty Morning?" Evaniese stared at him in awe.

Ellis nodded. "It was supposed to be *our* special place." He smiled quietly. Taking Evaniese's hand, he guided her over to a comfortable spot. Setting down, he extended his hand, and invited her to sit beside him.

Evaniese cautiously sat down close to Ellis. He wrapped his arms about her shoulders, and tenderly cradled her in them. Their faces were close enough to bridge, but they just stared intimately into each other's eyes. Evaniese frowned in sadness as she considered, "You bought this house for us last spring, and that's when *I* decided to pull away." Guilt overwhelmed her.

"That was just a very difficult time all around. I had hoped and prayed you and I would come together, but then *everything* went awry. I lost my dad, and I had to go out to my family..." Fresh tears gleamed in his eyes, as he detailed the events.

"I'm so sorry, Ellis. I had no idea." Evaniese frowned in commiseration, and explored his beautiful but sad eyes. "That must have been the most difficult time for you and your family. I wish you and I could have been together then."

"I wanted that more than anything else," Ellis's voice wavered, as he took in just how truly beautiful Evaniese was. "I thought I'd die when we were disconnected. The air was thinning all around me, and I couldn't breathe. I thought I'd never find you again."

"I'm so sorry that I put you through that, Ellis," Evaniese said softly. She reached up, and set her hand on his face. "There was so much I *didn't* understand."

Ellis planted kisses to the palm of Evaniese's hand and smiled hopefully. "I'd like to share *everything* with you. I want you to know it all, baby, because you mean the world to me!" Ellis bridged his mouth to Evaniese's, and planted warm sugar kisses to it.

Evaniese closed her eyes, and just treasured the moment of being with Ellis. She was still finding it difficult to wrap her head around the fact that she was with *Ellis Roman*. "I would like to know *everything* there is to know about you too, Ellis," she said wispily, totally captivated. "I love every single one of your movies!" she championed, with an excited smile.

"Really?" Ellis chuckled, delighted. "Which is your favorite?" he rose playfully to the occasion.

"That would have to be *Deadly Roulette*," Evaniese admitted, blushing. "I love that scene where you confront that cartel boss. '*Not* today…and *not* on my watch…,'" Evaniese parodied.

Ellis laughed. "That was actually *pretty good*. I like *Deadly Roulette* too. But it wasn't my favorite-at least not until now…," Ellis admitted, spellbound.

"Aww... You're so sweet. The tabloids paint you as this raging playboy. They said you calmed down when you started dating Kierra Spalding. But, then they said you were dating Laura Morgan Fields...," Evaniese detailed.

Ellis chortled, and shook his head in negation. "The lies told by the tabloids and social media, have of way of taking a life all their own. No, Evaniese... The truth is that I haven't been with anyone. We talked about my faith. I've *honestly* been waiting for God to bless me with the right person.

"Kierra and I have graced a lot of red-carpet events together, but we're just friends," he admitted. "And as for Laura Morgan Fields, we worked together on a project or two. But, at the end of the day, my heart belongs solely to *one* woman." Ellis stared avidly into Evaniese's eyes.

"I love you, Ellis!" Evaniese said softly. She moved in, and pressed a sweet kiss to his mouth.

"I love you too, baby...so much!" Ellis secured Evaniese in his arms. "I'm also so proud of you for being brave enough to go through with the surgery! You look amazing! Still, Evaniese, you've always been-and always will be, the most beautiful woman *I've* ever seen!" Ellis propped a kiss to her forehead.

"Even if I've gained fifteen pounds?" Tears shimmered in Evaniese's eyes.

Ellis's face creased, pertained. "*Especially* because you have," he heartened. "You're so beautiful, baby!" His mouth bridged ardently to hers. Once more, he tried to quench his thirst from the source of sugarcane, but found himself at an impasse. He just couldn't get enough to drink. "You're beautiful in every way shape or form! Understand?" he reminded her in between butterfly kisses.

Evaniese nodded, overpowered by the way Ellis loved her. This icon of an individual stared at *her* as if *she* was one of the great wonders of the world. It was taking a moment to process the fact that Ellis Roman was the same man she'd chatted with, the same man who'd loved her so simply and unrestrainedly.

The humiliation and pain she'd suffered with Brent, Jeremy and Nathan still resonated. These men had treated her atrociously. And yet, Ellis Roman-world renowned celebrity, who was in a category all his own, adored her. On that very special day-a day of dreams, God deposited something into Evaniese's heart. The teachable moment was that the *status* of a man didn't really matter. What truly mattered was that man's heart. And, Ellis had the *right* heart.

Being who he was, he could have been just as pretentious and aloof as the others. However, he was kind, down-to-earth, loving and personable. After all, Evaniese had endured, she couldn't believe someone like Ellis Roman loved *her*. She'd been belittled and mistreated by her friends, her work colleagues, and the men she thought would be good to her. But, God was honoring her with a man most women only dreamed about. And, she was quite frankly blown away!

***

Misty Morning felt more like *Stormy Morning* on Wednesday in the early a.m., as Ellis and Evaniese sat in the limo. Torrential downpour issued from the lead-painted skies. Lightening flashed, and thunder clapped furiously on their way over to the airport. For Evaniese, the day before still felt like a dream. Meeting the love of her life for the very first time, and discovering he was her celebrity crush, was indeed a fantasy.

Nevertheless, last night, Evaniese received a text message from Deanna. As it would seem, she and Ginger were victims of a horrible car crash. And whereas Deanna had a few bumps and bruises, Ginger was in serious condition at the hospital. So, Evaniese felt constrained to return to Amber Hills right away.

Ellis was heartbroken over Evaniese's terrible news. He was even more disappointed, because they had to say goodbye again. As the limo whirred silently on the pavement, he held Evaniese securely in his arms. But, neither of them spoke.

It broke Ellis's heart to see the woman he loved so distraught. There wasn't anything he wouldn't have done to take away the pain. Tears glinted in his eyes, in reflection of the pain he saw on Evaniese's face.

"I'm so sorry, baby," he said gutturally, stroking her arm in comfort. "Are you sure there isn't anything I can do?" His face warped in compassion.

"No, sweetie," Evaniese said demurely. "You've been so great! I'm just sorry we have to cut our time together short." She frowned in sadness.

"Don't even worry about that, baby." Ellis squeezed her closer to himself. "Your friends need you a lot more right now." He kissed her forehead. "We'll be together soon enough. I promise."

"Promise...?" Evaniese asked shakily.

"I promise, baby," Ellis reassured, staring intuitively into her sad eyes. "Do you really think I'm *ever* going to let you get away again?" Weightiness masked his handsome face. "Well, in case you were wondering, the answer is no. I will *never* let you go, Evaniese!" Ellis covered her face in tender kisses. "I love you!"

"I love you so much, Ellis!"

"I hate that you're hurting," he admitted, as they nestled. "You're my heart and my baby. If you're hurting, that means I am too."

"I'm going to be okay," Evaniese told him. "Thank you so much for being with me this morning, *and* for understanding."

"Of course, my love." Ellis kissed away her tears.

Evaniese contemplated the heaven she felt with Ellis. They'd spent most of yesterday together, but now had to say goodbye. Yet, even if she didn't harbor any ill feelings towards Ginger and Deanna, Evaniese felt conflicted. They weren't her *real* friends. Though, she couldn't see herself abruptly cutting them out of her life. And, she certainly couldn't walk away, until she knew for sure they were going to be all right. God had asked her to distance herself from them, and so she had to be obedient. Perhaps, cutting ties would be a lot easier, once she saw them at the hospital, and was assured of their recovery.

Ellis held Evaniese's hand, as they stepped out of the automobile on the curb of the busy airport terminal. He held a sizable black umbrella over their heads. With his free hand, he cradled Evaniese's face, and pressed kisses repeatedly to her mouth. "I love you so much, baby!"

Evaniese had to tiptoe in order to link her mouth to Ellis's. She set honey kisses recurrently to his mouth. Ellis was over six feet tall, and she was only 5'6." They were both in tears. "I love you too! I don't want to leave you, Ellis," she groused, and her face twisted in sorrow.

"Oh, baby, I don't *want* you to go, but you have to. All right, my love?" Ellis caressed her cheek. "I promise it won't be for long." His tear-filled eyes delved sensitively into hers. All at once, the realization that she was leaving overpowered him. Ellis was already experiencing some form of separation anxiety. "Go on, baby... I promise we'll be together soon," his voice broke.

"Promise?" Evaniese's face puckered in melancholy.

"I promise, my love. I promise to drop by with another *package* for you." He winked.

Evaniese gasped in shock. "That was you?" she questioned, incredulous.

Ellis laughed. "You were so adorable in your navy-blue floral print top and cute leggings."

Evaniese kept shaking her head in disbelief. "I can't believe all you went through."

"And, I would do it again in a heartbeat, if it means having you in my arms forever." Ellis stroked fondly on her cheek. "You sure you don't want me to go inside? I have my trusty baseball cap and shades handy," he teased.

"No, I don't want to risk creating a frenzy, and having everyone mob you at the airport. So, this has got to be goodbye for now." Evaniese sighed.

"Not goodbye, my sweet Evaniese. See you later," Ellis said optimistically. Arching down, his lips bridged to hers shortly. "I love you! Please, text me the moment you're off the plane."

Evaniese nodded, trying to keep a stiff upper lip, as Ellis led her over to the doors. With the umbrella draped over them, no one could really see his face. "Bye, sweetie." She frowned glumly just before slipping inside the airport.

"Bye, baby," Ellis said, and watched Evaniese disappear through the glass doors. He stood outside the bustling terminal with his eyes fastened to her, until she was no longer discernable. For a moment Ellis found himself frozen. He couldn't budge, as hurried patrons went in and out of the airport. There was such a sense of emptiness on the inside. Once he got his bearings, he crossed back over to the limo, folded the umbrella, and slipped inside.

There were tears in his eyes on the ride back over to the mansion. He reached into the pocket of his jeans, and retrieved the black jewelry box he'd kept concealed from Evaniese. In it was a 40-carat emerald-cut diamond engagement ring. That very morning, he'd planned on proposing to her. Picking up the custom-made ring, was the most pressing errand he had to run the day before.

However, in light of the circumstances, his proposal would have to take a back seat. Evaniese's friends had been traumatized in horrible car crash, and she had to be there for them. Ellis assented to the fact that he needed to let her go for just a little while. Still, in her absence, getting enough air to his lungs, was proving to be a real challenge. Once again, he was finding it difficult to breathe. There was no way he could live without her. So, he knew he had to find a way to keep her in his world forever.

Chapter Eleven

Evaniese lingered in front of Ginger's hospital room door. From what she was told, Ginger could now receive visitors. Because she'd been discharged from the hospital, Evaniese hadn't seen Deanna yet. Based on Deanna's text, she was now at home, and would return to the hospital later on to visit Ginger. Evaniese considered dropping by Deanna's to check in, because she had no intention of hanging out at the hospital all day.

After whispering a prayer, Evaniese gently pushed open the hospital room door. Her heart plunged in sadness the moment she saw Ginger laid up in the bed. There were bandages covering her upper body, and extreme swelling and edema to her lower extremities. The inflammation was so severe, anyone could have concluded she was suffering from some rare disease.

Tears immediately brimmed over in Evaniese's eyes to see Ginger that way. Also, as a result of the black and purple bruises and the distention, Ginger's face looked deformed. Her eyes were opened, but it was difficult to discern her facial expression.

Evaniese allowed the door to close softly, then edged in closer to the hospital bed. Sympathy and commiseration veiled her sweet face. "Hey," she said, standing to the side of Ginger's hospital bed.

"Hi," Ginger said, through gritted teeth, seemingly irritated.

"I'm so sorry this happened, Ginger," Evaniese said in earnest, with tear-filled eyes. "I'm even sorrier that I didn't know until last night."

Ginger tried not to be angry or bitter, but resentment stirred on the inside. She wasn't upset because Evaniese had been MIA for the past couple of days. She was just fine with that. What she *was* upset about was the accident. Ginger blamed the car crash and her injuries on Evaniese. Still, before she tore into Evaniese, there were a few things she had to know.

"You heard about the accident just last night?" Ginger's misshapen face turned crimson, making her look all the more grotesque. "It happened on Sunday night," she slurred.

"Yeah, I'm sorry I wasn't there," Evaniese said plainly, and offered no other words.

She hardly felt ready to disclose how she'd been out of town for the day, and had spent the night in Misty Morning, Georgia in Ellis Roman's mansion. She would *never* tell Ginger that she and Ellis Roman were now an item. At some point, Ginger and Deanna would find out, along with the rest of the world.

"Where were you, Evaniese?" Ginger asked snippily.

"I had an out-of-town engagement," Evaniese relayed, perceiving Ginger's frustration.

"You were going out of town, and you never said anything to me or to Dee?" She rolled her eyes reproachfully.

"Something came up," Evaniese defended, resenting Ginger's interrogative tone. "Ginger, I'm so sorry I was out of town when I found out about the accident. I had no idea what happened. Dee only texted me last night. She told me that neither of you were in any shape to text anyone after what happened," Evaniese justified.

"Yeah, right..." Ginger's head veered in the opposite direction. She couldn't stand to keep looking at Evaniese. Everything about her irritated Ginger, and got under her skin. She hated the fact that, in spite of the weight gain, Evaniese still looked gorgeous!

The WLS wasn't the flop she'd hoped for. Evaniese had only suffered a minor setback. On the other hand, Ginger wasn't sure that her own *bloated* body would recover from the injuries sustained from the car crash.

"What's wrong, Ginger?" Evaniese walked around the hospital bed to look at her. "I apologize for not being in town at the time of the accident, but I'm here now. Please, don't be mad at me." She set her hand on her heart in appeal.

Ginger's scowl swerved towards Evaniese. "I'm not *mad* at you, Evaniese," she hissed, clearly embittered. "I can't stand you," she spat out.

Evaniese flinched, and instinctively took steps away from Ginger's bedside. Tears immediately gathered in her eyes, and her throat felt scratchy. And, there it was again! Ginger's dark twin with the onyx eyes had reemerged. She looked just as threatening and odious as she had on Sunday night. "Wow!" Evaniese said, stunned. "You hate *me*, Ginger?" she asked incredulous.

"Yes I do, and I blame *you* for this." Ginger showcased her injured, and broken body with the three fingers on her right hand, protruding through bandages. "I blame you, because of your love for Jesus!" Ginger recriminated inordinately, and gave Evaniese the death stare.

Tears rolled down Evaniese's cheeks, and she kept shaking her head in disbelief. "Wow! Why don't you just tell me how you *really* feel, Ginger?" her voice wavered, and she breathed spasmodically.

"I can't *believe* the weight loss surgery worked for you." Ginger sneered and scowled in vexation.

Evaniese wiped tears away from her eyes. She took deep breaths to steady her voice. "Well, guess what, Ginger? I already *knew* that you hated me. God showed me all about *you*...about Dee." She was trembling. "You were hoping my weight loss surgery would be a complete failure, right?" Evaniese's face warped in regret.

"You think you're really something, right? You think you're *hot stuff*, because those three guys paid a *little* attention to you? Well, guess what? To me, you're still *fat*... You're the fat one, the one without a boyfriend, and the oldest...," Ginger denunciated, but recoiled in shock and indignity over her own words. She'd just *outed* herself, and exposed her wicked and jealous heart.

Evaniese kept shaking her head in denial and incredulity. "Thanks, Ginger. Wow! I guess, the mask has fallen off, hasn't it? The Lord showed me who you *really* are. I know you're not a real friend, even if you've been masquerading around as one for a very long time. I get that you hate me." Evaniese's breathing was short. She shook her head in irony, and gave Ginger a pitiful look. She couldn't understand Ginger's acrimonious behavior, especially after having suffered such a trauma. It didn't make sense that she was still so full of hate and animosity.

"You want to know the sad part? The sad part is that I trusted *you*, and I trusted Dee. I truly thought you were my friends..." Evaniese diffidently kept her distance from Ginger's hospital bed.

Ginger idly stared out the window. She was too ashamed to reestablish eye contact, after exposing her ugly heart.

"I feel sorry for you, Ginger. I thought we were friends, and that you had my best interest at heart. I see now how I couldn't have been more wrong." Melancholy and disillusionment were on Evaniese's face and in her eyes. "But, you aren't my friend at all. Friends don't hurt each other the way you and Deanna hurt me. Furthermore, true friends aren't jealous and evil. Neither do they chomp at the bit to see one another fail."

Evaniese nodded acquiescently. "Honestly, the only reason I came here today is to make sure you're okay. I *am* truly sorry about the accident, and I wish you nothing but a complete and total recovery. But, this is the end of the line for us, Ginger."

"Good..., cause I'm tired of looking at you," Ginger retorted, turning her head to glare at Evaniese. "I hope you regain all your weight. You're never going to have a good boyfriend like I do, no matter how long you 'wait on the Lord.' Nobody wants you," Ginger berated.

Evaniese smiled musingly to hear Ginger's words. Recalling the way Ellis had held her in his arms, and refused to let her go, she just nodded compliantly. "Thank you for your well wishes, Ginger. I really appreciate your *friendship*," she scoffed. "But, it's time to say goodbye." Unspeakable pain radiated inwardly, and changed her sweet face.

"More like good riddance, Evaniese! I don't care how much weight you lose, you'll never be better than me or Dee."

"Wow! Okay, you're *right*, Ginger. I will *never* be as good as you or Dee. Thank you," she assented. "Before I leave here today, I will say this. Ginger, God showed me about you and Deanna engaging in witchcraft, and how you've both been plotting my downfall. I'm begging you to stop messing around with that stuff. You're only securing your own destruction, and *possible* demise." Evaniese pointed out Ginger's current state.

"Kiss off, Evaniese," Ginger hollered. "You're in no position to preach to me."

"You're right, Ginger. I am not in a position to preach to anyone. And yet, I'm smart enough to know that anyone who attends church, and calls on the name of Jesus Christ, has no business dabbling in the demonic and practicing witchcraft. (2 Timothy 2:19) 'And Let everyone that nameth the name of Christ depart from iniquity.' You're just heaping up curses and calamity on yourself. Case in point." Evaniese showcased Ginger's condition yet again.

Growing even angrier, Ginger began to spout a string of obscenities at Evaniese. "Get out of my hospital room. Get out now!" she said brusquely.

"Goodbye, Ginger. I will keep you in my prayers." Evaniese surrendered to tears.

"Get out, you witch," Ginger bellowed. "I don't care if I ever see you again..."

Evaniese moved away from Ginger, and crossed over to the hospital room door. She was still extremely emotional. After all, for many years, Ginger had been *like* family. Nevertheless, Evaniese had prayed a great deal. Also, she was currently in the middle of a fast. And, the power of God at work within her, had stripped the mask off from Ginger's face, so to speak. Before Evaniese slipped out of the hospital room, she turned once more to look at her *lost* friend. However, this time around, she saw the demon which had manifested at her front door on Sunday night.

Evaniese vowed to pray for Ginger. It seemed, she had wholeheartedly committed herself to the infernal forces. Evaniese had left Ellis out in Misty Morning to ensure that her *friends* were Okay. It was a decision she now regretted. Now, more than ever, she missed Ellis, and longed to be in his arms again.

***

"She came right out, and admitted she hates me, Ellis," Evaniese told Ellis over the phone. She was home from visiting Ginger at the hospital, and Ellis had called to check in.

"I'm so sorry to hear that, baby. That breaks my heart for you. I *know* how much you love your friends. You always talked so endearingly about Ginger and Deanna whenever we chatted," Ellis commiserated.

"It hurts so badly," Evaniese admitted, as tears meandered down her cheeks. "I can't believe someone I love and considered a friend, could *ever* speak to me in that way."

"I'm so sorry, baby. Please, don't cry. Don't let it break your heart. What happened with Ginger is God's way of protecting you. God wanted you to see who you were dealing with. So, he exposed her heart. The relationship was toxic, and quite frankly very dangerous. You don't need anyone like that in your life, baby," Ellis explained. "God will bring the right people into your life, my love. He will give you friends with the right heart."

"Thank you, Ellis. You're right." Evaniese tried to pull herself together. "Thank you for being such a great friend..." She guffawed. "I can't believe *we're* actually *friends*," she said, still dumbfounded.

"*Friends?*" Ellis questioned. "Evaniese, you're my *everything*!" he declared.

Stirred beyond words, Evaniese choked up again, and her eyes flooded with tears of joy. She was head-over-heels in love with Ellis Roman! The fact that A-lister and Hollywood icon, Ellis Roman was her boyfriend, was taking a moment to sink in. "Oh, Ellis, I love you so much!" she affirmed.

"I love you too, baby...*more* every minute," Ellis emphasized. "So, are you feeling better?" concern resonated in his tone.

"I *always* feel better when I'm talking to you." Evaniese beamed.

"What are you doing right now, baby?" Ellis dallied.

"I'm just in my room talking to you...," Evaniese flirted.

"Are you missing *me* as much as I'm missing *you* right now?" Ellis's voice was husky.

"More...," Evaniese echoed.

"Did you have dinner yet, baby?" he tested. "With all the running around you did today, I doubt you had time for a decent meal."

"I *am* a little hungry," Evaniese confessed. Her stomach was actually in knots and growling. She hadn't had a bite to eat since leaving Misty Morning earlier in the day.

"Well, I took the liberty of ordering a nice dinner for you," Ellis said impishly.

"You *did*?" Evaniese was impressed and overjoyed. "Oh, you sweet, wonderful man!" she praised. "I love you so much!"

"I love you too, baby!"

Just then, Evaniese's doorbell rang. "I think my delivery's here!" she told Ellis over the phone.

"Oh, all right, babe. Go on and get the door," Ellis encouraged.

"We can keep talking while I walk over to the front door, sweetie." Evaniese coasted spiritedly over to the door, with the phone cradled to her ear.

"Alright, my love. I'm not going anywhere."

Evaniese opened up the front door, and nearly passed out to see Ellis standing beyond it. He looked incredible in dark slacks and gray sweater. With a mischievous grin, he held up a large brown paper bag. Shocked, she dropped the phone. "Ellis!" she announced, and instinctively threw her arms around him.

"Hi, baby!" Ellis crushed Evaniese in his arms. Tears of joy pooled in his eyes to have her close to him again. He'd tried to stay away, but couldn't.

"Ellis...?" Evaniese trembled, overwhelmed and overjoyed. "I can't believe you're here! What are you doing here?" She pulled away a bit to look into his beautiful amber eyes. Cradling his face in her hands, she brushed softly on his cheeks. "What have you gone and done?" She gave him a curious but skeptical look.

"I tried really hard to say goodbye this morning." Ellis shook his head emphatically, and his face warped emotionally. "I really did, baby."

"Oh, I *know* you did, sweetie..." Evaniese's face wrinkled in compassion.

"But, I had a little problem." Ellis pressed kisses to the palms of Evaniese's hands.

"What's that, sweetie?" Tears brimmed over in Evaniese's eyes.

"I honestly couldn't breathe, because you weren't near me," he admitted.

Ellis hunched down, and his mouth melded to hers. Taking his time, he covered every contour of hers with tender kisses, extracting honey from its source. "I love you so much!" he kept reminding her in between fiery kisses.

"I love you too, sweetie!" Evaniese squeezed Ellis affectionately in her arms, and plowed her fingers through his torturous bed of hair. "I can't believe you're here."

"And, I have dinner…" Ellis's grasp tightened about her. "I missed you the moment you slipped through those airport terminal doors," Ellis said thickly, and secured her in his arms.

"How did I ever get to be so lucky?" Evaniese lovingly explored his eyes. In her estimation, he was one of the most beautiful people on the planet. She kept her arms draped around Ellis's neck, and refused to let go.

"I've asked *myself* that question every day since we've met," Ellis admitted. Hunching down, he pelted her face with affectionate kisses.

Evaniese basked in the joy of being in Ellis's arms. A part of her still could fathom that *he* loved her. After all the rejection she'd known with other men, God had finally visited her. Needless to say, none of the other men could hold a candle up to Ellis.

"Thank you so much for coming over." Evaniese took Ellis's free hand in hers, and guided him into the house. "How long can you stay?" she asked, turning to face him.

"I love your home, Evaniese!" Ellis sized up the living room. "It's beautiful!"

Evaniese guffawed. "You've probably seen the most lavish houses out there, and you like this little one?" She kept shaking her head in irony. She led the way into the kitchen, and Ellis rested the bag of food on her counter.

"This *is* lovely, baby," Ellis heartened, staring all about the room in awe.

"Thank you, sweetie." Evaniese beamed. "I'll get us plates," she said, turning to walk away, but Ellis took hold of her right hand, and pulled her close to himself.

"Niece...?" Ellis said urgently, staring intently into her eyes.

"You're *not* hungry?" Evaniese questioned, bewildered. She was captivated by the way Ellis stared at her. Anyone would have guessed he was watching a fireworks display.

"Of course, I *will* join you for dinner, baby." Ellis's piercing eyes probed into Evaniese's soul. He wanted her to understand the depths of his loneliness, and how he could no longer live apart from her. Tenderly taking her hands into his, he moved in as close as he possibly could.

"But, I would have to get us plate...?" Evaniese said, adrift and stunned. Her relationship with Ellis had been passionate from the outset. Even when they'd chatted using the *Chat Channel* app, Evaniese had felt his enamoring energy with every exchange.

"Yes, in a moment..." Ellis smiled quietly. "Evaniese, you just asked how long I can stay." His eyes weightily explored hers.

"You're *not* staying?" Evaniese frowned, confused.

"I'm afraid I can't stay for very long. However, there are a few things I'd like to say," his voice was gravelly.

On impulse, Evaniese reached up, and pressed a kiss to his lips. "I love you!" she reaffirmed.

"And, I love *you* more than anything, baby!" Ellis smiled into her eyes. "That's why I'm here."

"Okay...," Evaniese said, winded, and with a drubbing heart.

"How devoted are you to staying in the lovely town of Amber Hills?" Ellis brought up.

"Are you asking if I have some kind of an emotional attachment to this town?" Evaniese clarified.

Ellis nodded. "Would you be willing to leave here tonight...with me?" He desperately searched her eyes.

"What...?" Evaniese kept shaking her head in skepticism.

"I have a private jet ready to take us back to Misty Morning. I'd like for you to stay out there for just a couple of days. There's this film festival I have to be a part of on Friday night out in L.A. So, I'd have to leave Georgia tomorrow afternoon."

"Ellis...," Evaniese began to say, overwhelmed. "I don't..."

"Niece," he smiled, "I'm not finished, honey."

"Okay..." Evaniese gestured for him to finish his train of thought.

"I'd like for you to stay out in Misty Morning for a couple of days. I promise I'd only be gone a couple of days. However, when I get back, I'd like for us to fly out to Southern Italy...together."

"Ellis, what are you saying?" Evaniese gasped, stunned. "You want to take me on a vacation...?"

"Not just any vacation, baby. There's this breathtaking vineyard out there."

"A vineyard?" Evaniese questioned, muddled.

"Yes, baby. I'd like for us to get married," Ellis said straightforwardly.

"You want us to get married?" Evaniese's eyes widened in shock, and her mouth gaped.

"Yes, baby... I'd like for us to get married just as soon as possible." Ellis kept his hold on Evaniese's hand, but genuflected down to one knee. "This is what I wanted to do this morning, but it felt all wrong in light of the circumstances." Ellis searched Evaniese's eye with great love and admiration.

Evaniese gulped, and reflexively set her free hand over her gaped mouth. She found herself trembling and in tears. "Ellis, what...? I can't believe this."

"Evaniese Catherine Spencer, will you marry me?" Ellis asked formally. This time, he reached into the pocket of his slacks, and retrieved the custom-made ring.

Emotionally overwrought, Evaniese wept, as she stared down at the most beautiful man she'd ever laid eyes on. There he was in prostration before her, displaying the biggest and clearest diamond ring she'd ever seen! This was the stuff fairytales were made of, but she knew this was no fairytale or dream. Ellis Roman was asking her to become his wife. Evaniese frenziedly nodded before muttering "Yes... Yes, of course, I will marry you, Ellis!"

"Yes...? Is that a yes, baby?" Ellis celebrated.

Standing upright, he collected Evaniese in his arms, and held her acquisitively. On impulse, he picked her up from off the floor, and spun her around. Once he set her down, he took his time to lavish kisses to her face and lips. "You *will* marry me?" his voice broke.

Evaniese draped her arms about his neck, and stared intently into his golden-brown eyes. "Yes, of course, I will marry you, Ellis. I'm not dreaming, am I?" she tested. "I'm not going to wake up, and find you gone?"

"Even if we were both dreaming, I'd find a way pull you out of my dream. In fact, I think I already *have*..." Ellis grinned. "I love you so much!"

"I love you too, Ellis!" Evaniese kept thanking God.

"What I feel for you, Ms. Evaniese Catherine Spencer, is difficult to define. And yet, I want to spend the rest of my life trying to express the great love I have for you."

Ellis's lips bridged to Evaniese's. And, in a deliberate and gentle rhythm, he massaged them lovingly with his. Ellis tenderly caressed the contours of Evaniese's waist, and her back, as he drank exigently from the confectionary rivulet.

Evaniese found herself responding hungrily to Ellis's sugar kisses. He kissed her like a person on life support, and she was the only thing keeping him alive. Breathless and overcome, Evaniese whispered in between ardent kisses, "I love you, Ellis!"

"I love *you*, Evaniese!" Ellis cradled her head in his hands. "So, you're leaving with me tonight?" he asked, searching her eyes. "I actually came out here to help you pack." He smiled.

"Oh, so you *knew* I'd say yes?" Evaniese set her hands cheekily on her hips.

"I prayed really hard that you would." He planted a kiss to her forehead. "Is there anything keeping you in this town?" Ellis asked more urgently.

Evaniese thought it through. She'd only considered Ginger and Deanna *family* out in Amber Hills. Needless to say, that was no longer an issue. Now that she knew how they *really* felt about her, she was more than ready to distance herself from the pain. She no longer tussled with guilt. As it would seem, both of her former friends would more than likely recover from the car accident.

Then, there was Brent Peterson. Years ago, God had shown her Brent loved her. However, Brent had never been strong enough to defy society, and risk his reputation by dating her. Evaniese had cared a lot about Jeremy Carter, but he'd broken her heart, and had *married* someone else.

Furthermore, Doctor Nathan Andrews had strung her along, and had subsequently abandoned her. Evaniese remembered what Dr. Sylvia Lester had said during her psych evaluation for the VSG. In a lot of ways, Evaniese realized she was right. Perhaps, somewhere down the road, she would cross paths again with the three men. Regardless of that notion, she wasn't holding her breath, because she couldn't see herself loving *anyone* the way she loved Ellis Roman.

Evaniese reasoned, if the other men were meant to be in her life, they would need to play catch up. However, in the interim, the plan was to follow God's leading. She would open up her heart to the most wonderful gift she'd ever been given. A stark contrast to the suffering and humiliation, the silver lining on her cloud, radiated with such an intensity it was blinding.

Any minute now she'd awaken from the sweetest dream. Even so, after a while, Evaniese perceived, such a blessing was God's way of wiping all her tears away. Heaven knows she'd shed so many over the years! The irony of it all was that Ellis was her junior by eleven years. Evaniese had always worried about her age. She'd groused that God had made her wait utterly too long for her soulmate. Nevertheless, even that concern was now a nonissue.

"All your bags are in the limo, babe," Ellis told Evaniese, as he ventured back inside the house to get her.

Evaniese examined the familiar setting she'd known as home for many years. There should have been a nostalgic tug-of-war on the inside, but she was *over* it. Scrutinizing the breathtaking and sizable diamond ring on her finger, she found herself in awe.

Ellis shifted over to the living room, and subtly slipped his arms around Evaniese from behind. "Hey, baby," he said hoarsely, "we're all packed." He pressed loving kisses to her cheek. "We can worry about renting, leasing, or even selling the house later on." He gently turned Evaniese to face himself.

Securing his arms about her waist, he stared lovingly down at her. "Are you scared?" he questioned, pertained.

Evaniese set her arms around his neck, and shook her head in negation. "Not even a little," she confessed, with tears shimmering in her eyes. "I know what we share is a gift from God. God has allowed me to cry a lot, but he's never steered me in the wrong direction."

"Well, guess what, beautiful? It's my *job* to wipe away all of your tears, and to keep you smiling and happy forever." Ellis stared sentimentally into her eyes.

"Oh, Ellis…" Evaniese found herself getting emotional. "I'm so ready to start this new chapter of our lives together."

"I'm so glad to hear that, because I'm ready to show you off to the world! I'm excited for everyone to see just what a precious and rare jewel I've found!" Ellis pressed his lips to hers.

"I can't wait," Evaniese encouraged. She took Ellis's hand, and entwined them in hers.

"Come on, baby… The limo's waiting," Ellis said softly, leading Evaniese outside. "Are we locking up?" he asked before they strolled down the walkway.

"Just close the door, and it'll lock on its own," Evaniese turned to tell him.

Ellis did as Evaniese asked, and closed the front door. Slipping his arm around her waist, the pair walked down the lane lovingly sustaining each other.

Ellis secured Evaniese inside the limo, and took his place beside her. The two cuddled, as the automobile pulled away from Evaniese's *former* home.

"I knew that I wanted you to be my forever love the very first time I saw you," Ellis whispered into Evaniese's ear, holding her tightly in his arms.

"How lucky am I!" Evaniese's face bridged to his. The pair nuzzled, as they were conveyed across town to the heliport, where Ellis's private jet awaited.

"No one's luckier than I am, babe! You've agreed to marry me, and life doesn't get any better than that!" Ellis lost himself in the throes of Evaniese's loving kisses.

***

Luckily, Brookline's Emergency Room was more or less tame on that particular Saturday afternoon. It gave the doctors, the PA's, nurses, and other members of the ER staff, a moment to gather together in the breakroom. All eyes were affixed to the Flat-screen T.V. mounted to the wall. There was tomblike silence, as they listened to the entertainment news broadcast.

The woman they'd all known as Evaniese Spencer, was now Evaniese Spencer-Roman. She'd married A-list actor, Ellis Roman in a secret ceremony in Southern Italy. Furthermore, the 40-carat diamond ring on Evaniese's finger flashed recurrently throughout the segment.

There was a somber tenor in the air. ER staff, who'd work closely with Evaniese, felt all the more humbled. When she'd worked through the hospital, they'd impugned, mocked and had fat-shamed her. And now, they were all forced to eat their words. Not only had she married Ellis Roman, but she was no longer plus-sized.

She looked like a queen in her elegant wedding gown, standing next to one of the most successful and handsome actors in the industry. Those who worked through the ER with Evaniese, hardly recognized her as the same person. No one dared to say she didn't belong on Ellis Roman's arm, because Evaniese dazzled just as brilliantly as her new husband.

Evaniese's former rivals, gave one another blank stares, as they watched the broadcast. Long time Hollywood bachelor Ellis Roman was now married. And, he'd married someone they'd belittled, undermined, and had plotted against. They were grieved and stunned over the turn of events. Mostly, they regretted the way in they'd treated Evaniese. Not a sound could be detected for a prolonged lapse.

Yet, they were all reminiscent of Evaniese's seven-year stint of working through the hospital. They'd underestimated and undervalued her. At that point, she was further removed from their reality than the cosmos. Evaniese was now the wife of a wealthy and handsome celebrity. Even if no one there had found a way to express it, they were all thinking the same thing. Evaniese's former coworkers were beside themselves, as they watched footage of the secret wedding. After years of looking down on Evaniese, their mouths remained tightly shut, and there was total silence.

Paula Rivers and Ann Ridges were also working through Brookline Hospital that weekend. Both had seen YouTube videos, and Google images capturing bits and pieces of Evaniese's secret wedding to Hollywood elite Ellis Roman. Furthermore, they'd seen the ring on Evaniese's finger.

The diamond was essentially the size of a marble. Paula sat in her office armchair feeling insignificant, dazed and overwhelmed. *How on earth had Evaniese Spencer landed Ellis Roman? How had she gone from being completely overlooked, to being sought out by a man like Ellis Roman?* Paula just couldn't wrap her head around it.

She was suddenly seized with a sense of fear and dread. She had misused, mistreated and gas-lighted Evaniese while she'd worked there. Besides, she had set Evaniese up with Human Resources, and compelled her to prematurely quit her job.

Now that Evaniese was the wife of a very powerful man, Paula worried she would seek out some form of revenge. *Would Evaniese return to Amber Hills looking to make trouble for her?* Paula's thoughts raced, as she internalized her evil and devious actions.

"Did you see the entertainment news?" Ann stood outside of Paula's office. Ann was still amazed that Evaniese Spencer was now married to Ellis Roman. She was also extremely happy for her. "Evaniese married…"

"Yeah, yeah, yeah…" Paula rolled her eyes in annoyance. "I know, I know… Evaniese married Ellis Roman. Yada, yada, yada… Now, don't *you* have those demographic reports to complete before you leave this afternoon?" she asked acerbically.

Ann's smile immediately turned to a frown. "Yeah, I guess. I'll have them ready as soon as I can." She made a face, and looked heavenward. Ann prayed for God to bless her with another job, so that she'd be emancipated from having to deal with Paula's.

"You're just jealous and upset that something good happened for Evaniese. We put her through a lot when she worked here. So, she deserves to be happy," Ann muttered, keeping a taut smile on her face, as she looked straight at Paula.

"You say something, Ann?" Paula glared over at her.

"Not a thing…" Ann turned away, and sauntered down the hallway in the direction of her office.

***

"Is everything alright, Brent?" Denise scrutinized Brent in concern. She and Brent had plans to go out to dinner, but they remained stalled outside in his car. There was a confused expression on Brent's face, as he sat behind the wheel. His eyes remained fastened to his smartphone.

Brent had just watched a brief YouTube video. The video detailed Evaniese's travels to Southern Italy, and her secret wedding ceremony to Hollywood icon Ellis Roman. Brent was flabbergasted, and he found himself blinking back tears. It took all the self-control he had not to fall apart in Denise's presence.

Sickened by the news, all Brent wanted was to be alone. After doing all he could to micromanage Evaniese's life, he'd failed miserably. Brent had done everything in his power to ensure that *all* men keep their distance from the woman he truly loved. In his assessment, he *did* do a great job at keeping all the men at bay, *including himself.* How on *earth had this happened right under his nose? How had Evaniese connected to, and wound up marrying Ellis Roman?*

"Brent...?" Denise frowned in apprehension.

"Yes, sweetheart." Brent finally looked at her.

"Are you alright?" The frown lines on Denise's face deepened.

"Sure. Of course," Brent said offhandedly, feigning total aplomb. Inwardly, he was falling apart. "Would you be terribly upset, if I asked for a raincheck tonight?" Brent was out of sorts and agitated. "Something's come up," he added.

"Are you sick?" Denise reached over, and set her cool hand on Brent's forehead.

"No, I'm fine, sweetheart," Brent reassured with a wavering voice. "I just forgot there was something I had to do tonight." He gave her a sympathetic smile. "I promise to make it up to you."

Denise surrendered to a slow nod. "Okay, Brent. It's fine." She pointed an accusatory finger at him in censure. "You *will* make this up to me."

"Of *course,* I will." Brent set his right hand to the side of her face and caressed it.

Soon after, Brent drove Denise. He couldn't remember ever driving so fast in his entire life. Perfunctorily walking her to her front door, he pressed a quick kiss to her lips.

"Brent, I forgot to...," Denise called out, as she watched him dash down the walkway.

She wanted to remind him of their shopping date tomorrow afternoon. However, her heart plunged in disappointment watching Brent hop back into his car, and rip away from the area.

Brent took a drive out to Nettles Park, which overlooked the river. After parking his car, he crossed over to the river barricade. Hunching over the enclosure, he wailed like an animal caught in a trap deep in the forest.

***

Nathan Andrews had spent the weekend all alone. His girlfriend had taken a trip down to the city to visit family. Nathan was close to polishing off an entire bottle of whiskey. He was so tired of seeing footage of Evaniese's secret wedding ceremony to Hollywood movie star Ellis Roman. It made him feel like an even bigger fool. He still loved Evaniese, and hated himself for allowing Brent Peterson to bully him from following his heart.

Now, it was much too late. Because of Brent's intimidation, he'd lost the most wonderful woman in the world. Nathan realized his failure to step up to the plate. He recounted the times Evaniese had shown romantic interest in him. He, in turn, had treated her appallingly.

His flippant and cavalier attitude towards their connection now haunted him. There were instances where he'd neglected to respond to a simple text message. Nathan readily acknowledged the times he'd made Evaniese feel as if she just wasn't good enough. Inversely, Hollywood icon, Ellis Roman, had clearly recognized the *diamond* he'd once treated like *junk*.

The adage, one man's junk is another man's treasure resonated that day. Nathan contemplated just how true the proverb was. Understanding exactly what that axiom meant, was something he'd have to sit with for the rest of his life. He'd lost someone truly special, and there wasn't anything he could do about it. On the other hand, at least for the moment, he had his trusty bottle of whiskey. He would use the deceitful libation to temporarily stifle the pain screaming so loudly on the inside.

***

"Can you shut that thing off?" Jeremy bellowed, addressing his wife. "How many times do we have to see the same footage?" His face reddened in frustration, because he could no longer stand to watch the coverage of Evaniese's and Ellis Roman's wedding.

"It's like the biggest event of the year, and *so* romantic," his wife gushed. "Didn't you work with Evaniese Spencer-Roman at the hospital a while back?" She turned the volume up on the T.V.

"Yeah, I worked with her briefly," Jeremy roared. The woman he'd married had very little knowledge of his and Evaniese's true history.

Jeremy and his *former* girlfriend had terrorized Evaniese a while back with a number of disparaging text messages.

"Must be exciting to know someone who just married the hottest, and most good-looking movie star in Hollywood!" Jeremy's wife declared.

"Yes, it's *very* exciting," Jeremy said dismissively.

Inwardly, he stewed in jealousy and disillusionment. He still loved Evaniese with all of his heart. However, he wasn't man enough to go against Brent Peterson's threats. Brent Peterson was an enemy to any man who showed the slightest bit of interest in Evaniese. Jeremy recognized how he'd taken the easy way out. Not only did he take Brent Peterson's money, but he'd denigrated and impugned Evaniese in the process. He'd undoubtedly hurt her in the worst way.

Realizing Evaniese would never be a part of his life again, was indeed a hefty price to pay. Jeremy was introspective, and couldn't even bring himself to watch footage of the lavish secret wedding. He readily acknowledged that Ellis Roman was strong enough to do for Evaniese what he himself had failed to. Therefore, because the Hollywood icon had honored Evaniese in the way she deserved, it was only fitting that he'd won her hand. The world-renowned movie star had *earned* the right to be her husband! There was no going back at that point. Jeremy acquiesced to the fact that he'd made his bed, and now he was forced to sleep in it.

***

Evaniese felt like royalty in her glistening white gown in the loveliest vineyard in Southern Italy. The view was breathtaking and romantic. Never had she seen such a beautiful stretch of radiating greenery. The wedding ceremony had been very small. Only immediate family was made privy to the secret ceremony.

Ellis took care of the arrangements, and had provided travel accommodations for everyone. Evaniese's mom, her sister, and her brother were shellshock! In awe of Ellis Roman, they were still trying to wrap their heads around the fact that *their* Evaniese was married to one of the most notable celebrities in the world. Ellis's pastor, Wade Sterling, had flown in from California in order to officiate the ceremony.

Now, Evaniese stood on the balcony of a hotel suite overlooking Southern Italy. The view was spectacular! It had been a long, but extremely wonderful day! She was still reeling from the whirlwind experience of flying out to such a lovely destination, to marry the man of her dreams. The word *happiness* tenuously described how she really felt. As the warm breezes caressed her face, tears surfaced in her eyes. Overwhelmed, Evaniese lifted up her hands in praise to God for being so gracious. God had blessed her beyond her wildest dreams!

She teared up to remember some of her past experiences. For so long, it seemed God had forgotten and overlooked her. Evaniese had watched others-including her *former* friends-be blessed with good guys. Such blessings had always evaded *her*. However, she'd failed to apprehend the process. God had an even greater miracle in mind.

As she stood out on the terrace, Evaniese felt Ellis's strong arms about her waist from behind. He secured his grasp, as they looked out into the vastness of the city. It was indeed a majestic view! "What are you thinking, my love?" Ellis's voice was throaty.

Evaniese turned towards her husband, and draped her arms around his neck. Staring dreamily into his honey brown eyes, she was captivated. "I can't believe we did this," she admitted.

"Did what, baby?" Ellis explored her face and eyes lovingly.

"I can't believe you're the *one* man in my life who followed through." Tears gleamed in her eyes.

There was a bewildered but involved expression on Ellis's face. "What do you mean, angel?" He gave her a befuddled stare, as he propped her chin to look up at himself.

"No one else took the time to get to know *me*, love *me* and not walk away," her voice wavered.

Ellis smiled fondly into the eyes of his new wife. He shook his head amusingly. "I'm *so* glad all the others *didn't* follow through." His eyes shone in affect, as he tightened his hold about Evaniese's waist.

"God gave *me* the grace to follow through, because you were created for me. You're *my* soulmate. I knew it from the first time I laid eyes on you. My love for you has only grown since then," Ellis admitted, devotedly searching her eyes. "Evaniese Catherine Spencer-Roman, what I feel for you is so overpowering, it's got to be a gift from God!"

"Oh, Ellis…." Evaniese cried, and surrendered to his arms. "I love you so much!"

"This gift God from God is what the entire world dreams about." Ellis crushed her in his arms, and tenderly rubbed on her back. "I'm never letting you go," he avowed.

"I can't believe I've found someone who loves me in this way." Evaniese pulled away to look into her husband's eyes.

"Well, then… It's my solemn *duty* to show you each and every day how real this love is. I'm not going anywhere," he said emphatically. "I'd be a fool to *ever* let you go, and I'm no one's fool," he quipped, chortling.

Evaniese laughed lightly, and marveled, as she scrutinized her beautiful God-given gift. In the past, she'd been the *fat* one, the *lonely* and the *old* one in her inner circle. Nonetheless, God reminded her yet again. The opinions of others didn't matter. What mattered was the way her heavenly father saw her. "I love you so much, Ellis!" she reiterated, overjoyed.

"You love me, baby?" Ellis teased. In a gentle manner, he took her hand, and guided her back inside the hotel suite. "How much do you love me?" Ellis shut the balcony doors, while simultaneously holding Evaniese's hand in his.

"A lot…," Evaniese whispered, as Ellis enfolded her in his arms.

"I'm not convinced, angel." Ellis covered her in kisses. "You're just going to have to show me," he murmured, losing himself in her embraces.

"I love you, Ellis!" Evaniese cradled his face in her hands, and ministered great love to every contour.

Moments later, Ellis drifted away in order to dim the lights. In the shadows, he set down on the bed, and held his hand out to his wife.

Timidly, Evaniese gave Ellis her hand, and he manipulated into his arms. Devotedly and affectionately, he secured her within the confines of his stalwart arms.

"Are you okay, baby?" Ellis tested, exploring unchartered territory with his new wife. The horizon held a great deal of promise. It was a sky full of love, passion and fire. The spectacular panorama invited them to take flight.

"With *you*, I feel completely safe and content," Evaniese whispered, in between ardent embraces.

"You *are* safe with me, angel. You are *everything* to me! I will spent the rest of my life doing all that I can to show you just how precious you are to me." Ellis immersed himself in the blazing embers of the love he felt for Evaniese.

"You promise?" Evaniese asked, before the conflagration.

"Oh, baby, I promise. I promise to love you today, tomorrow and forever…"

Their affection radiated keenly for some time. In Ellis's heart, he knew the truth. No matter how many times he was with Evaniese, he'd never be able to get enough of her love. No doubt, their fervent love story would set the universe ablaze for all eternity. This was indeed the beginning of a forever love.

***

"Does it still hurt when you try to walk around the house?" Todd Monahan, Ginger's physical therapist asked.

Ginger was still in rehab months after the critical car accident. The distension and engorgement to her lower extremities was paralyzing. Sadly, she was so large, anyone would have guessed she was suffering from Elephantiasis. In short, she was a balloon. The doctors and specialists were still racking their brains trying to figure out a way to restore her to her former self.

"Yes," Ginger yelped in irritation, because Todd had touched the right leg, "it still hurts."

"All right, dear. I'll talk to Dr. Preet, and recommend he increase the dosage of your painkillers," Todd explained temperately. Hating to be around her, the therapy session couldn't come fast enough.

"Yeah, thanks," Ginger said rancorously. "Are we done?"

"We're done for today." Todd sighed in relief. Ginger was the most miserable patient he'd ever worked with. "Well, I guess, I'll see you in a week," he emphasized.

"Yeah, sure," Ginger said dismissively.

Gathering up her things took quite a bit of time, because ambulating was excruciating. Ginger was still incredulous about the bitter, and unexpected twist her life had taken. Dragging along a heavy duffle bag, she trudged over to her car. Popping the trunk open, she tossed the bag inside, then ambled over to the driver's side.

Opening up the car door, it took forever to raise her bloated right leg into the car. Ginger flinched in discomfort. However, with a little more effort, she managed to get in, and shut the door. After tossing her pocketbook against the driver's side window in frustration, she rested her head on the steering wheel and cried. The car accident months ago had ruined her life. Also, the fact that Evaniese was no longer a part of her life tormented her.

Ginger had exposed the ugliness of her heart, and Evaniese was no longer a part of her world. Fundamentally, Evaniese was further removed than another galaxy. In fact, she was married to filthy rich and extremely handsome A-list actor, Ellis Roman. Ginger was still devastated, and reeling over the turn of events.

Her doctors were stumped, and couldn't figure out her condition. Her lower extremities were significantly inflamed. They couldn't figure out why the distention persisted. However, Ginger knew exactly why she was suffering from such a calamity. Practicing witchcraft to ensure Evaniese's weight loss surgery failed, was the cause and effect. Ginger had wanted Evaniese to remain fat. And now, *she* was fat-too fat to fit into anything.

The swelling was such that she'd ballooned up to a size twenty-four. Adding insult to injury, every time Evaniese and Ellis graced magazine covers, were on television, or on social media, Ginger was reminded of how miserably her plan had failed. Evaniese radiated all the more with a vibrant glow. She'd also managed to exceed her weight loss goals. Contrarily, the specialists had yet to find a remedy for Ginger's *mysterious* illness.

In spite of her mistakes, Ginger was trying to find her way back to God through a relationship with Jesus Christ. Shortly after the car crash, Deanna repented of her wrongs, and chose to rediscover faith in God. Recognizing her egregious mistakes, she begged God's forgiveness, and turned away from witchcraft. Thus, she was slowly but surely on the mend. Deanna had a new job. And, after her failed relationship with Scott, she met someone new. In fact, Deanna and Bryce Woods were engaged to be married.

It took quite a while, but Ginger finally understood. After losing it all, she realized only God could help her find her way back. Claiming that her issues were too much for him to handle, Ginger's boyfriend, Aaron had jumped ship two months ago. Ginger now grasped the fidelity of God when all others turned away. She'd learned some hard but invaluable lessons. Everyone who calls on the name of Jesus Christ, must do so wholeheartedly, and follow the narrow path (2Timothy 2:19, Luke 13:24).

"I know I messed up, God. I've made so many mistakes. I was selfish, cruel and stupid. It was foolish of me to think that Satan wouldn't take back *everything* he promised to give me (John 10: 10). I've dealt deceitfully with your word, God, but I'd like to come back. Please, give me another chance. Let me come back to you," she pleaded with tears in her eyes.

Moments later, Ginger managed to pull herself together. Turning on the car radio, she listened to music. However, during a commercial break, there was an announcement. *"Hollywood A-lister, Ellis Roman and wife Evaniese Spencer-Roman, are set to collaborate on an independent project. Roman says his wife inspired him to invest in, produce and to direct the film. The title of the duos collaborative project is not yet known, but details should be known soon."*

Ginger's face warped in misery, and fresh tears blazed in her eyes. Nevertheless, just then she received an impression from God's Spirit. *"You asked to come back to Me, Ginger. However, the first step to coming back is to get rid of all the bitterness and to forgive. Try to be happy for Evaniese…"*

Ginger wiped tears from her eyes, and nodded compliantly to the still, small voice of God's Holy Spirit. With her back pressed up to the car seat, she listened to the entertainment buzz about Evaniese and Ellis. This time around, she tried to do so with an open heart, rather than a heart full of envy, jealousy and rage.

***

Hollywood elite gathered in droves for the premier of Evaniese and Ellis's first movie project. The glitz and glamor of the red carpet was all new to Evaniese. It was the first time Ellis had her on his arm for a premier. There was Oscar buzz swirling around their shared film, *Of Weight Loss and Witches.*

Evaniese looked amazing in a hibiscus red designer gown. Whenever the press and media got too close, Ellis kept a firm grasp on her hand, and stood protectively in front of her. Evaniese found herself falling deeper in love with her wonderful husband every day.

"Ellis, Ellis, how does it feel to know that this project, which you worked on with your beautiful wife, has received ninety-eight percent on Rotten Tomatoes?"

"It feels wonderful, and I couldn't be prouder!" Ellis said like a champ. Squeezing Evaniese's hand, he affirmed, "Getting to do what I love, and sharing that with my brilliant wife, was truly an amazing experience! I wouldn't have wanted it any other way!"

"It must be like icing on the cake to be escorting your lovely wife to the premier of the movie you worked on together," an entertainment news reporter commented.

Ellis stood protectively in front of Evaniese. However, before he answered the press, he stared fondly at her with a great deal of dignity and respect. "I can't even describe how elated and proud I am to be here tonight with my baby!" Tears sparkled in his eyes, as his eyes fastened to his wife's.

Evaniese stared at her husband with equal devotion.

Ellis pressed a fond kiss to her lips. "Can you tell how over-the-top proud I am of my wife?" he asked, beaming.

The press went ballistic over Evaniese and Ellis's affectionate exchanges. They took a gazillion pictures capturing the couple's first red carpet event.

"Evaniese, Evaniese," reporters addressed. "*Who* are you wearing tonight?" They asked referring to her hibiscus-red gown.

"It's an *Angelique Rivierre* Original," Evaniese said meekly, trying to process being mobbed by the media.

"Evaniese, how does it feel knowing you've won the heart of one of the most elusive bachelors in Hollywood?" Another reporter asked.

Just then, Ellis pulled Evaniese even closer to himself. He had to keep the wolves at bay, because she was precious cargo. Staring admiringly at her, he anticipated an answer to the question she'd been asked. In fact, it seemed everyone was holding their breath until she responded.

Evaniese stared devotedly into the eyes of the man who'd transformed her entire life. Ellis Roman hadn't only *said* he loved her, he'd proven it in so many ways. Tears glimmered in her eyes as they fastened to Ellis's. "It feels like a dream come true every single day," her wavered.

For a lapse, the press and media stood still, and gushed over the gorgeous couple's doting glances and loving interactions.

Stirred by Evaniese's words, Ellis pressed his lips to hers repeatedly. "It's a dream come true for me too, babe," he said throatily, lavishing her face with tender kisses.

The media hailstorm temporarily ceased. Entertainment news reporters were mesmerized by the couple's display. It was obvious. Although rare, in such a crazy industry-and as lonely a place as Hollywood could often be, two honestly good people had found each other. Furthermore, the fire of their love radiated more fervidly than the sun.

"Are you ready to go inside, baby?" Ellis decided to move quickly, while the paparazzi remained more or less subdued.

"I'm all set, sweetie."

Evaniese slipped her am through her husband's, and allowed him to guide her into the Cobalt Theater. They would see the movie together for the first time. Evaniese realized she truly had a unique story to tell. The movie, *Of Weight Loss and Witches*, was an interpretation of her struggle prior to, and post having weight loss surgery.

Evaniese illustrated her challenges when she worked through Brookline Hospital out in Amber Hills, Indiana. She chronicled being rejected by Brent Peterson, Jeremy Carter and Nathan Andrews. The betrayal of several others, including her closest friends was also narrated. And yet, in spite of the pain and the suffering, God had given her a silver lining, and had blessed her beyond her wildest dreams.

Surrounded by Hollywood's finest, Evaniese sat in the dimmed luxury theater holding her husband's hand, and marveling over just how far she'd come. Humbled, she readily acknowledged God's favor at work. Life never guaranteed, or promised a happy ending. Nevertheless, Evaniese was convinced. If a person put their trust in God through faith in Jesus Christ, there was always a silver lining after the horrible storms of life. And, standing back to admire the view, she needed a pair of shades to shield her eyes from God's resplendent blessings.

Other titles from Higher Ground Books & Media:

Of Love and Witches by Marjorie Joseph

Erin & Oliver by Marjorie Joseph

Max by Marjorie Joseph

Destiny Revealed by Marjorie Joseph

Destiny Challenged by Marjorie Joseph

Destiny Fulfilled by Marjorie Joseph

In the Wash: The Rona Shively Stories by Rebecca Benston

The Bottom of This by Tramaine Hannah

A Summer Love series by Becka L. Jones

The Story I Tell by Rebecca Whited

Bloom by Robin Stone

My Name is Sam by Joe Siccardi

Raven Transcending Fear by Terri Kozlowski

The Power of Knowing by Jean Walters

Journey to the Mountaintop by Terra Kern

Chronicles of a Spiritual Journey by Stephen Shepherd

The Real Prison Diaries by Judy Frisby

The Words of My Father by Mark Nemetz

Add these titles to your collection today!

http://www.highergroundbooksandmedia.com

HIGHER GROUND BOOKS & MEDIA IS
AN INDEPENDENT PUBLISHER

Do you have a story to tell?

Higher Ground Books & Media is an independent Christian-based publisher specializing in stories of triumph! Our purpose is to empower, inspire, and educate through the sharing of personal experiences. We are always looking for great, new stories to add to our collection. If you're looking for a publisher, get in touch with us today!

Please be sure to visit our website for our submission guidelines.

http://www.highergroundbooksandmedia.com/submission-guidelines

HGBM SERVICES IS OUR CONSULTING FIRM

AUTHOR SERVICES

HGBM Services offers a variety of writing and coaching services for aspiring authors! We can help with editing, manuscript critiques, self-publishing, and much more! Get in touch today to see how we can help you make your dream of becoming an author a reality!

*****

We also offer social media marketing services for authors, small businesses, and non-profit organizations. Let us help you get the word out about your book, your projects, and your mission. We offer great rates, quality promos, consistent communication, and a personal touch!

http://www.highergroundbooksandmedia.com/editing-writing-services

Need Bulk Copies?

If you would like to order bulk copies of this book or any other title at Higher Ground Books & Media, please contact us at highergroundbooksandmedia@gmail.com.

We offer discounts for purchases of 20 or more copies. Excellent for small groups, book clubs, classrooms, etc.

Get in touch today and get a set of great stories for your students or group members.